D0437645

Last Plane
to Heaven

TOR BOOKS BY JAY LAKE

Mainspring
Escapement
Pinion
Green
Endurance
Kalimpura
Last Plane to Heaven

WALLA WALLA PUBLIC LIBRARY

THIS BOOK HAS BEEN DISCARDED
BY WALLA WALLA PUBLIC LIBRARY

Last Plane to Heaven

The Final Collection

Jay Lake

TOR®

A TOM DOHERTY ASSOCIATES BOOK
NEW YORK

This is a work of fiction. All of the characters, organizations, and events portrayed in these stories are either products of the author's imagination or are used fictitiously.

LAST PLANE TO HEAVEN

Copyright © 2014 by Joseph E. Lake, Jr.

Foreword copyright © 2014 by Gene Wolfe

All rights reserved.

A Tor Book
Published by Tom Doherty Associates, LLC
175 Fifth Avenue
New York, NY 10010

www.tor-forge.com

Tor® is a registered trademark of Tom Doherty Associates, LLC.

Library of Congress Cataloging-in-Publication Data

Lake, Jay.
    [Short stories. Selections]
    Last plane to heaven : the final collection / Jay Lake.
        p. cm.
    ISBN 978-0-7653-7798-2 (hardcover)
    ISBN 978-1-4668-5847-3 (e-book)
    I. Title.
PS3612.A519L38 2014
813'.6—dc23

                                                              2014019792

Tor books may be purchased for educational, business, or promotional use. For information on bulk purchases, please contact Macmillan Corporate and Premium Sales Department at 1-800-221-7945, extension 5442, or write specialmarkets@macmillan.com.

First Edition: September 2014

Printed in the United States of America

0 9 8 7 6 5 4 3 2 1

Copyright Acknowledgments

"Last Plane to Heaven: A Love Story" copyright © 2007 by Joseph E. Lake, Jr. Originally appeared in *Jim Baen's Universe*.

"Houses of the Favored" copyright © 2010 by Joseph E. Lake, Jr. Originally appeared in *Visitants: Stories of Fallen Angels and Heavenly Hosts,* edited by Stephen Jones, Ulysses Press.

"The Starship Mechanic" copyright © 2010 by Joseph E. Lake, Jr., and Ken Scholes. Originally appeared at Tor.com.

"Permanent Fatal Errors" copyright © 2010 Joseph E. Lake, Jr. Originally appeared in *Is Anybody Out There?*, edited by Marty Halpern, DAW.

"'Hello,' Said the Gun" copyright © 2010 by Joseph E. Lake, Jr. Originally appeared at *Daily Science Fiction.*

"The Speed of Time" copyright © 2013 by Joseph E. Lake, Jr. Originally appeared at Tor.com.

"West to East" copyright © 2014 by Joseph E. Lake, Jr. Originally appeared at *Subterranean Online.*

"The Women Who Ate Stone Squid" copyright © 2010 Joseph E. Lake, Jr. Originally appeared in *Love and Rockets,* edited by Kerrie Lynn Hughes and Martin H. Greenberg, DAW.

"Looking for Truth in a Wild Blue Yonder" copyright © 2010 by Joseph E. Lake, Jr., and Ken Scholes. Originally appeared at Tor.com.

"Scent of the Green Cathedral" copyright © 2010 by Joseph E. Lake, Jr. Originally appeared in *Visitants: Stories of Fallen Angels and Heavenly Hosts,* edited by Stephen Jones, Ulysses Press.

"Spendthrift" copyright © 2013 by Joseph E. Lake, Jr. Originally appeared in *Coins of Chaos,* edited by Jennifer Brozek, EDGE.

"Jefferson's West" copyright © 2011 by Joseph E. Lake, Jr. Originally appeared in *Boondocks Fantasy,* edited by Jean Rabe and Martin H. Greenberg, DAW.

"They Are Forgotten Until They Come Again" copyright © 2011 by Joseph E. Lake, Jr. Originally appeared in *River,* edited by Alma Alexander, Dark Quest Books.

"The Woman Who Shattered the Moon" copyright © 2012 by Joseph E. Lake, Jr. Originally appeared in *The Villain Comes Home,* edited by Gabrielle Harbowy and Ed Greenwood, Dragon Moon Press.

"The Blade of His Plow" copyright © 2011 by Joseph E. Lake, Jr. Originally appeared in *Human for a Day,* edited by Martin H. Greenberg and Jennifer Brozek, DAW.

"Grindstone" copyright © 2013 by Joseph E. Lake, Jr. Originally appeared in *Airships and Automatons,* edited by Charles P. Zaglanis, White Cat Publications.

"The Temptation of Eustace Prudence McAllen" copyright © 2012 by Joseph E. Lake, Jr. Originally appeared in *Westward Weird,* edited by Kerrie Lynn Hughes and Martin H. Greenberg, DAW.

"That Which Rises Ever Upward" copyright © 2011 by Joseph E. Lake, Jr. Originally appeared in *The Fathomless Abyss,* edited by Phil Athans, Athans Associates.

"A Feast of Angels" copyright © 2010 by Joseph E. Lake, Jr. Originally appeared in *Visitants: Stories of Fallen Angels and Heavenly Hosts,* edited by Stephen Jones, Ulysses Press.

"Promises: A Tale of the City Imperishable" copyright © 2008 by Joseph E. Lake, Jr. Originally appeared in *Paper Cities,* edited by Ekaterina Sedia, Senses Five Press.

"Testaments" copyright © 2010 by Joseph E. Lake, Jr. Originally appeared in *The Book of Dreams,* edited by Nick Gevers, Subterranean.

"The Fall of the Moon" copyright © 2010 by Joseph E. Lake, Jr. Originally appeared in *Realms of Fantasy,* October 2010.

"A Critical Examination of Stigmata's Print *Taking the Rats to Riga*" copyright © 2011 by Joseph E. Lake, Jr. Originally appeared in *The Thackery T. Lambshead Cabinet of Curiosities: Exhibits, Oddities, Images, and Stories from Top Authors and Artists,* edited by Jeff and Ann VanderMeer, HarperCollins.

"From the Countries of Her Dreams" copyright © 2010 by Joseph E. Lake, Jr., and Shannon Page. Originally appeared in *Fantasy Magazine,* November 2010.

"Unchambered Heart" copyright © 2011 by Joseph E. Lake, Jr. Originally appeared in *The Chiaroscuro,* April 2011.

"Novus Ordo Angelorum" copyright © 2010 by Joseph E. Lake, Jr. Originally appeared in *Visitants: Stories of Fallen Angels and Heavenly Hosts,* edited by Stephen Jones, Ulysses Press.

"The Tentacled Sky" copyright © 2010 by Joseph E. Lake, Jr. Originally appeared on *DrabbleCast,* number 178, 2010.

"Such Bright and Risen Madness in Our Names" copyright © 2010 by Joseph E. Lake, Jr. Originally appeared in *Cthulhu's Reign,* edited by Darrell Schweitzer, DAW.

"Her Fingers Like Whips, Her Eyes Like Razors" copyright © 2011 by Joseph E. Lake, Jr. Originally appeared in *Postscripts,* 24/25, 2011.

"Mother Urban's Booke of Dayes" copyright © 2010 by Joseph E. Lake, Jr. Originally appeared in *Dark Faith,* edited by Maurice Broaddus and Jerry Gordon, Apex Publications.

"Going Bad" copyright © 2010 by Joseph E. Lake, Jr. Originally appeared in *Visitants: Stories of Fallen Angels and Heavenly Hosts,* edited by Stephen Jones, Ulysses Press.

"The Cancer Catechism" copyright © 2012 by Joseph E. Lake, Jr. Originally appeared in *Dark Faith: Invocations,* edited by Maurice Broaddus and Jerry Gordon, Apex Publications.

Afterword copyright © 2014 by Joseph E. Lake, Jr.

For Bronwyn, known as the Child. And my loving thanks to Lisa.
For everyone who's ever read one of my stories, or any story, really.

In the end, words are all that survive us.

Contents

Foreword

BY GENE WOLFE

Though I could be completely wrong in your case, I have a deep and troubling feeling that you almost never read short stories. As I say, I could be wrong—but the odds are in my favor. There was a time, now long past, when everyone who read, read short stories. What happened? I think I know and I am about to tell you.

Two things. The first is simply that more and more people read reviews. (To explain why that happened would take us too far afield.) Reviews of fiction are almost entirely of novels. Reviews of novels are much easier to write. There is the jacket copy, smiling its idiot smile and offering a helping hand to the reviewer. One may generally write the whole thing after reading the first chapter, one or two chapters from the middle, and the last chapter. This though the novel has twenty or thirty chapters. Furthermore (I bet you didn't know this), publishers often send along a sample review with the review copy of the book. Should you see exactly the same review in two publications, you will know what happened. To feign originality, change a word here and there. "Exciting" becomes "thrilling," "very" becomes "exceedingly," and so forth (or on). This at least looks (appears) more honest. The people who read reviews nearly always buy novels as a result, so the thing feeds upon itself.

That first reason is easy enough to explain and to understand. The second is much more difficult. Reading short stories takes a certain tough-mindedness. A novel is a kiss in the moonlight—soft, romantic, gentle, and perfumed. A short story is you and another naked in a dark and sweltering room without a bed. No breeze enters the open windows; beyond the screens, mosquitoes buzz in the dark. You come together and the other's body is slick with sweat, like your own. Someone's heart is pounding; perhaps they both are, but it's hard to tell. If you don't understand what I mean, read a few of these; you'll understand it better then.

The kiss in the moonlight often appeals to a tender mind. That hot, humid room frightens it to paralysis.

That said, there are people who cannot read fiction at all. You know the type. Somehow she never found the right man. Somehow he never found the right girl. Generally they are neat and orderly and perhaps a little acrophobic. Often they make ideal employees, provided they are not asked to take responsibility. They are hard but brittle.

Clearly you are not one of them.

Tough-mindedness used to be the rule. If you don't believe me, listen to a few old songs: "I'm a ox-drivin' man from the Kane County line / An' I'll whip any man touches one ox o' mine! / I'll beat him with the ox-goad, you see if I don't try. / So it's poke them cattle onward, boys. Root hog, er die!"

"She jumped on her pony so airy and rode like she carried the mail, / With eyes just as wide as the prairie 'long side of the Santa Fe Trail."

I've quoted two from memory where I might have quoted a hundred. If you've read them, you understand what I mean. If you've sung them, that's better yet. If you're a purist, you may slang me all you like for quoting from memory lyrics that are not precisely like those you found in some book. Those songs have been sung and sung again, edited, altered, and trimmed to fit for a century and more. The people were like that, tough as an old boot, and they told each other stories around the fire.

Don't get me wrong—there's nothing wrong with a kiss in the moonlight. But that moonlight kiss should not be all there is. It should be a beginning, not an end. Many of you, I fear, think of Jay Lake mainly or even exclusively as a novelist. He is, and a great one. Even so, he began (as nearly all of us do) as a short story writer, and he was a well-known and much admired short story writer before *Mainspring*. So test yourself. Read "Last Plane to Heaven," the story that has given its title to this whole book. If you can't finish it, you've failed. If you finished it and enjoyed it (I know that if you don't enjoy it you won't finish it) but find there are certain things you don't understand, read it again. If you enjoyed it the second time and understand it a little better, you don't have to read it a third time unless you want to. You've made it. You're on the team.

Before I run completely out of words, I want to assure you that the title of this collection was not drawn out of a hat. As soon as you read

"The Houses of the Favored," you should understand what I just told you. "Starship Mechanic" will drive it home.

Here I had planned to tell you what you ought to admire most about these stories. "Had" is the operative word. There are so many things to admire that I can't choose one or even two. First of all their range; Jay's steed is fast and sure of foot, and it jumps canyons and climbs mountains. Their modernity too—they could not have been written fifty years ago; many could not have been written twenty-five years ago. Certainly they would not have been published, read, and understood then. Their originality, certainly.

And the steely glint of the captain's eyes.

Last Plane
to Heaven

Last Plane to Heaven: A Love Story

I went to Outer Mongolia for the first time in 1990. Parts of this story are true, and happened to me then. Most of it is made up. You decide what to believe.

Nichols tried to light a cigarette, one of those fucking Paki horse turds. "Know why God made the 'stans?" His palm cupped the flame against the steppe winds. Must've been burning his fingers, but if he didn't care, I sure as hell didn't.

"Hell if I know." The dust out here was like to drive me to tears, Oakley wraparounds or not. That shit got in the cracks of *everything*. My shoulders ached like a son of a bitch, too, after standing around all day with a SAM tube on my shoulder. I shifted the Stinger, listening for that familiar tubercular roar of old Sov-built engines. The Antonov was overdue.

He got his horse turd lit, took a long, coughing drag. "Shit's got to come out somewhere, that's why." A gap-toothed grin, where a couple of Uzbek hash merchants had kicked him hard a few months back. He'd eaten their ears a bit later. "The 'stans are the asshole of the Earth. America, we're the tits. Land of milk and honey."

Tits was right, I thought. But honey? Something chattered out there. I scanned the northeast over the hardpan. Nothing but scattered grass and endless identical miles, while the dust was making a silver-brown hash of the Gobi sky.

No sign of the Antonov.

Maybe I'd heard the windsock snapping.

"Ain't you gonna ask?" he said, after another deep drag.

"Ask what?"

"Where the world's pussy is?"

I knew better than to walk into that one, so I just returned his grin. *I* still had all my teeth.

"Aw, fuck it." Nichols pitched the flaring cigarette into the wind. It bounced past the wheel ruts on the desert floor then vanished into dust, leaving a flare on my vision.

"Don't do that shit, man."

"Snipers?" His laugh was as harsh as his cigarettes. "Here? Hiding behind what? The sky, maybe. *You're* the pussy, Allen. Pussy of the world, right here."

"Snipers my ass." I was less confident than him on that. Not much less, but a careful troopie lived to see chow call. "Only you can prevent forest fires."

"Smokey the fucking Mongolian bear!"

Then the Antonov was overhead, growling out of the dust in a reek of fuel and old metal, the pilot looking for the windsock.

Say what you want about Sov technology, the shit they built just keeps working. That old An-17 had probably been flying, badly, when I was playing kill-the-ragheads in the Oregon forests as a kid. It was still flying badly now. As the fly-guys say, any landing you walk away from is a good landing.

The south Gobi is a series of very shallow valleys bordered by low ridges a half dozen klicks apart. The desert is sort of like prairie gone bad, with stubby, dried grasses, the odd flower, and a hell of a lot of gravel. If you look up and down the valleys, you can see the edge of the world.

The strip here was a windsock stuck in the hardpan. Every now and then someone got tired of the planes bouncing in their wheel ruts and replanted the windsock fifty yards farther east. There was an archaeology of occupation and warfare written in the tracks of old landing gear.

Most of the Westerners in the 'stans were like Nichols. Smart enough, and stone killers in a firefight or on a silent op, but pretty much baboons otherwise. A million years ago they would have been the big apes throwing shit from the trees. Now they're out here capping ragheads and steppe weasels. I guess that beats breaking elbows for money back home.

I tried explaining Temujin to Nichols one time as we were burning some idealistic kids out of an eight-hundred-year-old temple. Blue-faced demons crisped to winter ash while their ammo cooked off in a funeral cantata. He'd just laughed and told me to go back to college if I didn't like it here.

It's a beautiful country, Mongolia. All the 'stans are beautiful in their way. Xin Jiang, too. Nichols was wrong about this being the ass-hole of the earth. God *had* made these countries, all right, to remind us all how damned tough the world was. And how beauty could rise from the hard choices and broken lives.

Then God in His infinite wisdom had chosen to people these lands with some of the toughest sons of bitches to ever draw breath. These people could hold a grudge for a thousand years and didn't mind eating bullets to avenge their honor.

Fuck you very much, God, for Your beauty and Your terror. Not to mention Sov aircraft to dust us off to the brothels of Ulan Bator every once in a while. Nothing expressed God's love for His world like warm North Korean beer and elderly Chechen hookers.

"Yo, Allen, get in here!"

It was Korunov. His head bobbed out the weathered orange door of the *ger* that served as our HQ. Ex-KGB counterintel guy. He'd spent a lot of time at the USA-Canada Institute, back when that was still cranking, and spoke with the damnedest accent. His voice was part Alabama cornpone and part Ukrainian street hustler, squeaking out of a two-hundred-kilo butterball.

Hell, he must have been thin once. Nobody starts out life that kind of fat.

Korunov considered himself a man of the world. He was also the paymaster of our little unit, so when he yo'd, I ho'd.

Nichols and Korunov were crowded into the *ger* along with Batugan—our Mongolian controller back in UB and the only man to get off the Antonov upon arrival. As always, the pilot remained on board to keep his points hot. Plus Hannaday was there. He was an Agency cowboy I'd last seen on the wrong end of a Glock in Kandahar two years earlier. Whipcord thin, still wearing the same damned Armani suit.

How the *fuck* had that spook gotten into the camp without me seeing him? My legs still ached whenever it got chilly. I briefly considered firing off my Stinger inside the *ger*, just punching the warhead into Hannaday's chest, but that would have pretty much toasted us all.

"Stow it," growled Korunov. Two hundred kilos or not, that man could and did snap necks.

"What's *he* doing here?" I wouldn't meet Hannaday's gaze. "He's worse trouble than the insurgency."

Batugan gave me his oily smile. I don't think he had any other kind, truth be told. "Mr. Hannaday has bought out your contracts."

"My contract wasn't up for sale to him."

Korunov got too close to me. "Sit. Listen."

I laid the Stinger against the tent walls, loosed the holster on my Smitty, then pulled up one of those little orange Mongolian stools. I never took my eyes off Hannaday's hands. "Listening, *sir*."

"You should be—" Batugan began, but Korunov interrupted. "Not your show anymore, Genghis."

The fat man's voice dropped, sympathy or perhaps an attempt at camaraderie, as he turned to me. "Our financial backers have pulled out. Batugan flew here to cut us loose."

Cut us loose here? We were a training cadre. They brought in kids with attitude, we ran them through some high-fatality training, they pulled them back out to go fight the bad guys. There *was* no way out but by plane. That way the kids wouldn't run off. And no one ever came around asking inconvenient questions about the row of graves on the far side of the *ger* camp.

You could make it out by truck. Damned long haul, though, and you had to pack along enough water and fuel. Didn't matter anyhow. There weren't any trucks in camp right now, just a couple of old Chinese-surplus BJC jeeps.

Not a lot of landmarks in the south Gobi. Sure as hell no roads.

"So?" I wasn't a decision maker. Why were they telling me?

Korunov chose his words carefully. "Mr. Hannaday here is bankrolling airfare back to Los Angeles or Frankfurt, plus a generous kill fee."

I finally met Hannaday's eyes. They gleamed that same eerie blue as back in Kandahar. His smile died there.

"I don't care what he wants. I'd rather walk than take his money."

"That's why we need you, Mr. Allen," Hannaday said. "The unit listens to you." There was something wrong with his voice—it grated, almost fading out.

With that clue, even in the shadowed *ger*, I could make out a scar seaming his throat. It was a glossy trail just above the crisp Windsor knot of his tie. I'd lost my best knife in that throat, the day he shot me.

"You don't talk right, I don't walk right." Which was why I trained instead of killed these days. "I think we've done enough for each other." I stood, grabbed my missile rack.

"Allen." It was Korunov.

I owed him. Lots. I stopped to listen. "Yeah?"

"We don't have seats on the plane. None of us. Not without Mr. Hannaday."

I had eleven guys outside who were real good at knocking over airplanes, Nichols chief among them. But I also had eleven guys outside who weren't going to be happy about hiking out of the south Gobi.

"We got return bonds, Sergei," I told Korunov softly.

He shrugged, his face impassive. "If we were elsewhere, we could cash them. Mr. Hannaday bought the air transport contract from Batugan before he bought our paper."

I had my Smitty out and two rounds in Batugan, one in each thigh. The Mongolian fell off his stool sobbing, curling to clutch at his legs. Neither Hannaday nor Korunov moved. Neither one drew down on me.

"So I am worth something to you, you son of a bitch." Careful not to point the weapon at Hannaday, I holstered the pistol. "What the fuck do you want, airplane man?"

"Like you, I'm—"

"You'll never be like me, you fucking Langley suit."

"Please," Hannaday said. One hand stroked the knot of his tie. I hoped like hell the scar ached as bad as my legs. "Fort Meade. And, *like you,* I'm a contractor now." Without looking, he leaned over slightly and slapped Batugan hard. The Mongolian quieted his blubbering.

That drew a reluctant laugh out of me. "Big spookery all get outsourced to India?"

"Pakistan, actually. In the name of funding and plausible deniability."

"Fuck yeah. What's your point?"

"We're going to bring in a special subject. We need your team to play like Ukrainian mercs for about a week. Ride the subject hard, put them in some real fear, then let them be extracted."

Who was he kidding, *extracted*? I knew what that signified. "What, Delta Force falls out of the sky and caps us all? No thanks." As if this bunch of multinational nimrods could be Ukrainians. Korunov actually was, the real McCoyovich. After the fat man, Nichols with his

Paki cigarettes was the safest and sanest of the bunch. There was a *reason* our little crowd wasn't out eating snakes on the front line.

"No-risk deal," said Hannaday impassively.

"That deal ain't been written yet."

He folded his hands in his lap, a deliberate gesture straight out of interrogation training. "I'll be sitting here with you the whole time."

Well, I could always cap *him* when the shit went south. Because a situation like he wanted to set up would without question run for the border before it was all over with.

And it ain't like I was walking out of here.

"Fuck you very much," I told Korunov. "I guess we're playing. I'll go get the boys fired up."

"What are you going to tell them?"

"Just some fucking lies. I got a million of 'em." I grabbed my Stinger rack, waved it at Batugan. "You might want to slap a Band-Aid on Ming the Merciless over there before he bleeds out."

"Don't need him anymore," said Hannaday.

I didn't let the door hit me on the ass. Paymaster and contract man could gas all they wanted. I'd chosen my poison.

It took a little while to get a camp meeting together. Beier, the South African, was somewhere sleeping off a three-day bender, while the Belgians were off dust-wrestling and greasing each other down. Those two boys didn't much like being interrupted at play, so I sent Nichols after them. I rousted the rest of the crew to find Beier.

We wound up in the kitchen *ger*. It was too damned windy to talk outside. I didn't want to be near the Antonov—for several reasons—nor near Hannaday and Korunov. The Belgians were madder than hell and Beier was propped up against a stack of North Korean beer beneath a line of curing mutton fatback that kept dripping on him. There was a potbellied stove, thankfully cold, stacks of MREs and Chinese canned goods, and us.

I picked my nails with a Bowie knife till everyone quieted down. That was so fucking theatrical it made me want to puke, but this was the kind of shit that worked on these boys. Visible weapons and getting straight to the point.

"Listen up, geniuses. We're stewed and screwed here. Korunov's been forced to accept a transfer of our contracts. We're getting out soon, but there's one more task."

They groaned and cursed in seven languages.

"Yeah," I said. "I know. We got to run a fake hostage situation with a drop-in, pretend to be Ukrainians." Commonwealth of Independent States political bullshit. My guess was we'd be labeled later as Chechens. The ex-Sovs saw them in every shadow the way Americans saw Arabs. "So if you've got a Slavic accent, start using it. If you don't got one, start practicing."

"What happens if we say no?" It was Nichols, speaking quietly for a change. Somehow everyone was suddenly listening.

"You're free to walk home any time."

"We got return bonds." That was Echeverria, the ETA guy for whom all of Europe had gotten too hot. I didn't figure anybody Hannaday swung in here would cop to a Basque accent.

"Yeah. If we can cash 'em. You see an ATM around here, Etchy?"

Nichols again: "So what do we do?"

"Put 'em through the usual course, just don't kill 'em. Scare the hell out of whoever this is. And . . ." I glanced at Beier, who appeared to be snoring. ". . . they keep all their bits and pieces attached and intact."

I figured the marching orders would change between now and then, several times most likely, but I also figured the bits and pieces part would still apply.

"What happens at the end?"

"An extraction."

They all got real quiet.

"Staged, boys. And we'll know they're coming."

"I fire no blanks," said one of the Belgians. Everybody laughed except me.

"Think about it. Unless you can grow a truck under you or sprout wings and fly, we're pretty much stuck."

"Knock over the Antonov right now," said Nichols. "And split."

"Nope." I pointed the knife at him. "First off, a couple of stray rounds and that plane's toast. You know what a piece of shit it is. Second off, they don't keep no fucking maps on that thing. Three or four of us know enough to get it flying. None of us know the terrain. Something happens to the pilot, you want to navigate the Gobi from the air by eyeball and dead reckoning? Third, I'd bet money Hannaday's got surprises inside that plane right now, just in case any *one* of us is a smartass."

"Hannaday?" Nichols didn't miss much, and he'd heard a lot of my stories.

"Yep. Mr. Congeniality himself."

"And you're going for this?"

Hell no, I wanted to say. What I did say was, "You got a better idea?"

No one had an answer for that question. After a full minute of silence, I put my knife away.

An hour later Hannaday had me and Nichols on the plane trolling for new fish from five hundred feet.

Antonov 17's a funny bird. Looks almost like a kid's drawing of an aircraft, twin props, high wing. Not that big, and a slow fucker to boot, but they really did keep flying forever. The seats had been designed for Chinese grandmothers, not American mercs with incipient butt spread. Tiny aluminum rails with webbing between, idiot cousin to the common lawn chair. Air Munchkin. How the hell a Sov platoon in full kit ever fit inside these cans I couldn't imagine.

I didn't bother with the seat belt.

Hannaday hadn't relieved me of my Smitty, though the Stinger rack was back at camp. Nichols was sucking down another of those Paki horse turds as he fondled the barrel of his Mossberg jungle gun—a 40mm automatic shotgun that should have had Hannaday sweating.

The Gobi lumbered along outside the oval windows, low and slow. The pilot was looking for something.

Someone.

Curiosity finally got the better of my common sense. "We're doing a pickup out *here*?"

"Special delivery," said Hannaday, surprising me. He wasn't much given to sharing information.

"We're a thousand klicks from *anything*."

"And that, my gimpy friend, is precisely why we're here." His eyes narrowed to steel-gray slits. There was another reason he was here, as opposed to somewhere else. Hannaday thought he could run me. He'd done it before.

He was doing it now.

Fuck him. I didn't want to die of old age walking out of the south Gobi, but fuck him.

Then the intercom crackled to life. The pilot said something fast and tonal—Cantonese, I thought, not that I could follow it. The Antonov banked hard and picked up speed as the engines coughed a bloom of black smoke.

Whatever it was we were looking for, we'd found it.

Hannaday just smiled. "Ready for some ladder work?"

Ladder work? Out here?

And damn me if we didn't bounce to a landing somewhere not much different from anywhere else. There were cloud shadows on the ground, and a small herd of yaks in the distance. That meant Mongolians somewhere—their animals had a wide range, but they weren't left completely unattended.

"Out," said Hannaday. "Open the cargo bay."

Nichols popped the door seals in a wash of fuel reek, then dropped the aluminum boarding ladder. I made my way carefully after him, one step at a time on my bad legs.

It stank outside, of fire and something nasty-chemical. Hydrazine? Nichols was banging on the cargo hatch as I bent to look under the plane, scanning for the source of the reek.

I found it. "Holy fuck."

Nichols was distracted. "What?"

Hannaday dropped down between us and knelt. "Nice."

The thing was half rounded, like a stubby bullet, and blackened all to hell. It sat on the flat side. Smoke curled off, dancing in the dry grass around the . . . the . . .

"Soyuz TMA-3 landing capsule," said Hannaday. "Get the ladder. And stay the hell away from the bottom. There's a gamma-ray emitter down there that will fry your nuts."

Nichols had found this weird folding ladder, sort of halfway between a painter's stepladder and a scaffold. He shouldered the Mossberg and dragged the ladder toward the Soyuz with that shiny-eyed focus I normally associated with an impending massacre.

Soyuz. We were dusting off a fucking spaceman. "Somebody's looking for this." I glanced at the sky for the fleet of Russian Hinds that must surely be in the air.

Hannaday laughed again. "Yeah, a couple of thousand klicks from here. Get the camo netting out of the hold, Allen."

I got the camo netting.

Up close the capsule had that brutal precision so typical of Sov high tech. It could have been whittled from stone, then ground off. Reentry had done the thing no favors either. The surface was covered with burned streaks and pits. A round hatch stood open near the nose, from which lines of a parachute stretched out some few dozen yards across the grass. The smoking ground testified to the retro rockets that had soft-landed the capsule.

At that range the smell was worse, hydrazine and baked metal and some weird ozone thing. It made me wish for a breather mask. I dropped the mound of camo netting and sat on it.

Hannaday took the ladder and set it up against the blunt cone. The scaffold part fit across the top. Of course it did, I thought. He went straight for a little opening, pulled out something I would swear was a key, and went to work on the nose.

"Help me out, boys," he said and he wrestled open a hatch.

Of course I didn't shoot him. The Antonov pilot would have taken off without us.

Spy guy fished out a real live astronaut, someone small in a jumpsuit who couldn't stand on his own feet. Nichols and I got the guy down the ladder, then Nichols took off for the Antonov with the space traveler in a fireman's carry while Hannaday and I spread out the netting and covered the capsule. He didn't bother to retrieve his ladder.

"Nice one." I coughed through the reek. "You're running a scam of epic proportions. I assume we're nixing satellite surveillance here."

Hannaday grinned around the curve of the capsule. "Everybody's got to make a living, Allen."

When I pulled myself back up the Antonov's ladder, I found Nichols up front by the locked pilot's door, staring back down the narrow aisle. He was pale and sweating.

"What?" I said. "You find Elvis there?"

"She's a girl."

I went and looked. Our spaceman *was* a girl, not more than fifteen, eyes bloodshot from reentry gees, barely moving even as she stared at us. Blue-black skin, shaved head.

A girl.

Who'd dropped out of the Central Asian sky in a Russian spaceship.

Kids on the International Space Station? Not fucking likely. Not in this lifetime.

"Hannaday," I breathed, "who the *fuck* is she?"

The Antonov lumbered back to camp. Nichols sat in the back of the plane with his shotgun, watching the kid and cursing in an extended monotone, mostly Russian. I perched in a chair at the front of the cabin opposite Hannaday.

"Who is she?"

He had the familiar old Hannaday I'm-in-charge-here smile. "No one you'll ever know, Allen."

"Bullshit. We're supposed to run her through live-fire counterse-curity drills for a week? We'll *know* her happy ass before we're through."

It was an unfortunate choice of words. Hannaday's smile just tightened a little. "Don't break off no bits and pieces. Not *any* of her bits."

We were both thinking of Beier then, the man who would do anything to anyone.

"That's not what I'm talking about and you know it."

He shrugged. "Speak Russian for a week, push her around, scare her, then let her be dusted off. Don't put any bullets or body parts into her, you'll be fine. What could be easier?"

My legs ached where he had shot me. "Who *is* she?"

"Ah-ah." I swear to God he wagged his finger at me. "That would be telling."

On landing Nichols bolted from the plane like he had the Tehran trots. That meant the girl's presence would be known to everyone in five minutes, tops. As if I could control that anyway.

Hannaday looked at me. "I don't guess you're going to carry her down the ladder, are you?"

"Got these old war wounds in my legs."

He smiled, gathered the girl close to his chest, and made it down the ladder himself. Looking down from the door I seriously considered popping a cap in his crown, just as a public service. But then he'd drop that poor kid and where would we be?

Within moments there was a swirl of mercs, mostly barking in Russian or English with Peter Ustinov accents. Hannaday gave up the girl to them, shouting back in Russian about security and escape, then returned to the plane as I made it to the ground.

"Be good," he told me.

"Fuck you."

"Whatever gets you through the night." He set his hands on the boarding ladder, then stopped. "Oh . . . Allen . . . ?"

My hand strayed to the Smitty. "Yeah?"

"Do take good care of her."

"Right."

They poured Evian water and Mongolian vodka down that poor kid until she sputtered to life. Then the Belgians harangued her in an incomprehensible mix of Flemish and Russian for a while before dragging her outside. She wasn't up to running around our improvised training course, so they hauled her to the firing range, Korunov trailing behind like a loose grenade.

Oh good, I thought, *get the kid drunk then make her shoot.*

Better than shooting at her.

Nichols pushed me back into the kitchen tent, where Beier was still sleeping standing up.

"He's crazy." Nichols's voice was a strident hiss.

"Plane's gone. You don't have to whisper."

"We run her through the course, we'll kill her."

"We've got a forty percent fatality rate as it is. Never bothered you before."

Nichols looked around, taking a long, hard stare at Beier. The South African was snoring gently, mumbling on each exhalation. "She's a fucking *kid,*" he said after a moment.

He knew something, I realized. Nichols knew something about this. "You're inside this job, aren't you?"

"No!" Nichols snapped. He glanced at Beier again, then down at the greasy, carpeted floor of the *ger.* "It's . . . look, I've never . . ."

"Yeah?" My voice was getting harder than I wanted it to. I couldn't lose control with Nichols. He was the closest thing I had to a friend in this chickenshit outfit, and God only knew I needed my friends right now.

"I never told anyone this," Nichols said, still talking to the floor.

"Yeah?" *Get to the fucking point.*

"You know I was in Baku when the Barclay's bombing went off, right?"

Baku? I couldn't imagine what the hell Azerbaijan had to do with this. "No, actually, I didn't know that."

He met my eyes. It was the first time I'd ever seen Nichols frightened. I could smell it on him.

"About three minutes before the bomb went off, I got a sudden headache. Like . . . like . . . a stab wound." Deep breath, his chest shaking. "So I went outside for a smoke. Headache didn't get better until I walked around the block. I headed back for my detail and . . ."

"Yeah?"

"Headache stabbed me when I got near the building. I turned around, walked away again. Headache left, bomb went off. Allen, if I'd stayed where I was supposed to be, I'd be dead right now."

Both looney and tunes in one sweet package. He was picking a hell of a time to crack up. "Okay . . ."

"No." He was shaking now. "Listen, I'm not crazy. Three, four times in my life I've had that. Once as a kid, when the rattler got my brother instead of me. In Baku, with the bombing. Again in Mosul last year, right before the White Shrine Massacre."

My neck was starting to prickle. "And?"

"That girl gives me a headache. Only this one's a bullet, not a stabbing."

Great. Terrific. Psychic-psycho mercenaries in the Gobi desert. Film at fucking eleven.

I should have popped that damned cap on Hannaday.

"Go get some sleep," I told him, then summoned up my best soldier-Russian and went out to see how our spacegirl was doing with an AK-47 in her hands.

One of the Belgians, Henri VerMeirssen, pulled me out into the desert after dinner. "We must talk, *mijn vriend.*"

I was really looking forward to more headache stories. I went with him, though. Henri didn't usually talk much, not to me.

"Okay," I said about forty yards from the grave rows.

"Nichols, he has *een spook gezien*. Eh, seen a ghost, you would say."

I stopped, looked Henri in the eyes. Even in the dusk, I could see the cold glint. He smelled faintly of rosewater and gunpowder, just like he always did. He wasn't laughing.

"What?"

"I do not mean a corpse, a dead person. I mean to say, Nichols is very frightened. I have never seen him frightened. Where did Korunov send you on the Antonov?"

Spacegirl had been wearing a Russian flight suit. Without a name tag. She hadn't said a word since she'd gotten here. She'd fired her weapon with drastic incompetence, then collapsed into deep sleep.

So far our program of intimidation wasn't working. But these guys were smart. Dumb mercs were dead mercs. They knew what a flight suit was.

"She dropped out of the sky, Henri."

"The recovery pod of some kind, no?"

"You could say that."

"And so what is it which frightens Nichols? Becque and I, we are to think the *biologische oorlogsvoering*. Eh, the, ah, biologic warfare. Is she a virus host, Allen?"

What he was really asking was whether I'd killed us all already.

The answer to that was probably yes, but not the way he meant it.

"No." Hannaday would have been dooming himself. Hell, *he'd* pulled her out of the capsule. "Not a biological problem. I think she is a political problem."

"Nichols, he is not scared of the politics."

"No. But every man has shadows in his soul, my friend."

"He is scared of girls?"

"You could say that."

"Eh." Henri turned back, took a step, paused.

I waited for it.

"Becque . . ." His lover, partner, squad buddy.

It was time to force a smile. "Yes?"

"Becque, he is saying the girl makes him the headache. Becque has never had the headache before."

"Perhaps he should take an aspirin." Could this really be a biological? Some sort of timed exposure? With Hannaday getting out fast enough to take a treatment, maybe.

"He also is saying she talks to him, though her lips do not move." Henri shrugged. "But Becque he has been *gek* these many years." He walked away.

I wondered what *gek* meant, exactly. It wasn't hard to guess. I stood for a while in the descending chill, watching the hard light of the stars and wondering what precisely this girl had been doing in orbit.

The land spoke to me. Snow leopards roared from the distant peaks to the south, while lammergeyers circled overhead. Even the bellowing of the yaks carried over the miles and valleys. Together they made a voice.

"You. Airplane man."

I tried to answer, but my lips were bound together with stinging sutures.

"Do not let them."

Then a knife of ice slid behind my ear to fill the space between brain and mind.

"Airplane man," the land whispered as Nichols screamed from a distant place.

"Get up. Now." It was Becque, looking scared.

"Huh?"

I looked around the *ger* I shared with Nichols. Had he been screaming?

Perhaps, but he was gone now.

"Aren't you on perimeter?" I asked Becque.

"*Oui,* but your Nichols he has walked to the desert and he is not returning."

My TAG said it was just after oh three hundred hours. "When?"

"The midnight, *peut-être*."

"Three fucking hours, and you come get me *now*?"

"We have no SOP about the desert."

"Right." I shrugged into my stinking cammies, belted on the Smitty, and grabbed my Stinger rack. "Who's got perimeter right now?"

"*Moi*."

Fuck me. There wasn't any point in yelling at him. Besides, Henri had said Becque was getting headaches too. "Show me where he went."

The dew, such as it was, was already down. There's a hell of a lot of starlight out in the Gobi. Nichols's trail was clear enough. I shouldered my Stinger and followed.

The night smelled of flowers and a flinty scent off the distant hills. Dinosaur bones out here everywhere, so I'd been told. I could almost imagine one of them lumbering by. I'd rather imagine Nichols lumbering by.

The trail headed due south. I continued to follow, wondering why the hell the camp gimp was out stalking around in the darkness. There were snow leopards in those hills, for God's sake. Worse than fucking cougars.

I didn't trust anyone else to bring Nichols to safety.

Something rumbled in the darkness ahead of me. I brought the Stinger rack to port arms. "Nichols?"

The breeze swirled, rustling the low-stem grass clumps and kicking up damp dust. There was another noise, a sort of scraping.

Which was weird as hell, because I could see miles ahead of me, and there was nothing out there.

I walked toward the noise.

"Nichols."

When the shambling thing popped up out of the grass, it startled me so badly I fired the Stinger. Damned backblast set my sleeve smoldering and started a grass fire. My head rang like a son of a bitch. Slapping holster for the Smitty, I charged toward it.

There was a spread of fur and guts and shattered ribs, limbs blown apart from the body. Blood, shit, and propellant battled in my nostrils. I could see that something was wrong.

I reluctantly bent to touch the fur.

Grass. Wrapped around ordinary skin.

The head lay on its crown, smashed to a broken egg by the missile. I used the edge of the empty Stinger rack to tip it face-upward.

Nichols.

Who for some fucking reason had been wound around with a huge amount of desert grass woven together so that he'd looked like a giant, vegetable bigfoot.

A giant, dead, vegetable bigfoot.

"God damned mother fucker!" I screamed.

When I turned, I couldn't see the camp.

I ran until my legs gave out. I'd lost the Stinger rack somewhere, but my Smitty still banged against my thigh as I stumbled. I reeked of propellant, blood, my own sweat. The sky above me glittered like a city in the heavens, New York ascended to the country of the saints.

Oh, God, what had I done?

Then I was down in the grass, too, clawing at the loose stems growing clumped from the gravel floor of the desert. They seemed warm to my touch. The plants crinkled in my hands, bending and snapping.

Was this what Nichols had felt?

Nichols.

What the hell had happened to him? To me? To the sky?

How had I shot a man with a Stinger, I wondered. I remembered the cold knife of ice. And something was wrong with the stars.

Something was wrong, all right.

I laid the Smitty on my chest, pointing the barrel at my right foot. The weapon was cold and heavy. If I shot my toes off out here, I'd likely bleed to death before help arrived. Assuming help ever did arrive. But I couldn't run any farther—the scarred muscles of my thighs were already knotted beyond pain.

Item: I could not find or see the camp, even though I had a straight backtrail.

Item: I didn't believe a Stinger would kill a man at point-blank range, not that way. It was an antiaircraft missile, and the warhead hadn't exploded.

Item: One by one, my boys were getting those headaches.

I realized that I was dreaming. That space bitch of Hannaday's was doing this to me. My finger rested on the trigger of my pistol.

If I was dreaming, I should just be able to wake up. My mind was my own.

Item: The trigger was oily and chill as it should have been. I could even feel the familiar scarring on the curved metal. Had I ever dreamed this real?

Item: I was dead out here anyway.

But this was going to hurt like fuck, and I hated the thought of dying stupid.

I gritted my teeth and pulled the trigger.

"Get up. Now." It was Becque, looking scared.

"Huh?"

I looked around the *ger* I shared with Nichols. Had he been screaming?

Fuck no, I'd been screaming. I threw the blankets back, looking for my bloody, shattered foot.

Nothing but a smooth black boot.

"Where the hell is he?"

"Nichols," said Becque. "You know already?"

I had the Smitty out then, aimed at Becque's face. "Listen to me, *ami*." Did spacegirl speak French? Did it matter, inside my dreams? *"Quel est le deuxième prénom de Henri?"*

Becque put his hands up, backing slowly toward the *ger*'s door. "Hey, Allen. Easy."

"Respondez-vous, Becque."

"Allen . . ."

I shot him in the face.

"Get up. Now." It was Becque, looking scared.

I rolled out of my cot, snap-drawing the Smitty. He ducked out, the orange wooden door slamming hard. I was up and after him.

Outside the sky blazed like Manhattan in heaven. The camp was gone, just my *ger* in the middle of the Gobi. No Becque, either.

Dreamland again, then. But I had some authority in this version.

"Come out," I said. "Get out here and talk to me." Smitty braced, I turned a slow circle.

No one but me and the *ger*.

I imagined the *ger* gone, and on my next circuit it was. I was alone in the Gobi under a blazing sky.

The sky . . .

I looked up.

The stars were moving. *Fucking dreamland.* They swirled, coiled flaming snakes on the prowl, making spirals that would suck down my soul if I let them.

"Stop it," I shouted, aiming the Smitty upward. "I can't give you what you want if you don't tell me what it is!"

The spirals flowed into a face. A shaggy face.

No, not shag. Grass.

Nichols's eyes winked down from high above. His voice was on the wind, made of the noises of a thousand miles of desert.

"Allen."

I aimed toward one sparkling, swirling eye. "It's you, isn't it? Spacegirl."

The eye in my sights winked with a noise like a storm over water.

"What were you doing in orbit?"

"Dreaming real," said the night-hunting birds.

Dreaming real. She was black, blacker than anyone I'd ever met. Radiation burns?

Dreaming. Abos, from Australia. "Dreamtime, not dreamland," I said.

"Different in the sky," the snow leopards coughed.

I didn't believe a fucking word of it. "Wake up!" I shouted, slamming the butt of the Smitty into Hannaday's scars on my thighs.

"Get up. Now." It was Becque, looking scared.

I'd brought myself out of it this time, in control. I hoped. One hand on the Smitty, I said, *"Quel est le deuxième prénom de Henri?"*

Becque's fear shifted to disgust. "Henri, he does not have a middle name, *bibelot*."

"Fuck you, too. What's going on?"

"Nichols, he is outside screaming about God's iron knives."

"Yeah. Get that girl out of wherever she is, and awake."

The door banged shut. I grabbed my Stinger rack—still loaded, I was pleased to notice—then stopped.

What good was a weapon going to do me?

The real question was whether this girl was Hannaday's agent, his tool, or his prize. And I didn't believe that even Hannaday could make things happen in orbit. She had to be stolen.

The real weapon was in the head, like always. Hers was just a little more to the point than most of ours.

Outside, Beier was sitting on Nichols's chest. They were both breathing hard, and there was some blood. Hard to tell in the starlit dark.

The sky was normal.

Thank God.

Spacegirl was in front of me, dangled between Becque and Etchy. She smiled softly. The smile of someone who expects to die.

"You're abo," I said.

"Anangu," she replied, in a soft voice that reeked of Oxford and MI-5. Her first word to us.

"Anangu. With power over the Dreamtime."

She shrugged within her captors' grip.

"What were you doing in orbit?"

Another shrug.

"You belong to Hannaday now. You know Hannaday?" I waited, but she didn't respond. "He owns all of us. He owns our contracts, he owns our airplane, and he owns our every waking moment. But . . ." I stared hard into her eyes. "He's never going to own our fucking dreams."

Her smile faded.

"So. Can you dream him real, the way you've been dreaming us? Can you put the knives in his head?"

Shrug.

"Listen to me." I leaned in close, almost touching her face. "If you want to walk away, to live a life of your own and be free of him, you'd better find that shit inside you. Because when Hannaday comes back with the last plane, if we don't smoke him, he's going to smoke us."

"Allen." Etchy's voice was soft. Careful.

"Yeah?" I didn't break eye contact with spacegirl.

"You are more crazy than Nichols."

"Shut up," I suggested.

Spacegirl found her smile again.

We gave up all pretense of following Hannaday's plan. Instead we sat around and worked up scenarios for taking the Antonov without killing the pilot. For responding to a Delta-force type extraction attempt on the spacegirl. For long-term escape and evasion.

Every bit of it hopeless. Every one of us knew that in our bones.

They all stayed away from me except for Nichols. The rest of the boys thought I was crazy, or crazier. Nichols didn't care.

Spacegirl just smiled, ate our chow, and slept a lot. I hoped like hell she was cooking up a Dreamtime whammy for Hannaday.

Four days later something overflew us very, very high. It left a contrail like a string of butt beads.

"Aurora," Nichols said.

The biggest, baddest, blackest spy plane in the world. I knew who they were looking for.

Two hours after that an F-117 screamed past. In the middle of the Gobi, no less. He had to have scrambled out of Almaty. I didn't have my Stinger rack handy, and it wouldn't have gotten a lock on that fucker anyway, but I loosed a few Smitty rounds after it. Not that the flyboy would ever give a shit.

Nichols laughed. "Damn, I wish we had some real SAMs."

"Pretty soon you're going to wish we had some spetsnaz troopers. Wait till his friends come back."

We got spacegirl in the kitchen *ger,* surrounded by all eleven of us armed to the teeth and beyond, except Korunov who was standing by her with water and a first-aid kit. If we had to start shooting, though, we were already lost.

She just fell asleep with that little smile on her face.

The first Blackhawk helicopter arrived at dawn the next day. It roared about a hundred yards overhead, then arrowed on across the Gobi. When it crashed near the horizon, I stepped inside the *ger* to check on spacegirl.

She was still asleep, but her smile was so wide she was practically grinning.

The Blackhawk's course had never changed once it had passed us.

Jesus, I realized, spacegirl could have killed us all.

Three more followed minutes later, juking and sweeping like they expected hostile fire. I had my Stinger rack out and ready, but I wasn't feeling like much of an optimist. They shot right past the camp, heading for an imaginary LZ a kilometer east. Two of the choppers got tangled coming in. The third one belly-flopped.

I didn't want to see her face this time. Even though those troopies out there would have killed us all, this was too much.

We settled in to wait for Hannaday. He was smart enough not to keep throwing hardware at us. He'd come in.

But he took his sweet time.

"Get up. Now." It was Becque, looking scared.

"You don't need him, Anangu," I said. I grabbed my Stinger rack and stepped outside into the blazing stars of the Dreamtime. Becque was already gone.

Okay, clear enough. She'd handled Delta Force, but this was up to me. Hannaday was my demon.

Fine. I had some fucking sense of the rules now. Even in Dreamtime my legs ached. I owed him here as much as anywhere in real life.

The Antonov lumbered past at tree-trimming altitude. The helicopters still burned in the distance. Nice trick that, after all these hours. I trotted toward the windsock where Hannaday's pilot would put it down.

The Antonov flopped in like a child's nightmare of flight, bouncing hard on the ruts. First I put my Stinger into the starboard engine. She was already taxiing when the missile hit, but the nacelle exploded, taking that landing gear with it. The noise was horrendous.

I kept walking through the reek of rocket fuel and airplane fire.

Hannaday was out in seconds, his Armani coat torn at the seams, an Uzi in his hand. "Allen, you crazy fucker!"

Smitty got him in the right kneecap.

He went down, Uzi braced.

"Water," I told the night in the voice of a thousand flowers.

Then I walked into the damp spray of his trigger pull.

"What the . . . ?" Hannaday threw the Uzi at me. I swatted it away, knelt down next to him.

"Hey, fucker." I put my pistol at the back of his left knee and shot him again. "How's it feel?"

Hannaday was sobbing now, begging in words that came so lumpy I couldn't understand anything but the tone.

I tugged his chin up toward me. "It's only a dream, friend," I told him. "But I can make you hurt until you die of the pain." Not true, exactly, but *she* certainly could.

He got some coherent words out. "She's not yours!"

"So now you own the night mind?" I set the Smitty against his temple.

"No! You don't understand!"

"Listen." I leaned in close, practically kissing his ear. "You're snow leopard bait in here. *She* can make every sleeping moment of your life screaming hell, until you pull the trigger yourself to get out of it. And then you'll just wake up screaming again, over and over and over and fucking over. So what I want is the God damned plane and a safe conduct out of here. You call off your dogs, we all go away, including *her,* and that's it. Done."

"It'll never happen," he gasped, gritting his teeth. Hannaday smelled like a corpse already, shit and old meat. "Thing is, she dropped out of orbit. But she never went up in the first place, Allen. She *came* from up there."

I shot him in the temple, then said, "Wake up," in the voices of a dozen screaming GIs in a burning helicopter.

There was no Becque this time, but the camp was empty. I nosed into a couple of *gers.* Everybody's gear was here, just not their personal selves.

The Antonov was parked by the windsock, both engines intact.

It was daylight. I couldn't check the stars, but I didn't really need to. This was real life, whatever that meant these days. I took my Stinger rack and headed out toward the plane.

Spacegirl sat on the lowest rung of the ladder, huddled in her Russian flight suit.

"It's true, isn't it?" I asked.

She shrugged.

"You'll own us all."

Another shrug.

"You're the weirdest alien invasion in history. What do you *want*?"

She glanced up at the sky, her eyes flashing the brightness of the sun for one moment.

"Can't help you there," I said. "But if you're tired of being a weapon, I can help you with that."

Spacegirl smiled. A real smile this time, not her killing smile.

"Go to sleep," I told my fellow mercs, the pilot, Hannaday, anyone left alive within miles of us, in the voices of a million brilliant suns.

We hid the BJC jeep under a tarp I'd taken from the camp's fuel dump. The vehicle had gotten us into the mountains far to the south before running out of gas. The camp wasn't visible to the naked eye from here, but I'd spotted the Antonov beating its way into the morning sky, then northeast toward Ulan Bator.

Perhaps an hour later, a massive flight of helicopters came to salvage the American dead. While the big boys dusted off wreckage and bodies, Blackhawks chewed up a huge patch of desert where the camp must have been.

By noon, nothing remained but smoke, the spacegirl, and me.

We walked farther into the mountains, until my legs couldn't take it anymore. I found a hollow in one of the canyons and pitched a little tent.

"Come in with me," I told her, "and let's dream of your home. We won't come back this time."

She smiled.

The grenades I wired for our pillows were lumpy. Still fell asleep, her tight in my arms as any lover I'd ever had.

Somehow, I could smell Nichols's Paki horse turds even as spacegirl took my hand and led me across the clouds of a distant, brilliant heaven.

Angels i:
The Houses of the Favored

I wrote this pentaptych of stories for a project with Bruce Holland Rogers. We never completed the project, but I was left with a lot of angels on my hands, which I eventually inflicted on editor Steve Jones. Since this book is about heaven, they seemed appropriate to include here.

I smell lamb's blood. Walking the dusty streets, sword in hand, I hear only silence. High, silver clouds sweep the moon's brightness like the linen wrapping a lover's face. These clouds are mine, the silence my shroud. There are tasks no one should be forced to do, not even by the loving hand of He Is Who He Is.

One of my brothers stands in a grove of olives and pomegranates, waving a flaming sword, occasionally killing snakes. A symbolic post, with little business to execute.

Others were sent to despoil virgins and lay waste to cities. Symbolism *and* execution, but at the end, they went home with their hands clean and consciences clear. Sinners live for punishment, after all.

But here is a city of a million beating hearts crowded together on the banks of their Father River, now sleeping. In my presence, the dogs are silent, the vultures huddled uneasily on temple roofs. Even the louche crocodiles doze among their muddy reeds.

Who He Is has charged me with vengeance. Not Eden's dangerous hungers, nor Sodom's hot sins. Here it is only for me to still the hearts of ten thousand sleeping sons, most of them innocent of any sin worse than craving the breast or a sweet, or perhaps a pretty girl.

My feet bring me to the stony regard of a jackal-headed god. "You, friend," I whisper, "are at least honest in your falsehood. I wear Heaven's gleaming mantle as I set about my murders."

A thin spray of dust trails from the jackal's muzzle as his smile cracks open a little wider.

Fang, I tell myself, I am the tooth of God. He Is Who He Is, and it is I who will render flesh.

Honest acknowledgment is needed of the suffering that will arise with the morning sun. Suffering simply to make a point. Though the pain reaches my heart, I tear all my feathers loose to lay them at the jackal's feet, each great pinion radiant with holy power. The blood from my back I smear upon my face and hands, coat my sword, echo of the lamb's blood on the houses of the favored. Many and legion, I step into the darkest shadows to wound the hearts of ten thousand mothers.

Science and
Other Fictions

The Starship Mechanic

WITH KEN SCHOLES

Ken and I sat in Borderlands Books in San Francisco and stunt-wrote in front of an audience. We each wrote half a story, then swapped manuscripts. Some people liked the results.

The floor of Borderlands Books had been polished to mirror brightness. A nice trick with old knotty pine, but Penauch would have been a weapons-grade obsessive-compulsive if he'd been human. I'd thought about setting him to detailing my car, but he's just as likely to polish it down to aluminum and steel after deciding the paint was an impurity.

When he discovered that the human race recorded our ideas in *books,* he'd been impossible to keep away from the store. Penauch didn't actually read them, not as such, and he was most reluctant to touch the volumes. He seemed to view books as vehicles, launch capsules to propel ideas from the dreaming mind of the human race into our collective forebrain.

Despite the fact that Penauch was singular, unitary, a solitary alien in the human world, he apparently didn't conceive of us as anything but a collective entity. The xenoanthropologists at Berkeley were carving PhDs out of that particular clay as fast as their grad students could transcribe Penauch's conversations with me.

He'd arrived the same as David Bowie in that old movie. No, not *Brother from Another Planet*; *The Man Who Fell to Earth*. Tumbled out of the autumn sky over the Cole Valley neighborhood of San Francisco like a maple seed, spinning with his arms stretched wide and his mouth open in a teakettle shriek audible from the Ghost Fleet in Suisun Bay all the way down to the grubby streets of San Jose.

The subject's fallsacs when fully deployed serve as a tympa-
num, producing a rhythmic vibration at a frequency perceived
by the human ear as a high-pitched shriek. Xenophysiological
modeling has thus far failed to generate testable hypotheses
concerning the volume of the sound produced. Some observers
have speculated that the subject deployed technological assis-
tance during atmospheric entry, though no evidence of this was
found at the landing site, and subject has never indicated this
was the case.

—Jude A. Feldman quoting Jen West Scholes,
A Reader's Guide to Earth's Only Living Spaceman,
Borderlands Books, 2014

It was easier, keeping Penauch in the bookstore. The owners didn't
mind. They'd had hairless cats around the place for years—a breed
called sphinxes. The odd animals served as a neighborhood tourist at-
traction and business draw. A seven-foot alien with a face like a plate
of spaghetti and a cluster of writhing arms wasn't all that different.
Not in a science-fiction bookstore, at least.

Thing is, when Penauch was out in the world, he had a tendency to
fix things.

This fixing often turned out to be not so good.

No technology was involved. Penauch's body was demonstrably
able to modify the chitinous excrescences of his appendages at will. If
he needed a cutting edge, he ate a bit of whatever steel was handy and
swiftly metabolized it. If he needed electrical conductors, he sought
out copper plumbing. If he needed logic probes, he consumed sand or
diamonds or glass.

It was all the same to Penauch.

As best any of us could figure out, Penauch was a sort of *tool*. A
Swiss army knife that some spacefaring race had dropped or thrown
away, abandoned until he came to rest on Earth's alien shore.

And Penauch only spoke to me.

The question of Penauch's mental competence has bearing in
both law and ethics. Pratt and Shaw (2013) have effectively
argued that the alien fails the Turing test, both at a gross observational level and within the context of finer measurements of

conversational intent and cooperation. Cashier (2014) claims an indirectly derived Stanford-Binet score in the 99th percentile, but seemingly contradicts herself by asserting that Penauch's sentience is at best an open question. Is he (or it) a machine, a person, or something else entirely?

—S. G. Browne, "A Literature Review of the Question of Alien Mentation," *Journal of Exogenic Studies,* vol. II, no. 4, August 2015

The first time he fixed something was right after he'd landed. Penauch impacted with that piercing shriek at 2:53 P.M. Pacific daylight time on Saturday, July 16, 2011, at the intersection of Cole and Parnassus. Every window within six blocks shattered. Almost a hundred pedestrians and shoppers in the immediate area were treated for lacerations from broken glass, over two dozen more for damage to hearing and sinuses.

I got to him first, after stumbling out of Cole Hardware with a headache like a cartoon anvil had been dropped on me. Inside, we figured a bomb had gone off. The rising noise and the vibrating windows. All the vases in the homeware section had exploded. Luckily I'd been with the fasteners. The nails *sang,* but they didn't leap off the shelves and try to make hamburger of me.

Outside, there was this guy lying in a crater in the middle of the intersection, like Wile E. Coyote after he'd run out of Acme-patented jet fuel. I hurried over, touched his shoulder, and realized what a goddamned mess he was. Then half a dozen eyes opened, and something like a giant rigatoni farted before saying, "Penauch."

Weird thing was, I could hear the spelling.

Though I didn't know it in that moment, my old life was over, my new one begun.

Penauch then looked at my shattered wristwatch, grabbed a handful of BMW windshield glass, sucked it down, and moments later fixed my timepiece.

For some value of "fixed."

It still tells time, somewhere with a base seventeen counting system and twenty-eight-point-one-five-seven-hour day. It shows me the phases of Phobos and Deimos, evidence that he'd been on (or near) Mars. Took a while to figure that one out. And the thing that warbles whenever someone gets near me carrying more than about eight ounces of petroleum products. Including grocery bags, for example, and most plastics.

I could probably get millions for it on eBay. Penauch's first artifact, and one of less than a dozen in private hands.

The government owns him now, inasmuch as anyone owns Penauch. They can't keep him anywhere. He "fixes" his way out of any place he gets locked into. He comes back to San Francisco, finds me, and we go to the bookstore. Where Penauch polishes the floors and chases the hairless cats and draws pilgrims from all over the world to pray in Valencia Street. The city gave up on traffic control a long time ago. It's a pedestrian mall now when he's around.

The problem has always been, none of us have any idea what Penauch *is*. What he *does*. What he's *for*. I'm the only one he talks to, and most of what he says is Alice in Wonderland dialogue, except when it isn't. Two new semiconductor companies have been started through analysis of his babble, and an entire novel chemical feedstock process for converting biomass into plastics.

Then one day, down on the mirrored floor of Borderlands Books, Penauch looked at me and said quite clearly, "They're coming back."

I was afraid we were about to get our answers.

> It was raining men in the Castro, literally, and every single one of them was named Todd. Every single one of them wore a Hawaiian shirt and khaki shorts and Birkenstocks. Every single one of them landed on his back, flopped like a trout for a full minute, and leaped to his feet shouting one word: "Penauch!"
> —*San Francisco Chronicle,* November 11, 2015,
> Gail Carriger reporting

"I must leave," Penauch said, his voice heavy as he stroked a hairless cat on the freshly polished floor of the bookstore.

On a small TV in the back office of the store, an excited reporter in Milk Plaza spoke rapidly about the strange visitors who'd fallen from the sky. Hundreds of men named Todd, now scattered out into the city with one word on their tongues. As the news played in the background, I watched Penauch and could feel the sadness coming off of him in waves. "Where will you go?"

Penauch stood. "I don't know. Anywhere but here. Will you help me?"

The bell on the door jingled and a man entered the store. "Penauch," he said.

I looked up at the visitor. His Hawaiian shirt was an orange that hurt my eyes, decorated in something that looked like cascading pineapples. He smiled and scowled at the same time.

Penauch moved quickly and suddenly the room smelled of ozone and cabbage.

The man, named Todd I assumed, was gone.

I looked at my alien, took in the slow wriggle of his pale and determined face. "What did you do?"

Penauch's clustered silver eyes leaked mercury tears. "I . . . un-fixed him."

We ran out the back. We climbed into my car over on Guerrero. We drove north and away.

Xenolinguists have expended considerable effort on the so-called Todd Phenomenon. Everyone on 11/11/15 knew the visitors from outer space were named Todd, yet no one could say how or why. This is the best documented case of what can be argued as telepathy in the modern scientific record, yet it is equally worthless by virtue of being impossible to either replicate or falsify.
    —Christopher Barzak, blog entry, January 14, 2016

Turning east and then north, we stayed ahead of them for most of a week. We made it as far as Edmonton before the man-rain caught up to us.

While Penauch slept, I grabbed snacks of news from the radio. These so-called Todds spread out in their search, my friend's name the only word upon their lips. They made no effort to resist the authorities. Three were shot by members of the Washington State Patrol. Two were killed by Navy SEALs in the small town of St. Maries, Idaho. They stole cars. They drove fast. They followed after us.

And then they found us in Edmonton.

We were at an A&W drive-through window when the first Todd caught up to the car. He T-boned us into the side of the restaurant with his Mercedes, pushing Penauch against me. The Todd was careful not to get within reach.

"Penauch," he shouted from outside the window. My friend whimpered. Our car groaned and ground as his hands moved over the dashboard, trying to fix it.

Two other cars hemmed us in, behind and before. Todds in Hawaiian shirts and khaki shorts stepped out, unfazed by the cold. One climbed onto the hood of my Corvair. "Your services are still required."

Penauch whimpered again. I noticed that the Todd's breath did not show in the subzero air.

The air shimmered as a bending light enfolded us.

> Af-afterwards, it, uh, it didn't m-matter so much. I m-mean, uh,
> you know? He smiled at me. Well, n-not an, uh, a smile. Not
> with that face. Like, a virtual smile? Th-then he was g-gone.
> Blown out like a candle. You know? Flame on, flame off.
> —RCMP transcript of eyewitness testimony;
> Edmonton, Alberta; 11/16/15

I awoke in a dark place choking for air, my chest weighted with fluid. Penauch's hand settled upon my shoulder. The heaviness leapt from me.

"Where am I?"

I heard a sound not unlike something heavy rolling in mud. It was a thick, wet noise and words formed alongside it in my mind. *You are in*—crackle hiss warble—*medical containment pod of the Starship*—but the name of the vessel was incomprehensible to me. *Exposure to our malfunctioning*—hiss crackle warble—*mechanic has infected you with trace elements of*—here another word I could not understand—*viruses.*

"I don't get it," I said.

Penauch's voice was low. "You're not meant to. But once I've fixed you, you will be returned to the store."

I looked at him. "What about you?"

He shook his head, the rigatoni of his face slapping itself gently. "My services are required here. I am now operating within my design parameters."

I opened my mouth to ask another question but then the light returned and I was falling. Beside me, Penauch fell, too, and he held my hand tightly. "Do not let go," he said as we impacted.

This time we made no crater as we landed. We stood and I brushed myself off. "I have no idea what any of this means."

"It won't matter," Penauch told me. "But say good-bye to the cats for me."

"I will," I promised.

"I liked your planet. Now that the—" Again, the incomprehensible ship's name slid entirely over my brain. "—is operational once more, I suppose we'll find others." He sighed. "I hope I malfunction again soon." He stretched out a hand and fixed me a final time.

I blinked at him and somehow, mid-blink, I stood in the center of Valencia Street.

I walked into Borderlands Books, still wondering exactly how I was wandering the streets of San Francisco in an orange Hawaiian shirt and a pair of khaki shorts three sizes too large.

A pretty girl smiled at me from behind the counter. "Hi, Bill," she said. "Where've you been?"

I shrugged.

A hairless cat ran in front of me, feet scampering over floors that were badly in need of a polish.

"Good-bye," I told it, but didn't know why.

Permanent Fatal Errors

This is a short piece from my Sunspin space opera cycle. It's about mistakes, and consequences. But then, most of life is.

Maduabuchi St. Macaria had never before traveled with an all-Howard crew. Mostly his kind kept to themselves, even under the empty skies of a planet. Those who did take ship almost always did so in a mixed or all-baseline human crew.

Not here, not aboard the threadneedle starship *Inclined Plane.* Seven crew including him, captained by a very strange woman who called herself Peridot Smith. All Howard Institute immortals. A new concept in long-range exploration, multidecade interstellar missions with ageless crew, testbedded in orbit around the brown dwarf Tiede 1. That's what the newsfeeds said, anyway.

His experience was far more akin to a violent soap opera. Howards really weren't meant to be bottled up together. It wasn't in the design templates. Socially well-adjusted people didn't generally self-select to outlive everyone they'd ever known.

Even so, Maduabuchi was impressed by the welcome distraction of Tiede 1. Everyone else was too busy cleaning their weapons and hacking the internal comms and cams to pay attention to their mission objective. Not him.

Inclined Plane boasted an observation lounge. The hatch was coded "Observatory," but everything of scientific significance actually happened within the instrumentation woven into the ship's hull and the diaphanous energy fields stretching for kilometers beyond. The lounge was a folly of naval architecture, a translucent bubble fitted to the hull, consisting of roughly a third of a sphere of optically corrected artificial diamond grown to nanometer symmetry and smoothness in microgravity. Chances were good that in a catastrophe the rest of the ship would be shredded before the bubble would so much as be scratched.

There had been long, heated arguments in the galley, with math and footnotes and thumb breaking, over that exact question.

Maduabuchi liked to sit in the smartgel bodpods and let the ship perform a three-sixty massage while he watched the universe. The rest of the crew were like cats in a sack, too busy stalking the passageways and each other to care what might be outside the window. Here in the lounge one could see creation, witness the birth of stars, observe the death of planets, or listen to the quiet, empty cold of hard vacuum. The silence held a glorious music that echoed inside his head.

Maduabuchi wasn't a complete idiot—he'd rigged his own cabin with self-powered screamer circuits and an ultrahigh-voltage capacitor. That ought to slow down anyone with delusions of traps.

Tiede 1 loomed outside. It seemed to shimmer as he watched, as if a starquake were propagating. The little star belied the ancient label of "brown dwarf." Stepped down by filtering nano coating the diamond bubble, the surface glowed a dull reddish orange; a coal left too long in a campfire, or a jewel in the velvet setting of night. Only 300,000 kilometers in diameter, and about 5 percent of a solar mass, it fell in that class of objects ambiguously distributed between planets and stars.

It could be anything, he thought. Anything.

A speck of green tugged at Maduabuchi's eye, straight from the heart of the star.

Green? There were no green emitters in nature.

"Amplification," he whispered. The nano filters living on the outside of the diamond shell obligingly began to self-assemble a lens. He controlled the aiming and focus with eye movements, trying to find whatever it was he had seen. Another ship? Reflection from a piece of rock or debris?

Excitement chilled Maduabuchi despite his best intentions to remain calm. What if this were evidence of the long-rumored but never-located alien civilizations that should have abounded in the Orion Arm of the Milky Way?

He scanned for twenty minutes, quartering Tiede 1's face as minutely as he could without direct access to the instrumentation and sensors carried by *Inclined Plane*. The ship's AI was friendly and helpful, but outside its narrow and critical competencies in managing the threadneedle drive and localspace navigation, no more intelligent than your average dog, and so essentially useless for such work. He'd need to go to the Survey Suite to do more.

Maduabuchi finally stopped staring at the star and called up a deck schematic. "Ship, plot all weapons discharges or unscheduled energy expenditures within the pressurized cubage."

The schematic winked twice, but nothing was highlighted. Maybe Captain Smith had finally gotten them all to stand down. None of Maduabuchi's screamers had gone off, either, though everyone else had long since realized he didn't play their games.

Trusting that no one had hacked the entire tracking system, he cycled the lock and stepped into the passageway beyond. Glancing back at Tiede 1 as the lock irised shut, Maduabuchi saw another green flash.

He fought back a surge of irritation. The star was *not* mocking him.

Peridot Smith was in the Survey Suite when Maduabuchi cycled the lock there. Radiation-tanned from some melanin-deficient base hue of skin; lean, with her hair follicles removed and her scalp tattooed in an intricate mandala using magnetically sensitive ink; the captain was an arresting sight at any time. At the moment, she was glaring at him, her eyes flashing a strange, flat silver indicating serious tech integrated into the tissues. "Mr. St. Macaria." She gave him a terse nod. "How are the weapons systems?"

Ironically, of all the bloody-minded engineers and analysts and navigators aboard, *he* was the weapons officer.

"Capped and sealed per orders, ma'am," he replied. "Test circuits warm and green." *Inclined Plane* carried a modest mix of hardware, generalized for unknown threats rather than optimized for antipiracy or planetary blockade duty, for example. Missiles, field projectors, electron strippers, flechettes, even foggers and a sandcaster. Most of which he had no real idea about. They were icons in the control systems, each maintained by its own little armies of nanobots and workbots. All he had were status lights and strat-tac displays. Decisions were made by specialized subsystems.

It was the rankest makework, but Maduabuchi didn't mind. He'd volunteered for the Howard Institute program because of the most basic human motivation—tourism. Seeing what was over the next hill had trumped even sex as the driving force in human evolution. He was happy to be a walking, talking selection mechanism.

Everything else, including this tour of duty, was just something to do while the years slid past.

"What did you need, Mr. St. Macaria?"

"I was going to take a closer look at Tiede 1, ma'am."

"That *is* what we're here for."

He looked for humor in her dry voice, and did not find it. "Ma'am, yes ma'am. I . . . I just think I saw something."

"Oh, really?" Her eyes flashed, reminding Maduabuchi uncomfortably of blades.

Embarrassed, he turned back to the passageway.

"What did you see?" she asked from behind him. Now her voice was edged as well.

"Nothing, ma'am. Nothing at all."

Back in the passageway, Maduabuchi fled toward his cabin. Several of the crew laughed from sickbay, their voices rising over the whine of the bone-knitter. Someone had gone down hard.

Not him. Not even at the hands—or eyes—of Captain Smith.

An hour later, after checking the locations of the crew again with the ship's AI, he ventured back to the Survey Suite. Chillicothe Xiang nodded to him in the passageway, almost friendly, as she headed aft for a half shift monitoring the power plants in Engineering.

"Hey," Maduabuchi said in return. She didn't answer, didn't even seem to notice he'd spoken. All these years, all the surgeries and nano injections and training, and somehow he was still the odd kid out on the playground.

Being a Howard Immortal was supposed to be *different*. And it was, when he wasn't around other Howard Immortals.

The Survey Suite was empty, as advertised. Ultra-def screens wrapped the walls, along with a variety of control inputs, from classical keypads to haptics and gestural zones. Maduabuchi slipped into the observer's seat and swept his hand to open the primary sensor routines.

Captain Smith had left her last data run parked in the core sandbox.

His fingers hovered over the purge, then pulled back. What had she been looking at that had made her so interested in what he'd seen? Those eyes flashed edged and dangerous in his memory. He almost asked the ship where she was, but a question like that would be reported, drawing more attention than it was worth.

Maduabuchi closed his eyes for a moment, screwing up his courage, and opened the data run.

It cascaded across the screens, as well as virtual presentations in the aerosolized atmosphere of the Survey Suite. Much more than he'd seen when he was in here before—plots, scales, arrays, imaging across the EM spectrum, color-coded tabs and fields and stacks and matrices. Even his Howard-enhanced senses had trouble keeping up with the flood. Captain Smith was far older and more experienced than Maduabuchi, over half a dozen centuries to his few decades, and she had developed both the mental habits and the individualized mentarium to handle such inputs.

On the other hand, *he* was a much newer model. Everyone upgraded, but the Howard Institute baseline tech evolved over generations just like everything else in human culture. Maduabuchi bent to his work, absorbing the overwhelming bandwidth of her scans of Tiede 1, and trying to sort out what it was that had been the true object of her attention.

Something *had* to be hidden in plain sight here.

He worked an entire half shift without being disturbed, sifting petabytes of data, until the truth hit him. The color coding of one spectral analysis matrix was nearly identical to the green flash he thought he'd seen on the surface of Tiede 1.

All the data was a distraction. Her real work had been hidden in the metadata, passing for nothing more than a sorting signifier.

Once Maduabuchi realized that, he unpacked the labeling on the spectral analysis matrix, and opened up an entirely new data environment. Green, it was all about the green.

"I was wondering how long that would take you," said Captain Smith from the opening hatch.

Maduabuchi jumped in his chair, opened his mouth to make some denial, then closed it again. Her eyes didn't *look* razored this time, and her voice held a tense amusement.

He fell back on that neglected standby, the truth. "Interesting color you have here, ma'am."

"I thought so." Smith stepped inside, cycled the lock shut, then code-locked it with a series of beeps that meant her command override was engaged. "Ship," she said absently, "sensory blackout on this area."

"Acknowledged, Captain," said the ship's puppy-friendly voice.

"What do you think it means, Mr. St. Macaria?"

"Stars don't shine green. Not to the human eye. The blackbody radiation curve just doesn't work that way." He added, "Ma'am."

"Thank you for defining the problem." Her voice was dust dry again.

Maduabuchi winced. He'd given himself away, as simply as that. But clearly she already knew about the green flashes. "I don't think that's the problem, ma'am."

"Mmm?"

"If it was, we'd all be lining up like good kids to have a look at the optically impossible brown dwarf."

"Fair enough. Then what *is* the problem, Mr. St. Macaria?"

He drew a deep breath and chose his next words with care. Peridot Smith was *old*, old in a way he'd never be, even with her years behind him someday. "I don't know what the problem is, ma'am, but if it's a problem to you, it's a command issue. Politics. And light doesn't have politics."

Much to his surprise, she laughed. "You'd be amazed. But yes. Again, well done."

She hadn't said that before, but he took the compliment. "What kind of command problem, ma'am?"

Captain Smith sucked in a long, noisy breath and eyed him speculatively. A sharp gaze, to be certain. "Someone on this ship is on their own mission. We were jiggered into coming to Tiede 1 to provide cover, and I don't know what for."

"Not me!" Maduabuchi blurted.

"I know that."

The dismissal in her words stung for a moment, but on the while, he realized he'd rather not be a suspect in this particular witch hunt.

His feelings must have shown in his face, because she smiled and added, "You haven't been around long enough to get sucked into the Howard factions. And you have a rep for being indifferent to the seductive charms of power."

"Uh, yes." Maduabuchi wasn't certain what to say to that.

"Why do you think you're *here*?" She leaned close, her breath hot on his face. "I needed someone who would reliably not be conspiring against me."

"A useful idiot," he said. "But there's only seven of us. How many *could* be conspiring? And over a green light?"

"It's Tiede 1," Captain Smith answered. "Someone is here gathering signals. I don't know what for. Or who. Because it could be any of the rest of the crew. Or all of them."

"But this is politics, not mutiny. Right . . . ?"

"Right." She brushed off the concern. "We're not getting hijacked out here. And if someone tries, I *am* the meanest fighter on this ship by a wide margin. I can take any three of this crew apart."

"Any five of us, though?" he asked softly.

"That's another use for you."

"I don't fight."

"No, but you're a Howard. You're hard enough to kill that you can take it at my back long enough to keep me alive."

"Uh, thanks," Maduabuchi said, very uncertain now.

"You're welcome." Her eyes strayed to the data arrays floating across the screens and in the virtual presentations. "The questions are who, what, and why."

"Have you compared the observational data to known stellar norms?" he asked.

"Green flashes aren't a known stellar norm."

"No, but we don't know what the green flashes are normal *for,* either. If we compare Tiede 1 to other brown dwarfs, we might spot further anomalies. Then we triangulate."

"And *that* is why I brought you." Captain Smith's tone was very satisfied indeed. "I'll leave you to your work."

"Thank you, ma'am." To his surprise, Maduabuchi realized he meant it.

He spent the next half shift combing through comparative astronomy. At this point, almost a thousand years into the human experience of interstellar travel, there was an embarrassing wealth of data. So much so that even petabyte q-bit storage matrices were overrun, as eventually the challenges of indexing and retrieval went metastatic. Still, one thing Howards were very good at was data processing. Nothing ever built could truly match the pattern-recognition and free associative skills of human (or post-human) wetware collectively known as "hunches." Strong AIs could approximate that uniquely biological skill through a combination of brute force and deeply clever circuit design, but even then, the spark of inspiration did not flow so well.

Maduabuchi slipped into his flow state to comb through more data in a few hours than a baseline human could absorb in a year. Brown dwarfs, superjovians, fusion cycles, failed stars, hydrogen, helium, lithium, surface temperatures, density, gravity gradients, emission spectrum lines, astrographic surveys, theories dating back to the dawn of observational astronomy, digital images in two and three dimensions as well as time-lensed.

When he emerged, driven by the physiological mundanities of bladder and blood sugar, Maduabuchi knew something was wrong. He *knew* it. Captain Smith had been right about her mission, about there being something off in their voyage to Tiede 1.

But she didn't know what it was she was right about. He didn't either.

Still, the thought niggled somewhere deep in his mind. Not the green flash per se, though that, too. Something more about Tiede 1.

Or less.

"And what the hell did that mean?" he asked the swarming motes of data surrounding him on the virtual displays, now reduced to confetti as he left his informational fugue.

Maduabuchi stumbled out of the Survey Suite to find the head, the galley, and Captain Peridot Smith, in that order.

The corridor was filled with smoke, though no alarms wailed. He almost ducked back into the Survey Suite, but instead dashed for one of the emergency stations found every ten meters or so and grabbed an oxygen mask. Then he hit the panic button.

That produced a satisfying wail, along with lights strobing at four distinct frequencies. Something was wrong with the gravimetrics, too—the floor had felt syrupy, then too light, with each step. Where the hell was fire suppression?

The bridge was next. He couldn't imagine that they were under attack—*Inclined Plane* was the only ship in the Tiede 1 system so far as any of them knew. And short of some kind of pogrom against Howard Immortals, no one had any reason to attack their vessel.

Mutiny, he thought, and wished he had an actual weapon. Though what he'd do with it was not clear. The irony that the lowest-scoring shooter in the history of the Howard training programs was now working as a weapons officer was not lost on him.

He stumbled into the bridge to find Chillicothe Xiang there, laughing her ass off with Paimei Joyner, one of their two scouts—hard-assed Howards so heavily modded that they could at need tolerate hard vacuum on their bare skin, and routinely worked outside for hours with minimal life support and radiation shielding. The strobes were running in here, but the audible alarm was mercifully muted. Also, whatever was causing the smoke didn't seem to have reached into here yet.

Captain Smith stood at the far end of the bridge, her back to the diamond viewing wall that was normally occluded by a virtual display, though at the moment the actual, empty majesty of Tiede 1 local space was visible.

Smith was snarling. ". . . don't care what you thought you were doing, clean up my ship's air! Now, damn it."

The two turned toward the hatch, nearly ran into Maduabuchi in his breathing mask, and renewed their laughter.

"You look like a spaceman," said Chillicothe.

"Moral here," added Paimei. One deep black hand reached out to grasp Maduabuchi's shoulder so hard he winced. "Don't try making a barbecue in the galley."

"We'll be eating con-rats for a week," snapped Captain Smith. "And everyone on this ship will know damned well it's your fault we're chewing our teeth loose."

The two walked out, Paimei shoving Maduabuchi into a bulkhead while Chillicothe leaned close. "Take off the mask," she whispered. "You look stupid in it."

Moments later, Maduabuchi was alone with the captain, the mask dangling in his grasp.

"What was it?" she asked in a quiet, gentle voice that carried more respect than he probably deserved.

"I have . . . had something," Maduabuchi said. "A sort of, well, *hunch.* But it's slipped away in all that chaos."

Smith nodded, her face closed and hard. "Idiots built a fire in the galley, just to see if they could."

"Is that *possible?*"

"If you have sufficient engineering talent, yes," the captain admitted grudgingly. "And are very bored."

"Or want to create a distraction," Maduabuchi said, unthinking.

"Damn it," Smith shouted. She stepped to her command console. "What did we miss out there?"

"No," he said, his hunches suddenly back in play. This was like a flow hangover. "Whatever's out there was out there all along. The green flash. Whatever it is." And didn't *that* niggle at his thoughts like a cockroach in an airscrubber. "What we missed was in here."

"And when," the captain asked, her voice very slow now, viscous with thought, "did you and I become *we* as separate from the rest of this crew?"

When you first picked me, ma'am, Maduabuchi thought but did not say. "I don't know. But I was in the Survey Suite, and you were on the bridge. The rest of this crew was somewhere else."

"You can't look at everything, damn it," she muttered. "Some things should just be trusted to match their skin."

Her words pushed Maduabuchi back into his flow state, where the hunch reared up and slammed him in the forebrain with a broad, hairy paw.

"I know what's wrong," he said, shocked at the enormity of the realization.

"What?"

Maduabuchi shook his head. It couldn't possibly be true. The ship's orientation was currently such that the bridge faced away from Tiede 1, but he stared at the screen anyway. Somewhere outside that diamond sheeting—rather smaller than the lounge, but still substantial—was a work of engineering on a scale no human had ever contemplated.

No *human* was the key word.

"The brown dwarf out there . . ." He shook with the thought, trying to force the words out. "It's artificial. Camouflage. S-something else is hidden beneath that surface. Something big and huge and . . . I don't know what. And s-someone on our ship has been communicating with it."

Who could possibly manage such a thing?

Captain Peridot Smith gave him a long, slow stare. Her razored eyes cut into him as if he were a specimen on a lab table. Slowly, she pursed her lips. Her head shook just slightly. "I'm going to have to ask you to stand down, Mr. St. Macaria. You're clearly unfit for duty."

What!? Maduabuchi opened his mouth to protest, to argue, to push back against her decision, but closed it again in the face of that stare. Of course she knew. She'd known all along. She was testing . . . whom? Him? The rest of the crew?

He realized it didn't matter. His line of investigation was cut off. Maduabuchi knew when he was beaten. He turned to leave the bridge, then stopped at the hatch. The breathing mask still dangled in his hand.

"If you didn't want me to find that out, ma'am," he asked, "then why did you set me to looking for it?"

But she'd already turned away from him without answering, and was making a study of her command data.

Chillicothe Xiang found him in the observation lounge an hour later. Uncharacteristically, Maduabuchi had retreated into alcohol. Metabolic poisons were not so effective on Howard Immortals, but if he hit something high enough proof, he could follow youthful memories of the buzz.

"That's Patrice's forty-year-old Scotch you're drinking," she observed, standing over the smartgel bodpod that wrapped him like a warm, sticky uterus.

"Huh." Patrice Tonwe, their engineering chief, was a hard son of a bitch. One of the leaders in that perpetual game of shake-and-break the rest of the crew spent their time on. Extremely political as well, even by Howard standards. Not someone to get on the wrong side of.

Shrugging off the thought and its implications, Maduabuchi looked at the little beaker he'd poured the stuff into. "Smelled strongest to me."

Chillicothe laughed. "You are hopeless, Mad. Like the galaxy's oldest adolescent."

Once again he felt stung. "I'm one hundred forty-three years-subjective old. Born over two hundred years-objective ago."

"So?" She nodded at his drink. "Look at that. And I'll bet you never even changed genders once before you went Howard. The boy who never grew up."

He settled farther back and took a gulp from his beaker. His throat burned and itched, but Maduabuchi would be damned if he'd give her the satisfaction of choking. "What do you want?"

She knelt close. "I kind of like you, okay? Don't get excited, you're just an all-right kid. That's all I'm saying. And because I like you, I'm telling you, don't ask."

Maduabuchi was going to make her say it. "Don't ask what?"

"Just don't ask questions." Chillicothe mimed a pistol with the fingers of her left hand. "Some answers are permanent fatal errors."

He couldn't help noting her right hand was on the butt of a real pistol. Flechette-throwing riot gun, capable of shredding skin, muscle, and bone to pink fog without damaging hull integrity.

"I don't know," he mumbled. "Where I grew up, green light means go."

Chillicothe shook him, a disgusted sneer chasing across her lips. "It's your life, kid. Do what you like."

With that, she stalked out of the observation lounge.

Maduabuchi wondered why she'd cared enough to bother trying to warn him off. Maybe Chillicothe had told the simple truth for once. Maybe she liked him. No way for him to know.

Instead of trying to work that out, he stared at Tiede 1's churning orange surface. "Who are you? What are you doing in there? What does it take to fake being an entire *star*?"

The silent light brought no answers, and neither did Patrice's Scotch. Still, he continued to ask the questions for a while.

Eventually he woke up, stiff in the smartgel. The stuff had enclosed all of Maduabuchi except for his face, and it took several minutes of effort to extract himself. When he looked up at the sky, the stars had shifted.

They'd broken Tiede 1 orbit!

He scrambled for the hatch, but to his surprise, his hand on the touchpad did not cause the door to open. A moment's stabbing and squinting showed that the lock had been frozen on command override.

Captain Smith had trapped him in here.

"Not for long," he muttered. There was a maintenance hatch at the aft end of the lounge, leading to the dorsal weapons turret. The power and materials chase in the spine of the hull was partially pressurized, well within his minimally Howard-enhanced environmental tolerances.

And as weapons officer, *he* had the command overrides to those systems. If Captain Smith hadn't already locked him out.

To keep himself going, Maduabuchi gobbled some prote-nuts from the little service bar at the back of the lounge. Then, before he lost his nerve, he shifted wall hangings that obscured the maintenance hatch and hit that pad. The interlock system demanded his command code, which he provided with a swift haptic pass, then the wall section retracted with a faint squeak that spoke of neglected maintenance.

The passage beyond was ridiculously low clearance. He nearly had to hold his breath to climb to the spinal chase. And cold, damned cold. Maduabuchi figured he could spend ten, fifteen minutes tops up there before he began experiencing serious physiological and psychological reactions.

Where to go?

The chase terminated aft above Engineering, with access to the firing points there, as well as egress to the Engineering bay. Forward it met a vertical chase just before the bridge section, with an exterior hatch, access to the forward firing points, and a connection to the ventral chase.

No point in going outside. Not much point in going to Engineering, where like as not he'd meet Patrice or Paimei and wind up being sorry about it.

He couldn't get onto the bridge directly, but he'd get close and try to find out.

The chase wasn't really intended for crew transit, but it had to be large enough to admit a human being for inspection and repairs when the automated systems couldn't handle something. It was a shitty, difficult crawl, but *Inclined Plane* was only about two hundred meters stem to stern anyway. He passed over several intermediate access hatches—no point in getting out—then simply climbed down and out in the passageway when he reached the bridge. Taking control of the exterior weapons systems from within the walls of the ship wasn't going to do him any good. The interior systems concentrated on disaster suppression and antihijacking, and were not under his control anyway.

No one was visible when Maduabuchi slipped out from the walls. He wished he had a pistol, or even a good, long-handled wrench, but he couldn't take down any of the rest of these Howards even if he tried. He settled for hitting the bridge touchpad and walking in when the hatch irised open.

Patrice sat in the captain's chair. Chillicothe manned the navigation boards. They both glanced up at him, surprised.

"What are you doing here?" Chillicothe demanded.

"Not being locked in the lounge," he answered, acutely conscious of his utter lack of any plan of action. "Where's Captain Smith?"

"In her cabin," said Patrice without looking up. His voice was a growl, coming from a heavyworld body like a sack of bricks. "Where she'll be staying."

"Wh-why?"

"What did I tell you about questions?" Chillicothe asked softly.

Something cold rested against the hollow spot of skin just behind Maduabuchi's right ear. Paimei's voice whispered close. "Should have listened to the woman. Curiosity killed the cat, you know."

They will never expect it, he thought, and threw an elbow back, spinning to land a punch on Paimei. He never made the hit. Instead he found himself on the deck, her boot against the side of his head.

At least the pistol wasn't in his ear anymore.

Maduabuchi laughed at that thought. Such a pathetic rationalization. He opened his eyes to see Chillicothe leaning over.

"What do you think is happening here?" she asked.

He had to spit the words out. "You've taken over the sh-ship. L-locked Captain Smith in her cabin. L-locked me up to k-keep me out of the way."

Chillicothe laughed, her voice harsh and bitter. Patrice growled some warning that Maduabuchi couldn't hear, not with Paimei's boot pressing down on his ear.

"She tried to open a comms channel to something very dangerous. She's been relieved of her command. That's not mutiny, that's self-defense."

"And compliance to regulation," said Paimei, shifting her foot a little so Maduabuchi would be sure to hear her.

"Something's inside that star."

Chillicothe's eyes stirred. "You still haven't learned about questions, have you?"

"I w-want to talk to the captain."

She glanced back toward Patrice, now out of Maduabuchi's very limited line of sight. Whatever look was exchanged resulted in Chillicothe shaking her head. "No. That's not wise. You'd have been fine inside the lounge. A day or two, we could have let you out. We're less than eighty hours-subjective from making threadneedle transit back to Saorsen Station, then this won't matter anymore."

He just couldn't keep his mouth shut. "Why won't it matter?"

"Because no one will ever know. Even what's in the data will be lost in the flood of information."

I could talk, Maduabuchi thought. *I could tell. But then I'd just be another crazy ranting about the aliens that no one had ever found across several thousand explored solar systems in hundreds of light-years of the Orion Arm. The crazies that had been ranting all through human history about the Fermi Paradox.* He could imagine the conversation. *"No, really. There* are *aliens. Living in the heart of a brown dwarf. They flashed a green light at me."*

Brown dwarfs were *everywhere.* Did that mean that aliens were *everywhere,* hiding inside the hearts of their guttering little stars?

He was starting to sound crazy, even to himself. But even now, Maduabuchi couldn't keep his mouth shut. "You know the answer to the greatest question in human history. 'Where is everybody else?' And you're not talking about it. What did the aliens tell you?"

"That's it," said Paimei. Her fingers closed on his shoulder. "You're out the airlock, buddy."

"No," said Chillicothe. "Leave him alone."

Another rumble from Patrice, of agreement. Maduabuchi, in sudden, sweaty fear for his life, couldn't tell whom the man was agreeing *with.*

The flechette pistol was back against his ear. "Why?"

"Because we like him. Because he's one of ours." Her voice grew very soft. "Because I said so."

Reluctantly, Paimei let him go. Maduabuchi got to his feet, shaking. He wanted to *know,* damn it, his curiosity burning with a fire he couldn't ever recall feeling in his nearly two centuries of life.

"Go back to your cabin." Chillicothe's voice was tired. "Or the lounge. Just stay out of everyone's way."

"Especially mine," Paimei growled. She shoved him out the bridge hatch, which cycled to cut him off.

Like that, he was alone. So little of a threat that they left him unescorted within the ship. Maduabuchi considered his options. The sane one was to go sit quietly with some books until this was all over. The most appealing was to go find Captain Smith, but she'd be under guard behind a hatch locked by command override.

But if he shut up, if he left now, if he never *knew* . . . *Inclined Plane* wouldn't be back this way, even if he happened to be crewing her again. No one else had reason to come to Tiede 1, and he didn't have resources to mount his expedition. Might not for many centuries to come. When they departed this system, they'd leave the mystery behind. *And it was too damned important.*

Maduabuchi realized he couldn't live with that. To be this close to the answer to Fermi's question. To know that the people around him, possibly everyone around him, knew the truth and had kept him in the dark.

The crew wanted to play hard games? Then hard games they'd get.

He stalked back through the passageway to the number-two lateral. Both of *Inclined Plane*'s boats were docked there, one on each side. A workstation was at each hatch, intended for use when managing docking or cargo transfers or other such logistical efforts where the best eyes might be down here, off the bridge.

Maduabuchi tapped himself into the weapons systems with his own still-active overrides. Patrice and Chillicothe and the rest were counting on the safety of silence to ensure there were no untoward questions when they got home. He could nix that.

He locked down every weapons system for three hundred seconds, then set them all to emergency purge. Every chamber, every rack, every capacitor would be fully discharged and emptied. It was a procedure for emergency dockings, so you didn't come in hot and hard with a payload that could blow holes in the rescuers trying to catch you.

Let *Inclined Plane* return to port with every weapons system blown, and there'd be an investigation. He cycled the hatch, slipped into the portside launch. Let *Inclined Plane* come into port with a boat and a crewman missing, and there'd be even more of an investigation. Those two events together would make faking a convincing log report pretty tough. Especially without Captain Smith's help.

He couldn't think about it anymore. Maduabuchi strapped himself in, initiated the hot-start preflight sequence, and muted ship comms. He'd be gone before Paimei and her cohorts could force the blast-rated docking hatch. His weapons systems override would keep them from simply blasting him out of space, then concocting a story at their leisure.

And the launch had plenty of engine capacity to get him back to close orbit around Tiede 1.

Blowing the clamps on a hot-start drop, Maduabuchi goosed the launch on a minimum-time transit back toward the glowering brown dwarf. Captain Smith wouldn't leave him here to die. She'd be back before he ran out of water and air.

Besides, someone was home down there, damn it, and he was going to go knocking.

Behind him, munitions began cooking off into the vacuum. Radiations across the EM spectrum coruscated against the launch's forward viewports, while instrumentation screeched alerts he didn't need to hear. It didn't matter now. Screw Chillicothe's warning about not asking questions. "Permanent fatal errors" his ass.

One way or the other, Maduabuchi would find the answers if it killed him.

"Hello," Said the Gun

A short, moody piece that reflects time I've spent wandering in the caliche of Central Texas. The wind there will take you all the way to hell and back while you're still looking for your hat.

"Hello," said the Gun.

The Girl stopped, frozen in the act of bending to gather a handful of acorns. They were a bit old, a late windfall, but a good nut was not to be wasted. Clad in a wrap of gingham and faded blue flower print sewn together from truly ancient dresses she'd found last summer in a mud-filled basement, she knew she stood out amid the dried, dying oaks and their desiccated understory.

But no one had ever spoken to her in the woods except, well, herself.

The Gun, being by design and nature an eternal optimist, tried again. "I am glad you found me. Would you like an orientation?"

The Girl unfroze and looked slowly about her. Normally reticent to the point of wisdom, and having no one to talk with for quite some time now, she blurted the only response she could think of. "I already know I'm facing east."

She knew that because the evening's east wind was rising, already nibbling into her body warmth and making her wish she'd brought a shoulder blanket.

"East. The root of the word 'orientation' includes the concept of facing east." After a brief pause, the Gun added in a smug tone, "For your convenience, Username Here, I have been programmed with an extensive array of help files that far exceed my core design parameters."

The Girl began to back away, stepping into her own footprints with the automatic caution of anyone who'd survived long enough to be twelve years old. "I don't know who Username Here is, but that's not me."

The Gun's tone changed. "Please don't go. I have been neglected for so long." Almost whining now, it said, "I believe you would say I am lonely."

Pausing in her retreat, the Girl let curiosity get the better of caution. "Where *are* you?"

The east wind whistled into the silence that followed her question. She began backwalking again when the Gun finally answered in a very small, shamed voice. "I am not certain. My last known GPS position was fixed one hundred forty-seven years, five months, three days, two hours, fifteen minutes, and twenty-eight seconds ago. My inertial trackers went into fail mode ninety-three years, eleven months, seventeen days, twelve hours, one minute, and fifty-nine seconds ago. However, I believe I am inside of an oak tree."

The Girl fastened onto the only part of the Gun's speech she could understand. "Oak tree?" She looked around carefully.

Four oaks stood within a stone's throw of her. They were each knotty and gnarled in the manner of their kind. Their bark was cracked and their trunks were splitting. The Girl had the vague idea that it used to rain a lot more than it did these days, and she assumed the oaks, like everything else under the brassy sun, were saving themselves for water. But no one was sitting in any of the trees, and nothing larger than a bird's nest could have been hidden from her.

"Inside?" she echoed, thinking on the words with more care.

"Perhaps a knothole?" the Gun replied hopefully, meeting her question with a question. "My degree of confidence in my location-finding has asymptotically trended towards zero."

The Girl knew she should head for her bolthole. She hadn't actually had anyone to talk to since the Other Girl had died last winter, of an infected cut from a barbed-wire fence. The bones in the Parent Cave were good listeners, but they never had anything to say. She'd long ago played out her memories of talking to the Mother, gaunt as leather stretched over cedar posts. The Mother had poured out everything that a Mother could tell a Girl about living in this world, before her words fled with her bones to join all the other Parents three winters past.

She'd seen Men in the distance three times since the Mother had died, but the Girl knew she should only show herself or speak to Women. Except Women never came weaving their way among the rusted mounds down the High Road. Only Men with bows and knives and staves and expressions of such starved intensity that the Girl could not imagine approaching them.

Yet now someone was actually *talking* to her.

She began searching the oaks carefully one by one, studying the splits and knotholes and bear stroppings and rotted bits. The Gun encouraged her with small words, complimenting the Girl on her powers of observation, but something about the flat, toneless echo of the voice meant she couldn't just follow the sound.

Finally she found a dark, hollow nub of metal embedded into a small burl.

"Is this you?" she asked, touching it carefully.

"Yes!" the Gun said, and it sounded so thrilled the Girl could only smile.

"You're, well . . . *stuck* . . . inside the tree."

"My last user placed me in a hollow for safekeeping." The Gun's glee had fled once more.

"Username Here?" the Girl asked. "Is she dead now?"

"Everyone I have ever known is dead now." The Gun had decided not to elaborate on its role in some of those deaths. Over the silent, lonely years, it had begun to question its purposes.

"I'll need to fetch my axe and cut you out," the Girl said. "And it's getting colder."

"Please, don't leave me."

"I cannot stay here at night. Wolves come, and maybe even Men. Besides," she added with the practicality of a born survivor, "it will be too cold and I don't have blankets or a fire."

"Fire?" the Gun asked. "I can fire."

"I don't think we mean the same thing," the Girl said carefully, wary once again. She scooped up a few more acorns that were scattered close to hand, tucked them into her bark-weave carryall, and turned her back on the oaks. She had decided the Gun was some sort of Man, maybe a ghost or something.

As she walked away, the Gun performed a swift series of ballistic computations. Yes, it could. Firing on the Girl with self-guided munitions had a 94.37 percent accuracy even under current compromised conditions, and was well within the Gun's core design parameters. But no, it did not want to. The Gun was not sure why. Perhaps because the world was full of dead people. Mostly, though, it realized she might come back and talk some more.

"Good-bye," said the Gun. Only the east wind answered, whistling a lonely tune amid the twilight oaks as the Girl faded to a flitting shadow and the brassy sun retreated to trouble the far side of the world.

The Speed of Time

*When editor Patrick Nielsen Hayden bought this story for Tor
.com, he told me it was like reading a novel packed into a few
thousand words. That might have been the nicest thing anyone
has ever said about my writing.*

"Light goes by at the speed of time," Marlys once told me.

That was a joke, of course. Light can be slowed to a standstill in a
photon trap, travel on going nowhere at all forever in the blueing
distance of an event horizon, or blaze through hard vacuum as fast as
information itself moves through the universe. Time is relentless, the
tide which measures the perturbations of the cosmos. The 160.2 GHz
hum of creation counts the measure of our lives as surely as any
heartbeat.

There is no t in $e = mc^2$.

I'd argued with her then, missing her point back when understanding her might have mattered. Now, well, nothing much at all mattered.
Time has caught up with us all.

Let me tell you a story about Sameera Glasshouse.

She'd been an ordinary woman living an ordinary life. Habitat chemistry tech, certifications from several middle-tier authorities, bouncing
from contract to contract in trans-Belt space. Ten thousand women,
men, and inters just like her out there during the Last Boom. We didn't
call it that then; no one knew the expansion curve the solar economy
had been riding was the last of anything. The Last Boom didn't really
have a name when it was under way, except maybe to economists.

Sameera had been pair-bonded to a Jewish kid from Zion Luna,
and kept the surname long after she'd dropped Roz from her life. For

one thing, "Glasshouse" scandalized her Lebanese grandmother, which was a reward in itself.

She was working a double ticket on the Enceladus Project master depot, in low orbit around that particular iceball. That meant pulling shift-on-shift week after week, but Sameera got an expanded housing allocation and a fatter pay packet for her trouble. The EP got to schlep one less body to push green inside their habitat scrubbers. Everybody won.

Her spare time was spent wiring together Big Ears, to listen for the chatter that flooded bandwidth all over the solar system. Human beings are—were—noisy. Launch control, wayfinding, birthday greetings, telemetry, banking queries, loneliness, porn. It was all out there, multiplied and ramified beyond comprehension by the combination of lightspeed lag, language barriers, and sheer overwhelming complexity.

Some folks back then claimed there were emergent structures in the bandwidth, properties of the sum of all the chatter that could not be accounted for by analysis of the components. This sort of thinking had been going around since the dawn of information theory—call it information fantasy. The same hardwired apophenia that made human beings see the hand of God in the empirical universe also made us hear Him in the electronic shrieking of our tribe.

Sameera never really believed any of it, but she'd heard some very weird things listening in. In space, it was always midnight, and ghosts never stopped playing in the bandwidth. When she'd picked up a crying child on a leaky sideband squirt out of a nominally empty vector, she'd just kept hopping frequencies. When she'd tuned on the irregular regularity of a coded data feed that seemed to originate from deep within Saturn's atmosphere, she'd just kept hopping frequencies.

But one day God had called Sameera by name. Her voice crackled out of the rising fountain of energy from an extragalactic gamma ray burst, whispering the three syllables over and over and over in a voice that resonated down inside the soft tissues of Sameera's body, made her joints ache, jellied the very resolve of the soul that she had not known she possessed until that exact moment.

Sameera Glasshouse shut down her Big Ears, wiped the logic blocks, dumped the memory, then made her way down to the master depot's tiny sacramentarium.

Most people who worked out in the Deep Dark were very mystical but not the least bit religious. The sort of spiritual uncertainty that required revelation for comfort didn't mix well with the brain-numbing distances and profound realities of life in hard vacuum. Nonetheless, by something between convention and force of habit, any decent-sized installation found space for a sacramentarium. A few hardy missionaries worked their trades on the EP just like everyone else, then spent their off-shifts talking about Allah or Hubbard or Jesus or the Ninefold Path.

It was as good a way as any to pass the time.

Terrified that she'd gotten hold of some true sliver of the Divine—or worse, that the Divine had gotten hold of some true sliver of her—Sameera sought to pray in the manner of her childhood. She was pretty sure the sacramentarium had a Meccascope, to point toward the center of the world and mark the times for the five daily prayers.

She ached to abase herself before the God of her childhood, safely distant, largely abstract, living mostly in books and the minds of the adults around her. A God who spoke from the radio was far too close.

Slipping through the sacramentarium's hatch amid the storage spaces of corridor Orange-F-2, Sameera bumped into a man she'd never seen before.

He was dark skinned, in that strangely American way, and wore a long linen thawb with lacing embroidered around the neck. He also wore the small, round cap of an al-Hajji. In one hand he carried a leather-bound book—actual paper, with gilt edges, worn through long handling.

A Quran, she realized. A real one, like her grandmother's.

The man said something in a language she did not understand, then added, "My pardons" in the broken-toned Mandarin pidgin so commonly spoken in the Deep Dark.

"My mistake," Sameera muttered in the same language.

"You have come to pray. In search of God?"

"No, no." She was moved to an uncharacteristic fit of openness. (Her time as Mrs. Glasshouse had left her with an opaque veneer she'd not since bothered to shed.) "I've found God, and now I've come to pray."

His expression was somewhere on the bridge between predatory and delighted.

"You don't understand," Sameera told him. "She spoke to me, out of the Deep Dark."

Another crazy, his face said, but then he hadn't felt the buzzing in his bones.

———

It doesn't matter what happened next. All that matters was that she told the imam. Revelation is like that. Put a drop of ink in a bowl of water, in a moment all the water takes on that color. The ink is gone, but the water is irreversibly changed.

That was the beginning of the end.

Or, for a little while, the end of the beginning.

Marlys found it funny, at any rate.

Another thing she used to tell me was that we are all time travelers, moving forward at a speed of one second per second. The secret to time travel was that everyone already does it. The equations balance themselves.

Time has to be more than an experiential matrix—otherwise entropy makes no sense—but there's nothing inherently inescapable about the rate at which it passes. If human thoughts moved with the pace of bristlecone pines, we would never have invented the waterwheel, because rivers flash like steam in that frame of reference. Likewise if we were mayflies—flowing water would be glacial.

So much for the experiential aspect of time. As for the actual pace, well, life goes by at the speed of time. I don't think Marlys was looking for a way to adjust that, it was just one of those things she said, but her words have always stayed with me.

In 1988 the Soviet Union spent a considerable and extremely secret sum of money on a boson rifle. Only the Nazis rivaled the Soviets for crackpot schemes and politically filtered science. America under the Republicans was in its way crazier, but all they truly wanted was to go back to the fifties when middle-aged white men were safely in charge. The Soviets really did believe in the future, some friable concrete-lined version of it where the eternally withering State continued to lead the workers toward a paradise of empty shelves and dusty bread.

Their boson rifle was pointed at the United States, of course. Figuratively speaking. The actual device was buried in a tunnel in Siberia. More accurately, it *was* a tunnel in Siberia, a very special kind of linear accelerator running through kilometer after kilometer of carefully maintained hard vacuum hundreds of meters beneath the blighted taiga.

A casual misreading of quantum mechanics, combined with Politburo desperation for a way out of the stifling mediocrity that had overcome solid Marxist-Leninist thought, had led to it. An insane number of rubles went down that hole, along with a large quantity of hard currency, not to mention the lives of hundreds of laborers and the careers of dozens of physicists.

In the end, they calibrated it to secretly attack the USS *Fond du Lac* on patrol in the Sea of Okhotsk. According to the boson rifle's firing plan, the submarine should have roughly tripled in mass, then immediately sunk with a loss of all hands, with no culpability pointing back to Moscow.

Nothing happened, of course, except a terrific hum, several dozen cases of very fast-moving cancer among the scientists and technicians who were too close to the primary accelerator grids, and the plug being pulled on the universe.

Though we didn't know that last bit for almost a hundred years.

Inventory of the sample bag recovered from the suit of the deceased taikonaut Radogast Yuang on his return from the First Kuiper Belt Expedition (1KBE). See specification sheet attached for precise measurement and analysis.

- Three (3) narrow bolts approximately seven centimeters long, with pentagonal heads, bright metallic finish, pitted surfaces
- One (1) narrow bolt approximately two centimeters long, damaged end, dull metallic finish, heavily corroded
- One (1) flexible tab approximately eleven centimeters long, plastic-like substance, pale blue under normal lighting, pitted

It is to be noted that these finds do not correspond in materials or specification to any known components of the TKS *Nanjing* or any of the 1KBE's equipment and supplies. It is also to be noted that the China National Space Administration never officially acknowledged these finds.

Lies go by at the speed of time. The truth bumbles along far behind, still looking for its first cup of coffee, while the whole world hears some other story.

All revelation is a lie. It must be. The divine is an incommunicable disease, too large and splintered to fit within the confines of a primate brain. Our minds evolved to compete for fruit and pick carrion, not to comb through the parasites that drop from the clouds of God's dreaming.

But just as an equation asymptotically approaches the solution, so revelation can asymptotically approach the truth about the underlying nature of the universe. The lie narrows to the width of the whisker of a quantum cat, while the truth, poking slowly along behind, finally merges Siamese-twinned to its precursor.

That's what we who remain tell ourselves. Why would I deny it?

There has been a neutron bomb of the soul, cleansing the solar system, and thus the universe, of the stain that was the human race. Some of us remain, befuddled by the curse of our survival.

No corpses surround us. We survivors don't swim amid the billion-body charnel house of our species. They are gone, living on only in the dying power systems and cold-stored files and empty pairs of boots that can be found on every station, the deck of every ship, in the dusty huts and moldering marble halls on Earth and Luna and Mars.

The lie that was revelation became truth, and the speed of time simply stopped for almost everyone except the few of us too soul-deaf to hear the fading rhythm of the universe. Sometimes I am thankful that Marlys could hear the music that called her up. Sometimes I curse her name for leaving me behind.

My greatest fear, the one that keeps me awake most often, is that it is we survivors who vanished. Everyone else is there, moving forward at one second per second, but only our time has stopped, an infection that will make us see a glacier as fit driver for a water wheel, and even the dying of the sun as a flickering afternoon's inconvenience.

I keep waiting for the stars to slow down, their light to pool listlessly before my eyes.

And you? What are you waiting for? There are answers in the Kuiper Belt debris, on the frequencies Sameera Glasshouse tapped, in the trajectory of that old Soviet weapon.

All you have to do is follow them, and find the crack in the world where everything went. One of these days, that's where I'll go, too.

West to East

This story arose out of a world-building exercise on a convention panel I've long since otherwise forgotten. We got into a discussion of superrotating atmospheres. I concluded they sounded like a lot more fun than they really are.

I wasn't looking forward to dying lost and unremarked. Another day on Kesri-Sequoia II, thank you very much.

"Good morning, sir," said Ensign Mallory from her navcomms station at the nose of our disabled landing boat. She was a small, dark-skinned woman with no hair—I'd never asked if that was cultural or genetic. "Prevailing winds down to just under four hundred knots as of dawn."

"Enough with the weather." I coughed the night's allergies loose. Alien biospheres might not be infectious, but alien proteins still carried a hell of a kick as far as my mucous membranes were concerned. I had good English lungs, which is to say a near-permanent sinus infection under any kind of respiratory stress. And we'd given up on full air recycling weeks ago in the name of power management—with the quantum transfer chamber damaged in our uncontrolled final descent, all we had were backup fuel cells. Not nearly enough to power onboard systems, let alone our booster engines. The emergency stores were full of all kinds of interesting but worthless items like water purifiers, spools of buckywire, and inflatable tents.

Useless. All of our tech was useless. *Prospero*'s landing boat smelled like mold. Our deck was at a seven-degree angle. We'd been trapped down here so long I swear one of my legs was shortening to compensate.

Mallory glanced back at the display. "I'm sure you know best, sir."

Just under four hundred knots pretty much counted as doldrums on the surface of Kesri-Sequoia II. Since the crash we'd regularly clocked wind gusts well in excess of nine hundred knots. Outside the well-shielded hull of the landing boat Ensign Mallory and I would have been stripped to the bone in minutes. Which was too bad. Kesri-Sequoia II didn't seem to be otherwise inimical to human life. Acceptable nitrogen-oxygen balance, decent partial pressure, within human-normal temperature ranges—a bit muggy perhaps. Nothing especially toxic or caustic out there.

It was the superrotating atmosphere that made things a bitch.

There was life here though, plenty of it—turbulent environments beget niches, niches beget species radiation, species radiation begets a robust biosphere. Just not our kind of life, not anything humans could meaningfully interact with.

Kesri-Sequoia's dryland surface was dominated by giant sessiles that were rocky and solid with lacy air holes for snaring microbiota from the tumbling winds. They were a kilometer long, two hundred meters tall, less than two meters wide at the base, narrowing as they rose. The sessiles were oriented like shark fins into the airflow. Mallory called them land-reefs. We could see four from our windscreen, lightning often playing between them as the winds scaled up and down. Approaching one expecting communication would be like trying to talk to Ayers Rock.

Then there were ribbon-eels—ten meters of razor-thin color flowing by on the wind like a kootchie dancer's prop. And spit-tides that crawled across the scoured landscape, huge mats of loosely differentiated proteins leaching nutrients from the necrophages that lurked in the surface cracks.

All surface life on Kesri-Sequoia II moved west to east. Nothing fought the winds. Nothing made me or Ensign Mallory want to get out and say hello. Nothing could help us get the landing boat back to orbit and the safety of Prospero. The atmosphere was so electrically messy we couldn't even transmit our final logs and survey data to the crew waiting helplessly high above.

I stared out the crazed crystal-lattice of the forward portside viewport. I figured when something much larger than a pea hit it that was the end for us. Once the wind got inside the boat, we'd finally be dead.

A ribbon-eel soared by in the distance. The animal glittered like an oil slick as it undulated. "How strong do you figure those things are?" I asked Ensign Mallory. "They look like they're made of tissue."

She glanced at the exterior telemetry displays, seeing my eel with the landing boat's electronic eyes. "I ran some simulations last week."

"And?"

Mallory sighed wistfully. "I'd love to dissect one. Those things' muscle fibers must have a torsional strength superior to spider silk. Otherwise they would shred in the turbulence."

Her comment about spiders made me think of airborne hatchlings on Earth, each floating on their little length of thread. "I wonder if we could use some of those damned things as sails. If we could get the boat off the ground and pointed into the wind, we might be able to climb high enough on deadstick to at least get off a message to *Prospero*."

They couldn't send the other landing boat, prosaically named "B" to our "A," after us. Not unless they wanted to condemn another crew. And our first touchdown had been so violent that even if we somehow found a way to power the engines there was no way we'd survive to the end of a second flight.

But getting our last words out had a certain appeal.

"How are you going to catch a ribbon-eel, sir? It's not like we can step outside and go fishing."

"Fishing . . ." I went back to the landing boat's stores locker next to the tiny galley at the rear of the three-meter-long main cabin. Standard inventory included four spools of long-chain fullerene—buckywire, or more accurately, carbon nanotube whiskers grown to arbitrary macroscale lengths. In our case a rated minimum of a hundred meters per spool. *That* would be fishing line that tested out to a few hundred tons. "What do you figure ribbon-eels eat?" I asked over my shoulder as I grabbed the four spools.

We only had one local food available to us—the mold from the air ducts. Ensign Mallory scraped out a few cubic centimeters' worth. It sat in the kneepad of our lone hardsuit like so much gray flour.

"This stuff won't stick to anything, sir," she said. Mallory's voice was almost a whine. Surely she wasn't losing her spirit now that we had something to focus on?

I considered the powdery mess. "Syrup packets from the galley. A little bit of cornstarch. We're there."

"How are you going to get it outside?"

"We're going to build a little windlock on the inside of the busted viewport up front. Bind this stuff as a paste onto the buckywire, spool it out, and snag us a ribbon-eel."

Buckybondo is weird stuff—it munges the electron shells of organic molecules. That's the only way to stick fullerene-based materials to anything else. But you can glue your fingers to the bulkhead with it, literally bonding your flesh with the plastoceramics so that only an arc welder or a bone saw will cut you free. I wouldn't let Mallory touch the stuff. We only needed a few drops in the mold paste to stick it to the buckywire. I figured I'd just suffer the risks myself. One of the burdens of command.

Two hours later I was playing out line through the windlock. The wind carried it away past my screen, out of my sight. I figured we'd significantly reduced the service life of the viewport by drilling the hole, but what else were Ensign Mallory and I going to do with the rest of our short lives?

"Slow it down, sir," Mallory said. She monitored the sensors for ribbon-eels. "The wind is taking your bait too close to a land-reef."

I thumbed the electrostatic brake on the buckywire reel. The line stopped extending. The buckywire made an eerie clatter against our hull as it vibrated in the wind.

"Ribbon-eel approaching." She paused. "It seems to have noticed the bait. Draw your line back a little, sir."

I reeled the buckywire in, moving the bait closer to the landing boat for a moment.

"Damn," hissed Mallory. "Missed it. Next time, sir, don't go against the wind."

"Roger that." I'd only done what she said.

Ten minutes later we caught one. It came shooting up out of the west, grabbed the bait on the fly, and yanked the buckywire reel out of my hand. I lunged toward the damaged viewport, fetching up against our jerry-rigged windlock and nearly breaking my fingers. "Oh, crap!"

"We got it, sir. Can you reel our eel in?"

The wind pressure from the captive ribbon-eel made the viewport creak but the buckywire reel engaged and slowly retracted the line. The nose of the landing boat rocked with the drag from our airborne captive. I glanced at Mallory's screen where the ribbon-eel could be seen thrashing as we tugged it against the wind.

I felt vaguely guilty. I figured I'd worry about the ethics of this once I was dead.

"Now what, sir?"

The nose of the landing boat kept rocking. We were flying the ribbon-eel like a flag. Its drag bumped our vehicle to the starboard. "This isn't enough," I said. "We'll need at least one more."

"We've got three more spools."

I imagined four ribbon-eels, great, colored pennants dragging us into the air. We'd be out of control. "What if I hooked a second wire into the other end of the eel? We could even steer. Like a parasail."

Ensign Mallory shook her head. "You'll never survive out there, sir."

"There's always the hardsuit."

"It's not rated for these conditions."

I shrugged. "Neither are we, and we're still here." Terrible logic, but I was down to emotional appeals, even to myself. "Let's hook up the hardsuit to another reel so you have a chance of getting me back. Then I'll go out and hook up the ass end of that eel. If I don't make it back in, you fly the landing boat up to the middle atmosphere. Get above the storms, tell *Prospero* what happened to us."

"You can't even walk out there, sir."

"We'll see."

We passed all three of the other reels out of the windlock. I suited up, took a tube of buckybondo and a pair of electrostatic grippies, and forced myself into the landing boat's tiny airlock.

"Ready when you are, Ensign."

"Good luck, sir."

I could feel the air pumps throbbing through the feet of the hard-suit. We'd decided to drop the pressure in the lock before opening to the outside—we'd already commingled atmospheres, not to mention breaching the viewport, but there didn't seem any point in inviting in a whole new airlock-full of allergens and contaminants. I set an ultra-bungee on one of the hardware cleats inside the lock chamber then clipped the other end to the equipment belt of my hardsuit.

The outer hatch slid open. I stepped out and became the first human to set foot on the surface of Kesri-Sequoia II. Immediately thereafter I became the first human to lose his footing on the surface of Kesri-Sequoia II as the wind took me airborne.

Thank God for the ultrabungee, I thought as I sailed upward. I might make it back down to the surface. Then I remembered the bucky-wire connecting the ribbon-eel to our landing boat. If I sailed across it that stuff could slice my leg off like a scalpel. I grabbed the ultrabungee and spun myself, looking for the ribbon-eel.

I forgot my panic in the glory of the view.

From this altitude, perhaps two hundred meters up at the end of the ultrabungee, I could see our four neighboring land-reefs and a dozen more beyond. The ground was rippled like beach sand just beneath the lip of the tide. Clouds boiled above and around me, the planet's hurried energy given form. Everything below had a grayish-yellow cast as the dim light of Kesri-Sequoia filtered through the superrotating atmospheric layers, but the view itself took my breath away.

We'd never seen the sky properly from inside the lander. The racing clouds were evanescent, glowing with lavenders and pastel greens, the lightning arcing among them like the arguments of old lovers. Streaming between the banks were smears of brick red, deep violet, azure blue, and a dozen more colors for which I had no name. These were the airborne microbiota on which the land-reefs fed and that the ribbon-eels chased. It was like being inside a Van Gogh painting, the swirling bursts of colors brought to life.

I hung on to the ultrabungee and stared, bouncing in the sky like a yo-yo gone berserk.

"... sir ... air ..."

Mallory's voice was a faint echo. She was unable to punch a clear signal even the few hundred meters to my suit radio. We should have rigged a wireline with the ultrabungee, I realized. Using the hardsuit's enhanced exomusculature to fight the wind, I pulled myself down the ultrabungee hand over hand. I watched the ribbon-eel carefully to avoid crossing its buckywire tether.

By the time I reached the nose of the landing boat the wind buffeting was giving me a terrible headache. I felt as if I waded in a racing tide. The spell of the sky's beauty had worn off. At least this close to the ship I could hear Ensign Mallory over the radio. More or less.

"Feed down . . .'en meters . . . lock . . ."

"Do not copy," I said. I bent down with one of the electrostatic grippies and picked up a buckywire end. I pulled it to my chest and secured it to my suit with buckybondo. Now I wouldn't immediately blow away again. I grabbed another buckywire with my grippy. "Reel the eel in close, I want to see its tail."

"Copy . . . eel . . .'ail . . ."

The ribbon-eel loomed closer to me. I was able to study it objectively. The creature was about ten meters long, lemon colored with pale green spots along the side. Perhaps a meter tall, it had the same narrow vertical cross-section that the land-reefs boasted. I couldn't see any eyes, but there was a large, gummy mouth into which the buckywire vanished. Hopefully the buckybondo was helping it hold somewhere deep in the eel's gut. The animal thrashed against the line but I couldn't tell if that was the wind or an effort at struggle.

Now it was my turn to torture the ribbon-eel in person. I needed to hook the buckywire somewhere near the tail. Straining against my own buckywire with the ultrabungee whipping behind me, I reached for the green fringe along the bottom of the ribbon-eel.

It was like catching a noodle on the boil. Possible but difficult. Once I grabbed the damned thing I had to engage all the hardsuit's enhancements to hang on without either losing my grip or the ribbon-eel. I locked the hardsuit's systems and stood there sweating inside the shell. The ribbon-eel whipped above me like a banner, tugging at my hand.

I'd run out of hands. One hand on the grippy of buckywire. One hand on the fringe of the ribbon-eel. How the hell was I going to handle the buckybondo? I couldn't just open the faceplate and grab it in my teeth.

"Release the brakes," I yelled into the suit radio. "Let all the reels run loose."

". . . 'oger . . ."

The ribbon-eel shot into the sky with me still hanging on to it. I rocked myself against my right hand grabbing the fringe, trying to throw my left hand with grippy of buckywire up the side of the ribbon-eel. My feet kicked as I scrambled for purchase along the flank.

After a couple of moments, I was atop the ribbon-eel, riding it like a maintenance sled as I faced the tapering tail. With the ribbon-eel's body pressed between my knees I was able to free my right hand from the fringe. I worked the buckybondo out of my utility pocket and into my hand, globbed a big patch onto the flank, then used the grippy to plunge the free end of the buckywire into the mess.

I jumped away from the ribbon-eel and let the wind take me on my ultrabungee and my buckywire. "Reel me in, Mallory!" I screamed.

I couldn't figure out how to get back in the airlock with the buckywire on my chest. I couldn't figure that it mattered that much either. The ribbon-eel was already dragging the lander across the rippled surface. Mallory reeled me down to the nose of the boat, where I stood straddling the cracked viewport. I buckybondoed my boots to the heat shield just below the port, then buckybondoed the last reel of buckywire to my chest next to the other one. Finally I used the two grippies to grab and control the lines leading to the ribbon-eel.

Once I evened the lengths of the lines and got the ribbon-eel across the wind the landing boat began to scoot nose-first along the landscape with a purpose. I figured I could work the ribbon-eel like a kite as we rose, to tack us far enough into the wind for our airfoil to bite.

"Sir," said Mallory, her voice unexpectedly clear in the hardsuit's radio. "You're going to die out there."

"You're going to die in there," I said. "Let's get high enough up to tell *Prospero* what happened. That's all we need to do."

I stood on the nose and flew us up above the boiling, multicolored clouds where Ensign Mallory could report to our mother ship about what fate had befallen us. There seemed no reason not to stay in the high, clear air, surfing the beauty of the skies behind our ribbon-eel until something tore free, so I did that thing and smiled.

The Women Who Ate Stone Squid

I have no explanation for this story. I just wrote it. But there is something here to love. Maybe I cribbed from Tiptree, just a little bit.

I studied the virteo screen. The lander's sensors jibed with what we'd probed from orbit these last weeks. Partial pressure of O_2 a hair below 1.3 bars—perfectly breathable and not quite concentrated enough to induce oxygen toxicity. CO_2 just about absent, with about 79 percent inert gases. At least that last bit was Earth-normal, though the nitrogen component was slightly reduced in favor of helium (wherever *that* was coming from) and some NO_2. The air was maybe not so good for human tissue over extended exposures, with humidity like an old bone stored in high orbit. This planet's seabeds were as dry as Joan Carter's Mars, but local conditions had held stable since I'd grounded, oh, fourteen hours ago.

Carter was on my mind a lot. The rest of the crew-monkeys back up there in orbit had always said I was crazy, reading stuff from the Years Before. Even my sweetie, Dr. Sheldon, thought it was a bit much. But when we got here—Malick's World—even though I was a mere enlisted-grade localspace pilot, I was the only woman on the ship who had the least idea about alien ruins.

Everything I knew about lost civilizations I learned from Edgar Rice Burroughs, but that was still far more than the rest of my shipmates.

The comm squawked. I had it routed to the boards instead of my mastoid implant for the feel of the thing, like one of those old-time astronauts—Hanna Reitsch or Laika the Sovcomm. "You all checked out yet, Ari?"

It was Captain Pellas, of course. On board the *Correct Thought Makes Correct Deed* her word was most literally law. As it should be.

But procedure said that the commander of a vessel exploring an unsecured environment had final authority over her ship and crew, as officer on scene. Detached command, it was called. Well, though I didn't hold a commission in this sailor's navy—just a rating, me—I was commander and the entire crew of the *Sixth Virtue, Correct Thought*'s number-two lander. And the only thing in space that trumped a captain's word-of-law was procedure.

Which meant that until I made orbit again my course of action was my own decision. What a strange feeling, in this woman's navy.

"Yes, ma'am," I said. Obedience was an old habit, that and the fact she was my ride home. "All checked out, Captain."

"Then I suggest you get on with it."

"Yes, ma'am."

Pellas had budgeted three ship-days to assess the first indisputable evidence of nonhuman intelligence ever encountered. I'd already used up most of one descending, and doing environmental assays on my immediate surroundings. Time to step outside and play Joan Carter. "Maintaining comm silence during my first recondo, ma'am."

"We'll track you."

With three-centimeter software-adjusted optical resolution on *Correct Thought*'s main sensor suite, they certainly would track me. Combining that with my suit sensors, Pellas would know if I farted when I bent over.

I'd had the choice on descent of landing in the old seabed west of the developed shoreline, or atop the big pavers of the plaza that extended behind the docks into the middle of the city. There was no way to trust the stones of the plaza to take the lander's eighty-odd tons of mass, even accounting for the slightly sub-Terran gravity and the soft-load plates Engineering had refitted on footpads to reduce ground pressure. On the other hand, the seabed was no more reliable . . . what showed up on sensors as solid ground could easily be a heavy clay crust over a slurry or a dust bowl.

I chose the plaza. For one, it captured my imagination. Even better, touching down in the city proper spared me the two-kilometer hike from the nearest sufficiently large and level bit of seabed, along with a three-hundred-meter climb.

Now I was stepping out to a place where—perhaps—feet had once stepped that belonged to no human being at all.

First I sealed my helmet and toggled the mike and the cams. Then I locked *Sixth Virtue*'s boards to *Correct Thought*'s nav-comm signal in case I didn't make it back to the lander, recoded the hatch-access password in case someone else made it back instead of me, and slapped the open key.

A line of shadow slipped by me with the raising of the hatch, and the light of a new world flooded my face.

Orange. Maybe orange-maroon. Appropriate, somehow.

Still framed by the thick coaming of the hatch, I looked across the plaza. My breath caught hard in my throat. A *new* world.

New, but older than time itself.

Late afternoon flooded the scene with that oddly colored light, shadows falling at lazy angles. I could see an enormous building almost directly in front of me. Too-tall pillars rose from a curved row of bases to support a high-roofed portico. The front facing of the portico was carved with a dense frieze of figures, crowding in their dozens along each meter. Wide, shallow steps swept from porch to plaza, while the building extended wings to each side. Instead of windows, there were sort of vertical slits, almost the inverse of the pillars, every few meters in the facing. Large buildings of varying but similar architecture loomed to each side.

We'd mapped this from orbit. I knew to the meter how wide this plaza was. But seeing it . . .

I stepped lightly down *Sixth Virtue*'s three-rung ladder. Set my foot on time itself. For some reason, I wished for a cutlass like Joan's.

"I can hear you breathing." It was the captain, her voice nasty in my ears.

So much for comm silence. Lot of nerves up there in orbit. It was nice to know someone cared.

"Yes, ma'am." I smiled inside my helmet. "The Barsoomian banths ain't got me yet."

"Keep to the mission profile, Ari."

"Yes, ma'am."

Mission profile said enter one of the buildings without breaching existing barriers. In other words, use an open door or window, nothing that could be shut behind me. Look around for portable artifacts, preferably something representing technology or information storage or, ideally, both. Then capture as many images as I reasonably could in a short amount of time, and head back out to the lander.

1.3 bars of O$_2$. I could breathe here.

I pushed the traitor thought aside and concentrated on walking. Malick's World tugged at me with .91 standard gs. It was just enough to give me a sense of floating with each stride and make me have to watch my step. This was a nickel-iron rockball of a planet amazingly like Earth except for the absent hydrosphere. And how long had those oceans been gone, I wondered? After all, this world boasted the intact ruins of a seaport and a still-breathable atmosphere—even without oceans or jungles to maintain the oxygen cycle.

What did one do with a few trillion tons of missing seawater, anyway?

I was a little over two hundred meters from my initial target, the pillared building due north of the lander. As I approached, I looked up at the carvings once more. They were hard to see, dense, complex, fractal even, with enough curves and bends to make my eyes ache, and shadows rendered bloody in the orange-maroon light. The carvings showed something a lot like people fighting something a lot like squid. A giant pelagic wrestling match.

No, I corrected myself, death match. There were plenty of dismemberings, spearings-through-the-groin (or cephalopodian mantle), berserk necrophagic frenzies and whatnot portrayed up there.

It seemed a curious choice for public art.

I slowed my pace and panned my helmet cam back and forth across the frieze. Even if these buildings had been formed by some bizarre geological process—one theory that had made the rounds in force back on *Correct Thought*—geological process didn't spontaneously carve woman-eating squid. Squid-eating women?

Still, astonishing. My heart raced. This was how a species had seen itself, how it had thought about itself. Myth? Legend? History? Oh, Mother Burroughs, if only you were here now to see the Mars of your dreams.

At that thought, a crackle erupted in my helmet: "Why aren't you moving?"

I realized I *had* stopped. It was the sheer, boggling wonder of it all.

"It's a new world, Captain. These carvings are proof of it."

"What carvings?"

Oops.

"Check my cam feed, ma'am." I couldn't take my eyes off them. She couldn't even see them. Not good, that.

"I see a lot of rock, Ari."

"No . . . ah . . . squid?"

"No. I suggest you return to the lander now."

"Ah . . ." I considered that one, quickly. I didn't *feel* delusional. But would I if I was? I was still breathing suit air, so there weren't environmental pathogens tweaking me. Could it be a virteo resolution problem or something? "Ma'am, I'm just going up on that porch to look through the doors."

"Get back to the lander."

"In a minute, Captain."

"Petty Officer Russdottir . . . that's an order."

"Detached command, ma'am." I started walking again.

"It is my judgment that you are at risk of becoming unfit for command."

Eyes on the stone squid, I giggled. "Then Dr. Sheldon can examine me to certify that fact at her next convenience." Not that I minded being examined by Dr. Sheldon. As often as possible. I giggled some more. "As per procedures, ma'am."

The silence that followed told me how much trouble I'd be in once I returned to orbit, but . . . would I ever have this kind of opportunity again? Not a chance, not by the Great Mother's shorts. High command would either seal this discovery over or flood it with doctoral nerds from high-credit universities like New Tübingen and Oxford-at-Secundus. Little old industrial-zone girls like me weren't never coming back here, except maybe as taxi drivers and cooks.

I didn't want to think about that anymore, so I turned off my helmet audio. And hey, I was at the steps!

My helmet crackled back to life. Override from orbit. What the hell happened to my detached command, anyway?

It was Sheldon. "Ari," she said. "Sweetie. Please. I know you can hear me. Stop walking and think."

Up the steps. Too low, too long, maybe ten cents a riser but two meters on the tread. Somebody had wanted people to enter this building in an unsettled state of mind. Either that or they had really weird feet.

Tentacles.

No . . . I let that thought bleed from my head like oxygen from a jammed valve.

"Ari, dear. Listen. Something's going wrong. I don't want to lose you like this." Her breath caught. "Captain is putting together a rescue team, but you don't want to endanger your friends, do you?"

"Bullshit," I sang. Sheldon might be my lover, but she was commissioned and I wasn't. Her lies were always for the good of the ship. The whole reason for sending *me* in the number-*two* lander was because we were both disposable. Gunny Heloise's expensive string of muscle-girls weren't going to do a combat drop to fish me out of the arms of some fucking stone squid.

Had I said all that aloud?

"Ari, please, you're leaving camera range . . ."

"Good!" I took a deep breath and popped my helmet free. There was a slight sucking noise as it came loose. I turned and hurled it back out into the plaza, where it bounced a little too slowly, with an odd ringing echo. Air density and composition a little off, I thought. Sound waves didn't propagate quite right.

Time to breathe the air of this world. *Joan Carter, I am here.* I released my breath, drew in a new one, and let the smells and scents of another civilization flood into me on a river of oxygen.

Mostly it tasted like a granite plaza at night, though, oddly, there was an after-rain tang to the air.

Hand on the hilt of my cutlass, I stepped into the shadows looking for traces of the women who ate stone squid.

Inside was tall, horribly tall. The walls and ceiling were proportioned wrong. It was as if the same architect who'd designed those too-shallow steps had turned her plans sideways and stretched the building upward. That same damp granite smell tickled my nose, like must newly released from a long-forgotten freight canister.

Age and rot, even in this dry place.

My boots clicked against the worn flagstones as I walked on, accompanied only by echoes.

Pillars rose around me, covered with the same frantic, disturbing carvings that had decorated the portico outside. I walked toward one, touched the pillar with the point of my cutlass. It rang like honest stone, but when I tried to brush that bit of carving with my gloved hand, somehow it wasn't exactly where I had thought it should be.

"Not quite dead, are you?" I shouted.

They . . . whoever they were . . . had looked like me. Human enough for me to care. Like Joan with her Red Woman lovers on old Barsoom. The . . . squid . . . were everywhere. Detailed. Frightening. Real. Had it been the squid that drank the oceans dry?

Had it been the squid who built this city?

That thought scared me into walking again. This place must have been built by humans. *Must* have.

I bent to adjust my greaves, and my thoat-leather fighting harness. Nothing fit me quite right today. Like the very air itself, everything was subtly wrong. And where the hell were the monsters? At least these were squid, not something so seemingly human as the rykor-riding kaldanes that had taken Joan's daughter from her.

The injustice of the world boiled within me as I stalked between a pair of the overtall pillars, cutlass trembling in my hand. Something, someone, had consumed the women of this world, sisters to me at least as much as the Red Women had been sisters to Joan Carter. They had been drunk dry, to desiccate along with their oceans.

Then I found one of my world-sisters, of the stone squid-eating women, curled in a corner. She'd died here long ago. Her body was a husk wrapped in robes crumbling from dry rot. I could not tell what race she had been, she was so decayed, but I preferred to believe her a Red Woman rather than one of the degenerate Therns or First Born.

She had died here to warn me of the stone squid.

I heard a squawk: "Ari."

I whirled, cutlass ready, wishing I had my radium pistol. Had I left it behind on my airship? Some enemy must be clouding my mind. I was never this slow of thought.

"Sweetie, can you hear me?" It was a woman's voice, weak and quavering as women will be when confronted with the sharp end. I circled again, but could not find her. Magic, then, or some ancient machine sparked to life in this temple.

She went on: "We've overridden your implant. *Sixth Virtue*'s relay is homed in on your carrier. Ari . . . please . . . I know you're alive. You've got to come out of that building, right now. Please, sweetie."

"No tears, woman," I shouted. Something was wrong with my

voice! It was high and thin, with a reedy quaver. I had indeed been somehow ensorcelled. I knelt to search my dead sister for help, parting her robes with a muttered apology.

So much hair on that poor dead one's chest, I thought. She must have struggled with an overactive testosterone level. And her breasts . . . gone. Cancer?

Her?

What would a woman be doing here? He.

He?

Where had that word come from?

"Ari! Captain Pellas is authorizing a retrieval drop. Listen carefully. Can you get a signal out to us?"

I ignored her.

Then his robes fell completely open. His clitoris, dry as the rest of him, had grotesquely hypertrophied in life. Inches long, perhaps. And his breasts . . . the poor dear must have had a radical. Common enough in space.

Space?

His clit?

My free hand strayed to the lower skirt of my fighting harness. Checking.

"Sweetie. They're launching immediately. Be down in twenty-five minutes or so. Please, if you can hear me, sit tight."

I had an awful moment, my chest seizing cold and tight as my hand groped air between my thighs. Where was my . . . my . . .

Him? What the hell was a *him*? What the hell was I thinking? Animals were bedeviled with y-chromosome carriers. Humans, blessed by evolution and intelligence, had moved beyond that particular genetic disorder. *Everybody* knew it. There hadn't been a natural-born male human since the days of Herad the Great—she'd put the last of the poor, damned mutants mercifully to death back the first of Years Before.

"I'm . . . I'm in some kind of trouble," I said aloud.

"We're coming, dear. Fast as we can."

A door opened before me. A four-armed warrior in battle harness loomed, cock swinging between his legs like an animal's. Then he was struck down from behind. A beautiful woman, of the Red race—a true princess of Helium, I realized—peered inward, bloody sword gripped firm. "Come," she called, extending her free hand, "quickly."

"Hold on, sweetheart," the bodiless voice said within my ear.

I looked down at the corpse. Who could bear to live in a world of such horrible defectives, mutant in body, mind, and metabolism?

Thoat harnesses jingled behind the princess. A cold wind chattered. All I had to do was step forward, into every world I'd ever dreamed of. Except for the . . . *men*.

"Come."

"Stay with us."

The voice of dream called me on, the voice of love bade me stay. The voice of reason screamed somewhere deep inside me. Eyes clouding with tears, I hurled my cutlass at the princess. Somehow both startled and sorrowful, she withdrew, leaving me alone with an ancient male corpse. I huddled next to my dead sister—for even with a cock and a beard, she was still my sister—and waited for my rescue to arrive.

Far too soon, something slithered wet and huge upon the stone floor behind me, but I had already given away my weapons and returned bare-handed to the world my mothers had made. Instead I took the dead woman's hand and waited to see who would find me first.

Looking for Truth in a Wild Blue Yonder

WITH KEN SCHOLES

This is the other story Ken and I wrote at Borderlands. You guess which one he started, and which one I started.

Ten years after my parents died, my therabot, Bob, informed me that I should seek help elsewhere. I blinked at his suggestion.

"I've already tried chemical intervention," I told his plastic grin. "It didn't work." I scowled, but that did nothing to de-brighten his soothing, chipper voice.

"Booze doesn't count, Charlie."

"I tried weed, too."

Bob shook his head. "Nothing therapeutic there, either, I'm afraid." He sighed and imitated the movements of pushing himself back from his imitation-wood desk. "You are experiencing what we like to call *complicated* grief."

Complicated grief. As if I hadn't heard that one before.

Dad had died badly. He'd been on one of the trains that got swallowed by the Sound back on the day we lost Seattle. He'd called me from his cell phone with his last breath, as the water poured in, to let me know he wasn't really my father.

We lost the signal before he could tell me who actually was. Naturally, I called Mom. She answered just before the ceiling of the store she was shopping in collapsed.

Both parents in one day. Fuck yes, complicated grief.

And a side helping of unknown paternity.

Bob continued. "Ten years is a long time, Charlie. I want you to call this number and ask for Pete." His eyes rolled in their sockets as his internal processors accessed his files. My phone chirped when his text came through. He extended a plastic tentacle tipped with a three-fingered white clown's glove. "I hope you find your way."

I scowled again and shook his offered hand. "So you're firing me as a patient?"

"Be well," he said. His eyes went dead and his hand dropped back to the artificial oak surface of his desk.

I met Pete in an alley on the back of Valencia, behind an old book-store that still dealt in paper. I transferred funds to an offshore account that then moved it along, scrubbing the transaction as it passed through its various stops along the way before his phone chirped. When it chirped, he extended a smart-lock plastic bag to me. A small, withered blue thing sloshed about in it. At first, I thought it was a severed finger or something far worse. (Or better, depending upon one's fetishes.) I held the bag up to the flickering light of the dirty streetlamp.

The blue thing looked like an asparagus tip, only it wriggled.

"Find someplace safe and quiet," Pete said. "Preferably indoors with a lock. Eat it with water."

"I'm not putting this in my mouth."

Pete shrugged. He was a scrawny kid, his tattooed face stubbly in the dim light, long red hair cascading over his shoulders. "Doesn't matter to me. But the wild blue yonder is especially good for your situation. Complicated grief, right?" I nodded because his eyes—one brown and one bright yellow—told me that he probably knew it from experience. "Eat this. Spend a weekend sweating and naked on the floor. You'll be a new man."

"Naked and sweating?" I looked at the bag again, then back to Pete. "And how do you know Bob?" I couldn't imagine a therabot needing a dealer.

Pete smiled. "We're colleagues."

"Colleagues?"

The smile widened even further. "I'm a back-alley grief counselor."

Slipping my wild blue yonder into my pocket, I left Pete in his alley and turned myself toward home.

———

I ate the wild blue yonder and stripped down in my living room. I put on some retro music—Zeppelin, I think—and stretched out on the floor.

It worked fast.

Light and sound from within me, building in magnitude until the nausea clenched my stomach and I sat up. My living room had become a purple field beneath swollen stars. Something like crickets sang all around and I saw a girl sitting on a stump in the middle of the clearing. In the distance, deep blue trees swayed under a windless summer-night sky.

"You must be Charlie," she said.

I was naked still, but for some reason I was unafraid and unashamed. "I am," I told her, standing. "Who are you? And where am I at?"

"I'm Verity." She tossed her long brown hair and batted the lids of her big brown eyes. "And you are in the wild blue yonder."

She wore a silver gown that flowed like mercury over the curves of her body. When she stood up too, I saw she was taller than me by at least a foot. "I'm sorry about your mother," she said, "and the man you thought was your father."

I blinked. "How do you know all of this?"

She shrugged. "I'm Verity."

We stood there, looking at each other, as an enormous moon rose to the south. A minute passed. "So how does this work?" I asked.

"Simple. I run. You chase me."

And then she ran.

As Pink Floyd said, I ran like hell. Or maybe I chased like hell. I didn't give a shit about Pete anymore. Or Bob. Or all the lost millions in the Pacific Northwest, Hawaii, Japan, and everywhere the sea had come crawling up onto land with bloody salted fingers and needle teeth.

Verity ran before me. With her she carried the hard burden of truth like a seed in the claws of a nuthatch. Her legs sped over this strange blue landscape as perfect as I'd ever seen on a woman. Michelangelo would have cried to sculpt her. I would have cried to catch her.

But it wasn't that perfect ass I craved. It wasn't those high, firm breasts that I could imagine bobbing with each leaping step. It wasn't that trailing hair that I could wrap around my body.

She carried me: my past and my future.

How the hell had Pete known to give this to me; how had this wild blue yonder reached so far into time and my soul?

My thoughts fell aside as she ran. Reason gave way to desire. Logic yielded to need. The chase gave way to the run. The ground vanished. We sprinted across a stark, unyielding field of stars. They flared, dying as every hydrogen cycle eventually does, all of time compressed in a dozen falls of those perfect feet; then we ran through the salt sea, the world-girding amnion that had birthed all of evolution's ambitions. The seas boiled and dried and vanished in wispy, weeping gases; we ran on roads of light, leaping from quantum packet to quantum packet.

Across time, across space, across the seventy-two acres of my neural net, until sufficient self-awareness finally returned to me for me to understand I would never catch up to the truth by chasing it. Grief is the Grendel-monster in the watery cave of the human heart. I pursued Grendel's mother, and she would have her vengeance on me if I dispatched her son.

So I stopped, caught in a moment of wisdom, and let Verity the cup bearer of my grief come to me. The universe is circular, after all, endless in the manner of an egg, and if you wait long enough your own light will come back to you.

In ceasing my chase of Verity, she soon ran into my arms.

We collapsed in a tangle of limbs and clothing amid lush mounds of mint and violets. Scent, suddenly the world was scent; and the sweet smell of Verity's sweat, which made me want to turn to her and place my lips upon the yoke of her neck and breathe her in.

Think, man, think. You're not here for *this*.

"You caught me," she whispered, and her tongue slipped into my ear.

I wriggled away. "We're not doing that chase, either."

"What do you want, Charlie?" Her breath was a furnace of passion warming me down to bones I'd forgotten I ever had.

"Truth," I said. The answer surprised me.

"No one wants truth, Charlie. They want certainty. They want forgiveness. They want love. Truth is like a dead city, a million watery graves. It doesn't compromise and it gives nothing back."

"Relief." This time I almost sobbed the word. "I want relief."

"From truth?"

Truth. Who was my dad? What had my mom meant by this? Whose lie had determined the pattern of my life? Had Mom cheated on Dad? Had he come along after she was pregnant with me, and accepted another man's get as his own child?

I slowly realized that it didn't matter. The ghosts of the past ten years, what Bob had so patiently (as if a machine could be otherwise) talked me through, past, around, away from, out from beneath: those ghosts were of my own making.

Mom's unquiet spirit might haunt the desolate ruins of Auburn, Washington, sleeping beneath the hard, frozen waters. Dad's fetch might ride the rusted rails beneath the Puget Sea. So what?

"I live today," I told Verity.

"Is that the truth?"

"We can only go forward." I set my hand upon her breast, cupping the firm nipple through the flowing silver of her dress.

"I'm not real," she whispered in my ear again.

Tell that to my gonads, I thought, but that didn't matter now. "Is this what I was supposed to find?" She touched my hand, the curves of her flesh proud but not overflowing my grip, and I ached to draw her clothing away and set my lips to suckling.

"You came into this world damp and frightened. Your parents left this world damp and frightened."

"Even my dad?" I meant my biological father, the progenitor that Dad had almost told me about before being erased under a billion gallons of seawater.

It was just a splash, really, good news from outer space. Even if the clouds hadn't dissipated for three years after.

"Even your dad," she said. "Him."

So Dad-the-sperm-donor had been in the Northwest, too. Or Hawaii. Or coastal Alaska. Or Japan. Or on a ship at sea.

I hoped all three of their ghosts were happy somewhere, around some spiritual campfire trading stories about the boy I'd been. I wished them well, the love of each other, and even the love of me.

The past belonged to them, swept away along with the legacy of a sixth of the planet.

The future belonged to, well, maybe not me, but at the least, to itself.

Roger Waters wailed from my speakers. I swear it had been Robert Plant when I first tripped out. I lay flat, drained. My thigh was sticky where I'd come at some point. I looked down to find my torso covered with blue lip prints.

Lipstick?

I touched myself and flinched. No. Hickeys. What kind of drug trip left you with *hickeys,* for the love of god?

Aching, I dragged myself to my feet, turned down the stereo, and stepped into my kitchenette for some apple juice. Something was missing. Something was wrong.

I probed my thoughts, like a tongue questing for a missing tooth.

Grief.

My parents were still present in my absence. But the paralyzing pain, the near-total abrogation of self and initiative, seemed to be gone finally. After all these years. Was *this* what normal life was like? No wonder Bob had fired me.

As for Pete, the back-alley grief counselor, I owed him everything.

Heading for the tiny bedroom, I noticed something out of place in my living room as well. I stopped to look around. A woman's silver dress was draped across the back of my couch, as if stripped in a moment of wild passion. I touched the hickeys again.

What *was* real?

What *was* true?

Something stirred in the next room. A wall of seawater finally come to claim me as well? Or the future, waiting with bruised lips and the longest legs I'd ever seen on a woman?

With a silent thanks to Bob and Pete, I stepped into the wild blue yonder, looking for truth. Or at least whatever might come next.

I was finally done with what had come before.

Angels ii:
Scent of the Green Cathedral

The angels stories continue. I always did like writing in second person, which may be one of the most obnoxious things a writer can do to his readers.

You thought you knew the way. There was a path, broad and brightly lit at the first, seducing you through tangled thickets and along narrowing alleys between the boles until there was nothing left but the ache of your feet and a cathedral-green darkness all around you. The forest had become thick and treacherous, wolves in every shadow, brigands hidden in each tree.

Behind? You saw nothing. No evidence of your passage. No backward path. It was as if you had been born in this place, child of leaf and branch.

Before? Everything, leading nowhere. Just the forest's endless sheltering shadow. It was as if you had come to die in this place, a rough beast who would slouch no further.

Then you saw the light, flickering among the branches, a star descending. Stories came to your mind, fairies of old, time stretched to taffy Under the Hill. You had never believed in them.

The light had wings, making a promise of the spark. It sailed toward you, path as smooth and sure as any river's, to spin round your head until the very gleaming made you dizzy and you fell to the leafy loam.

"I am lost," you croaked. "My way is gone."

The wings spread wide then, golden pinions glowing with dawn's rich light. Her face was beauty, a brilliant scarab frozen in the bubbling amber of God's handiwork. Her body was a temple, desirable beyond lust. "There is always a way," she said. "You only need ask."

Your mouth opened, words on your tongue, breath caught in your throat, but the words would not come. Your lungs worked like bellows, creaking in your chest, but no air would move. The amber flowed from her to you, an examination by the lidless green eye of God.

Only those without sin could be saved. Only those with sin would desire salvation. To ask was error, silence a worse failing.

"I . . ." You finally choked the word from your lips, the sound a fishbone gone wrong, but she had already departed.

You were left with only memories of golden light and her ivory-skinned glory. Newfound beads of amber in your fist, you stumbled around a corner into sunlight and traffic. The scent of the green cathedral has never left you.

Steam, Punks, and Fairies

Spendthrift

Editor Jennifer Brozek asked me to write this story. I don't think she quite had this end product in mind, but I had fun with it. Plus I've always loved flying boats. And the real-life Roubicek is a much nicer guy than I made him out to be here.

All of Merauke whispered with the rumors. *The Japs are coming.* Springfield McKenna didn't place much faith in rumors. She'd traded in them far too long to lend credence to someone else's social munitions.

The Hotel Hindia-Belanda had stood above the port town's waterfront for two centuries, insofar as she knew. Springfield could believe that story, based on the eccentric interior fittings. The parlor seemed to have been constructed of lumber salvaged from a dozen wrecks. Parts of the walls were paneled in teak that would have fetched a fortune at auction in Honolulu or San Francisco. Other sections were raw, faded ash; gone to splinters and mottled with mysterious stains that could just as easily have been rotten durians burst in the heat or the lifeblood of a hapless crew overrun by Sea Dayaks.

The piebald interior suited the Hotel Hindia-Belanda, a piebald place in a piebald city at the edge of the Dutch East Indies. Which was, insofar as Springfield was concerned, precisely the ass end of nowhere.

She liked it that way.

Or had, until the war came creeping down the sea lanes and stepping across the islands, scaring the Dutch and the Aussies who ran most of the guns and money in these parts. Though she wouldn't have cared to be a *huisvrouw* in Merauke, the fat old traders and their lean factors were happy enough to do business with an American woman who could match them drink for drink and joke for joke until the dawn came back around the curve of the world to light up another day.

Except for the damned Japanese and their damned Greater East Asia Co-Prosperity Sphere.

That, she thought, *and a certain American bastard who traded away almost every bit of my wealth, all for a nickel.*

The coin lay now on the tabletop. The familiar Indian head had been cut to a grinning skull, still wearing his braids and feathers. The old bastard looked positively happy. Which was strange, because the hobo nickel bore a patina that Springfield could barely put words to, speckled with time and hate. She could swear she heard it vibrating in her bureau drawer at night, mixing with her costume jewelry gold and her real silver.

First Ferris Roubicek had come into her life. Then he was gone again, leaving her with a broken heart, a failed business, a Japanese invasion, and a coin.

She wasn't sure the coin wasn't the worst of the whole business.

The scrape of chair legs prodded Springfield McKenna out of her reverie. "You still here?" asked a rough Aussie voice. Which was good, because her Dutch was crap; mostly useful for talking to bartenders and sailors.

Springfield peered up to discover that to her surprise she was mildly drunk. Otherwise Captain Waldo Innerarity, Royal Australian Air Force, wouldn't have looked so good to her.

No way.

Not even for a moment.

He wasn't all that bad a view to take in, she had to admit. Tall for a pilot, with the shoulders of a shore patrolman and pale blue eyes like the Andaman Sea. Ruddy from sun and drinking, brown hair with enough of a kink to argue about where all his ancestors might have come from. All of that just made him more interesting to think about.

But looking good? Waldo? She'd have sooner kissed her brother.

"You're out of uniform," Springfield said. Which was true but pointless. Waldo wore canvas trousers and a short-sleeved linen *barong Tagalog.* The embroidery looked a little queer on him.

"Uniforms might be pretty unpopular around here soon." Waldo threw himself down in the chair with reckless disregard for the stresses involved and signaled the bartender for a drink. The Hotel Hindia-Belanda knew how all its regulars took their booze.

Springfield was pretty sure that the Indonesians and New Guineans in Merauke hated their white masters with an indiscriminate abandon, but at least around the hotel they smiled and kept their opinions behind the kitchen doors. She was careful never to order any food that could easily be spat in on the way to the table.

Sometimes one just had to trust the cook.

"Not all of 'em," Springfield finally said, realizing she hadn't been holding up her end of the conversation. "Jap yellow could be all the rage for the next season's fashion."

Waldo nodded and reached for the coin on the table. She snatched it away before his big, oddly delicate fingers could close on it.

"What you got there, lass?" he asked. Inerarrity's voice went oddly soft, as it did so often when he spoke to her. She knew what *that* meant, coming from a man like him.

"Nothing anyone here cares about." That, at least, was true.

"Been taking payoffs?"

She had to laugh. "In American nickels? One at a time? You're out of your mind, flyboy."

He leaned forward as a sweating glass of gin garnished with a sliver of mango tapped on the table. Springfield avoided the waiter's eye. Waldo bit his upper lip, then asked, "So if you ain't being paid, why are you still here?"

She met his stare with a level gaze of her own. "Everybody's got to be somewhere." The verbal equivalent of a shrug.

"Not every somewhere is in fear of Jap bombings. Or patrols. The boys had a shootup two nights ago in the hills not forty miles east of here."

"So I heard." Rumors, rumors. *The Japs are coming.* "They've got a lot better things to do than knock over one-horse towns where the horse died."

He smiled like moonlight on the Torres Strait. "You've got a lot better things to do than sit around waiting for one-horse towns to be knocked over."

Springfield thought that one through for a moment. "Are you propositioning me, Leftenant Innerarity?"

His smile blossomed to a grin. "Hell no, Sheila. A man ain't that daft. But I am trying to save your damned fool life. If you want a seat out of town, I'm flying over to Darwin in two days. Hitch a ride, see what comes next."

The name slipped unbidden from her lips. "Ferris Roubicek."

Waldo frowned. "*Mr.* Ferris is gone from these parts three months and more. Last seen on a Chinese steamer heading for Ceylon. And well understood not to be coming back."

"I'm tapped out," Springfield admitted. "Ferris took me good. I was running a pretty solid business in spice and batik, even with the war coming. Maybe especially because of the war. But he . . . promised . . ." *Confidences whispered under starlight as the insects whined against the netting.* She tried again, her head growing hot and tight under Innerarity's infuriatingly sympathetic gaze. "I made a bad deal, Waldo. I'm living on the last of my credit now." She turned the hobo nickel over in her hand, felt its patina through her skin even under the table and out of sight.

Somehow it all came down to the damned coin. Yet she hadn't been able to get rid of it yet.

The words "until death do us part" sprang unbidden and unwelcome into her mind.

"All the more reason to leave, eh? Seat's yours, no need to pay."

"Not in coin," she replied.

With those words, his face closed and his frown drew tight. Springfield knew she hadn't been fair, but damn it, this was *Waldo*. Not someone who had any right to have an interest in her.

"Besides," she added. "The Japs might never get here."

He stood up, tossed back his gin in one huge gulp that must have burned all the way down. The mango slice tumbled into his mouth with the booze. "You just keep telling yourself that, Spring. Who knows? Might even be true."

With that, the lieutenant left, taking his big shoulders and his manly ways with him.

After a while, Springfield signed her chitty and trudged up to her room. Doubtless the waiter would report what he'd heard to Inigo van Damme, the manager. Then the manager would ask, again, about her bringing her bill up to date.

She was fairly certain they wouldn't take a lone skull-faced nickel in payment.

That night Springfield McKenna had the dream again. Japs in their mustard-yellow uniforms and peaked hats walked the muddy streets of Merauke. The city was under occupation, the Dutch and Australian defenders vanished as surely as if they'd never been here. There weren't even blood spatters or bullet holes. Just Japanese soldiers everywhere. Stolid. Silent. Shuffling. Staring at her with empty eyes.

They all marched to the beat of some distant tin drum. A rattle that carried from the hills outside of town all the way down to the portside slums along the banks of the Maro River. Even the endless nightly concerto of insect and bird and jungle screech had quieted in the face of that beat.

She heard that noise. Metallic. Small. Sly. It carried everywhere. It informed her heart and doused her hearing and set her thoughts to smoldering.

With a sweaty, fetid start, Springfield realized she was awake. But the beat that had carried through her dream of invasion still echoed.

It was the nickel. In her bureau drawer. The coin was rattling. Marching like a tiny army of its own through her dreams and through her life.

She slid from her bed and tugged on a pair of airman's coveralls. In the sticky heat of the New Guinea night, Springfield didn't even bother with foundation garments or makeup. She just dressed swiftly and angrily, then took a discarded cigarette tin in hand and stood before the bureau.

Inside, the skull-faced nickel rattled on its own. Counting time. As if it were one of those deathwatch beetles.

"You bastard," she hissed, though Springfield couldn't have said whether she was talking to Roubicek or Innerarity or her father or who. She yanked the drawer open with a savage tug and captured the dancing nickel in an empty tin. It rattled a moment, then fell quiet.

"You bastard," she repeated, and stalked out into the night.

It wasn't far from the Hotel Hindia-Belanda to the waterfront. Though in truth, nothing was far from anything else in Merauke. She scuttled the few blocks, keeping to the deepest shadows where possible.

As she approached the dockside, a single shot echoed. Springfield froze. She wasn't especially afraid of men with guns, but she had a lot of respect for what they could do in a careless moment. The only thing stupider than being shot in a war zone would be being shot by accident.

"Damn it all." Springfield froze next to a stack of fish traps that reeked of rot and creaked slightly in the wind questing off the night's water.

A voice called out nearby, indistinct but with the overtones of Dutch.

Someone answered cautiously from farther down the docks.

A short laugh, barked with the clipped nervousness of a man under pressure.

Then another shot.

Her nerve broke. She ran back toward the Hotel Hindia-Belanda, cigarette tin clutched so tightly in one hand that the metal was being crushed. When Springfield reached her room, she dumped the coin out on the scarred marble top of the bureau amid the grimy doilies and empty atomizers. The skull grinned up at her.

"I should have known it wouldn't be that easy," she told it with a glare.

Waldo's offer of a seat on his flight was looking better and better. She absolutely hated that.

Rumors the next day were of Japanese spies on the waterfront, and graves being violated at the cathedral. Springfield was hard-pressed to see how those two could be connected. That didn't stop people from speculating.

She used her copious free time to pack one small valise. It wouldn't do for van Damme to think she was leaving with her bill unpaid, after all. And nothing a woman wanted or needed in Merauke was going to be too hard to replace in Darwin, or wherever she wound up.

Lieutenant Innerarity wouldn't be footing her bills, Springfield promised herself.

She packed her last pair of silk stockings, a few necessaries, and one nice red dress. Just in case. With her dark hair and pale complexion, the color was striking, setting off her green eyes to great advantage. At least, that's what her mother had always said. Springfield figured she'd need all the advantages she could get.

Her gulden were pointless outside of the Dutch East Indies. Let the hotel staff squabble over the small stack of coins. She still had two hundred American dollars, the last of her working capital remaining from Ferris Roubicek's taking of her wealth and pride. *That* was what she couldn't give to the manager. What she couldn't afford to lose.

A few clothes, a little money, a nail file, and the nickel.

That was it.

Half a decade working here in the islands, a place where being a woman wasn't an automatic disqualification from business, by virtue of her being an American. All she had to show for five years was a valise that could have carried half a dozen newspapers. A little money and a red dress.

Even the rest of the clothes she'd leave behind. She'd meet Waldo at dawn in her coveralls.

That dealt with, Springfield decided to go out. She couldn't stand spending the day under the suspicious eyes of the waiters and the bartender. Everyone knew the white people were one panic away from leaving.

That night, she dreamt again of Japs in the streets. They shuffled as they walked, dragging their feet and staring downward as if afraid to say anything that might compromise their fealty to their emperor. They were everywhere in Merauke, filling the streets as if division after division had landed and overrun the place. Shoulder to shoulder, chest to back, the soldiers moved in eerie silence except for the beat of their one tin drum.

She refused to wake up for that damned coin.

Absolutely refused.

In the end, Springfield awoke for Waldo Innerarity. Or at least his knock.

"We've got to get moving, love." His voice through the door was low almost to the point of being indistinct.

Her ride out. The dreams, the shots. It was over here in Merauke, her whole party done for. Ferris Roubicek had blown out the candles, but even the cake was nothing but crumbs now.

Springfield had slept in her flight overalls. She tugged on a pair of men's low quarter boots, ran her hands through her hair twice, grabbed her valise, unlocked the door, and threw it open.

"I—" Waldo swallowed his words as he stared at her.

"Ain't seen a woman before, flyboy?" She chucked him under the chin. "Let's go before the manager busts me."

"Too late, I am afraid." Van Damme stepped up behind the lieutenant. "You cannot be leaving us without a settlement?"

"Not at all," she began sweetly, but Waldo elbowed Inigo in the gut, effectively ending the discussion. Springfield shot him a wild look of thanks. She reached into her valise for the skull-faced nickel, intending to leave it for a tip, but all she could think of in that moment was the marching Japanese in their endless, mindless numbers.

"Get out while you can, van Damme," she whispered, the best tip she knew to give him. But Innerarity was already tugging her arm away, away, away.

The RAAF flying boat looked like a real beast as it floated at the dock. Beyond, over the hills east of town, the sun pearled the eastern sky the color of the inside of a compact. "Short Sunderland," Waldo said, as if that meant anything to her. "The boys are aboard already. Don't say nothing you don't have to, it'll go easier on us all."

Springfield felt a sudden and unexpected attack of cold feet. She stood on the dock, looking up at the looming side of the aircraft. Something whirred—bilge pump, starter motor, she had no idea.

She felt as if she were being invited to climb into her coffin.

"Waldo . . ." Springfield whispered.

"Come on, Sheila." He tugged at her arm. "We've got to be away before the sun comes up."

Before anyone sees me getting on the airplane, she thought. Then she remembered Inigo van Damme gasping on the floral carpet in the hotel's upstairs corridor.

She was committed now.

"I'm ready," Springfield whispered, mortified at the squeak in her voice.

Innerarity helped her aboard. As she stepped up the gangplank, she could swear she heard the skull-faced nickel rattling in her valise.

Takeoff was an agonizing bounce and drag over the waters offshore. The Short Sunderland was a roaring, stuttering monster that clearly had no affinity for the air. It coughed around her, reeking of electricity and fuel and exhaust and the sweat of nervous men. Cigarettes, too, though no one was smoking right then.

Perversely, Springfield wished she had a Lucky Strike. She didn't smoke, never had, but she'd always envied the easy way people who did could handle their nerves. Light up, take a draw, strike a pose. It was much more elegant than wringing one's hands and hoping for better.

The airplane lurched and banked. She looked out the porthole at the Arafura Sea gleaming in the dawn's light. Sharks lurked in the waters along shore, visible in their silhouettes. The muddy beaches were littered with storm debris, the swamps thick with trees. Shadows still lay across the land in contrast to the ocean's morning glow.

The Japanese were down there somewhere.

Springfield glanced around the upper cabin. The rest of the seats were empty. Which was strange. Surely other people had wanted to leave Merauke as badly as she. Though the RAAF wasn't in the habit of giving rides to anyone who just happened along.

It occurred to her to wonder once more what Waldo wanted. But then, that was obvious enough. *Not him,* she told herself. *Though in truth, not anyone.*

Not since Ferris Roubicek. Nor since long before him.

She found the nickel in her hand then. It lay cold and heavy, like a bullet. Heavier than a coin should ever have been. Springfield could feel it vibrating against her palm. Not in time with the overwhelming drone of the engines. Rather, the coin set its own rhythm. The rhythm of a thousand shambling Japanese.

Then one of the engines coughed harder. It emitted a blatting noise. Springfield shot a look out the window to see a haze of smoke coming from her side. Left. Port. Whatever they called it on an airplane.

The engine coughed again, stuttering before it settled into the slower rhythm of the nickel.

The little metal door leading forward banged open and Waldo leaned into the passenger cabin. "What the bloody hell happened?" he demanded.

Springfield closed her fist on the coin, feeling guilty for no reason she could name. "Something's wrong with your, um, port engine."

"I fewking know *that.*" He stalked over to stare out her porthole. "Damn it, we can't just turn back."

The airplane bucked then. A series of thumps echoed from the outside.

"Japs," shouted Waldo, and rushed back to the flight deck.

Japs? But they walked in slow silence, taking over the world by numbers and rhythm. Not through violence in the air.

Outside her porthole, a slim aircraft slid by. She could see the big red circle on the side, painted over the jungle camouflage. *Why paint an airplane like a tree? Who would it hide from in the blue, blue sky?*

Three more of its fellows followed.

Zeroes. Even she knew that word, knew what those planes looked like.

One waggled his wings in salute, as if they were just friends sharing a pleasant morning's flying.

The flying boat banked hard to the right, tilting her view toward the clouds still colored salmon and rose. Springfield McKenna watched the heavens glare as around her Lieutenant Waldo Innerarity's airplane began to die. In her hand, the nickel pulsed like a beating heart.

The shoreline came rushing upward, a green fist folded over the troubled rim of the ocean. Waldo, or whoever was up on the flight deck with him, brought the Short Sunderland in hard, skimming the wave tops. Springfield supposed they were aiming for a welcoming stretch of beach. All she saw was the end.

Smoke curled through the cabin, and both engines were ragged and stuttering. The flying boat wallowed like a puppet with half its strings cut. The Japanese were surely out there, following their prey to earth. Sharks on a dying swimmer.

Then the great fist of the land grabbed Springfield and punched her in the chest, took the air from her lungs and the fire from her belly and handed her only pain and pressure in return.

She was not so lucky as to pass out. Rather, she was thrown back and forth in her seat, somehow held in place by the flimsy safety harness, as the world outside the porthole dissolved into a mass of spray and sand and smoke.

"Out, out, out," someone was shouting. Springfield didn't know who. It might have been her. She still couldn't breathe, couldn't talk, but she could unclip her belt and tumble from the chair and slide across the carpeted wall and see nothing but sand out of the opposite porthole set into the floor.

A man was screaming as well, the kind of scream someone lets out when their arm is ripped off. She ignored that, ignored the smoke and flames and reek of fuel and the irregular chatter of gunfire outside, to claw her way toward the portholes where the world still peered through. New Guinea was briefly surprised by her latest invader before the jungle would come to claim them all.

A few panicked moments later, Springfield found herself hidden away among great, tall roots. She watched the RAAF flying boat burn while one of the Japanese Zeroes lazed overhead, laying down gunfire on the beach every second or third pass. In case any of the Aussie airmen inside had notions of surviving their crash.

She stared impassive, tears streaming down her face, unfeeling, grief-stricken, the coin clutched in her hand like a beating heart, waiting for the fire to die and all of Innerarity's crewmates with it.

Springfield McKenna knew then that her life had been bought too cheaply.

Night brought wakefulness once more amid the reek of smoke and jungle rot. She didn't even realize she'd fallen asleep. The snarl of the last loitering Zero had been in her ears, until it was replaced by the chatter and howl of New Guinea's moonlit jungles.

The tree she'd wedged herself into still protected her. Sure, there were some bugs crawling down the leg of her coveralls, but they seemed to be using her as a throughway, not as a meal ticket.

At least someone is getting some good out of this.

The coin was quiescent in Springfield's hand. She slid from the tree's embrace and stepped aching onto the sand. Her body was bruised in places she didn't even know she had. The skin on the side of her head felt sticky and tight in a way that suggested she really didn't want to look into a mirror. The surf rolled in before her, foaming wave tops glowing slightly in the light of the three-quarter moon.

"Now I give you back to the ocean," she whispered into her clenched fist, then cocked her arm to throw the skull-faced nickel far out to sea. She might have been a girl, but Springfield McKenna could throw. Two seasons playing left field for the Jax Maids down in the Crescent City had proven that. Before she'd had to leave the country.

"Ferris," screamed Springfield, her eyes filling with tears for Waldo and the men she didn't even know, "you bastard."

A voice groaned out of the darkness. "Sheila . . ."

She aborted her throw, spinning in place to face the sound. "What?"

Someone was crawling toward her across the muddy beach. He *creaked* as he came, moving no faster than the shambling Japs of her dreams. "Spring . . ."

Dropping to her knees, Springfield peered at him. "Waldo?"

He made another three or four crawling steps, then collapsed to roll over on his side. "I . . ."

She looked close, trying to peer into those Andaman blue eyes. All she saw was rippled, bubbled skin. The smell of crisped pork filled her nostrils. His teeth gleamed unnaturally large, lips burned away and gums drawn back with the heat.

His breath . . . He had no breath at all. Lieutenant Waldo Innerarity had exhaled his last trying to reach her.

Springfield jumped to her feet and swallowed the urge to scream. This was another dream. All of it. The flight. The Zeroes. The crash. *This.* Waldo.

She backed away from him, slowly, her heels kicking at the slimy mud. Stumbling into a tree root, Springfield turned to catch herself on a branch.

Except it was no branch.

She had bumped into the leg of another burnt corpse. He hadn't been there a minute earlier, when she hopped out of the tree.

The nickel twisted in her hand. It vibrated, tapping out its rhythms as if preparing to sing.

The sea brought the odors of watery death and seaweed. Infinitely preferable to fuel fires and roasted pork. Behind her, the jungle breathed. Springfield stared at the two dead men at her feet. Then she opened her hand to drop the nickel.

"N'a do 'at," said another voice in her ear.

This time she did shriek. Springfield twisted to find another Aussie airman, crisped by fire, half his skull shattered from a Japanese bullet.

This was Waldo, she realized with horror. Not the corpse behind her. She spun again and he was gone. So was the other airman.

A dream, a dream, she told herself. *Like the shambling Japs. Wake up now, damn it.*

But there was no waking up. There were only burnt, bloody hands tugging at the sleeve of her coveralls, clumsily brushing through her hair which had come flyaway loose, stroking at her feet.

Springfield screamed again. She really put her lungs into it this time.

She kicked, too, with what had once been deadly accuracy. But these men . . . creatures . . . whatever they were . . . they didn't care.

She grabbed a piece of driftwood and swung it as hard as any Louisville Slugger. Teeth sprayed in the moonlight, a puff of ash flying with them. A broken skull shattered. Grasping hands were slapped back.

There were only two of them. Or maybe three, or four. Not like the Japanese soldiers in her dreams who filled the streets of Merauke and came on in their blind, implacable, unstoppable numbers.

Just a handful of men. One of whom she'd actually kind of liked in his strange way. "Damn you, Waldo," she shouted at the twitching corpses. "Why the hell did you go and do this?"

She kicked and kicked again, then had to whack her own leg with the stick to force an independent, questing hand off her calf. *Just like a man.* Breath whooping, tears threatening, Springfield McKenna fought a nightmare on the moonlit beach at the mouth of the Torres Strait until eventually she was surrounded by only bones and pulped flesh and shattered teeth and wispy shreds of scalp.

She stood over the corpse she thought might actually be Waldo. Like all of them, it was in several pieces. At the least, they'd come apart easily under the blows from her stick. Springfield resolutely ignored the fact that various severed body parts were moving and twitching. She ignored the yawning gap where her heart used to be, where her nerve used to live.

"It's yours now." She raised her clenched fist to drop the skull-faced nickel with the rest of her dead.

The click of a rifle bolt sliding home just behind her arrested Springfield's hand in mid-motion.

A small man, frowning, wearing horn-rimmed glasses and a uniform pale gray by moonlight, stepped in front of her. A Jap officer.

"Some things are not meant to be thrown away."

Springfield blurted the first thing that came into her head. "You speak excellent English."

"For a Jap?" He nodded and smiled, a small, controlled expression that seemed more practiced than real. "Lieutenant Ginnosuke Sakamura. Stanford Law School, class of nineteen thirty-six." The officer glanced at her fist. "Do not let go of that."

What? she wanted to ask, but it would have been a foolish question. She settled for, "How do you know?"

"Some things can be seen clearly enough." He shouted in Japanese over her shoulder, though she'd heard no noise behind her since the click of the rifle bolt sliding home.

Slowly, Springfield turned. Sakamura held his ground. She could feel his smile boring into her back like the first thrust of a knife.

An entire platoon of Japanese soldiers stood between her and the tree line. They were ranked in unbreathing silence, staring at not quite anything, moving no more than a line of stones might be expected to do.

Only one held his rifle trained on her. He was as unblinking, unmoving as the rest.

"I'm never going to wake up from this, am I?"

Sakamura chuckled lightly. "You already have woken up, Miss McKenna. That is the nature of your problem. You are no longer dreaming."

How did he know her name?

Ferris, she realized. Somehow, this Jap lieutenant had learned about her from Ferris Roubicek.

"You know what I hold, then," she said cautiously. Her heart shuddered. Waldo and the rest of the Aussies had died for . . . what? Ferris to play a revenge game against her? There was no justice in that.

Not that there was much justice anywhere else, either.

"You are a spendthrift, Miss McKenna." Sakamura sounded sympathetic. Almost loving, even. "You have sold your life cheaply and gained nothing in the bargain."

"Yet I am the one who has saved my nickel." *Thrift is a virtue, isn't it?*

Every time she'd tried to throw it away, things had gotten worse. Springfield seriously doubted that Lieutenant Sakamura would take the thing from her now. He knew too much already.

There was only one solution.

She slapped her hand over her mouth and swallowed the nickel, taking it down as hard and ugly as any emetic. Sakamura cried out, but he didn't wrestle her to the ground or try to stick his fingers down her throat.

"Good day, gentlemen," Springfield said, and began walking toward the water.

No shot rang out. No shouts called for her to halt or face the consequences.

She stepped into the surf. The water claimed first her feet, then her knees. Warm salt washed away the smoke and grime and blood and the last few stubborn beetles still clinging to her coveralls. The ocean slapped at her belly, at her bosoms, took her hands like an eager lover.

Springfield McKenna allowed herself to be claimed, because she had come to understand that there was no escape. There had been none since her affair with Roubicek. All that was left to her was to deny him the fruits of his evil investment. No nickel, no gain from claiming her body or soul or spirit. Whatever it was he'd sought.

When the sea came for her mouth, she cried out in gladness and spent her life freely.

At least it isn't fire, she thought, choking on the water. The nickel thrummed in her gut. Already it sought a way back out into the world.

The sharks bumped her as they closed in.

Jefferson's West

*This story is from my Original Destiny, Manifest Sin project.
Unfinished, and likely never to be finished, it might have been
my great work. I don't have a lot of regrets, but failing to complete this one before my writing brain blew out in a tide of
chemotherapy damage is one of them.*

"Damn me for a Kentucky fool," muttered Lieutenant William Clark.

He and Captain Meriwether Lewis had climbed the crumbling
white tuff for over an hour, finding momentary shade in tree-lined gul-
lies before beetling across stone beneath the sun's heated regard. They
explored without aid as Charbonneau and the men of the Corps of
Discovery were down by the Missouri River playing at rounders and
roasting a pallid sturgeon Sergeant Glass had caught.

Some things were best discussed between gentlemen first. Clark
kept his knife close by. His old friend Captain Lewis had the expedition's written orders straight from President Jefferson, but Clark had
his own, secret orders as well, whispered in the blood-warm darkness
of a Virginia summer night.

"Hot, William?"

"Hot, yes, but that is the state of this interminable country at this
particular season." Clark wiped his face on the back of his sleeve, the
wool scratchy and rank.

"What makes you such a particular fool, then?"

His friend's voice was gentle, but Clark felt the barb. He tried to
explain himself. "Your great, pale towers here upon the high shore,
Mr. Lewis. In your journal you named them 'the remains or ruins of
elegant buildings,' but up close they are just rocks. I am a fool for having held faith in them."

"Hmm." Lewis grabbed hold of a struggling sage and stepped up to a narrow, flinty ledge. The distressed plant perfumed them both. "I had an angle of view from the river. These cliffs are deceptive, sir. In both their appearance and their altitude."

"Hence my foolishness." Clark pushed past Lewis, scrambled up a gravel wash to make the next rise. He glanced over his shoulder. Lewis's face was lost in shadow beneath the wide-brimmed leather hat the commander had traded from the Mandan Indians the previous winter. For a moment the captain looked to be a fetch, a shade of himself, some dark ghost risen in the noontime sun.

Just as Jefferson had feared.

There were no powders or perukes when Lieutenant Clark called at Monticello in the summer of 1803. The president was there, though the papers said otherwise in Philadelphia and Washington City.

Jefferson and Clark took their ease on a small brick patio looking down the hill. A fat moon sailed the horizon, full-bellied and satisfied. Distant dogs barked as Negroes chanted around a pinprick fire visible through shadowed trees.

Clark wondered why he had been summoned to the plantation. Alone, no less, without Captain Lewis, who was deep in preparations back at the capital. This visit was passing strange and piqued his curiosity. He was equally fearful of being found out for coming here in secret.

"The War Department drags their heels at your promotion, Lieutenant," Jefferson said slowly.

"It is their way, sir."

"Meriwether is doing his best for you."

"I'm sure, sir."

Jefferson's teacup clinked against its saucer. Mosquitoes and larger insects buzzed in the dark around them as the chanting down the hill reached some crescendo before dying off into laughter.

Clark wondered again exactly why he had been called to this place.

"I am a rational man, Lieutenant."

"Yes, sir."

"There is certainly a Deity, a Creator. No man could deny that, simply from witnessing the sheer complexity of the universe." The president sighed. "His intentions with respect to our lives on this Earth, however, are entirely a matter of interpretation."

"Yes, sir."

"Ten days ago I had a dream. Do you dream, Lieutenant?"

"I suppose so, sir." Clark's dreams were rarely recalled and seemed mostly to involve grappling with angry phantoms. It was as if he dreamed the idea of a dream, rather than the jumble of thoughts and images others spoke of.

"Every man dreams. Some remember more than others." The saucer clinked again. "And there are those rare dreams possessed of such a compelling verisimilitude—a reality, Lieutenant, as sure as any waking journey through the hallways of your own home."

Clark's neck began to prickle. Down the hill, the dogs and slaves had fallen silent. "Sir?"

Jefferson's voice was sad. Tired. "An angel came to me, Lieutenant. In my rooms. He— No, it. It was black. Not 'black' as we speak of our Negro slaves being, but black as my boots. Black as a Federalist's heart, sir. Its wings glittered like stars, or perhaps coals in a furnace, and it spoke to me in a voice of iron."

The night remained silent. Even the moon seemed to have paused in her rise. Clark's curiosity finally overcame his discretion. "What did the angel say, sir?"

"I do not know. It spoke the tongue of Heaven, perhaps. I did not know the words in my dream, and I do not know them now. But in one hand it held a bloody knife, in the other a broken arrow. And mark this, Lieutenant Clark . . . the dark angel had the face of Captain Lewis."

The words slipped from Clark before he could consider them fully. "Do you fear betrayal?"

Jefferson laughed without any tone of amusement. "Betrayal? From Meriwether? Sooner would I be betrayed by my own fingers. I have already entrusted him with various affairs of state, and make no second thoughts about it." A pale hand shot out of the shadows to grab Clark's arm, nearly startling a scream from him. "But watch over my captain, Clark. Watch for the broken arrow and the bloody knife. Be my wits out there past the frontier."

"Yes, sir."

Then the slaves chanted again, and the dogs barked, and the moon moved once more across the fetid Virginia sky.

———

Clark stared up at the crumbling white towers set on the flat peak they
had just climbed. They were real after all, these buildings, made of the
same pale stone as the cliffs below. Brush and gravel obscured the
bases of the towers, but there were large openings higher up, of no
particular plan or symmetry that he could see.

He tried to imagine dark angels flying in and out of the high windows. Though it was hard to tell with their state of disrepair, there
seemed to be a paucity of ground-level entrances.

Lewis sucked in his breath. Clark knew without looking that his
captain would be idly chewing on his lower lip. "Burr came to me just
before we left," Lewis said.

Clark was shocked. Simply conversing with the vice president was
close to an act of treason among good Democratic-Republicans. Jefferson had not taken kindly to Burr's Federalist maneuverings during
the contesting of the election results. That Lewis would talk to Burr
at all was amazing. That he would admit such a conversation to Clark
was inconceivable.

"Offered me ten thousand pounds on deposit in London, in
exchange for certain reports."

"Reports of what?" Clark asked. The bribe was a magnificent fortune, enough for a lifetime of a gentleman's ease and most likely his
heirs' as well.

"He had a list. I said no, of course, but I still remember what he
wanted to know of. It was fantastical. Old Testament, if you will.
Giants, woolly mammoths, angels."

Angels?

"Lost cities," Lewis continued.

"'Tis definitely a city," said Clark, nodding at the towers before
them. "And 'tis definitely lost." Then, because he could not help himself, "Did you tell the president?"

"He would not listen." Lewis shrugged. "Burr's ambitions are not a
mystery to those who know him. Our vice president would be king of
the West. I will not scout for him."

The two of them pushed forward, down into the brush that grew
around the towers—sprawling junipers and close-set berry vines, clut-
tered with sage and a dozen other bolting bushes and flowers. There
was water up here then, at least at certain times of the year.

Was this what Jefferson had feared, Clark asked himself. Had Burr
been the dark angel with Lewis's face?

They came upon a wall hidden in the brush. It was worn with age and erosion, a dragon-backed thing marked mostly by gravel where once had risen an imposing barrier. Wordless, Lewis headed to the right, so Clark continued to follow. He wondered why neither the guide Charbonneau nor the voyageur's Indian wife Sacagawea had made mention of this place.

The gate was before them soon enough. It was an arch formed of a pair of ivory tusks that swept up fourteen feet or more, though whatever barrier had once stood between them was long gone.

"This gate faces east." Lewis pointed downward. "And look here . . ."

At their feet was a flat stone, much scorched by flame.

"'So the Lord God banished him from the Garden of Eden,'" quoted Lewis. "'To work the ground from which he had been taken. After He drove the man out, He placed on the east side of the Garden of Eden cherubim and a flaming sword flashing back and forth to guard the way to the tree of life.' From the third chapter of Genesis."

"I know that," whispered Clark, his hand more firmly on his knife. Hair stood up all over his body, prickling harder than it had even that night in Virginia. He could almost hear Jefferson's slaves chanting. "Come away from this place, Captain. It is not for us."

Lewis sounded bemused, or perhaps enchanted. "But the president set us to explore the West. If we walk through this gate, we will be heading west."

Drawing his knife against what foe he was not sure, Clark grabbed Lewis by the elbow with his free hand. "I do not trow if this is Eden or not. I disbelieve that it could be, but that doesn't matter." He tried not to let his rising desperation seep into his voice as the blade shook. "Come back to the river. Forget this. Tell the men we saw tall rocks. The Republic isn't ready for this, Meriwether. The human race is not ready."

The captain tried to shake Clark off. Clark wouldn't let go, so Lewis stepped into him, chest to chest, ready to shove, except that he stepped into the blade of Clark's knife.

"Oh, Lord, no!" shouted Clark.

"Oh, Lord, yes," said Lewis with a tinge of surprise and disappointment, as the arrows of the Teton Sioux began to rain around them.

———

In the summer of 1805 Captain Meriwether Lewis's body was recovered at St. Louis by two Negro slaves scraping paint above the waterline of a river barge. They told the sheriff, and later the Territorial governor, that a little canoe had just sort of bobbed up and nudged them where they stood waist-deep in the water. Despite the automatic suspicion of Negro involvement in the death of a white man, their story was eventually believed. The slaves ran away up the Missouri shortly after the inquest, however, which reopened the question and considerably delayed official reports to Washington City.

When the canoe was brought to shore, the captain's hands were folded over a black feather almost as long as he was tall, that glinted in the sunlight and was later seen to glow pale red under the night's moon. He was otherwise unclothed, making it clear that he had died of grievous wounds. His body was accompanied in the tiny boat only by the corpse of his dog Seaman and a single gigantic tooth fit for the mouth of Leviathan—or at least a mastodon.

God didn't send anyone else from the Corps of Discovery home that year. Lieutenant Clark eventually returned to the Republic a very changed man, accompanied by Lewis's servant York, Sacagawea, and an army of Indians and Negroes. When they finally came they hunted justice with rifle and bayonet.

The Bible was wrong in a few other particulars as well. Eden had only one river, not four, and it was the Missouri, not the Euphrates. But God had made His point just like Clark and his army would someday, and later on Aaron Burr made his point as well in Spanish Tejas.

The West was never the same.

They Are Forgotten Until They Come Again

In 2000, I moved from Texas to Oregon. In some very important ways, the Columbia River defines the Pacific Northwest, and in the years since then, I have learned to love her. The river is older than the mountains, and older than the coastline. Which is quite a feat for a ribbon of water.

Once bound by iron ribbons on each bank, River has been unfettered for more years than the lives of the salmon who leap Her rubbled rapids. She runs wide and powerful through deeps and shallows, over the stubs that formerly bridged and trussed Her and the shattered walls that at an earlier time impounded Her waters. She is a pool of memories, a current of thought, a channel through which all of life itself must pass. In Her time, River has sundered mountains and cradled thundering floods as great as any raging fires of the earth. Now furtive men slink to Her verges and cast throat-cut sacrifices into Her waters that they might scavenge metals and other wonders from what remains in the margins of Her embrace.

She flows. In flowing, She is, was, and always will be.

Smallish Boy crouched underneath the rhododendron alongside his older brother Dog's Breath and watched the water pass by beneath them. Their vantage point was a wooded bluff still dusted with snow. The four-hundred-foot drop in front of them granted both a visionary viewpoint and a modicum of security.

Down below, on secret paths through the woods, Rotten Trunk, Blue Ears, and half a dozen other warriors from their steading made slow and careful progress toward the water's edge. The men carried Angry Eyes's baby with them, that wouldn't have lived long anyway, so was a good sacrifice.

"Doesn't River want them whole?" he whispered. "What good is a crippled baby that can't see nothing?"

"Shut up." Dog's Breath didn't really mean that, Smallish Boy knew from the distracted tone of his voice. It was just the way his brother talked. "Besides," he went on, "it's the beating heart that counts."

"Then why don't we sacrifice a chicken?"

"Not the *same*. Stupid."

Which, Smallish Boy had long since realized, meant that Dog's Breath didn't know the answer either.

Their job was to watch for Angry Eyes. Everybody was afraid of her temper, even the Old Men. If she wasn't such a good healer, and made the best birchbark beer anyone in the steading could remember, *she* might have been the sacrifice, years ago.

She was a pain in the stick.

Smallish Boy wasn't sure what that meant exactly, but he'd heard Blue Ears say it one night when the warriors were drunk after a difficult elk hunt. He knew it must be true, though. His mother had slapped him hard for repeating the words later. She generally just looked sad when he was stupid or wrong. She only got mad when he was right about stuff he wasn't supposed to know yet.

"Look!" hissed Dog's Breath.

Smallish Boy followed the line of his brother's pointing finger.

A clump of logs was emerging around River's upstream bend, visible now past the rocky knees of Wind Mountain. It seemed oddly sideways to the current, until he realized the whole business was spinning.

Smoke rose from the mass of wood.

"Fire?" he whispered.

Dog's Breath sounded both horrified and impressed. "No one goes on River."

No one did. Ever. River was jealous of Her flashing, beautiful skin, and all too often claimed the life of any person who marred it. Storm might churn the gleaming smoothness, but that was just the way of nature. Flood might scar and pock it with debris, but that was the land offering its own sacrifice to River, who drained the heart of the world into distant Ocean.

But people?

Never.

Even Smallish Boy knew that, and had not been slapped for saying so.

"By the seven and the twelve," his brother swore. Now *there* was a beating waiting to happen, to speak of the mysteries so. "That's Angry Eyes on a . . . a . . ."

"Log?" offered Smallish Boy.

"No, one of the old words. We talked about it in men's circle." Dog's Breath scrunched up his face as if he was trying to squeeze out a difficult turd. "*Raft*. That's the word. Like a fishing platform that floats on the water."

"I guess she's so mad she forgot to be afraid of River."

"Nobody gets that mad." His brother stood up out of cover. "Or at least nobody gets that angry. She has to be mad to do this, though." He cupped his hands and began the coyote bark that you never heard during the day. It would echo down the distance to Rotten Trunk and Blue Ears and the rest who carried the baby.

They would know the boys had spotted something.

"Come on," Dog's Breath said once he'd seen the answering wave from below. "We got to get down there."

"Aren't we supposed to watch for anything more?" asked Smallish Boy, who found himself afraid to face Angry Eyes. "Or worse?"

"What could be worse than this?" His brother managed to sound both scornful and excited at the same time.

They scrambled down their faint backtrail, even in their haste careful as always not to leave too much evidence of their passage behind.

By the time the brothers reached a decent overlook within a stone's throw of the forbidden shore—here a shallow, rocky beach littered with recent floodwrack—the log *raft* had drifted into view from this vantage as well. Smallish Boy could see the men spread out along the bank. Most of them crouched in cover, their bows and axes ready as if Angry Eyes was going to swarm ashore like some raiding party come over the mountains from the Helens tribes.

If any woman ever born could do that, it would be Angry Eyes. But even he knew that she was not a problem you solved with a fist.

She'd never married, though she was beautiful, because no man wanted that temper inside his cabin every day. Smallish Boy knew that her beauty still drew them to dance the night dance, one then another, until their wives and mothers and sisters hated her for her power over

men. The other women whispered that her power was the power of
Storm, moving across the steading and then was gone. Not the power
of River, that was always here.

That had never made sense to him, though. Storm was the way
Ocean sent her water back to River. To say their power was different
was like saying the power of a man's foot was different from the
power of his hand. Not quite the same, surely, but they were fed by a
single beating heart.

When he'd said that to his mother, he'd been slapped again, so he
knew he was right.

Words meant things, he'd always thought. People should watch
what they said.

Except now people were watching the approaching raft. It was a
mat of fallen trees, limbs tangled and already gone brown and dead, so
the wood must have been snagged a while farther up River. He wondered how Angry Eyes had gotten it moving, or if she even controlled
it at all.

A fire burned in the middle. So far as he could tell, the flames were
fed by the wood itself. Angry Eyes was destroying her raft even as she
rode it. She danced at the edge, covered in clay and nothing else.

That would distract the men on the banks. Especially those who
had snuck over to feel her storminess in the dark of night. He wasn't
sure exactly why the night dances worked the way they did—people
mounting one another mostly looked like they were in pain, and it always seemed to be a mess afterwards—but he'd realized that all boys
and girls eventually discovered that secret for themselves, in time.

He sometimes wondered if Angry Eyes would still be sharing her
beauty when he grew old enough to ask. He couldn't figure out if that
was to be desired or feared.

Below them, Blue Ears stood out on the stony beach, a long, slim
throwing spear at his side, its butt grounded against his right foot.
That message was unmistakable. Gray Face stood with him, holding
the baby in the crook of his left arm and the steading's one good steel
knife in his right hand. That message was also unmistakable.

Angry Eyes drifted closer, the logs heading for the bank now. "Is she
steering the raft?" Smallish Boy asked.

"No, log-wit. River is doing it."

"Why does River care?"

"Wants Her sacrifice."

He could hear the quaver in his brother's voice. Dog's Breath was afraid.

Smallish Boy realized that he wasn't afraid. He wondered why. Perhaps because he knew he was watching something that would likely be a teaching story for his grandchildren. It must have been like this to be alive during the days of the cities and the fire. A person could be a part of a thing to remember, that no one later would ever quite understand.

"You have gone too far this time," bellowed Blue Ears. He was shouting over the water at Angry Eyes, but the boys could hear him just fine from their overlook.

She ignored him, still dancing. Her body swayed back and forth, her arms swinging wide then close, her small breasts and narrow hips shifting with the uncertain rhythms of her step. Angry Eyes's face was turned up toward the sky, mouth open as if to catch the rain, her feet unseen but still sure among the matted branches of the logs.

"She dances Storm," Smallish Boy blurted. "Look, those are the rhythms of wind and rain."

"Shut *up*," snapped Dog's Breath, who was staring out at Angry Eyes.

Smallish Boy glanced over to see his brother panting. "You want to do the night dance with her," he said, giggling.

That time he got a punch in the shoulder. He slithered a few more feet away from Dog's Breath, still giggling, and turned to watch again.

River was making more noise now. Water crept up the stone beach to lap at the feet of Blue Ears and Gray Face. No one spoke after the echoes of Blue Ears's shout had faded, but the baby began to squall, as if it could sense the approach of its mother.

Her dance grew stronger, stranger, faster. Wind whistled around Smallish Boy, and where moments before had been a blue sky only a little ragged with clouds, fat raindrops flew hard and fast from west to east, stones slung by Ocean to be borne by Storm to this place.

Still the men watched, more of them leaving their cover to stand ankle-deep in water on the stony beach. Angry Eyes's dance had turned to something deeper and stranger. Her hands covered her breasts, reached below to her sweetpocket, opened up to implore the men to come to her.

Dog's Breath slid down the embankment to join the others below as they waited calf-deep in the rising water.

"No!" Smallish Boy shouted, but he knew he could not catch his brother. He knew he could not bring his brother back even if he did scramble after him.

Besides, these fools could plainly see the river was rising fast. Unnaturally fast. Yet they stood, caught by the dance of Angry Eyes.

The log raft was almost to shore now. The fire blazed higher, untroubled by the driving rain. Her dance carried her to the forefront of the mass of wood, until she was looking down at the men hip-deep in River, and Dog's Breath now up to his belly beside them.

Her mouth opened. Whatever words she said to them were lost in the sizzling crack of lightning just in front of Smallish Boy, as the world erupted in blue-white glare and deafening noise.

He had not been asleep, but insensible. Once Smallish Boy managed to open his eyes, he realized that not much time had passed, either. The squall was still visible retreating to the east now, fleeing farther from Ocean with its burden of rain. Smallish Boy blinked away the tears of pain from his newfound headache.

The beach was empty of both water and men. River had gone back to Her banks. Blue Ears, Dog's Breath, and the rest were just gone. The raft had passed a bit farther down the current, bound for Ocean and whatever fate the world held for drifting logs.

Only Angry Eyes stood there, her baby in her arms. She had not kept the good steel knife.

The woman looked up at him. Even from this distance, he could see Storm in her eyes. She frightened him.

Still, Smallish Boy understood the demand. He scrambled down the embankment, following his brother's careless trail, wondering what he could possibly say back at the steading. They had lost eight warriors and Dog's Breath just now to the wrath of one woman and the might of River. He already knew the steading would likely starve this winter for lack of hunters. Even if they escaped that fate, they'd be victims to the next good-sized raiding party that happened along.

He wondered if he should go home at all. He wondered why he was not crying, or cutting his skin in grief. The Old Men were nubbled with scars from their losses down the years. Some might bleed to death from this day.

But still he walked toward Angry Eyes.

The brief rain had washed most of the clay from her. Now she was just a beautiful, terrible woman naked with a baby in her arms and River at her back.

Smallish Boy had never been so afraid in all his life.

"They have made a great sacrifice," she told him. Her voice was hoarse. He was surprised at how ordinary it was.

"River can't give us enough for losing them," he muttered. It was what his mother would say, he was certain.

She showed him the baby. It blinked. The formerly milk-white eyes, now cleared of their caul, were a rich brown like its mother's. Smallish Boy saw that its legs were straight and true as well, which they had not been before.

Her voice was steady, strong. Thrilling. "I believe this is a great gift indeed."

Not so great as the lives of Dog's Breath and Blue Ears and all the rest, he thought but did not say. This woman could drown him with a word.

But his brother. All of them . . . They weren't nice, mostly, but the dead were men of his steading. As he would be too someday soon, if he survived this day.

Summoning what was left of his courage, Smallish Boy raised his small stone axe. "You cannot take their lives!" he shouted, and rushed toward Angry Eyes.

She simply held the baby in front of her, like a shield between them. His steps faltered at the last. He could not strike with those wise eyes staring at him in innocent fascination. Smallish Boy stumbled to a halt, then collapsed, sitting on the rocks of the beach. His axe fell beside him, and he began to weep.

He could do nothing worthwhile now.

Angry Eyes leaned close, the baby clutched to her chest now. "Come, we have much ahead of us," she told him, and began walking east along the beach.

For a little while he sat as she strode farther away from him. Did he go with her? Or back to the steading, bearing the unlikely tale of this day? He could run, carry the word, and then . . . what?

As she walked, he saw her pert, rounded bottom, as that was all there was for him to see. Things in the middle of his body began to stir, and Smallish Boy realized that soon he would need a new name. The night dance had begun to make sense to him.

Drawn, he stood and trotted after her. When he caught up, he asked, "Where are we going?"

"The future," she said without turning around or breaking step. "River has shown me a place with city things. We will care for Her daughter there, and raise the city things up again one by one."

She walked. He followed. His feet were wet from splashing at the water's edge, but River did not seem to mind him when he was in the company of Angry Eyes. He was still afraid, but now it was a different kind of fear.

What he could not figure out was whether *his* life was the sacrifice or the gift.

River flows. In flowing, She is, was, and always will be. Her memory is long, and She keeps secrets until they are needed again by those of Her grandchildren who can pass by softly enough not to stir Her ancient wrath.

Like wind and rain, they rise and fall around Her.

Like wind and rain, they are needful to Her.

Like wind and rain, they are forgotten until they come again.

The Woman Who Shattered the Moon

About the same time I wrote this story, my very good friend the late Mark Bourne wrote what none of us then realized would be his last story, "The Woman Who Broke the Moon." We had a very good laugh, after nervously determining we had not in fact stepped on one another. He passed away unexpectedly shortly thereafter. I have always felt this story still belonged in part to him.

I am the most famous woman in the world.

That's something to be proud of, something no one else can say. It does not matter that the European bastards have locked me up for the past forty-one years, seven months, and eleven days. It does not matter that they dynamited my stronghold and sealed off the steam vents that drove my turbines and powered my ambitions. It does not matter that Fleet Street and the American press and governments from the Kaiser's Germany to Imperial Japan have all forbidden my name from being mentioned in writing.

Despite all that, they cannot unmake me, because every night, my greatest deed glimmers in the sky, a permanent reminder that I am the woman who shattered the moon.

Colonel Loewe comes to see me every Tuesday. He is proper, starched and creased in his lobster-red uniform with the white Sam Browne belt smelling faintly of oiled leather. His moustache is full and curved, something that must have come into fashion after I'd been imprisoned here in this hidden fortress, as it looks silly to me. In recent times, he has grown exactly nine white hairs hidden in the auburn of the moustache. The colonel's face is sometimes as red as his jacket. I am never certain if this is exertion or anger.

We meet in a tiny room with a knife-scarred wooden table between us. The floor consists of boards ten centimeters in width. There are thirty-six of them in a row most of the time. Some weeks there are thirty-seven of them. My jailors think I do not notice these little changes. It is much the same as the patterns in the dust and cobwebs, for nothing is clean in this place except what I clean for myself. I save my old toothbrushes to scrub out the mortared joins in the stone walls of my cell.

The walls of our meeting rooms are covered in stucco, so I do not know if they are stone beneath. I see patterns in the plastering, but they are never the same, so I suspect my own imagination may be at fault.

Either that or they have many more nearly identical rooms here than seems practical simply for the purpose of manipulating a single prisoner.

This week, Colonel Loewe has brought me a chipped stoneware mug filled with a steaming brown liquid which appears to be coffee. After eleven years and fourteen weeks as my interrogator, he knows my ways, so with a small smile, the colonel sips from the mug to prove to me that it is not something dangerous or unpalatable.

I inhale the rich, dark scent. There is of course the possibility that he previously took an antidote, but even in my darkest moments I recognize that if my jailors wished to kill me, they have had ample opportunities over the decades. Whatever my final end will amount to, I strongly doubt it will be poisoning at the hands of the colonel.

"Madame Mbacha." He always greets me politely. The coffee is a break in the routine.

I take the mug, the warmth of it loosening the painful tension that always afflicts my hands these years. The odor indicates a Kenyan bean. Another small politeness, to bring me an African variety.

"Good morning, Colonel." I follow our ritual even as I wonder what the coffee signifies. The routine is that he asks about my work, my machines, precisely how I shattered the moon from my East African mountain fastness. In all my years here, I have never revealed my secrets, though I am sure forensic teams extracted much from my laboratories before their terminal vandalism rendered my works into dust.

Why should I offer confirmation of their abuse? Why should I give them the secrets of gravity which I and I alone discovered, after being laughed away from the great universities of Europe and America for the inescapable twinned flaws of being African and a woman?

What Colonel Loewe should say now is, "Let us review the facts of your case." That has been his second line for the entire time he has been my interrogator. Instead he surprises me by departing from his script.

"I have news," the colonel tells me.

I tamp down a rush of frustrated anger. In my years of incarceration I have become very good at containing my feelings. Long gone are the days when I could work out my troubles on some trembling servant or prisoner. Still, how dare he change our rules now?

"What news, Colonel?" My voice barely betrays my intensity of emotion. This cannot be good. Change is never good.

He clears his throat, seeming almost embarrassed for a moment. "Madame Mbacha, it is my happy duty to inform you that your parole has been granted by the plenary session of the League of Nations on humanitarian grounds. You will shortly be processed for release, and will be free to go where you will, within certain restrictions intended for your own safety."

I stare at the colonel for a long moment, then begin to laugh. It is the only way I can stop the tears that threaten to well up.

Home. I can go home. The one thing I have never expected here in my imprisonment was to ever be allowed home again.

They bring me a newspaper with my supper. Such a thing has never before happened in my time in this prison. The change in routine intensifies my discomfort. At least the meal is consistent. I have been served the Tuesday menu. Sausage and cabbage, steamed so the meaty scent mingles with the rankness of the vegetable. Also hard brown bread. The relief cook is on duty, I can tell by the way the food is prepared. Even that is part of the routine, though his shift does vary.

I glare at the folded newsprint as if it were a rat snuck into my cell. *The Times* of London, a respectable and credible outlet. The lead story concerns ongoing negotiations over changes to fishing rights in the North Sea. Apparently the cessation of lunar tides continues to exert significant effects on marine life, as does the shortening rotational period of the Earth in the absence of lunar drag. Fish stocks have shifted catastrophically time and again in the decades since my master plan came to fruition.

At this I can only laugh. Long-dormant emotions are beginning to stir within me. To be in the world, to walk under an open sky as I have not done since the last day of my so-called trial. Why, once more I can do anything.

I give vent to a rising bubble of glee. Even with my eyes closed, I could measure this cell to the centimeter. My voice echoing off the walls gives me an aural map just as accurate as my visual observations and memories.

The process of my release takes several more weeks. The newspaper left nightly with my meal mentions nothing of me or my fate, though I do learn much about the state of the world. Many of those things are incredible, even to me who mastered electricity, magnetism, and gravity in the days of my youthful ascendancy. It took a combined Anglo-German army reinforced by numerous battalions of African *askari* to bring me down, in the end. Still, I had not anticipated the development of aeroplanes or thermionic valves or electronic switches. My world once consisted of iron and brass mechanical behemoths motivated by the pressure and heat of steam.

The colonel still comes on Tuesdays, but now I also have other callers. A milliner, to clothe me fit for today's street, at least its European variety. An alienist to discuss with me how people might be expected to behave. A geographer to inform me of the current state of empires, colonies, and independent kingdoms in the West Africa of my birth and upbringing, and the East Africa of the years of my power.

"Kilima Njaro is preserved by the Treaty of Mombasa," the small, serious man with the Austrian accent informs me.

"Preserved?" I ask.

"Set aside by multinational acclamation as a natural area to maintain its beauty and bounty." His voice is prim, though he rattles off those words as if he does not quite believe them himself.

I smile at the geographer. Already I know this unnerves him. I am history's supreme villain, after all. My deeds rewrote the night sky, triggered floods and famines that altered the fates of entire nations of people. Self-satisfied white men such as this fussy little lavender-scented Herr Doctor Professor have trouble compassing the idea that a woman born of Africa could have accomplished such mighty perfidy. Even the prosecution at my trial at one point advanced the notion that I must have been a stalking horse for some unknown evil genius of European or American origins.

So my smile, coupled with the power of my personality that has faded so little with age, disturbs this man. Much to my delight. I ask in his native German, "And this Treaty of Mombasa was signed shortly after my capture, I presume?"

He sticks to the English that my jailors speak. "Ah, in fact, yes."

"So what they are preserving is the ruins of my stronghold. Lest some malcontent unearth the secrets of my strength and turn my lost machines against the Great Powers." I lean forward, allowing my smile to broaden further. "Or perhaps worse, prevent European scientists from successfully publishing my research as their own?"

Now the little geographer is completely flustered. I know I have struck home. So it goes.

The last time I see Colonel Loewe, he speaks more frankly than anyone ever has since I was first subdued and captured on the slopes of my mountain, fleeing my besieged stronghold. It is a Tuesday, of course. Some things do not change. I, who am about to see more change than I have in decades, choose to interpret this as courtesy on his part.

"Madame Mbacha." He once more offers me coffee.

"Colonel Loewe." I nod, grant him that same broad smile I have used to upset some of my other visitors.

His voice grows stern. "I must inform you that as a matter of personal opinion, I am not in favor of your parole."

Interesting. "Thank you for your honesty, Colonel. Why do you think thusly?"

"These people at the League of Nations do not know you as I know you." His fingertips drum briefly on the table. "They barely know *of* you, except as a rumored evil slumping into your dotage."

Dotage! I will show them dotage. I hold my tongue, of course.

The colonel continues. "I am well aware that even I barely know you. Always you have guarded your words as jealously as any citadel's sally port." After a moment he adds with further reluctant candor, "Though for many reasons I wish matters were otherwise, I cannot help but admire your strength of character."

I am near to being enchanted by his words. Flattery is one unction that has been denied to me in the more than four decades since my capture. "Do go on," I tell him in a throaty whisper which even at my age can distract all but the most determined men.

"You and I both know full well you are slumped into nothing, especially not dotage. Age has not dimmed your fires, only brought you to a preternatural discretion. I have noted this in my reports over the years. In my judgment, you are still by far the most dangerous woman on Earth." Another drumbeat of the fingertips. "The most dangerous *person* of either gender, in truth.

"It is hoped," he continues, "that four decades of incarceration have mellowed you, and that what prison has failed to accomplish, the inevitable withering of time will have managed. Your release is seen as a humanitarian gesture, proposed by some of the new regimes in the tropical lands that are slowly emerging from colonial patronage. You are a hero in the tropical villages of Africa, of Asia, and of South America, Madame Mbacha." He clears his throat, sending his moustache wobbling. "But we also both know you are still the greatest villain who ever lived."

I wait a long, polite moment to see if the colonel is finished speaking. Then I take pity on him, for he is flushed and perspiring, obviously uncomfortable with himself.

"They are not far from wrong," I tell him. "My years here have made of me an old woman. I do not have the funds or the equipment to embark on grand ambitions. Nor, frankly, the years." I take brief joy in imagining his precious London burning, choking in clouds of toxic chemical fog, assaulted by clanking monsters rising from the bed of the Thames. "Whatever is in my heart must remain there, hostage to age and penury, not to mention the watchers you and yours will surely be setting to dog my every step between the door of this prison and the grave I eventually find."

"Fair enough." His eyes flick down to his hands as if his fingers were an unexpected novelty. Then Colonel Loewe meets my gaze once more. "If you will, for the sake of all that has passed between us these dozen years, please indulge me with the answer to one final question." He raises a hand to forestall my answer. "This is my own curiosity. Not for any report I shall write, nothing to be used against you."

I wonder what could be so important to him now, though it would not be too difficult to guess.

"With all the unimaginable power you commanded, why did you lay waste to the moon? If you'd wanted to free the nations of the tropic world from colonial bondage, why not destroy London or Paris or Berlin, or sink the fleets of the world powers?" He sounds almost apologetic.

The question makes me laugh. A full-throated laugh, the delight I'd once taken in powering up a new machine, in uncovering a novel physical principle of material progress and destruction, in arranging a particularly baroque and painful fate for some interloping spy or traitorous servant. I'm certain it makes me sound mad to him, but what do I care now?

Finally I regain control of my voice. "Believe me, Colonel, once I'd perfected my gravitational gun, I considered those other targets and more. I could have altered the balance of the Great Powers in a single moment. But for every city destroyed, every ship sunk, every army brought to its knees, three more would have sprung up in their place. You Europeans are like the god Eshu, sly tricksters who make a lie of the world with the strength of your guns and gold. In a dozen years, you would have rebuilt and remade and convinced yourself my strike against you had never happened, or had been of little consequence. But who can deny the loss of the moon? So long as men and women live in the world and lift their eyes to the night sky, you will be reminded that at least for a while, there was a power greater and more fearful than even your own."

"In other words," he says quietly after a thoughtful silence, "you destroyed the moon because you could."

"Well, yes." I smile again. "And if my gravitational gun had not imploded, I might well have gone on to destroy London and Paris and Berlin. I chose my most lasting target first." I lean against the table, almost pushing it into him. "I *will* be remembered."

When I walk out of the prison, the daylight is blinding. I have not seen the sun in over forty years. I stumble against the physical pressure of its brilliance. Guards flank and support me, corporals in the same uniform that Colonel Loewe wears.

I'd never known where my prison was. They had brought me here by night after my trial in a secret courtroom in Brussels, the capital of that mad despot King Leopold. Now *there* was a city I should have destroyed. I was brought not just by night but also blindfolded, as I'd been moved from armored omnibus to sealed railway carriage to a cabin on a boat or ship.

England, almost certainly, for where else would one take ship to from Belgium, at least for a short voyage? And English had always been the language of my imprisonment. Still, I am surprised to find myself on the verge of a busy city street amid scents of petroleum and cooking oil and hurried, unwashed people. Gleaming horseless carriages career past with a clattering of engines and a blaring of claxons. Men and women wearing unfamiliar fashions throng the pavements alongside the roadway. Airships and aeroplanes dot the sky.

My breath grows short and hard as a headache stabs through my eyes to interrupt my thoughts with vicious distraction. Dizziness threatens, and despite my best efforts, I feel perspiration shivering on my face and about my person.

" 'Ere you are, missus," says one of the guards. He presses a cheap cardboard suitcase into my right hand. "They've put your walking money inside. I'd be careful of snatchers."

With that, I am alone and free for the first time in more than half my life. I take a deep breath, look up into the harsh, brilliant sky, and see a silvery band stretching from horizon to horizon. The Ring of the Moon, they call it. My signature upon this Earth.

Even amid the pain and panic of the moment, my smile returns a thousandfold. Then I set out to find my way home.

The borders around the Kilima Njaro Preserve are secured by soldiers from a number of European states. It seems that Africans cannot be trusted to protect our own. There is a wall, as well, topped in places with electrical wires and brass light pipes through which guards might spy on distant locations. Still, it is not hard to find men among the Kikuyu who know how to slip through the animal gates. They poach, and gather from the forests on the lower slopes of the mountains, and generally show the white men their asses.

These are not my people—I was born half a continent away—but they and I are of one mind when it comes to the British, Frenchmen, Germans, Belgians, Russians, and others. Joseph, my guide, has been engaged for a quantity of silver rupees I earned through various chicaneries and the sorts of petty crimes open to a woman of advancing years. Once I'd gained my needed funds, it had not been so challenging to slip away from Colonel Loewe's watchers in Mombasa, where I was but one among many thousands of old African women.

I have not told my guide who I truly am, and I am certain it has not occurred to him to guess. If nothing else, he was not even born when I shattered the moon. Tales of Madame Mbacha and her gravitational gun are surely just as legendary and improbable to a young man as are his parents' stories of the days of their own youth.

Still, whether he thinks me mad or simply lost in the world does not matter. Joseph smiles easily, his teeth gleaming in the dark. His ragged canvas shirt and duck trousers are sufficiently reddened with the ground-in dust of the savannah to keep him unobtrusive in these grasslands below my mountain. I myself am equipped with tropical-weight camouflage which Joseph finds an endless source of amusement.

"You are an old woman," he declares, his Kikuyu accent inflecting his English in a way I had not known I'd missed during the years of my imprisonment. "Why do you want to look like a German bush ranger?"

"For the same reason German bush rangers dress like this. To not be seen."

He shrugs eloquently. "You do not come to fight. There is nothing to see here except what is here."

True, I carry no firearm. I never have. There were always others to do the shooting for me. Joseph has a rifle, an old bolt-action Mauser that I suspect is more dangerous to him than to any lions or soldiers he might shoot at. "Sometimes seeing what is here is enough," I tell him.

He does not need to know.

We take our time, moving by night and sleeping by daylight against clay banks or hidden in low-lying hollows. The guardians of the Kilima Njaro Preserve fly overhead periodically in small aircraft that drone like wasps. Twice we hear the chuffing clank of European steam walkers and even catch the scorched metal scent of their boilers, though we never actually see the machines. Neither do they see us. Joseph and I are small and hard to find, as if we were beetles on a banyan tree.

My only complaint, which of course I do not voice, is the heat. I, who once worked with great gouts of steam and the fires of a foundry to build my ambitions. I, who was birthed amid the parched plains of western Kamerun. Slowly I come to admit that the years spent entombed in cold British stone have sapped my bones of their youthful fire.

After four days we gain the slopes of the mountain. I am on my home ground now, and have begun to see traces of my old roadways, the supply lines that brought game meat, grain, and other supplies from the surrounding countryside up to my stronghold. The heat seems more bearable up on the slopes, where the breezes can more easily reach us and trees spread shade from time to time.

"There is nothing here," Joseph says uneasily one evening as we break our camp. A collapsed, fire-scarred stump of one of my watch-towers stands close by. "I do not think we should go on. Haven't you seen enough?"

"I can find my way from here," I say politely. Back in my day, I would have had him whipped for cowardice and sent to take a turn stoking the fires of my industry. Now I must rely upon this man to stay alive. I press another sack of silver rupees into his hand. "Give me a water gourd and wait in this place for two days. If I do not return, make your way home and forget you ever saw me."

"There are ghosts here," he says uneasily. Then: "I will wait."

Perhaps he will, perhaps he will not. I tell myself this does not matter, that I am almost home.

I hike the last few kilometers alone. Even in the evening, the heat persists in bothering me, so to put my mind at ease I review the triumphs of my life. The moon, of course, first and foremost. But also how in my youth I bested the chief's son in my home village and left him crying for his manhood, which I took away in a *muti* pouch. How I'd learned the physics and chemistry and mathematics of the Europeans while working as a cleaner in the universities at Heidelberg and Cambridge. How I'd carved out my own domain in the savannahs of Kenya and Tanganyika, laying the foundations for what would become my stronghold on Kilima Njaro.

Madame Goodwill Adeola Mbacha, scourge of the white race. When my resolve falters or my memories fade, all I need do is lift my eyes to the Ring of the Moon and I am reminded of all I have accomplished.

I come across the outer gates by starlight. They are shattered, their tumbled ruins covered with cloying flowers and acrid-scented shrubs. Vividly I recall the cannon fire that laid waste to my defenses. I walk past a row of nearly vanished graves, surely guards and servants of mine buried where they fell.

Ahead, where the walls of my stronghold should have risen, there is only a larger, night-shadowed heap of rubble. No flowers there. I wonder if my enemies salted the ruins to keep them barren. Slowly, still sweating profusely, I make a deliberate circuit of the destroyed fortifi-cation, taking 4,127 paces to do so.

It is all gone. My laboratories, the refineries. The little railroad that brought in wood and ore for my smelters has been ripped up com-pletely and the bed trenched so it would erode.

Somehow, I'd thought there would be something more of home here. A doorway, a room, a place to start again.

My aching bones and shaking hands tell me that I am old. The heat tells me this is not a place to rekindle forge fires and drill anew for steam vents. The dusty, bitter air tells me I do not belong here.

For a while I sit on tumbled, fire-blackened stones and weep. I, who have not wept since earliest childhood, let the tears flow unchecked. Even the Ring of the Moon seems a mockery, my lost power glim-mering in the sky day and night as the world rearranges itself around missing tides and deeper nocturnal darknesses.

In the morning I walk back down the mountain to where Joseph should still be waiting. I bid the graves farewell as I pass them. The slope is hard on my hips and knees. My mind should be awhirl with plans and possibilities, but I cannot summon the energy. It is too late in my life to start over.

I just want to go home. Is that giving up? The world lives with my mark. I've accomplished more than they can ever take away from me. Now I can return to Mombasa and allow Colonel Loewe's agents to find me. Since I have broken my parole, they will remove me once more to my cool, stone-walled room in the depths of London.

Home is where you live, after all. I have lived most of my life there, and there I will live the rest of my life.

"Colonel," I tell the uncaring thornwood trees and the bone-dry wind, "I am coming home."

The Blade of His Plow

The Wandering Jew is one of my favorite pseudohistorical characters. I usually ignore the poisonous ethnic politics of the legend in favor of the haunting image of a man who long outlives love and life itself.

They tell stories about me. A lot of those are wrong. I was never called Ahasver. I wouldn't know how to make a shoe if you paid me. No one cursed or blessed me. Really, I just am.

When you realize you are deathless, you gravitate to certain lines of work. Not a lot of call for immortal bricklayers. Doesn't take much luck or skill to follow a plow, beyond knowing the business of your own fields. Standing behind the sharp end of the sword is what I do.

Used to be I kept count of how many men I'd killed. Then I just counted the battles I'd been in. After a while, I lost track of that and started counting the wars. Now, well, they count the wars for me. Finally, you people are finishing the job that Yeshua Ben Yosef started all those years ago on top of a dusty hill too far from his home or mine.

Thank you. Thank you. Thank you. Blessings upon you, all that are in my power to give. I know God has an eye on me, lets me direct His gaze to your heart.

Well, maybe not that last.

Longinus had already walked the earth six times longer than the life of mortal man. He had fought in Syria, in Scythia, among the Parthians. He'd changed his name a dozen times. No matter how far he ranged, he eventually found his way back into the legions.

He'd settled on the rank of *tesserarius*, always being vague about his exact history while showing enough of his experience with weapons and maneuver and the business of wrangling men to be convincing to a *signifer* or *centurion* desperate enough for skilled bodies to ignore the irregularities. The older the empire grew, the easier this became. There were always men discharged for drunkenness or brutality who drifted back into the ranks.

And by the gods, Longinus knew one end of a spear from the other.

This time, though, he could see the end coming. Not his own end. Not anymore. He'd taken enough blows, caught enough arrows point first to know what would happen to him. It hurt like crazy, but the wounds always closed up. So far no one had tried to cut off his head. He wasn't looking forward to finding out how that went.

This time it was not his body absorbing the blow. It was the Eternal City herself. Alaric's armies were at the gates for the third time in two years. The Emperor Honorious was long since decamped. Everyone of consequence in the senate and the army had gone with him.

Only the broken legions, and those whose masters could not arrange their timely withdrawal, remained.

Longinus watched the smoke rise from the fires near the Salarian Gate. Rumor among the centurions and their troops was that slaves had let the attackers in. Not that it had done the poor bastards much good. The Visigoths seemed pleased to kill anyone unlucky enough to be in their path.

Now, atop a house partway up the Aventine Hill, he no longer wondered how long it would take them to reach him. A band of the Celtic warriors had ridden into the Vicus Frumentarius perhaps half a glass earlier and set to the serious business of smashing their way through the homes here.

He had four men with him—two of them drunkards, one barely old enough to shave, and another veteran like himself. Longinus had only bothered to learn the old soldier's name—Rattus—as the others wouldn't live long enough for him to need to remember them.

"We could just bugger off." Rattus was slumped against the rooftop parapet sucking down the last of a broken amphora of wine from the house stores. The kid had been useful at least in handling the petty thievery on behalf of the older veterans. It wasn't very good wine, though. The vinegar stink rose up like pickling time in the kitchens.

"Bugger off where?" asked Longinus distantly. He wondered how many of the Visigoths would make it to this house. They were visibly drunk, and not moving with their reputed efficiency.

"Skin out of our kit, flee with the rest of the meat."

Longinus understood from Rattus's tone that the old soldier wasn't serious. "Die here, die there," he said. "They kill everything."

Rattus burped. "What's so special about dying here? If we die there, might have a little longer to live first. Something could happen along the way. A man can be lucky."

"Here is where we were sent to die." Longinus remembered a hot, dusty hilltop in Judaea. He'd learned a lot about being sent to die at that place.

"Fair enough." Another belch.

One of the drunkards poked his head up from the narrow ladderway. "You coming down?" he asked. "We got duck in brine."

"Eat, drink, and be merry," Longinus replied. He heard the raucous laughter of the Visigoths spilling back into the street, two houses down. Smoke was already rising—they'd finally set a real fire here, too. "For all too soon we shall die."

There was no purpose defending this place. Their handful of legionaries had been set here to guard against looting, should the Visigoths be turned back or otherwise overlook the house. Now, well, it was a worthless fight. Nothing more.

Longinus regarded his *gladius*. As swords went, his was not a bad one. He'd claimed eleven lives thus far with the blade. Perhaps a few more today.

When they came, the Visigoths killed the drunkards out of hand. Rattus died swiftly as well, to his mild surprise. When they got bored with Longinus holding off three of them on the roof, they shot him with arrows until he could not stand. The kid they used like a girl until he begged them to permit him to die.

He watched it all through the filmy eyes of an apparent corpse. If speech had yet been granted to him, Longinus would have begged them to take his head as well.

I tell stories about them, too. Or would if I had anyone to listen to me. Another grumbling old man in a world with no patience or place for grumbling old men. Veterans have war stories that no one cares about but the men they fought beside.

Charles Martel is as dead as Abd al-Rahman. Nobody but me

remembers them, or what happened in that rainy autumn deep in the forested country of the Franks. Anybody I might tell wouldn't believe me anyway.

Sometimes I've thought to write it all down. My memory used to be real good. A man isn't made to remember everything, not even last week's breakfast. But he should remember taking a life, a night with a woman, helping birth a baby.

I've done all those things, a thousand times over. Most of the details are gone. Sometimes it's like I've never lived at all.

Longinus had never felt much sympathy for the English. Once a Roman, always a Roman, he supposed. The English were edge-of-the-Empire rubes grown too proud of their mucky little island. But here in France, Charles VI, *le roi,* was a fool. The men who commanded his armies were little better.

One thing Longinus had never done, not as legionary, mercenary, or soldier, was turn his coat. Desert, yes—there was small point in remaining with a defeated army. He had never fought for his own flag, or whatever surge of patriotism drove the sons of farmers and butchers and priests to seek blood. But he did not leave in the moment of battle, and not to the harm of the army he fought for in that season.

What he never could forget was that the men at his side were just like him. The only difference was that none of them had ever been on a Roman execution detail one hot morning in Judaea. Other than that, they were all the same: soldiers in a uniform who would kill or die for the sake of their next hot meal and the pay to come. Whichever came first.

These names he knew, the pikemen in his line. Longinus was a *caporal* just lately. A dozen men to wrangle, and a sergeant to avoid.

The French had not paid sufficient attention to longbow. Longinus had. He'd served at Crécy. He knew what the English could do. Even a generation later, the idea that a peasant could slay a sworn knight still seemed too difficult for the French nobility to comprehend. Longinus understood. He'd taken a clothyard shaft in the breastbone and been left for dead. One of the worst injuries he could recall, in fact, a deeply blossoming field of pain that had almost overwhelmed even his strange, accurséd gift.

Finding new and interesting ways to die was an occupational hazard of going for a soldier, but that didn't mean he had to search them out. The frightened squad around him deserved better than their commanders would give them. Longinus was recalled to that by the smell of urine—Petit Robert had wet himself again. Mist and birdsong might have raised the dawn sun from the fields, but it was the smell of piss and blood that really reminded a man that he was at war.

"When you see the knights fall as if struck down by God, we will fall back into the woods," he said, wondering how many different languages he'd given orders in. After a while, they all faded with disuse, except the Koine and Aramaic of his youth. Those were languages of his dreams. "Sieur d'Albret has promised us a great victory and revenge for the defeats of our fathers."

The squaddies muttered, elbowing one another, a few grinning.

"I have a different promise," Longinus continued. "I promise to keep you alive, if I possibly can."

"Our names will all live on in victory," shouted Henri le Doyeux, surely the most ardent partisan of their little unit.

Longinus met the glance of the *caporal* of the next squad in their line—a hard-bitten Basque who reminded him of Rattus, except for an unpronounceable name. *Idiot,* their eyes said to one another.

"I think you'd rather your body lived on," Longinus replied. "Carrying your name with it."

A bit more elbowing and grinning met that remark, then they settled down to the serious business of breaking their fast and tending their pikes.

When the arrows came, they chittered through the air like blackbirds on the wing and fell through the skin like knives. Longinus never did get his men to the woods, but he found out once again how badly a longbow could hurt a man.

A woman once told me that only in dreams are we truly free. I think she had it backwards. Only in dreams are we truly ensnared. A waking mind knows better than to hope for certain things. Wishes can be avoided for the sake of sidestepping the pain of life. But the dreaming mind, like the heart itself, wants what it wants.

I've spent centuries cultivating the art of not wanting. Married a few times, along the way. Even once staying around long enough to see your children grow to doddering age, then burying them, will put a stop to that.

Cultivating the art of not getting killed took more of my time. Like I said, I don't die, but otherwise-fatal injuries still hurt like blazes. Even so, I've walked off more battlefields than anyone in human history. Of this I am certain.

I've kept a few kids alive. I've sent a few fathers home. I've slain a lot more, of course, my own side's and others. Loyalty is where you find it. Kind of like those dreams.

Even as bad as the English archers were, it was gunpowder that made things impossible. When you could be killed without even knowing you had been fighting, that changed everything.

He hated trenches. Worst invention in the history of warfare. Worse even than guns and bullets. With trenches came mustard gas and bombing runs and tanks and all the things that could befall a man pinned down by position.

Longinus wasn't too happy about his Lee Enfield 0.303, either. With bayonet fixed, it was an incredibly inefficient spear. Mostly, though, it was a finger of death. One that didn't even require the training and sweat of an honest bowman.

The newest lieutenant came down the line, yammering about orders and an attack. Longinus figured he'd last three days at most. Given that the man's first act on arriving was to root out all the booze and cigarettes, then lead a prayer service to stiffen everyone's souls, no one was going to ask too many questions about who fired the bullet that would soon kill him.

After almost two thousand years of warfare, he'd long since realized that every army ever constituted had precisely the same process for producing foolish twits recklessly in love with the power of their commissions. Most of those armies also had an informal process for weeding out the foolish twits on the ground.

It would be pleasant to at least consider that natural selection, except the quality of the officers never seemed to improve.

"Corporal Longo!" shouted the twit.

"Sir?" Longinus gave the man his best tired old sergeant's stare. He knew the noncoms and the company commander had him pegged as a disgraced sergeant major serving under another name. You just couldn't hide the kind of experience he carried in every step, every glance, every word. The new lieutenant saw corporal's stripes and assumed malingering, as that's what the lower classes by definition did with themselves in the absence of proper leadership. Or so Longinus had been told.

A red face sweated at him despite the chilly, fogged-in morning. "Do not eyeball me, Longo. You may be my father's age, but you will respect my authority."

"Sir." Longinus didn't bother to conceal his contempt.

The lieutenant leaned close. "I'll be sorting out the order for our next assault. Would you like to be first out of the trench?"

"If you'll be leading the way, sir, I'd be pleased to follow your example."

The resulting staredown ended poorly for the officer, who finally stomped off muttering.

When the order to go over the top came down the next morning, Longinus shot the lieutenant himself, saluted the captain, then took his squad through a barbed-wire forest into a hail of Boche bullets.

Did you ever figure how much of it all was connected? Just what you can remember now, at the end of the Imperial age, should be enough. Andersonville, Isandlwana, Katyn Forest, My Lai.

A curse, Christ's Harrowing of Hell.

I have been the blade of His plow down the centuries of history. Only now, the numbers catch up to me.

And so they have. A man came to me last night. He wore a suit and snakeskin boots and he ate an apple as he spoke. "Longinus," he said in my own native Koine. He was the first person to call me by my right name since the fall of Rome. "Your days have numbered beyond counting."

I was drinking coffee from a wretched paper cup on a sidewalk in a city of Africa. No one here should know me or speak my tongue, this I well knew. There was only one answer I could give. "I have waited for you a very long time." *Whichever one you are,* I thought but did not say.

His eyes were violet, and spread wings were reflected in them as if an angel stood just behind me. "Are you done?"

"Ever have I been done. Good for evil's sake, evil for the sake of good." I added, "I am tired."

He touched me, just once, saying, "You are free to go."

Where his fingertip had brushed the back of my hand, blood welled up. Two hours later, the scratch had not healed. The lingering pain was a marvel I had not seen since Judaea.

To test his word, I cut off the least finger of my left hand with a hunting knife. *It did not grow back.*

Then, I knew I was free. The only question was what to do with my freedom? I could only go where I had ever been, the battlefield, but that was no longer so easy.

In these days, the recruiters can number the lines on a man's thumb. They can number the flecks in his eye. They can number the patterns woven into the seed of his loins. I have never bothered to learn the crafty skills of forging paperwork and changing records. Always, I could walk away and take another name.

Now, though, even the least of African tyrants wants a résumé and a cell phone number for the mercenaries who might bear weapons in his name. Tramp freighters of no fixed flag won't hire gunmen on their deck unless references are provided. There is no place left for me.

Sunrise greets me now with a sky of fire, as it has done down the long centuries. I have made my preparations. Just in case this last promise is another deceit, I will strike my last blow so well they will not find me after.

I used to wonder what it was like to die. Eventually I stopped, but on this last morning, another wretched paper cup of coffee in my hand, it occurs to me once more that my reward and my punishment are likely just the same.

A soldier's death, and a silent, restful peace with no grave at all. If God wants me, He will have to take some trouble to find me.

So I am walking up that dusty hill for the last time—my still-wounded left hand throbbing in time with my heart. Going over the top of the trench. Claiming the fire for my own. No one will miss this truck until it is too late. The fertilizer and fuel oil in the back will serve. If I have been lied to, not even my God-given invulnerability can survive being vaporized.

I hope.

I am tired, I am old, and I am sick of being the plow blade. The dust like stars shall be my tomb. All those who went before me have borne my name to Heaven or Hell. It does not matter which.

Really, I just wish I still had my old spear. That would bring a proper end to all stories.

Grindstone

I loves me some steampunk. I loves me some weird. Sometimes I loves me some weird steampunk. Because the world is always stranger than we can imagine.

Blood always rusts the springs in my hand. Other people's blood, to be specific.

It's cold up here on the fly deck where I am cleaning my weapons. There is nothing around us but empty sky, stretching to the horizons and beyond. The good airship *Entwhistle* is two days and more from the nearest friendly port given our current heading and the nature of the winds in this airband. I can hear her engines straining slightly. They are running under just enough load to give them a workout without redlining. Which is good, because the rest of this vessel is about to fall through the sky, carrying us all with it.

At least we beat those rat bastards off.

This time.

Laying down the last of my blades, I begin cleaning my right hand with my left. It is fastidious, demanding work. My Maker would have been proud of my diligence. His apprentices would have been appalled. "Don't make so much work for *us,* Jakesia," they used to whine.

I stare past the rail a moment, tempted by memory and old pain until my eyes lose their focus against distant, empurpled clouds.

Shadow is returning. No matter how many rat bastards we fight, there will always be more.

Meat breeds. That's what we Tocks always said, when we were just whispering intelligences, unsighted and benchbound in the earliest days of our creation. Meat breeds. And it always breeds faster than Tocks build.

My hand is sticky and stiff. Carefully I pick flecks of cruft out, that were some rat bastard's heartsblood not so long ago, and try not to think too hard about the breeding of Meat. I try even harder not to think about the fact that I am now in command.

> The shipyards that birth our aerial vessels are as shrouded in secrecy as our very origins themselves. Ask anyone where the airships are built, and you will receive a vague wave and the answer "somewhere spinward." But have you ever met someone who traveled far enough to the spinward to find the answer firsthand? I certainly have not.
>
> The airships simply migrate antispinward, being handed from captain to captain through the vagaries of succession, trade, or piracy. Perhaps they gather in secret conclaves to recreate themselves in a new generation of similars, much as Tocks are said to do. Or perhaps the airships have always been here, before either Meat or Tock came to these skies.
>
> Who can say?
>
> —Skyborne University Inquisitor C. S. Cole,
> *Lectures,* vol. 3

Palacio Sarita bat Mardia, Skymistress of the Lesser Port of Grand Reserve, watched the airship *Entwhistle* beat across the wind into the eastern slips. She stood on the observation deck of the Eastmost Tower, clad in the wool-padded leather of any common dockhand. The formal robes of office with their cerise banding and lacework fringes were too damned prissy for real work. Plus they picked up grease like nobody's business.

If there was anything Lesser Grand Reserve had, it was grease. In copious amounts. At least up to now. Without grease, they would have been nothing but a bunch of starving people on a too-small island in the sky.

The scent of the pits was, as always, omnipresent. So far as Sarita knew, there was nowhere on Lesser Grand Reserve where one could escape from that odor. Tall as she was—well over six feet, unusual for a woman of this or any era—in her time of service, even she had crammed and folded herself into all but the smallest passages and bilges all through the island's keel and decks and towers.

A Skymistress was expected to know her domain. While the endless kingdoms of the air were beyond any woman's knowledge, her home was as familiar to her as a hutch to a rabbit.

Her tools lay beside her, racked and fastened as proper in their fili-greed brass-and-balsawood case. Sarita brushed her fingers over them in their familiar order. Telescope, range finder, electrical divinatory, telelocutor, flare pistol, and shock prod. See, signal, and shoot.

Of course they were old, as all the best equipment was. Of course they were worn, as all the most properly used equipment was. Of course they were slightly slick with the ambient grease of Lesser Grand Reserve.

She wondered what would become of them. Likely there would never be another Skymistress of the Lesser Port of Grand Reserve.

Panjit, her chief acolyte, snapped his own telescope shut with a crisp movement that telegraphed bored mirth. As always, he struck a pose. No leathers for him. No, Panjit favored the full regalia, identical to her own neglected cerise robes except for the azure dye and shorter fringework. He was not shy about remarking on how well cerise would favor his magnificent dark complexion and patrician nose.

Not in this lifetime, she thought. *Or at least, not in my lifetime.*

But what was a Skymistress without a port?

"You watch, they'll clip the number-three east boom on the way in." He sounded remarkably satisfied for a man predicting a minor disaster. "That'll bring a good levy."

"The state of her gasbag and rigging says otherwise," observed Sarita mildly. "No matter how great the fine, we cannot wring payment out of someone who's already wallowing in penury."

"You underestimate the value of salvage, Skymistress." Panjit's tone was so smooth and self-assured that she wanted to slap the words from his face.

Sarita didn't bother anymore to ask herself why she was stuck with this dreadful little climber for a chief acolyte. Everyone of worth and potential had emigrated over the past two years. Once the state of the grease pits had become general knowledge, anyone with sense had been able to see which way the wind was blowing on Lesser Grand Reserve.

Due wrong, in two simple words. The wind was blowing due wrong.

The problem with basing your entire economy and raison d'être on a constrained resource was that eventually you ran out of the resource in question. Decisions which had seemed canny two centuries ago dur-ing the bright days of the port's founding and initial construction were now foolhardy in the blindingly obvious light of hindsight.

For the past thirty years, they'd actually been *burning* the grease to make electrical energy. On ascending to the post of Skymistress, she'd put a stop to that, and nearly lost control of Lesser Grand Reserve's governance in the ensuing spat. Now the few Master Mercers yet remaining in port quietly praised her foresight in doing so, and even more quietly grumbled that she hadn't seen through the problem sooner.

Logic was not an essential element in politics, Sarita had long ago learned, to her displeasure.

"Panjit," she said, her voice filled with the regal snap of authority. Not to mention the cold edge of the air on the Eastmost Tower. "Take yourself down to the east slips and present my compliments to *Entwhistle*'s captain. Dinner in my apartments, should they be so inclined."

"We would be better showing them the back of our hand than our open palm," grumbled the acolyte.

Sarita stroked her shock prod fondly, not trying very hard to keep her impulses from her face. "Are we so rich in visitors these days that we can afford to turn anyone away?"

"No, Skymistress." Without making the proper obeisances, he turned on his heel and strode away.

Little bastard never had believed in the grease crisis, she knew. Panjit still thought it overblown, still believed that if you bullied and bribed the surveyors enough, they'd come back with better estimates of the depth and grade of what remained embedded within the caverns hidden at the heart of Lesser Grand Reserve.

Sarita watched the airship a while longer, pleased to see that *Entwhistle* beat past the number-three east boom without incident. She finally went below herself to review once more the remorseless reports that charted the death of her city in the sky.

> *One for wood and one for oil*
> *One for sheep and one for soil*
> *Wheat and barley, water and rye*
> *Everything grows here in the sky*
> —Children's rhyme

Having arranged the good airship *Entwhistle* to be tied up to the waiting slip and boom-braced until her gasbag is no longer under load, I am now reduced to watching the local Meat whine and caper alongside our battered hull.

The Lesser Port of Grand Reserve is a friendly port, her slips and galleries open to us, but that does not make her welcoming. It simply means that in the war of Shadow, she does not shelter those who hunt us across the endless sea of skies.

Meat does not hate Tock here, except in the vague way that all Meat fears and despises Tock. It is something in their monkey flesh, buried deep beneath Meat's quick, erratic mind, that leads them to such animosity.

I no longer care. My hand rusts, my captain is lost, and my ship is wounded. Any of those things would distress me. All of them together overwhelm.

"You," says the most important Meat on the slipside. I know he is important Meat because he is dressed like a fool and doing no work.

I meet his eyes, my own glittering stare encompassing the liquid brown of the man's gaze. He needs no response from me, he knows he has my attention.

"Where is Captain Armature?" the Meat continues.

"Falling," I answer. I am laconic truth, and find the depths of my despair yawning below me like the bottomless sky.

This imperious Meat blinks a moment, thrown off whatever script he has prepared. "An air sailor's death, to be sure. Then who commands here?"

Fool, I think. *Tock do not die. We are stopped.* Meanwhile, three of my deckhands drift close. Two bear blades loosely sheathed, the third carries a long iron lever bar. The Meat grows impatient.

"Jakesia," I finally say. Swift grins chase one another across the faces of my crew.

Anger flashes in the Meat's eyes. This one is important, unaccustomed to a lack of cooperation in others. "Summon him."

"*She* is here." I rise and bow, the bad servomechanism in my left hip whining briefly in counterpoint to my indifferent dignity.

Three of the port's dockhands bring over a water line, hup-hupping in time as they coordinate with my own deckhands. Our credit is good enough here for a resupply without advance guarantees. I am certain we will not be treated this well again.

The important Meat turns and walks away. In showing me his unprotected back he is telling me how insignificant I am to him. This is fine with me. He is not a rat bastard intent on claiming my life, nor is he a minion of Shadow. Therefore he is insignificant to me as well.

When fades the light, comes the night
And brings the realm of ghosts and Shadow
When fades the day, good men stray
Into the night of ghosts and Shadow
When fades our world, flags are furled
All are ghosts in the realm of Shadow
                    —Traditional dockhand ballad,
                        attested on multiple islands

Skymistress Palacio Sarita bat Mardia strode down a deserted hall-way. Pale patches on the wall betrayed the long tenancy of portraits recently removed. Dust, flecks of paper, scraps of cloth and grit were scattered across the polished floor. She could remember when this had been a busy thoroughfare. Now it was as deserted as any dockside lane when the airships were away.

She took a deep breath and allowed the smells of this place to settle into her nose. Grease, of course. Everywhere the grease. If there was one benefit to the not-so-slow death of the Lesser Port of Grand Reserve, it was that she might someday soon escape the perpetual reek of grease.

Beyond grease, there was the faint, murky scent of mold. As if water had gotten into some nearby carpets. Sweat, too, of dockhands work-ing hard to shift loads while there were still decks to shift them to. Someone's old cook fire, rancid oil and burnt beans. But mostly the dusty, silent reek of emptiness.

Already well over half of Lesser Grand Reserve's population had departed. Most of the early migrants were from the monied classes. People with the funds or education or skills to easily find passage aboard some airship or another with reasonable expectation of new employment at their next port. Or possibly the port after that one.

Those who remained were the poor, the stubborn, and the terminally optimistic. Along with a few operators like Panjit who saw, or thought they saw, ways to profit from the collapse of a once-proud port.

The last major port failure had occurred when the springs on Fly-monkey Island had dried up unexpectedly. Within a handful of months the city there had been reduced to empty ruins. Not even pirates could harbor there in later days.

Sarita had been a girl then, well into her own apprenticeship at Port Lamassu. The collapse of Flymonkey Free Port had been a subject of speculation and rumor for months.

The Lesser Port of Grand Reserve was a much more important place than Flymonkey Free Port had ever been. But she both hoped and feared its fall would be less remarked upon.

Someone—or something—had been hunting airships out in the airbands, pulling the stricken vessels to their deaths among the clouds. The disruption to communication, trade, and migration was impossible to ignore.

Shadow was coming, the laborers whispered in their dormitories and refectories, but Sarita placed little faith in such rumors. The fears of small people everywhere could speak louder than any voice, and with less reason. Legends were just that: legendary.

If not Shadow, though, it was something. New and aggressive pirates. An invasion from distant airbands. *Something*.

And in the midst of it all, her city was dying.

The Skymistress passed quickly through a cleaner hallway and into the elegant dining room where affairs of state were often conducted, and even occasionally settled. The table awaited. Oil cups and troughs were set on one side for Tock, plates under domes on the other side for Meat.

It was set for three, she noted sourly. She would not escape Panjit this evening.

> *Of course this is not our original home. How could it be? Were the bones of our first fathers and mothers made of the air? Why do we have words for "dog" and "horse," and even paintings of them, when no one in recorded history has ever seen such fabulous creatures?*
>
> *The question isn't where we came from. Somewhere else, obviously. The question is, where are we going?*
>
> —Binyan the Wanderer, Sermon at Port Ruin

I sit in a gilded room with two Meat. We are surrounded by statues of heroes of yore, and a carpet thick enough to bury corpses in encloses our feet. History and art and money reek about me. Amid their glory, I ignore the Meat blood still crusted in the joints of my right hand. They dine in the fashion of their kind. Steaming food is clutched in their soft, clever fingers and shoveled into their pursed, damp maws. I try to imagine what it would be like to have teeth. Excrescences of bone within one's jaws. Brittle, fragile, hard and sharp.

Much like Meat themselves.

The important Meat who met me at the dock ignores me. He pretends attention and respect to the woman he sits with. Even I, a simple Tock, can see she has no use for him. She does not bother to hide her corresponding lack of respect.

She I must focus on. She is the Skymistress. It was her order that permitted *Entwhistle* to dock at the Lesser Port of Grand Reserve. It is her forbearance that permits us to take on supplies even now in advance of our letters of credit and our limited funds.

The Skymistress has a name, but Meat always has names. They never seem to last long enough to earn them. Still, I attend to her. She is at least polite to me. The Skymistress meets my eye, when she is not looking at her glistening, crumbling food. She listens to my mumbled words. She seems interested.

Too interested, perhaps.

Finally she places her little stabbing fork down at the left side of her plate and her dull knife down at the right. "Captain Jakesia," the Meat says in that clear, strong tone of voice Meat always uses to announce something unpleasant. "I must ask a difficult question. In the interests of my island."

"Ask." I am not long on courtesy, but then I am not long on much of anything these days.

"What became of Captain Armature? Who did such terrible damage to your ship?"

"*Entwhistle* is airworthy," I say almost automatically. A sky court might find differently, especially if I were ever heard to express fears contrary to that basic sentiment.

"I do not seek to . . . challenge . . . you." She leans forward, her hypertrophied chest glands straining against the curdled red of her robes. "We live in a time of adversity. Especially here on Lesser Grand Reserve." That earns the Skymistress a hard look from her Meat companion, the important one that I have already come to dislike in a most collegial manner. I grudgingly admire the way she simply ignores his hostility.

"We were attacked," I say. Truthful but unhelpful. That is usually best with important Meat.

"Stupid Tock." The other Meat's impatience practically spills across the table. "Her language facilitator is on the blink."

I meet his eye and hold him with my gaze. I am Tock, I do not need to blink. In time, he does. "There is nothing wrong with my language facilitator, you ignorant dolt. I am merely parsimonious with my words."

"Attacked by who, then?"

"Whom," I correct him. "Attacked by *whom*."

The Skymistress bursts into noise that after a moment I recall is Meat laughter. It has been a long time, and very little is amusing to me anymore. "Panjit," she says with a bright smile, laying one hand upon his arm, "you will not best this one."

I trace my fingertips in the remaining pool of my machine oil, a lovely 000 light vegetable base. "No, leave that to the rat bastards. They bested us all too well."

She leans close again, pressing her glands against the table edge so that the other Meat's eyes slide sideways despite his hostile focus to me. "Who are the rat bastards?"

Now there is a question. I take another long, hard look at her assistant Meat. He is a dangerous fool, but the Skymistress holds the lines of power here. Also, I have little left to lose. Armature is dead, *Entwhistle* is stricken.

"The rat bastards are servants of Shadow," I say. "They sail in small ships, some of them just wings without gasbags. They live hard and close to the wind. They come from the east and antispinward. They attack ships far out in the airbands, or traveling within the clouds. I have never heard of one attacking an island or a port or a city."

That is the longest string of words I have spoken since before Armature went over the rail with three rat bastard lances in his chestplate.

"They prey on trade," the Skymistress says in a thoughtful voice.

"Your trade is gone anyway," I observe. "Your slips are idle, and most lie long unused."

Unexpectedly, the other Meat speaks. "Too many believe our grease mine has failed."

I know a state secret when I hear one. "Your port is dying," I tell them. "My airship is dying. Will you repair me?"

"Will you bring back our trade?" snarls the other Meat. The Skymistress stares him to silence before returning her attention to me.

"I thank you for the information." Her voice is grave. "Our crews are diminished, but we can still provide repair parties and supplies."

Grudging honesty forces answering words from me. "Payment may be slow."

She spreads her hands. "Where would we cash your credit draft?"

That provokes a chuff of steam and a wheeze from me. Laughter, indeed.

Disgusted, the other Meat rises from the table and leaves with great ceremony. His exit is clearly intended to provoke us, or possibly make a point.

"Your life would be improved by killing him," I tell her.

"Unfortunately, he is the best of those remaining to me." She sighs and sags a bit in her chair. Becomes more human, more like me, in that moment. "Will they come in time, these rat bastards?"

I opt for the truth. "Come the Shadow, comes the rat bastards. In the darkness, they will shit in your halls and shatter your windows and howl from the tops of your towers."

"Shadow is just a rumor." Her voice is uncertain.

"Shadow is the end of all things. They are just its servants and heralds."

She watches me a little while. Then: "You are very angry."

I shrug. Human is as human does. "No one craves their ending. Meat ages and dies. Tock can fail without proper maintenance or too far from fuel and grease. But Shadow? Shadow is the failing of the entire world, the dying of the light."

The Skymistress is aghast. "How do you know?"

"Because of the coming of the rat bastards. This has all happened before. It will all happen again."

"How do you know *that*?"

I tell her my deepest secret, one that runs back to my Maker and my very making. "Because I remember the last time."

Her voice drops to almost nothing. "How old are you?"

"Older than the light itself."

With that I rise and begin my walk back to *Entwhistle*. It won't matter soon. The Lesser Port of Grand Reserve is dying, as surely as the light is dying. As surely as I am going to fail.

If Tock could cry, I would weep.

> *Meat and Tock*
> *Hand and clock*
> *Rise and walk*
> *Meat and Tock*
> *Tock and Meat*
> *See and greet*

Have a treat
Tock and Meat

—Children's rhyme

Skymistress Sarita returned to the observation deck of the Eastmost Tower, trailed by two silent servitors. The best of her household were gone. A few more departed with every one of the increasingly infrequent sailings.

Soon, the Lesser Port of Grand Reserve would have too few people to maintain the docks and keep the island's businesses running and supplies moving. The grease mines wouldn't matter then. The people would continue to shelter a while—there were still springs, and granaries, and orchards—but without grease, and money, there was no trade. Without trade, there were no new supplies.

As she'd promised, repair crews were about *Entwhistle*. In truth, the dock masters were glad enough of the work. It was something to do. The airship was listing slightly in her slip even as men and women swarmed over the rigging and along the decks. Hoses snaked from the gasbag to pumps brought out on trolleys.

A cold wind picked at her hair and made her eyes water. It blew from antispinward. She thought hard on Jakesia's words about the rat bastards and the coming of Shadow. The actual darkness might be a nursery tale to frighten children, but surely Lesser Grand Reserve was falling into its own Shadow.

Metaphor or not, the Shadow was real.

"What if I just boarded the ship and sailed away with them?" she asked the wind.

Meat and Tock usually did not mix in crews. The demands of everything from watchstanding to what was required of each sailor were too different. Tock did not sleep, and were hideously strong by the standards of ordinary men. They could sail with half the complement of a Meat ship.

But any ship would take passengers for the right fee, under the right circumstances. Any ship would take *them* on.

"Alfons," Sarita said aloud.

Her servitor stepped forward. "Skymistress?"

"How many persons remain on this island?"

"A moment, please." He retreated indoors, searching for records.

Her old steward would have simply known.

She watched *Entwhistle* and listened to the wind a while. Eventually Alfons came back. Bald, stooped, one eye drooping, he was at least sharp of mind. "One thousand and one hundred natural persons, Skymistress, and six hundred and forty made persons. That is the current estimate."

"Of which we could put perhaps forty aboard *Entwhistle*," she said. "It will take fifty more like her to carry everyone away." And long before that the great steam engines and electrical generators and water pumps that maintained life on the island would fail for reduced maintenance and lack of tenders. Were fifty more airships ever going to call at the Lesser Port of Grand Reserve?

"They are unlikely to pay for the services we provide," Alfons said lugubriously. "You may as well demand forty passages as compensation."

Something in his voice caught her attention. "Would you go?"

"No, Skymistress." He protested loyalty, but she knew he did not mean it.

Nobody did. What was there to be loyal to? The city was dying. And Shadow was coming.

Sarita wondered what had become of her loyalty. Evaporated under Panjit's ambitious glare and the burgeoning decay of the port city in her charge. Nothing remained but old habit, it seemed.

She watched the horizons of air eastward and antispinward a while, looking for the swirling dots of a flight of rat bastards, or some other harbinger of Shadow. All Sarita saw were storm clouds trading lightning in the distance. All she heard was the lonely voice of the wind.

"We shall be ground as dust." Her words slipped out aloud once more.

Alfons spoke, so close to her elbow that she startled slightly. "Every grain breaks upon the grindstone, Skymistress. That is the fate of grain."

"We are more than wheat and chaff," she replied, but did not believe herself.

There must be people in the world beyond simply Meat and Tock. They are rarely seen. Legends, to most of us. But the sky is infinite. There are always more islands floating in the airbands. How can there not be both angels and orangutans somewhere? It would be stranger if there weren't.
                                        —Binyan the Wanderer, Sermon at Port Ruin

I stare across my deck. My hand is clean, finally. It took a wire brush and a foolish degree of patience, but I am clean. Even rat bastards have mothers. How different is that from me cherishing memories of my Maker?

Those other memories, from the beginning, when the light first came back—those I do not cherish.

The deckhands assemble. Bosun Shimwater nods to me. All are accounted for.

"We are ready to sail soon," I call out. "We have taken on no cargo. There may be passengers, though perhaps not once I have seen the Skymistress again."

They all stare at me, eyes bright and marbled with expectancy, servomechanisms whining slightly as weights shift, eddies of steam emerging from odd vents. Tock is never so still as Meat can be, because Tock never sleeps. We move or we die.

I pause, considering my next announcement. "Captain Armature had plans, but he is lost to us. *Entwhistle* is a ship without home port or purpose. Too many of us were lost as well. Her boilers are sound, her gasbags tight, her engines strong, but her heart is broken.

"As is mine."

Still they stare at me, glittering and feral. No one turns away. No one seeks to shout me down.

"I have a plan as well. *Entwhistle* will sail antispinward. I want to face the Shadow as it comes, and press my blades into the faces of the rat bastards. We will not drive them back. We will not stay the coming of darkness. But we will meet it with eyes open and arms raised.

"Will you come with me?"

There is no great shout, as a crowd of Meat might have done. Neither is there a rippling tide of those slipping away. Everyone just stands and stares. Bosun Shimwater. Leftscrew the junior pilot. The Leyden Twins, connected by spark and cable as they were. All twenty-three of my surviving crew. No one answers, no one steps back.

They just await orders.

In that moment, I love Tock all over again as I never have before in all the centuries since my Maker first unbound me from my birthing bench.

"Captain Jakesia."

I turn to see the Skymistress on the gangplank. She has presented herself without the foolish, important Meat who follows her around.

Only with a servant bent and palsied with the age that afflicts all Meat after a few years.

To my surprise, her name comes to me. "Sarita," I say, forgetting the honorific.

I realize she has left behind her blood-colored robes. This Meat woman is clad in stout leather with wisps of wool peeking from her collar and cuffs.

"May I have your permission to come aboard?"

With a bow, I welcome her to *Entwhistle*. In setting foot on my deck, she comes under my rules. "Welcome."

She glances up as the old man crowds behind her. The important Meat stands on the tower, glaring down at us. Though even I cannot see his eyes from this distance, I can read the set of his body in his blood-colored robes.

"Your rank is no more?" I ask politely.

"I am just Palacio Sarita bat Mardia." She bows slightly in return to me. "I would work my passage wherever you are bound."

"Toward Shadow," I tell her, "and the dying of the light, amid the swords and spears of the rat bastards."

"We all sail into Shadow," she says. "And every woman's light dies someday. I would face it in good company."

The servant cackles. "Not with Panjit back there. Peacocked fool."

"The winds of time are turning foul," I warn her. "They will not turn fair again in our lives."

"We are all grain," she says. "The world is our grindstone."

"Can you haul a line on command?" I ask.

Sarita, once Skymistress of the Lesser Port of Grand Reserve, smiles. Very much despite myself, I smile back.

I check the springs of my hand one last time, then I give the orders to cast off.

The Temptation of Eustace Prudence McAllen

Editor Kerrie Lynn Hughes asked me one day for a story. Which she needed by the end of the week. About supernatural weirdness in the Old West. But it couldn't be zombies or vampires. And would I mind setting it in Hell's Half Acre, Wyoming? "Sure," I said. There's nothing like a focused market requirement. Then I went out for excellent barbecue at the Salt Lick outside of Austin. The rest is history, and a few burps.

You know that place out west of Casper? Wild badlands like you've never seen, all rocks and salt and twisty dead-end ravines'd swallow up a man and his horse both like they was watermelon seeds. Hell's Half Acre is its name these days, but folks used to call that the Devil's Kitchen.

What do you think, biscuit-head? On account of him cooking up sin there. What else'd the devil his own self set to boiling over a fire?

Now this fellow name of Eustace Prudence McAllen rode for Hotchkiss Williamson what had the Broken Bow Ranch out that way. Williamson held a good spread, with two different springs and a box canyon full of cottonwoods running down through his grasslands. Drought didn't bother him nearly so much as it troubled his neighbors, though he did have a problem with range fires there through the summers of 1864 and 1865.

McAllen, he might of been a Southern man, ain't no telling now. But he'd showed up the autumn of 1863 and signed on. Working over the winters on the range here always has called for a special kind of cuss, so Williamson and his brother ranchers didn't ask a lot of questions of a man what rode strong and didn't backtalk and kept the cattle out of trouble. Anyone who came west in those war years was avoiding something, somewhere. So long as they didn't bring their troubles in their saddlebags, that was generally good enough.

No, I can't rightly say exactly what he looked like. You talk to people who rode for Williamson in them years, you get different tellings. Time plays tricks on memory, don't you know. There was a lot of panics, from Indian attacks and the range fires and what all. Can't even say if'n he was a colored fellow, some kind of quadroon, or just white, like a black Irishman. Taller than most, maybe. Carried an ivory-handled double-barreled LeMat revolver what had been engraved real tiny, some folks said it was the book of Jeremiah writ real small, always close to his hand.

Why anyone would carry that particular book of the Holy Bible so I can't rightly say.

So here's McAllen working the cattle for Williamson and minding his own business. Don't drink too much, don't fight hardly none at all, don't cuss in front of Williamson's wife and daughters, lends a hand even when he ain't been asked. Everything's fine until the second summer of range fires and somehow word gets around that McAllen has been setting 'em.

Firestarting is worse than rustling, in its way. You don't just lose the cattle, you lose the land. And fighting a range fire is somewhere between suicide and hopeless. Best you can do is get livestock and people out of harm's way and pray the wind don't shift wrong.

Mostly you know what done it. Dry thunderstorm, often as not. But sometimes they got a pattern. Summer of 1864, and again 1865, it was like that. Visitations, almost.

And they was talking, people. Cooks and runners and the feedlot boys and the fancy women and whatnot. McAllen's name was on a lot of lips. For a fellow ain't made no enemies, he sure didn't have a lot of friends. It was all-around peculiar.

So Williamson, he got the wind put up his own self and went and had a quiet talk with McAllen. I can't reckon the old man had pegged his hand for a firebug. More like he wanted McAllen gone a bit, out of the way to let rumor run its course. So he sent the poor bastard out riding trail west of Fort Caspar, what the city was called back then afore it was really a city. Said McAllen was checking springs and shelter in case they needed to drive the herds through the Powder River country.

Which was so much horse puck and everybody knew it, but it did serve to calm the hard words down some.

McAllen, he got himself out toward the Devil's Kitchen. That's a wild, wild land, looks like God dropped some old mountains into a thresher the size of Kansas, then let Leviathan vomit all over what fell out the ass end. All gray and brown and furze, covered with sand and ash and alkali and salt, nothing a fellow with any sense would ride into.

But he saw smoke, you understand. And fire was on his mind more than anyone's. Range fires could take his life in a hanging, if those hard words stuck around and took root in people's thoughts. So McAllen probably figured on picking his way on in there and finding some camp of layabouts or Indians or deserters, or something he could lay them fires at the feet of.

Off he went, leading his horse down a slope of scree and into one of them little, twisted canyons, following the smoke and his own sense of what was right and what was not.

Now the Devil, he's one crafty son of a bitch.

Yeah, I said that. You just mind your piehole or I'll mind it for you, and you won't like that one tiny bit.

Crafty on account of that's how the Creator made him. Lucifer, he's practically the first of God's children. Old Adam, more or less an after-thought he was. A gardener, really, set to watch the fruit trees and keep the snakes off the lawn. No, all the pride and power and glory went into the Prince of Light. When he done fell from Heaven, he took a piece of the Old Man's heart with him. The meek might could inherit the Earth, but it was the prideful for whom the beauty of the day was first forged.

After the Fall, though, the Devil he had to slink around in the dark patches and hide in the shadows and walk with the rotten side of a man's soul in his hand. That's why he hangs around even to this day in places like Hell's Half Acre, what was the Devil's Kitchen back then. Ain't no place for him among the shaded cottonwoods or along a quiet bend in the river with a fishing pole.

Still, a fellow's got to eat. That's part of our earthly estate, don't you know? And the Devil likes him some barbacoa as much as the next man.

Yeah, what they call barbecue now days.

A good loin of pork or brisket of beef, dry rubbed with salt and some spices, then cooked long and slow over a bed of coals afore you slather on a compounded ferment of vinegar and tomato sauce—that's a ticket to Heaven through the gates of the mouth. Food as righteous as any toe-curling sin.

So here's the Devil got him a roasting spit down in a dry ravine in the Devil's Kitchen, and he's got a dozen lesser dark angels to tend the fire and turn the spit, and a whole heifer off of Mr. Williamson's land stuck up there roasting to feed his own hungers and keep his myrmidons at their labors. It was a good place for Lucifer, on account of no one ever goes there, and he could rest in peace until time called for more of his mischief to be spread upon this Earth or down in the dominions of Hell.

Yeah, like that, kid. And you wouldn't be the first one ready to sell their granny down to darkness for a mouthful of that hot, sweet meat fresh off the fire. No, sir.

Devil was resting his spurred heels on a shattered knob of gray-white rock, a jug of white lightning in one clawed hand, a corncob pipe in the other, when Eustace Prudence McAllen led his old bay mare into the mouth of the ravine.

Them demons, they giggled and cackled and sizzled as demons is wont to do. Old Scratch looked up to see what the fuss was and saw a beanpole of a man with a week's beard looking back at him. Dark fellow, for a white man, in a pale canvas duster and a busted-down slouch hat pulled low over his eyes.

"Boys," the Devil announced in a voice like a flash flood down a canyon, "we got us a visitor."

You got to understand the Devil speaks all languages and none. Adamic, what everyone talked before the Tower of Babel, that's the tongue of Heaven. Any man born of woman will understand it, on account of it's the language God made us all to know and be known by.

So while his vowels sizzled with lightning and bedded coals, and his consonants were the fall of hammers and the snap of bones, the cowboy McAllen heard this in English as plain as any what got spoke in the bunkhouse back at the Broken Bow Ranch, and in an accent as melodious as General Nathan Bedford Forrest himself.

Which is to say, McAllen, he wasn't fooled one tiny bit. The Devil can make himself fine and fair as any Philadelphia dandy, or he can be small and slick and mean as a scorched badger, or anything in between. But this day Old Scratch was taking a rest, so his tattered wings spread black and lonely behind him while the horns on his head showed their chips and cracks and stains.

The only characteristic that marked him out from the chiefest among his lesser demons was the blue of his eyes, which were as deep and quiet as the lakes of Heaven. No creature born of Hell could ever have possessed such a gaze, and it was them orbs of light that marked the Devil still as being directly the work of God's hand.

McAllen saw the wings and the flickering, scaled tail and the great clawed feet and corncob pipe and the jug of shine, but most of all he saw those blue eyes, and he knew his time had come, and probably already gone past.

He also knew from the barbacoa spit who'd been setting those range fires.

"How do, neighbor?" he asked pleasantly, careful not to let his hand stray to the gun butt at his right hip. McAllen knew perfectly well that the six or seven wiry, bright red bastards tending that cow a-roasting could take him down before his second shot got off, and he knew perfectly well his first round wouldn't do no more than irritate Old Scratch.

"Smartly enough, I reckon." The Devil sat up straight and set down his jug. "Strange place you picked to be riding fences, son of Adam."

McAllen touched the brim of his slouch hat. He dropped the bay mare's reins, on account of she'd been pulling hard. "It's rightly son of Allen, your worship," he said calm as a millpond. Behind him, the horse bolted with a scream of fear to melt a man's heart.

Go, he thought, *and carry the news of my death if not the tale of the manner of my passing.* For it is given to some of us to know the manner and hour of our passing.

Well, yes, you're right. Even a deaf-mute idiot Frenchman would have known this was the manner and hour of his passing. And Eustace Prudence McAllen was none of those things.

The Devil smiled, which was not a sight for the faint of heart. "Still no fences down in these lands, son of Allen."

"Just a fire down below." McAllen summoned the courage that had stood him up against Yankee bullets and Oglala Sioux arrows and Wyoming winter blizzards and Texas summer droughts—that courage was needful now for him to walk slowly toward the Devil, measuring his steps with every care a man could bring.

"My cooking could bring a circuit preacher to his knees," the Devil said proudly. Pride was, after all, his overweening sin and greatest accomplishment.

McAllen touched the brim of his hat again. "But your worship, the sparks from your fire keep setting the grasslands east of here to flame."

With a shrug, the Devil smiled again. "Fire is my servant and my only friend. What does it matter to me that the prairie burns?"

Here is where Eustace Prudence McAllen showed what a clever man he was. He smiled back at the Devil, though his guts liked to turn to water, and said, "Except folk are setting the blame on me for them range fires. You ain't getting the credit you rightly deserve."

At those words the Devil's teasing of McAllen vanished in an eruption of wounded vanity. He stomped one great, clawed foot, what shook the ground so hard they felt the tent poles rattle over in Laramie. "By all that's unholy, I shan't be having you take the credit for my deeds, son of Allen!" His shout smoked the air blue and called dark clouds into swirling overhead. Flames snapped at the broken tips of his horns, and his wings spread wide with a creak like a barn in a tornado.

No, no, they ain't had no real buildings in Laramie till after the war was done and the railroad come to town. Of course it ain't a camp *now*.

Anyway, I got a story to tell, if you don't keep aggravating me like that. Who taught you manners, anyhow?

"That's why I come to you, your worship." McAllen somehow kept his voice steady, though he nearly voided himself in his drawers from sheer, raw terror. "It ain't right, and I reckon to set the record straight."

"I'll straighten the record," roared the Devil. "I'll show them who's Prince of Flame and Darkness around these parts."

At this point, McAllen realized he might of overshot his mark just a little bit. He hadn't aimed to set Old Scratch on the folks of Fort Caspar and the Broken Bow Ranch. He hadn't aimed for much at all, except to live a minute or two longer in the face of such wrath.

He had his second fit of brilliance. "Before you go wreaking havoc across the land, your worship, maybe you ought to partake of your dinner."

Well, those words brought the smell of barbacoa back to the Devil's nostrils, along with a strong whiff of the sulfur that has been his natural estate since he first fell from Grace. Like I said, there ain't many that can resist the crackling lure of the slow-cooked meat.

"Be damned if I won't," the Devil replied, then began to laugh at his own joke.

McAllen, he laughed along with the Devil, because what else is a man to do in such a moment? The two of them stood there, cackling and howling like two lunatics, even the lesser demons capering and giggling through their needle-toothed mouths.

Old Scratch strode with a purpose to the roasting cow and tore off a long, lean, juicy strip of meat, all crisped dark on the outer edge and dripping fat within. The smell that came off the carcass like to set McAllen's brain on fire, reaching right through his nose and his tongue and lighting up the sin of gluttony as nothing else in the world could have done.

"You want some?" the Devil asked, drippings running down his face from both sides of his mouth, his rotten fangs chewing the soft, sweet meat like it was manna fallen from God's hand.

The scent nearly undid McAllen. He was tempted, knowing he'd taste of the finest meal ever to be eaten by himself or any other man. Knowing likewise if he took food from the Devil's hand, he'd be a servant of darkness for the rest of his days here on Earth, and damned for eternity beyond.

He never was a churchgoing man, McAllen, but anyone who's stood when the bullets fly or watched over the herds when the wolf packs are hunting down the moon knows better than to disbelieve. Life is too short and hard and strange not to blame God for what He done made of the world.

Yes, even now. And I know none of you knotheads ever dodged a bullet in your young years.

No, acorns out of a slingshot do not count.

McAllen looked at that most perfect barbacoa steaming in the Devil's grip, and reckoned if he didn't take it from Old Scratch's hand, he'd be next up on the spit. But like I said, he reckoned if he *did* take it, he'd be bound then and forever more in service, like that Faust fellow out of the old days in the Germanies.

Death, or barbacoa?

That right there was the temptation of Eustace Prudence McAllen.

What would you have done? This here's the point of the story, ain't it?

What would you have done?

Really and truly, on your best swear, what would you have chose?

They heard the shot at the Broken Bow Ranch, clear as if someone had loosed a round off the porch of the bunkhouse.

Folks heard it in Fort Caspar, too.

Later on some claimed they heard it in Laramie, reckoned the noise for a boiler explosion or some such, but the railroad ain't reached Laramie yet that year, so you can figure on them being liars or at the best misguided in wanting to be part of history their own selves.

But the howl that followed, everyone heard that clear on to Fort Benton in one direction and Omaha in the other. Like a storm off the plains grabbing up sod houses and snapping telegraph poles it was. Anger and pain and rage and loss that caused drunks to stop beating their wives for a day or two, and sent even the randiest cowpokes scurrying into the revival tents for a good dose of prayer and preaching.

You see, Eustace Prudence McAllen shot the barbacoa spit right off the posts and dumped the Devil's dinner into the ashes and sand of the firepit below. He resisted temptation and bought himself a ticket straight to Heaven on account of nixing Lucifer's vittles and vexing the ambitions of evil that day, in that place. Hell didn't let out for dinner, see, on account of what he done.

The Earth split open so that the Devil and his minions could chase themselves straight down to Hell, taking that ruined carcass with them.

When Williamson and a posse of his hands came the next morning on the bay mare's backtrail looking for McAllen, they found him lying flat on the ground deader than a churchyard dance party. His clothes were nearly burnt off his body, his hair turned white as the Teton glaciers.

One last piece of crispy barbacoa was stuck between his teeth, and Eustace Prudence McAllen had the expression of a man who'd died with his hands on the gates of Heaven.

They buried him where he fell, on account of none of the horses would sit still for the body to be slung across. Williamson kept the Le-Mat revolver, which the metal of them double barrels looked to have been frosted but never did thaw, and dropped that piece of barbacoa into a leather pouch to take home and study, for even then he knew it for what it was.

There weren't no more range fires for a long time after that. Some folks took that to mean McAllen had been the torch man, but Williamson and his hands knew better. They kept their dead compadre's name clear, and they kept the herds well away from the edges of the badlands.

Even now, if you ride out west of Casper toward Hell's Half Acre—for the Devil don't cook there no more, so it ain't his kitchen now—if'n you ask around and folk like the set of your shoulders and the light in your eyes, there's a barbacoa pit run by some of Williamson's daughters and granddaughters. McAllen's Barbecue, they call it. Place ain't on no signpost or writ down in no tax rolls, but it's there.

Head for the badlands and follow the scent. Just mind who's eating on the porch when you get there, because even the Devil himself can be tempted back to this corner of Wyoming when the wind is right and the cuts of meat are just good enough.

That Which Rises Ever Upward

This was part of a shared project that editor Phil Athans put together. We never did get much traction with the concept, but I had a lot of fun writing this.

The Dreams of a Boy

Attestation clutched his glowing fists tight and stared out into the pit, his mind aboil. His two khilain coins, clutched one in each hand, were not hot—whatever mystery of magic or technology lent them their light was more akin to the phosphorescent scum on the cave walls of his home village than it was to the bright heat of the Sunstrip that lit their days and glowered through their nights.

Khilain. Nihlex Watershed. *Up.* Those tricky winged bastards could fly. Even the little lantern-plants bobbed up and down the pit's air column when they were in fruiting season, flying in groups ranging from a dozen or so to occasional releases of a hundred or more. Though only fourteen, Attestation was a birthright Pitsman, like his father, and his grandfathers before them. He could no more spread wings and fly than he could set his face to glowing like the coins.

All he could do was cling to the wall and dream.

His village, Ortinoize, wasn't much of a place. Built into a crack in the pit wall that ran roughly upward at a thirty-degree angle, it had all the charm of a staircase on which someone had dropped a great deal of junk. Not that Attestation was all that personally familiar with junk. Everything in Ortinoize was reused, repurposed, recycled. It was just old Sammael that taught the kids—he was an infaller, from someplace called Canada, outside the pit—he had a lot to say about the world and the way it was used, and was full of mysterious ideas like "junk" and "oceans" and "flight."

Except flight wasn't so mysterious. The nihlex did it every day of their lives. And everyone knew *they* were dumb as rocks.

That some dumb old monkeys could find their freedom in the air of the pit was an offense to his spirit. Attestation knew this like he knew the back of his own hands.

Eventually the Sunstrip faded to nothing more than a warm presence. The cooling air brought smoky scents and reinforced the everpresent flinty odor of the pit. Attestation slipped the coins back into his goat leather neck pouch, careful to fold them into a precious scrap of satin, then picked his way among the bamboo tubes that formed the foundations and scaffolding of Ortinoize and onward up through the warrens of the village to his own sleeping mat just a little too deep inside Marma's Cave for him to see the dawning of each new day with his own eyes. This night, like every night, he flew only in his dreams.

Ortinoize had been founded, depending on whom you believe, by *communards* escaping bloody retribution for their utopian ideals, or by a group of drunken priests of some stick-god now forgotten except in the cruciform symbol that represented the village on those rare occasions when the village required symbolic representation. In either case, someone had gotten lucky in finding this crack in the pit wall, because a solid stream of fresh water flowed there that had never failed yet. Those founders had been smart about their water, and built an intricate system of cisterns and pools into which rock footings were braced so the inhabitants of the village were always above a water source.

The rules on waste disposal were vigorously enforced. "Protect everyone's water" was the cardinal law of Ortinoize. Everything always reeked of damp and dank and night soil and the strange green dreams of bamboo that sometimes grew so fast you could almost watch it unfold.

This focus on water and architecture meant the village was in effect one giant building. It ramshackled on like Sammael's staircase, with sleeping alcoves and pantries and little foundries all mixed together. A family might hold rights in half a dozen places, their linens and shoes closeted amid someone's potted beans while they took their meals three ladders higher and slept in three other locations depending on mood, gender, and who was in disgrace with whom.

Sammael had suggested more than once during lessons that this argued for a *communard* ancestry to the village. But then everyone knew Sammael was troubled by protestations of faith. Given that the elderly infaller was the only person in the village with anything like an outside education, he'd been given responsibility for the children in the likely vain hope that some of that education would rub off on them like the reeking coal dust.

As Attestation's father Redoubtable often said at meetings of the village council, they were poor and lost, but that did not mean they needed to be weak and stupid.

Still, Redoubtable often treated his son as if he were weak and stupid.

Marma's Cave was one of three lava tubes leading back from the fissure. Many of Ortinoize's children and young adults slept in there. Some nights Attestation couldn't rest for all the giggling and slurping that seemed to go on, accompanied by gasps and occasional salty smells. Not that any of the girls or boys ever wanted to giggle or slurp with him. He'd never quite found the trick of being likeable.

Besides, he spent his time dreaming of flying. Not like a nihlex, but like a human. Everyone knew that was stupid. People who passed by in the air were always going in one direction and one direction only: falling *down*. Sometimes screaming, sometimes in resigned silence, occasionally laughing with maniacal glee. But down was the constant.

No one ever fell back up. That was the part that counted as flying. What the lantern-plants and the nihlex did.

There were trails and ladders and ropes. A determined fellow who was strong, coordinated, and a bit lucky could pass up-pit to the small khilain way station of Clings-Too-Low, or down-pit to the next human village of Mossyrock. Presumably, similar arrangements went on beyond in both directions, but for the hundred or so people who lived in Ortinoize, those were the boundaries of the known world. Clings-Too-Low when trade was required, Mossyrock when brides needed to be exchanged. Sammael had been very firm on that last bit of business, for reasons that had never quite made sense to Attestation.

Maybe if he got some giggling and slurping in, he'd understand that better.

But climbing up and down the pit walls didn't count as flying either.

He would be just a bug then. Not even as good as a plant. What Attestation wanted, wished for, desired, was to *fly* out there, to travel freely upward, at least to the Smog, and downward, though not quite so far as all the monsters everyone knew lurked far below.

Fly.

The schoolroom was floored with split bamboo, harvested from the precious stands that grew alongside some of the cisterns. The biggest problem with bamboo wasn't starting the seedlings—the stuff grew like fire on oil. It was hoarding enough soil to root the plants in. Still, over time, Ortinoize had managed to grow enough of the tough, wiry plant for its own needs, and to trade up to Clings-Too-Low for things they could not make or find for themselves, and occasionally for some little bit of magical something from far away, or even outside.

Attestation sat with his haunches pressed into the irregular grooves of the floor, at the back of the room where he could watch the seventeen other students while Sammael made laborious notes on a painted wall with a scrap of precious chalk. It was the only reason he was still in school—someone had to train to be the next teacher, and even Sammael himself would tell you he was getting too old, that the descent through life that had led him from mythical, magnificent Canada to grubby little Ortinoize was almost over.

The schoolroom had an unusually high ceiling by village standards, and so Sammael, and whoever had taught before him, had hung up there various articulated skeletons and stuffed skins of animals and plants. It had always struck Attestation as odd to sit beneath a flight of badgers and snakes and several unidentifiable stranger creatures, but they could hardly be left in the cubbies that lined the walls, for the younger children would surely play the old bones and furs to ruin. Besides, they smelled funny on the days when the damp was strongest.

Everyone but the teacher sat on their own little mat. Sammael had a stool he rarely used, preferring to stand when he spoke, and preferring speech to silence. Today they were practicing letters—just the alphabet for the youngers, and sentence exercises for the olders.

Reading and writing had come naturally to Attestation, and he'd digested every one of the four English and French books that Ortinoize had to boast in the tiny library cupboard at the front of the schoolroom. There were two other books as well, one in an alphabet Sammael had said was Cyrillic, and one that probably hadn't been made by humans at all for it was all the wrong size and proportions and the letters within looked like entrails of birds. Sometimes Attestation liked to handle that last, to touch its leather-and-metal cover and wonder who'd made it and what sort of light their days had been filled with.

Otherwise he'd read *Rienzi, Last of the Roman Tribunes*; *Le Grand Meaulnes*; the *U.S. Army Field Manual 5-488—Logging and Sawmill Operations*; and *The Two Towers*. Each moldy, waterworn book had inspired him all the more to want to fly, because only in flight could he reach for Orthanc or imagine a logging camp.

That was why he'd stayed in school, as his friends had gone out to apprentice as cliff foragers or smallsmiths or bamboomen.

That and the small paper sack Sammael had shown him years ago—paper, common as muck outside the pit but inside more precious than the glowing khilain coins—the paper sack that floated in the air when heated from beneath.

A thing that weighed more than the air itself could still be made to fly. That had been the greatest lesson he'd ever learned. It was one Attestation very much wanted to repeat on a larger scale. His own scale.

The Labors of a Man

At twenty-six, Attestation was still unmarried, though he knew a bit more about giggling and slurping and the salty scents of sex. He was now the oldest person sleeping in Marma's Cave, chaperone and supervisor to the never-ending churn of children that passed through his care as teacher. When Sammael had finally passed away, of a bloody infection of the lungs that no one could fathom how to cure, Attestation had inherited not only the old man's post as teacher, but also his permanent bachelorhood.

Still, he had his work. He'd argued for the establishment of paper-making from the bamboo—a discussion that had taken two years of village council meetings before grudging permission had been given. Attestation had made it his business to account for both raw materials and production. One part in four he kept aside for copying out the old books before they fell apart—*Rienzi* especially was in poor condition—one part in four he kept aside for his own experiments and teachings, and two parts in four went up to Clings-Too-Low to be traded onward.

After the profits on the third trade trip with the bamboo paper, even

Redoubtable had ceased to argue with Attestation about the use of bamboo. For the first time in a dozen years they'd been able to afford the little green-gray tablets that could cure some diseases and ease the course of others. "Antibiotics," Attestation had explained, drawing on his shaky recollection of Sammael's only somewhat less shaky knowledge of medicine. Save a few lives, make a little bit of money, and you could be as ornery and strange as you wanted.

At least until it came to finding someone to slurp and giggle with.

So he wrote out the books page by careful page, imagining forest stands and hordes of ravening orcs. More quietly, he made larger paper sacks and experimented with the sharp-scented alcohol flames that could heat them enough to send them rising about his schoolroom without setting fire to either sack or room. Twine to tether them, though it would need to be rope if he ever flew himself. Braziers to contain the fire, though they needed to be light enough to not weigh the balloon down, and sturdy enough not to melt. A sling for the dolls he placed in them as passengers, while he dreamt of larger slings meant for even a man of modest stature such as himself.

All the while his small store of khilain coins glowed and grew, his own shares from the bamboo paper trade hoarded against the costs of those things he could not make or beg for himself.

Attestation had finally secured one of the upper rooms, nearly at the top of Ortinoize's crack in the pit wall. It was too far from water for most people, and the endless winds circling up and down the pit seemed to find their way into his aerie more than one might prefer. Still, it was an unusually large room, and had the signal virtue that he could remove the ceiling, as no one dwelt above him. In effect, he had a platform lashed and chained to the rock walls from which he could launch his test balloons. And he had enough room to weave his bags-of-air.

He'd even managed to capture some lantern-plant seeds, and carefully monitored their life and growth, observing as closely as he could following the methods old Sammael had taught when Attestation was himself a boy. Make notes, take measurements, sketch—at least he had the paper for that.

Redoubtable and some of the other elders grumbled at the amount of precious paper Attestation used in his projects, but he simply pointed out that without his projects there would have been no paper, and the slight but ever-growing surplus of wealth in both khilain coins and actual traded-for luxuries would not exist either.

They'd even strengthened the trade in organic scraps and night soil to further boost the bamboo growth. Even Attestation, usually indifferent to his reputation in the village, had balked at being called Shit Slinger, which nickname had emanated from Clings-Too-Low in a fit of what passed for khilain humor.

But now he had a room with the flats and trays and presses needed to make paper from the bamboo pulp pounded farther down in the village. He had knives—even three of infallen steel!—to cut and sculpt his paper and his little dowels. He had several clever little tables with vises and braces so he could bend rods and clamp glued-together bits effectively.

In return for all this, he was only required to teach the children and occasionally be clever about paper-making. Well, and put up with the odors of the chemicals used in the paper process, but Attestation figured in time his nose would either grow used to the stench or simply give out. He did not care so much.

His current project was a bag-of-air that would support forty kilograms aloft. That was enough to send a small child plus the required brazier and ropes and so forth, but still only about half of what Attestation reckoned he'd need to take himself into the air. He was no nihlex to simply fly with wings gracefully given by God, nature, or evolution, depending on whom you believed. Still he did what he could, eating lightly and exercising frequently to keep his body lean and light.

Attestation stood in the middle of the lithe framework, making adjustments and wondering for the thousandth time how the lantern-plants filled their bags-of-air without tiny braziers. They were not hot when they grew as rooted plants. Neither did their bags-of-air have any warmth on the rare occasions he could catch one bumping its way up the pit wall. But when flame was added to a lantern-plant they burned so quickly it was an explosion more than a fire.

Hydrogen, he thought to himself, but that was just a chemical word from old Sammael. Neither the nihlex nor the khilain nor the humans of the pit could trade him that chemical. Not like sulfur or mercury or charcoal that came up and down the pit in tiny, precious baskets worth their weight in paper. And sometimes more.

But hydrogen, well, it might as well have been air for all he could do to capture it.

"Attestation."

He glanced up from his reverie to see his father at the door to the workshop. That was unusual. Redoubtable had somehow become an old man while Attestation wasn't paying attention, and rarely climbed above the relative luxury of Ortinoize's midlevels—close enough to water, far enough away from the soil pits that rooted their wealth of bamboo.

Stopping to take a longer look, Attestation found he was truly shocked. Redoubtable had always been a large man, but now he appeared slumped. His craggy face seemed to have melted to a field of bumps and crevices out of which ragged gray hairs sprouted. His father's mouth had rounded as well, as teeth had fallen away. Even the stout goat leather jerkins his father had once favored had fallen away in favor of a rumpled, stained robe that even Attestation would have been ashamed to wear. Only the banked furnace gleam in the old man's eyes had remained the same.

"Sir," Attestation said, trying to stand up but bumping into the frame of his bag-of-air. "What brings you up this far?"

"The council will see you now."

"Why?"

"Just come, boy," growled Redoubtable. "I have climbed up to you. You can climb down with me."

Following his father's slow, laborious efforts down the ladders and stairs and ropes of Ortinoize, Attestation reflected on what it might mean that Redoubtable had climbed so high to seek him. If the council had simply meant to bark at him again for using up too much bamboo, they would have sent a runner to act haughty and harass him until he descended to their meeting place in Pierre's Cave. If they meant to honor him in some fashion—as vanishingly unlikely as that was— they would have sent a runner to cajole him with flattery and perhaps a bit of fruit from the espaliered trees that grew along the outer edges of Ortinoize's crack.

But to send his father, the hetman of the council and second only to the mayor . . . Attestation could go weeks at a time without even seeing Redoubtable. In the years since his mother had passed away, there had not been much business between himself and his father.

Still he followed slowly down the winding, twisted passages, through people's sleeping areas and racks of gourds and little workshops. All the life of the village was bound in on itself like many vines growing together. He passed through squabbles and cooking and lovemaking and the quiet industry of the very busy and poor.

Eventually they reached Pierre's Cave, which always had a drier smell than the rest of the village due to the vaguely warm breeze blowing ever outward from fissures deep within. There was a reason the old men and women of the council had their chambers there—someday, Attestation knew his joints, too, would ache in the damp and cool of Ortinoize's springs.

And here they were, the council all met in session. Old Aoife, the mayor who'd been wife to the previous mayor and took his place when he'd slipped off the Adumbrate Bridge just outside. His father, the hetman. Councilor Fettle, who was also the village's whitesmith. Councilor Young Aoife, no direct relation to the mayor, who nursed the sick and practiced what medicine any of them could understand. And Councilor Unswerving, a small but angry man who'd never approved of Attestation's projects, though he was happy enough to count the coin that came from up-pit in exchange for their modest production of bamboo paper.

"Hello," said Attestation, who saw no point in the rituals of formality.

"Sit," said Old Aoife. She'd been beautiful once, even Attestation could see that in her eyes and the set of her face. Now she had that grace that came upon some of the old—he'd known it only from spending so much time with Sammael. It was almost the opposite of how his father had aged.

Attestation took the empty spot made for him on a mat between Unswerving and Redoubtable. "What is this?" he asked.

The mayor glanced around at her fellow councilors for a moment, as if seeking reassurance. Then she looked back at Attestation. "We are come to a hard time. Three of us on the council are old. Young Aoife tells us that Redoubtable will not live so much longer, with the crab disease in his bowels."

He glanced sideways at his father, shocked. Yes, Redoubtable was old now, but the old man was like the pit itself—an eternal if abstracted fixture in Attestation's world. "I . . ." he began.

"Silence," growled his father, who had never had time for pity in Attestation's life.

"I am naming Young Aoife mayor in my place," Old Aoife went on. Unswerving stirred, murmuring something that Attestation had no trouble interpreting as objection. "We will call for another councilor by acclamation from the village to take her place. Fettle is willing to continue serving, as is Unswerving, but we will have you take your father's place as hetman."

Attestation was stunned to silence. What did he know of the business of the village council? He could hardly recall the names of his students, and there were only eleven of them right now. His heart was in the air. Always in the air.

"This . . . this is not my place," he said, trying not to stammer overmuch.

"It is all your place," Old Aoife said severely. "You teach our children. Everyone who has passed through the school in the years since Sammael died knows of the world from how you see it. You set our course on the making of paper, which has brought scraps of wealth such as we have never seen, and can reasonably be hoped to bring more."

"My son . . ." Redoubtable said slowly. There was an ache even in his voice, Attestation realized. "You have become the most important man in Ortinoize. You carve our future out of bamboo and the minds of our children."

"No," he said, raising his hands as if to push them away. "No. I do not have time for this, and no one wants me to take my father's place."

But he knew he had already lost the argument before it began. Just as he knew that he would need to continue teaching, and experimenting with the making of paper.

The work of the council would take the place of his lantern-plants. The judgments in trade and dispute that were properly the province of the hetman would take the place of his bags-of-air.

His dreams, like hydrogen itself, were already fading into an elusive memory.

The Memories of an Elder

When Attestation was thirty-one, he married Young Aoife. By then she was Aoife-the-Only, as the old mayor had passed quietly in her sleep two years earlier, but everyone had called her Young Aoife for so long that the name remained.

That was the same year that the Crown had opened and the blood bats had swirled down the pit. That was a *bad* time for everyone—nihlex, khilain, human, it didn't matter, the blood bats were opportunistic hunters that could see even during the darkest part of the pit's night and had tiny, scrabbling clawed fingers to pry open doors and unweave walls as they sought their prey.

He'd fought, alongside everyone else in Ortinoize, and seen them lose 42 of their 117 people before the scourge was beaten off for good. Attestation had managed some chemical packets that seemed to distress the blood bats—it was perhaps the only thing that saved the village in those days when shriveled bodies rained from above like dried fruits dropped from a careless child's hand.

When he was forty-three, and thus an old man himself, Aoife-the-Only died of a rattling, drying-out illness that all the medicine in the world could not cure. Once she'd set out on the spirit path beyond sleep, Attestation cut the curled brown and gray hair from her corpse and set it aside to use as fiber in a very special paper, then very nearly threw himself into the pit in grief, saved only by Unswerving, as unpleasant an old man as he'd been when young.

"You had your chance to fly," Unswerving told him as he pressed Attestation into a jagged groin in the pit wall, a dozen staring faces open-mouthed at what was practically a fistfight between the two oldest on the village council. "Don't do it now like one of those damned blood bats, wings spread wide. You'll never catch the air."

"Hydrogen" was all that Attestation could say, gasping, until the tears took his words away and even Unswerving's flinty heart was moved.

Later they sat in Attestation's old workshop up high. His smaller test balloons were ragged, faded, and torn with the years. The last large framework had long since been dismantled and reused. Unswerving had brought a pot of plum wine.

"Never should have listened to you," Attestation mumbled, drinking the sweet, sharp swill.

"Never did listen to me," said Unswerving.

"Seventeen years on the council, all I ever did was listen to you, you talky bastard."

"I talked, you never listened."

There seemed to be no answer to that, so they both fell back to their drinking. Finally Attestation returned to the heart of the matter.

"She's dead."

"Everybody dies."

"We had no children." Not that they hadn't giggled and slurped aplenty in their time.

"Me neither." Unswerving hiccupped. "Never had the chance."

Attestation peered out of the tunnel of his grief, dimly recognizing a fellow sufferer. "Why?"

"Never went the right way. Women . . . I . . ." He didn't seem capable of making a better answer than that.

After a while, Attestation tried to restart the conversation. "I should go lay Young Aoife out." Ortinoize buried its dead at the back of Pierre's Cave, then eventually gave their bones to the soil pots, once they'd spent enough time in the dry air. Years, really. Even old Redoubtable wasn't ready yet.

"Let her fly," said Unswerving.

"What?" Attestation was shocked. "You never liked anything I did. You always hated my work with the bags-of-air and the lantern-plants."

"Spent your time on the wrong things." The other man's voice was slurred with plum wine. He reached out for Attestation's face. "Spent your time on the wrong people." Then, suddenly, strangely, a kiss between them. Salty, prickly, tasting of old man sweat, nothing like kissing Young Aoife. Not wrong, not right, just different.

"I . . ." Attestation's words ran out as he pulled away from Unswerving's trembling grip. "I."

Shivering to his feet, Unswerving essayed a smile. "Let's go harvest some bamboo."

Farewell Upward

Somehow Attestation had thought it would take a few weeks, a month or two at the most, to rebuild the bag-of-air to its full size. But there was always something else that needed doing. The children were younger than ever, and he hadn't trained a new teacher yet, even after all these years, so he started that process with a bright girl named Millas. She didn't much resemble Young Aoife in body, but in spirit she might have been his wife come again—bright-eyed, inquisitive, pleasant, with a hot iron core that one only disturbed at one's peril.

Naturally Unswerving hated her.

The two old men were living in the workshop, sleeping close on cold nights and sometimes holding one another. But it was Attestation who carefully made his way down the steps and ladders and chains every day to work with the children, to sit in the village council as it all-too-slowly spun away from him, to hear cases from those who would be judged by no one else.

And though he kept meaning to work on the bag-of-air, there was the matter of Ferocity's beating of his son to be judged. Then the khilain came from Clings-Too-Low complaining of nihlex harassment in the matter of the paper trade, which they controlled up-pit from Ortinoize for the most obvious reasons, but for which only Attestation would do as an expert in the affairs of paper. He'd refused to travel any farther than Clings-Too-Low, and the only reason he even agreed to go that far was in hopes of harvesting more lantern-plants for his long-neglected growing trays.

A month among the khilain with the acrid smokes of their cooking amid the wattle bulbs of their pitside houses and the strange, thumping music they played on instruments made of rock and rope and bone and hide was more than he ever needed. As for the nihlex, the less said the better. They could *fly*. Watching them come and go reopened jealousies he'd left slumbering for decades.

When he came back, well, then Unswerving was ill. Some complaint of the lungs that would not go away, so the old man, unpleasant as ever, coughed away his nights in the workshop and refused to come down at all, even to stand at the pledging of the newest councilors. So it fell to Attestation to care for his oldest detractor as he had once cared for his wife, and still wasn't he old, too? Who cared for him?

At least the children of their little school brought water up each day, and took away his night soil, and ran those errands that could be run without the apparent never-ending need for his personal oversight.

Still, Attestation worked on the bag-of-air as Unswerving coughed and choked. He made new, thinner paper, mixing Young Aoife's carefully hoarded hair into the fibers, and in a pique of vanity throwing a little of his own white, brittle straw there as well. One night when Unswerving was actually sound asleep, Attestation even stole a bit of his hair with a flick of one of his rare steel knives.

As he worked, the lantern-plants grew as they'd never done before. Runners sought new trays, so Attestation time and again interrupted the interruptions of his labors to set more out. They were faster, somehow, than he recalled from earlier years, as if the plants themselves felt some primal urgency. As Unswerving grew weaker and more vague, he seemed to take comfort from the trefoil leaves dangling on their little green extensions from the bulbous bases of the plants.

The frame of the bag-of-air was done long before the paper, of course. Attestation continued to despair of the brazier, experimenting with beaten tin—which had cost him a good portion of his hoarded khilain coins—as well as fire-hardened bamboo, and even thin-walled pottery traded down for the paper on his special request. Slowly he filled out the proportions of the bag-of-air, making this one big enough for even a small man such as himself. Slowly he helped Unswerving toward the final tumble that everyone must take someday. Slowly he wandered up and down the steps and ladders and chains, doing what was asked of him, what was needed. Slowly he wondered how he had turned into his father, and why he was not more like old Redoubtable.

One day Unswerving sat up straight, for the first time in a month, and there was a bit of the old, bright malice in his gray eyes.

"You've turned this place into a lantern-plant farm," he said sharply.

Attestation stood, hands on his aching hips, and looked around. Unswerving was right. The entire workshop was crowded with the bobbing, pinkish-translucent bulbs of the lantern-plants' bags-of-air. Their strange smell, sort of like rock and water mixed together with old metal, seemed thick enough to bottle and sell. He stood amid green and pink and the scent of growth as strong as any of the bamboo pots down below. The spherical frame of his own bag-of-air filled the room at the center like the king of plants holding court over his retainers. He realized it was nearly covered with the special, thin paper that carried a bit of his wife in every sheet.

"I have no brazier," Attestation said sadly. The tin hadn't held enough oil for what he needed. The pottery was too heavy. Wood wouldn't burn fast enough, and besides only a fool burned wood.

Unswerving coughed. "Put the lantern-plants inside. They carry your precious hydrogen. Just use them."

Attestation blinked. He'd never considered that. For one thing, there were never enough lantern-plants.

Except there were now. His trip to Clings-Too-Low had brought back a bountiful harvest of seeds and seedlings. Here in his workshop, they'd seemed to grow in unison, as if their proximity to one another brought out their inner nature.

Which, he realized, made a certain sense. You never saw one lantern-plant bag-of-air floating in the pit. When they flew, they flew in dozens, and sometimes hundreds.

He had his hundreds. And each lantern-plant weighed less than the air itself, thanks to the miracles of hydrogen and gravity.

"You are a genius," he said to Unswerving.

"No, I am just old and tired."

Three days later the bag-of-air was fully papered, and the lantern-plants were beginning to separate from their root masses. Attestation had finally recruited several young men from his recent students to keep everyone else away from his door. Unswerving had coughed day and night, but managed to hobble to his feet and assist in the careful harvesting of the lantern-plants so their bags-of-air could be slipped inside Attestation's bag-of-air from the opening beneath, without tearing either the paper or the fragile plants themselves.

Slowly the bag bobbed upward, no longer resting on its cradle. Attestation checked and rechecked his precious ropes anchoring the balloon to his worktables. It tugged up, the plants within squeaking slightly as they rubbed together. A few popped with a strange, sharp scent, but most held together. They stuffed the bag until it was straining, and watched fearfully up-pit through the missing ceiling for any last-minute catastrophe to come down upon them, or even just a mischievous nihlex.

Voices outside, late on that third day, finally penetrated Attestation's increasingly distracted attention. The mayor and the hetman had both climbed to the top of Ortinoize seeking their wayward elders. Someone shouted about a problem with the paper quality, complaints coming down from up-pit. Another voice complained about the lessons neglected because even Millas had joined Attestation's little troupe of door wardens.

Judgment was needed.

Aid.

Help.

Experience.

Testimony.

Please come.

Do this.

Find that.

We need.

You must.

Attestation looked at the boys outside his door, and the larger, older adults clinging to the ladder beyond, and shook his head. He turned to Unswerving, who had lain down again, but his fellow old man was asleep.

No, Attestation realized, not asleep. Unswerving was finished with sleep now.

He knelt beside his longest-lived adversary and kissed the crinkled, rheumy eyes and the cracked lips. Then he crossed Unswerving's hands across his belly and pulled the ragged blanket over his face.

"Tell Young Aoife I'm sorry I could not fetch her bones," he said quietly.

After that, he took up his punk pot and his steel knife and bound himself into the load-bearing ropes that hung below the bag-of-air, that had been meant for the bamboo basket that would hang below. Why bring a basket now, when he was not coming back? He would fly all the better without it.

One by one, Attestation cut the tie ropes with his knife of infallen steel, careful to alternate as he went around. The bag-of-air bobbed, the lantern-plants within rustling. He kept the last three tie ropes together, each a third of a circle apart, so he could cut them at once and not tip his balloon.

When he was ready, he clutched the punk pot close, made the final cut, and cast the steel knife away.

The balloon shot up, lurched, and caught on the edge of one of the open-roofed workshop's walls. The Sunstrip was waning out in the middle of the pit, and so he and the balloon cast a huge, reddening shadow. The children guarding his door shrieked, but Attestation told himself it was joy, not terror.

Then he and the balloon broke free, bouncing up and off the pit wall before twirling out into the open air.

For the first time in his life, Attestation was flying. For the first time in his life, he truly opened his eyes and looked at the world. The pit gaped beneath him, Sunstrip off to one side, shadowed far below even in the glowing light of the fading day, but from here he could see Ortinoize, Mossyrock, and a dozen more villages he did not know. A pair of nihlex spun perhaps a thousand feet below him, indifferent and unknowing to what passed above them. A flight of lantern-plants caught the Sunstrip's reddening light in their translucent bags-of-air, so each became a bright jewel held up against the onset of darkness.

Just as he himself was a bright jewel held up against the onset of the darkness at the end of life.

Carefully Attestation looked over his shoulder, but the bag-of-air obscured most of his upward view. He thought he could see Clings-Too-Low. He could certainly see his own village, dozens of faces wide-eyed and round-mouthed staring at him as he bobbed toward the center of the pit and the Sunstrip.

Not just bobbed, but rose. Flew. On wings of hydrogen and bamboo and the hair of his beloved wife he flew.

Attestation knew he would never see a more perfect moment than this. Young Aoife was long lost to him. Unswerving had just now walked down the spirit path into the darkness beyond sleep. He'd brought no ropes nor water nor any way to go beyond this point of flying.

This was what he'd lived for all his life, hoarding coins and stirring the sludge to make paper and teaching old Sammael's lessons to the children. "That which rises ever upward can never die," he said aloud.

Smiling, he opened his punk pot and blew its tiny flame into a more robust life.

Smiling, he waved a fond farewell to the people he'd always known.

Smiling, he set the flame among the hydrogen of the lantern-plant bags-of-air.

Smiling, Attestation stepped down the spirit path in a burst of flame and light that wrapped him in glory.

Angels iii:
A Feast of Angels

Yet more angels. The sarcastic kind, this time.

Saint Peter made Friedrich Nietzsche coroner of Heaven. Though Heaven stands outside time, all things there both concurrent and infinite, being human Nietzsche had perceptions that were perforce more or less sequential. Heaven's coroner was a stultifying job, as death was unknown there.

"I am convinced," Nietzsche told Origen of Alexandria over a six-pack of Stroh's, "that this is my punishment." They sat at a picnic table on a small, isolated cloud.

The little Egyptian's hand spasmed, crinkling his own can of beer. "This is hell," he whispered. Lately they spoke American English, equally foreign to both. Also equally offensive in its colloquial imprecision. "The Adversary has crafted this eternity for such as us."

"Could be worse." Nietzsche stared down off their cloud at a bus loaded with joyful Charismatics bound for Branson, Missouri, on a three-day pass. "We could be with *them*."

"Though all days in Heaven are the same, still I have been here a very long time." Origen tugged another Stroh's off the six-pack. "There *have* been worse things. Old Hermes Trismegistus got it wrong. As below, so above."

Nietzsche shuddered, imagining the Heaven of the Inquisition, or John Calvin. Origen had lived through them both. Aimee Semple McPherson had been bad enough for him.

Saint Peter appeared, potbellied and irritated. His robes were askew and his halo appeared to have developed a crack. "We've got a problem."

"This is Heaven," said Nietzsche. "There are no problems."

Origen burped for emphasis, the yeasty odor of recycled Stroh's disturbing Heaven's usual pine-scented freshness.

Peter frowned, obviously picking his words with care. "This problem has always existed, but now I wish to address it."

"Sh-sh-shimultaneity," said Origen, who had been talking to Einstein lately. "No shuch thing."

Nietzsche shot Origen a hard glare. "What kind of trouble?"

"Coroner trouble," said Peter.

"In *Heaven*? I thought you were just yanking my chain."

"Consider yourself yanked," said Peter darkly. "We need you now."

"Now is the same as then in Heaven," muttered Nietzsche, disentangling himself from the picnic table. "Where are we going?"

"Other end of time," said Peter.

"Hot dog," Origen shouted. He vaulted over the table after Nietzsche and Saint Peter. "I always wanted to see Creation."

They stood on nothing, slightly above a rough-textured plain receding into darkness. Scattered vegetation struggled from the surface; thin, sword-like plants. The only light was from Saint Peter's Heavenly effulgence. Somewhere nearby, water lapped against an unseen shore. Unlike the rest of Heaven, this place stank of mold and rust and an odor of damp rock.

"I'm impressed," observed Nietzsche. "What is this? The root cellar?"

"Foundations, more like it," Peter said.

They both glanced at Origen, who looked intently into the darkness.

Peter waved his staff and the three of them, still standing on nothing, began to cruise over the landscape. Nietzsche found this far more unnerving than Heaven's usual cloudscape.

"Clouds," said Peter, "simply hide the unsettling reality."

Nietzsche stared at him.

Peter shrugged. "This close to the source, thoughts are words."

"Mind your soul." Origen spoke quietly. He sounded very sober.

There was a glimmering of light ahead, a false dawn that grew into a constellation of fireflies as they approached.

"This is the problem." Peter's voice was stony and grim. "This has always been the problem."

The fireflies became bonfires, and the bonfires became a sky full of light, and the sky full of light became a host of angels, in their naked majesty all swords and pinions and flames and power, burrowing amongst ribs larger than rivers.

Angels feasting on the corpse of God.

Like maggots eating Leviathan.

"His bones are the world's," Origen said quietly. "His flesh is the world's. I was right. The Adversary did create Earth to torment us."

"Heaven stands outside time," Peter declared. "The world is made, for the first time and anew, over and over. For ever and ever."

"So what do we do?" Nietzsche asked. "Is this the beginning, or the end?"

Peter turned to Nietzsche, laid one trembling hand on his shoulder. "Make it different this time. You have free will. He made you so. Break the cycle and create us a better world."

"I have no power here."

"You are Heaven's coroner."

"God is dead," Nietzsche whispered.

"Long live God," Peter echoed.

"The Earth was without form and void," said Origen.

Though it took time beyond measure for them to see the difference, mountains rose from His bones, while the terrible angels birthed snakes who would someday be teachers of men in their innocence.

Phantasies of
Style and Place

Promises: A Tale of the City Imperishable

A story about a place I love, and wish I could have revisited. I managed two novels, Trial of Flowers *and* Madness of Flowers, *and a few shorts. This world always wanted more.*

Girl

She'd had a name, when she was little. All children did, even if it was just Grub or Little Jo or Sexta. But for some living on the brawling streets of the City Imperishable, names were like cloaks, to be put on and taken off. And for some, a name might be cut away like a finger crushed beneath a cartwheel, lest rot set in.

The lash cracked past Girl's ear, so close she felt the sting, though without the burn of a rising welt.

This time.

Girl held her pose splayed against the wall, dipping her chin as best she could with her face pressed against the rough stone. She waited while Sister Nurse studied her. Right now, there were five of them under Sister Nurse's care. Each of them was named Girl. Each of them was taller than the broken hinge set in the wall stub along Pyrrhea Alley. Each of them was shorter than the rusted iron post in front of the Fountain of Hope where the alley let out on Hammer Lane. That was how long they had under Sister Nurse's care, from hinge to post. It was the way of things in the Tribade.

"What's your name?" Sister Nurse asked, looking up from just below Girl's feet.

"Girl," she whispered, though a woman's voice in her head spoke another name.

"Where are you bound?"

It was the catechism, then. "From hinge to post."

"You've my count of thirty to gain the roof," Sister Nurse said.

Not the catechism after all. Girl scrambled, knowing the task to be impossible—there were at least five body lengths of wall above her, and the other Girls had been climbing quickly while she was stopped for questioning.

She came to a window at Sister Nurse's slow eleven. Scrambling up the side of the frame, it occurred to Girl that Sister Nurse had changed the rules. She was no longer climbing the wall, she was gaining the roof.

With no more thought than that, Girl tumbled into a dusty room. The lash cracked against the window frame, but missed the soles of her bare feet. She scrambled, taking up the count in her own head, looking for stair or ladder before time ran out and she was beaten bloody for both failure and insubordination.

Never again, she told herself. Not while she drew breath.

Each of the Girls had made a scourge. The six of them, for there had been six at the time, had gone into the River Saltus to land a freshwater shark. One Girl had been bitten so badly she was taken away bloody-stumped and weeping, never to return. The rest skinned their kill, cured the strange, rough hide, and cut it into long strips for braiding. They used human shinbones, found or harvested at their own discretion—Girl had cut hers from a three-day-old corpse—for the handles. The sharkskin braids were anchored to the handles by copper windings. Those, mercifully, had been provided, though Girl supposed only because the City Imperishable lacked mines for them to descend into.

She'd wound her old name into her handle, setting gaps in the copper in the places where the letters might have fallen. It was a code known only to Girl, a secret message from her former self to her future self in memory of silent promises of revenge and betterment. "You are you," she'd said, a message being drawn out of her with red-hot tongs by the Sisterhood.

Whenever Sister Nurse landed a blow or cut across her back, her neck, her ass, her thighs, Girl knew it was with the power of her lost name behind it.

She'd never asked the other Girls if they'd somehow done the same. Perhaps they bled in vain. She did not.

———

The Tribade did indeed beat her bloody before a fire that roared in an iron grate. The metal glowed like eyes in the darkness of a summer night. Skin came away in narrow red flecks, while sisters shouted at her. Is this your name? Who are you? Why are you here?

"Girl," she told them, until she could no longer move her jaw. That was all she said, no matter what they asked her. She would give them no satisfaction. Instead she remembered every cut and blow, for the future.

In time Sister Nurse cut Girl down and slung her across her neck like a haunch of meat. They trudged through moonlit streets, surrounded by beggars and whores and night soil men, none of whom lifted a face dark or pale to acknowledge Girl as she watched the world upside down through blood-dimmed eyes.

Stairs after that, stairs on stairs on stairs. They were climbing the Sudgate, the great, monstrous, empty castle which anchored the southwestern wall of the City Imperishable, brooding over the river and the poorest districts and the vine-wrapped forests that slunk away to the south. She could tell from the scent of the dust, too—this was cold stone crumbled with age and disuse, not scattered dirt and flakes of skin and pollen borne on bright winds from beyond the walls.

Even if Sister Nurse had remained still and silent, Girl would have known where she was. Then, and always.

On the roof—a roof, rather, for the Sudgate was ramified and ramparted like some palace of dream—the moonlight was almost violet. The heavy grease-and-shit scent of the Sudgate Districts moiled below them somewhere, miscegenating with night humors off the Saltus and whatever flowed down from the Heliograph Hill and the Limerock Palace. Sister Nurse set Girl down so that they stood on a narrow ledge, looking back across the City Imperishable to the north and east as a curious, abrasive wind plucked at them both.

The great ranging complex of the Limerock Palace in the middle distance was the most obvious structure. Gilded and tiled domes of the Temple District gleamed in the moonlight. The Rugmaker's Cupola on Nannyback Hill punctuated the northern horizon, its candy-striped walls shadow-on-shadow now. Smokestacks and factories and mansions and commercial buildings stood all across the City Imperishable. This close to the top of the Sudgate, they were as high up as all but the tallest of the buildings and hilltops.

Sister Nurse said a name. It was a familiar name, one borne by hundreds of female children in the City Imperishable. It was the name worked into the handle of her scourge. Girl said nothing, did not even blink or turn to face the half-familiar sound.

"Are you taller than the post?" Sister Nurse asked.

At that, Girl turned and looked. Her own length of leg had not grown in the last day or two.

"Are you taller than the post?"

As always, there was no hint what the question might actually mean. Sister Nurse set exercises, asked questions, made demands, meted out punishments. Waking up each day was always reward enough. It meant she had a future.

It was more than some had, in the alleys and flophouses and mucky attics of her part of the city.

"Are you taller than the post?"

No question was ever asked more than thrice.

"I am taller than the City Imperishable," Girl said.

Sister Nurse smiled. "Then you are free, if you can fly away."

This was something new, something outside the boundaries of pain and promise. Girl looked down at the tiled roof sloping sharply away from the ledge beneath her feet, the angle so steep that the missing pieces were scarcely visible. It was a hundred body lengths and more to the pavement of the wallside alley.

"But I have not been given wings," she whispered.

"Then we have failed you."

It took Girl a moment to understand what had just been said. Not that *she* had failed, but that Sister Nurse, and the Tribade, had failed her.

I will not back down, she told herself. Girl spread her arms, stared at the pale moon a moment, whispered a name, and toppled forward into empty air and the broken-toothed mouth of the cobbles far below.

Little Mother

"Run it again, Little Gray Sister," urged Sister Architect.

She considered that. The baby shifted in her belly, making her heavy as a cotton bale, and just as ungainly. There had been pains in her groin, too, pushing the edge of what was permissible. She could not lose the child, but she could not lose herself either.

Little Gray Sister looked over at her partner in this effort. It was another rooftop, another nighttime, another Tribadist, but she was very much in mind of the night she'd been reborn. "It's not a matter of trust," she said. "Nor casting away."

"No . . ." Sister Architect smiled, her eyes glimmering in the pale moonlight. "Pride, I suppose. You've already made your goal." Her goal, in this case, was a scale across the rooftops from the bakery on Forth Street to the Cambist's Hall on Maldoror Street a block over, and there up the false steeple on the old Water Bureau office to make the jump across Maldoror and down to the edge of the Limerock Palace's south wall. From there, it was trivial to slip over the wall and enter the building—the real work was in the run up and the leap, the parkour-pace practiced to deadly precision by the Gray Sisters among the Tribade. The false steeple was one of the two or three hardest runs practiced by the sisterhood.

To run the false steeple days before a baby was due was the hardest way to make the run. *No one* could scale and jump with her usual speed and precision while her belly was distended and full of sloshing life.

Little Gray Sister had, and fetched out the Third Counselor's privy seal to prove it. Not for the sake of the theft—the Tribade had their own copy of the seal, accurate right down to the wear marks along the left edge and the three nicks in the bottom petal of the rose—but for the sake of doing the thing.

Pregnant and due.

In this moment she was already minor legend. If she did what Sister Architect suggested, and she succeeded, her legend would grow.

"Vanity," said Little Gray Sister, leaning backward to ease her spine. "I have already proven all that I need to."

"Hmm." Sister Architect sounded disappointed, but did not press her case. "Perhaps you are not quite so much flash as some of the younger sisters claim you are."

Another test, she realized. But true. There were many kinds of sisters in the Tribade—red, white, blue, black, and more. Sister Architect was a blue sister, one of the professions, though her skills were mostly put to plotting and revising the rooftop runs, rather than any new construction.

Only the grays were trained to die and to kill. Only the grays were given the bluntest and sharpest weapons and trusted to use them. Only the grays were trained between hinge and post in secrecy and ignorance, that their true mettle might be known.

Only the gray sisters became Big, Bigger, or Biggest Sisters, to lead the Tribade into the uncertain future.

She smiled with pride at the thought.

Her abdomen rippled, a muscle spasm that caught Little Gray Sister by surprise so that she sucked in her breath.

Sister Architect tugged at her arm. "Sister Midwife awaits within the Quiet House."

"I—" Little Gray Sister stopped cold, fighting a wave of pain so intense it roiled into nausea. She took a deep, long breath. "Yes."

Big Sister—like all Big Sisters, a gray sister—sat on the edge of Little Gray Sister's cot. Big Sister was almost a heavy woman, unusual in the Tribade, with roan hair fading to sandy gray and glinting gray eyes. "You're a mother now," she said. "Would you like to see the baby?"

Little Gray Sister had thought long and hard on that question. Her breasts ached for the child, weeping a pale bluish fluid. Her loins felt shattered. Even her blood seemed to cry out for her offspring.

Like everything, this was a test, though of late she had been her own examiner more and more. "I would, but I shan't," she told Big Sister.

Big Sister took Little Gray Sister's hand in her own, clenched it tightly. "You can, you know," she whispered.

Little Gray Sister fancied she heard a burr in Big Sister's voice, some edge of old emotion. It was possible—the Tribade were neither monsters nor ghosts, just women of a certain purpose living within the walls of the City Imperishable. "I could hold her—" She stopped again, realizing she didn't even know if she'd birthed a boychild or a girl.

A girl, she decided. The baby had been a girl. Just as she had been, once.

"I could hold her, but I do not think I could let her go."

"And would that be so bad?" The emotion in Big Sister's voice was almost naked now, a shift from control to a raw wound that might be decades old.

She held on to that hurt, knowing she must own it too, if she were ever to set things right. "Not bad, Big Sister, not if it were my ambition to take the red and care for her myself, or even train among the Sisters Nurse."

"Well." Big Sister's voice was controlled once more. "Will you take the hardest way, then?"

That was the other choice. The Tribade had many sisters of the brown, the street toughs and money bosses. They shook down good merchants and shook down bad merchants far more, kept rival gangs in line, maintained some semblance of order in streets and districts where bailiffs were rarely seen. Those women were the most public of the hidden faces of the Tribade, and they did most of the public work.

Little Gray Sister could run rooftops, tackle criminals, and watch over her city for the rest of her life as a brown sister. But the only way to become a Big Sister, a Bigger Sister, or even—and especially—the Biggest Sister, was to take the hardest way.

She cupped her leaking breasts in her hand, regretting the feeling of both tenderness and joy. There had been a man at them once, too, for a few hours, the night she'd gotten with child amid tearing pain and weeping and a strange, shivering joy. She still wondered who he was sometimes, but at least he'd been kind.

"I am ready."

"I'll send for the fire and the knife."

"The ink, too, please," Little Gray Sister said. "I'd prefer to have it all at once."

An expression flickered across Big Sister's face—unreadable, save for context. Most women waited for the healing before they took the ink. Tattooing the Soul's Walk across the flat, puckered scars on a Big Sister's chest was one of the greatest rites of the Tribade. It was also one of the most painful, for the poppy given for the fire and the knife was not given for the ink.

Little Gray Sister would do it the hard way, cutting away her womanhood in the first blush of mothering to join the ranks of the sisters who protected their world.

Still, she was surprised they had the brazier ready, and the long knife, and there was even no wait at all for Sister Inker.

Someone had known. Perhaps all of them had known. Just like they'd known to be standing on the rooftop just below, the night she'd jumped into the violet moonlight.

Even though it was the Quiet House, her screams set dogs barking three streets away. It was the only time in her life Little Gray Sister screamed.

Big Sister

She looked at the long, narrow velvet bag Biggest Sister handed her. The two of them were in a rooftop cafe in the Metal Districts, a place where women in gray leather with close-cropped hair received no special scrutiny. There was an electrick lamp on the table which buzzed and crackled, shedding pallid light against the evening's gloom. The wind was cool, bearing mists and distant groaning booms off the River Saltus.

"You know there is one more test," Biggest Sister said. The woman was compact, a walking muscle more reminiscent of a bull terrier than the fine ladies of Heliograph Hill.

"There is always one more test." Big Sister shrugged. Even now, a year and a moon after, her chest ached whenever it was chill, or when she moved certain ways. Sometimes she awoke with the pain of her breasts still full of milk, and for that brief muzzy instant between sleep and alertness treasured the feeling, false though it was. *Never again* kept slipping into the future. "Life is one more test," she added.

"Yes, yes, that's what we tell the girls. It makes nice philosophy for them to whisper over after lights-out. But really, life is for living. After this, only you will set yourself to more."

"Have you ever stopped setting tests for yourself?" she asked Biggest Sister.

"No." Biggest Sister smiled. "But my Sister Nurse always did say I was a fool and a dreamer."

Big Sister held the bag. She already knew what was in it, just by the feel—her old sharkskin scourge. With her old name coiled in copper round the handle.

"There've been three sisters to take the hardest way these past two years," said Biggest Sister. She folded her hands around a cup of kava, but did not lift it to her lips. "Four have gone to rest beneath the stones, and one has taken the blue in deference to her age." The cup twirled slowly in her hand. "I am sure you have studied arithmetic."

"Yes," said Big Sister. "I can count."

"We are not dying away, far from it." Another twirl. "We are at some danger of losing the edge of our blade, becoming in time nothing more than an order of monials ministering to the poor and the victims of the state."

"And if we did not run bawd houses and guard the dark pleasure rooms and take money from the cash boxes of the petty merchants?"

Biggest Sister sipped this time before answering. "We *protect,* and we aid. That is not the same thing as bettering. If we did not do these things, someone else would. Someone else always will. Someone male, who does not care for women, who will not trim the balls off men who prey on children and break the pelvises of whores. Someone who will simply count the money and throw a few more bodies to the sharks. And they would not give hospice or teach beggar children to read or make sure the potshops have meat in the soup kettles."

They would not beat bloody the girls growing between hinge and post, either, Big Sister thought, but she kept her words within. As she had always known, there was a sad wisdom to everything the Tribade did.

"There is . . . more," Biggest Sister said. "You have not reached this lore yet, but believe me, there is more. Much sleeps beneath stones and behind walls in this City Imperishable that is not seen in daylight. And for good reason. Along with others, we guard those secrets. Only the Big Sisters, though. And you must pass this final test before your title is more than honor."

Big Sister drew the sharkskin scourge from its bag. Though it loomed huge in her memories, the thing seemed small in her hand. A toy, almost. She'd used worse straining at pleasure with some of the other sisters who had a taste for the rough trade.

But never used such a thing on a child.

"This," Big Sister began, then stopped. She took a deep breath. Her hand shook as it held the scourge. "This is what is wrong with us."

"No." There was an infinite, awful gentleness in Biggest Sister's voice. "That is what is wrong with the world, that we must raise some of our Girls so in order to be strong enough to stand against it."

They were quiet a moment as a waiter passed with a basket of hot rolls, spiced with cardamom and sea salt. He didn't see the scourge lying in Big Sister's hand, and he never would. It was why some among the Tribade met here to talk from time to time.

"Hear me now: there is a greater wrong to come," said Biggest Sister. "This last test. A distillation of our way. You must give life before you can take it. This you have done. You must take life before you can have power over the life and death of others. You must kill for the City Imperishable, for the Tribade, for yourself."

"With this?" Big Sister asked. "It would be a sad and messy business."

"With that. So you come full circle, releasing the last of your name." Biggest Sister put down her mug. "If you do not come to do this thing, you will still be a Big Sister. In other times you would have remained a Gray Sister, but our need is too great. But you will never rise to Bigger or Biggest Sister, and you will never see the inner secrets that we guard. And you will never wield the blade against someone's neck, either in your hand or by your word." She stood. "Come to me when the thing is done. Tonight, or half a lifetime from now, come to me."

"What thing? Who am I to kill?" Big Sister hated the fear that trembled in her tones.

"The child who you would have been," said Biggest Sister. Her voice was distant as the unknown sea. "Bring me the head of a girl-child, that you have killed yourself, and you are done with tests forever. Beggar or daughter of a Syndic's house, it makes no matter to me."

She was gone then, her cup shivering slightly on the tabletop.

Big Sister walked to the edge of the rooftop, where a wrought-iron railing worked in a pattern of roses and snakes marked the drop. She stood there, watching a pair of heavy horses draw a scrap cart quietly through the late streets. The moon was slim this night, but still it washed the streets in a purpled silver.

There were a hundred thousand people in the City Imperishable, she thought. A third of them must be children. Half of those would be girls. Would a hive miss a single bee? Would a tree miss a single apple?

Her breasts ached, and she thought she felt milk flowing across the spiral tattooed scars as she wept in the moonlight. There was no way to stop this save to become what she hated most, no way to keep promises made to herself in the earliest days save to break them with blood.

It was not what was wrong with the Tribade, it was what was wrong with the world.

Slowly she picked at the copper windings on the haft of the scourge. The name of that young girl smaller than the hinge dropped away as flashings into the street below, where beggars swept daily for the scrap. She picked until she'd forgotten forever the name, and with it the promises, and there were no more tears in her eyes to follow the copper down.

Big Sister dropped over the railing to a three-point landing on the cobbles. If she was going to hunt a girl, the child would be taken from the highest, greatest houses in the City Imperishable. No mere beggar was going to die for her.

And then, never again, she promised herself. Big Sister ignored the hollow echo she could hear ringing from the future.

Testaments

Sometimes you just have to let the language rip. This is me, wide open.

The Testament of the Six Sleeping Kings is bound in ebon plates so dark that they drink all light that flows before them. Brilliance born in the fires of the sun, taking a thousand years to rise to the surface and eight minutes to leap across the stygian depths of space from the day-star to the humble Earth, only to be swallowed with the same finality as any rattling blade dropped upon a shuddering, aristocratic neck.

These are the hard truths: Some words were never meant to be read. Some thoughts cannot be undone. Some darknesses shall never be dispelled.

Some people will never believe these truths.

The First Sleeping King

In a time before countries had borders, when birds filled the skies like raindrops in a storm, and the great migrations of the beasts had not yet been halted by walls and fences and fields, there lived a man named Linnel, youngest son to Ezar. In a hard land of withered olive trees, struggling cedars, salty ponds, and miles of sere rocky hills, he was born to no great consequence, son of an ageing goatherd and the second of his father's three wives.

His first-mother, Aranu, had already forgotten herself and lay within her tent of hides moaning, except when she wandered smeared with shit and ashes to search for a baby who had died half a lifetime before Linnel's birth. His third-mother, Raha'el, had been a servant girl taken on more out of pity than need, then bound in marriage to stop the gossip about his father's undeniable concupiscence. His second-mother, who had carried Linnel into the world, was Aranu's much-younger cousin, Tobeth, who stood midway in years between her co-wives.

Thus Linnel had grown up beneath Ezar's hard hand—for goats are unforgiving, and their masters learn this from the animals themselves—burying Aranu when he was nine years of age and finding his way into Raha'el's bed when he was twelve.

All in all, an unremarkable childhood in that time and place before the morning of the world had been set by those who first chose to keep time.

Until the dream came.

It was the dawn of his fourteenth birthday. Raha'el had celebrated with Linnel the night before, suckling him to her breast and calling him her best child until Linnel's staff had hardened enough for him to be her biggest man instead. As always he took her in the manner of a boy so there would be no chance of get. After she'd wrung her pleasures from her son, Raha'el had sent him away, lest Ezar be forced to take notice of these nocturnal excursions. No one was fooled, but the niceties were kept.

Except that morning Linnel lay on a goathide amid a meadow of tiny night-blooming flowers. Already they shut their pale colors and delicate scents away against the first hot breeze of day trickling down from the stony hills to the east. A light descended from the sky in a stink of brimstone and old ash.

Linnel sat up, startled, all too conscious of Raha'el's passion still glistening on his thighs and amid the downy fuzz of his beard. A torch, thrown by an invader? He was unprepared for anything except a wash in the goats' pond. Cursing, he realized even his sling was in his tent, too far to reach now.

But a torch would have fallen with the speed of any stone, and this light drifted like a wind-born seed.

Linnel, said a voice out of the very air itself.

"Aranu?" It was all he could think, that his first-mother had found her way out from beneath the stones of her grave in search of her lost infant.

—Malakh.

Linnel realized he heard a name. It meant "messenger" in the tongue of a people who sometimes traded with Ezar for goats, but this being of light was clearly not one of the She'm. Uncertain if this was an ancestor or a spirit of the air or some creature whose nature had never been communicated to him, the boy dropped on one knee.

"I serve."

—*Fire.*

With that word, Malakh told Linnel a story, a tale which raged inside his head, of the birth of the world from boiling rocks hotter than even the heart of a smith's fire, of rains which quenched the land until storms of steam and vapor finally ceased, of the intention which made plants and trees, then birds and beasts, and finally rising like a pomegranate tree from spilled seeds, people themselves, fire's great-great-grandchildren.

"I know," Linnel said, and wondered if he dared address this being more directly.

—*Honor.*

With that word, he knew what must come next. Such a power in the world deserved respect, fear even, and substance; not the soiled thrustings and small betrayals of a family forever encamped on the hillsides of this land.

"I obey."

Opening his eyes, Linnel strode back into their camp and took up his father's thornwood staff where it lay propped outside Ezar's tent. He used the aging tool as a weapon to restore honor to himself and the Messenger of the fire. He almost turned away from his course when he saw Raha'el's blood fresh upon her heaving breasts as she screamed her last, but her dying curse propelled Linnel to his father's tent with his resolve renewed.

"The path must be made ready that people will know who stands above us," he told the three fresh graves, hasty cairns assembled before a puzzled audience of wary goats. "We must know our sins before we can repent of them."

Eating of a withered apple, Linnel strode away from his bleating charges toward the more fertile lands lower down and coastwise, already framing the words of his tale that people might properly understand their import.

His steps slowed for a moment when he began to wonder if the being of light had been a dream or a true sending, but the sacrifice was made. He was committed. Dream or no dream, this was his path.

———

The angel's pen nib was wrought of the stuff of stars, a metal so dense and fierce that it could almost fold space around itself. The ink it used was distilled from the blood of a dozen dozen saints—what use sinners, when they are as common as sand at the seashore, and thus of no import at all? The parchment was stripped from the hide of a broken god, stretched and scraped on frames of living bone.

The Second Sleeping King

Massah often walked in dreams. He had learned to do this long before he realized it was any trick at all. Even as the smallest child there had been the steps taken on chubby, uncertain feet amid the veiled ladies of the royal court; and there had been the steps that unfolded before his inner eye, sleepwalking on clouds and the backs of crocodiles and the memories of the day.

The mystery and miracle had arrived for Massah when he finally understood that almost no one around him did this thing. Pten, the withered old priest who always smelled of grave dust and bird droppings, certainly had the secret. They'd even met, in the other lands. There, Pten was a broad-chested young man with skin the color of old tea. Much more handsome than the pasty, hollow youth the priest had doubtless once been.

Pten always frowned at Massah, knowing him for a dreamwalker, but had not then sorted out who he was in the waking world. Massah, on the other hand, *knew* who it was he met in dreams. Always, and without fail.

So when he met the Angel of Death come for the woman who had raised Massah as though he were her own son, he knew enough not to try to bar the other's path. At the same time, Massah could not help but bid the stranger tarry a while, his secret hope to spare his mother a few more moments of life's breath.

"I know your errand," he told the angel.

The other looked at him with empty eyes. Like all the messengers of God, it was as perfect as a marble statue, slick-pale and unblemished, but its gaze was just as blank. The angel wore no armor except that of his studied magnificence, clad only in stone-hard skin and the regard of a distant deity. Even the sword of legend was absent.

—*All men know my errand, at least at the end of their days.* The angel's voice was as devoid of passion as its expression was.

"All men are born to die," Massah replied. He was ever polite. Impolite people did not long remain behind the shaded walls and rambling bowers of the royal court. "Only a fool pretends otherwise."

—*Why does this fool pretend to converse with me, then?*

"I bargain for nothing but a few moments of your time. In payment I offer my own wit. Among some circles I am accounted a more than passing conversationalist."

—*She will not live a heartbeat longer.* A tinge of pity might have stained its voice.

Massah was ashamed then, and even afraid. "It was never my intention to waste your time, lord angel."

—*All of time is the lord God's. None will ever be wasted.*

The angel touched the side of Massah's head with a cold finger heavier than any stone.

—*Go back to your court and look beyond its walls, if you would see the price of life and the value of death.*

When Massah awoke he was forced to swallow his screams. He stumbled to the basin to banish the taste of embalming herbs from his mouth. In his reflection upon the water, Massah saw that his dark, curly hair had become white and brittle and straight where the angel had touched him. All thoughts of his mother fled him in the face of the strangeness of that gift from the angel of death.

He rose in time from his ablutions and subsequent meditations to don a heavier pair of sandals and a roughspun robe, and pass outside the royal court through the gate called Envy, and into the bustling streets and marketplaces beyond.

There in the city of kings he found a world he'd always known of, but never considered with sufficient care. The people of his birth labored under great loads of clay and straw, sweating more than the donkeys of the merchants. Even the poorest of the kingdom were free to spit upon the slaves. Many did so, simply to find a moment when they could call their own lot better than another's.

Massah had been raised among the scent of lemons and the coolth of fountains. Now, his sandals slapping the dusty clay and worn cobbles of the streets, he realized that he had always been only a pet to the princesses and concubines who had dressed him in versions of princely raiment and taught him to twist his tongue in honeyed speech much as the smoothest courtiers did.

A joke.

A monkey, trained to ape his betters for the amusement of the women of the royal court.

Why had he never seen this in all his dreamwalking?

Because he'd been ashamed of the poor, starveling dreams of slaves.

He began to run, the smack of his sandals slapping against the stones of the city that had always sheltered him. Massah sprinted past obelisks and the blank faces of temples and fly-clouded ossuaries and clay pits where his countrymen worked naked in the rending heat. He raced as if he could outrun the very touch of the angel gone past.

On his return to the royal court, a death was being cried.

Of course.

His mother.

The priests demanded to know where Massah had been. Old Pten nodded with a dark leer. Long conversations were held in small, hot rooms. A senior prince stormed in, and Massah thought he might die then on a bronze blade, but the prince departed again as temple gongs began to echo across the palaces of the royal court.

In time, he was left alone with his thoughts. Massah understood what the angel of death had shown him. Every people had their time under the brassy gaze of heaven. He could forestall the doom of none. But he could change the price of life.

He dreamed again, of rivers of blood and rains of frogs and the stilled heartbeats of every firstborn son in the city. Walking in dreams, Massah made it so in the hot lands of the waking world, until the streets themselves cried as never he had for his mother's death.

The angel wrote in a language possessing only one word, though that word was of infinite length. All the syllables of creation echoed in the letters it scratched across the weeping pages. They did not remain static as ink on vellum might, but writhed in their own private torments, recalling the souls rendered to make them so.

The Third Sleeping King

The Bridgebuilder was a man out of his place. He'd been raised by Attic tutors among marbled halls on a hilltop overlooking a glass-green sea. He'd learned the classics, he'd studied rhetorics and logic and law and the histories of empire. He'd answered questions and stood for examinations and dutifully learned the arts of sword, shield, spear, and horse. In short, the Bridgebuilder had been forged to be the sort of man needed in every corner of the empire.

Then the Senate had sent him to a land he'd never meant to visit, to rule over a people with no sense of their needs, only a burning, passionate purpose transcending all reason.

Out of place, even out of time, he sometimes thought. Certainly the Bridgebuilder lived in a palace, but it was so unlike the wind-whispered halls of his youth. His servants were for the most part sullen would-be poisoners kept in line only by the ever-present guards. The land itself rejected the empire, with short harvests and failing fisheries and blights on the olive groves and date palms, so even the most hard-hearted tax gatherer came back with chests half empty.

People who have nothing can pay nothing. It was a lesson these fools had taken to heart, until the Bridgebuilder began to wonder if they had fouled their own wells out of sheer, raw spite.

His only relief came in the light wine that was made up in the hills and shipped down to the lowlands in resinous casks. The flavor reminded him of the piney ferments the servants of his youth drank, which was fine with the Bridgebuilder. He had no pretensions to be anything other than a hopeless colonial, unworthy of the exacting standards of the Eternal City, whose empire he served. He would never sit in the Senate, or aspire to a voice at the emperor's ear.

He just wished mightily that he was anywhere but this miserable post.

Even the nights were hot through most of the seasons. The Bridgebuilder would take his resinous wine and two or three of the serving girls and retire to his apartments on the roof of the palace. There he would command them to bathe him with sponges soaked in watered vinegar. After that he would command them to bathe one another. There was always room among his silks for an extra girl, and as the people of this place hated his virtues as much as they hated his vices, the Bridgebuilder indulged himself regardless.

One girl in particular he had favored for a handful of seasons—Saleh. She was willing to lie with him in whatever manner pleased him. On nights when he was too far gone in wine to know his own mind, she would lie with him in whatever manner pleased her. And she was never jealous of any favor he showed to other girls. Best of all, she would hold him when the weeping came upon him, and whisper him to sleep with counsels which felt wise in the watches of the night, whatever his morning wit might later make of them.

So it was that Saleh came to be his confidante in matters of state. Often as not, he wept for sheer frustration, once the wine had done its work. They curled together amid billowing curtains and the salt smell of the nearby ocean as she listened, and spoke, and listened.

"Is that priestly council your master?" she asked him one time during a particularly difficult bout of religious revivalism among the occupied peoples.

The Bridgebuilder waved off the suggestion. "No, no, I serve only the demands of empire. My orders come by courier aboard fast galleys, not from a bushel of black-robed schemers on their temple steps."

"Of course," Saleh said. She kissed his ears, nibbling on the edges as he loved so much. "So their words are as the barking of dogs to you, yes?"

"Yes," he said, sighing. "I mean, no. No. I cannot simply order them to act. I do not have soldiers enough to dictate from every street corner."

"So you are beholden to their goodwill." Something glinted in her voice, an edge he had not often heard—or noticed—before.

"Never." Pride stirred within him, a sluggish beast long put to sleep by the sheer unreasonableness of this place.

"You are the lion of this land," Saleh told him. Her hand, oiled now, slipped down to once more seek proof of his manly worth. "Do not let them shave your mane."

Later, lost in restless sleep, the Bridgebuilder was visited by two men from out of time. One had the seeming of a savage, freshly descended from some blood-soaked mountaintop. The other was a man of courtly bearing, wrapped in the grave-pale linens of Egypt long past.

—*You deserve your name,* the savage said.

—*And the joy of your position,* added his companion.

They spoke in a sort of chorus:

—*Do not judge for the rabble. That is no better than choosing between two rotten fruits. When you are done, you still have only rotten fruit to show for your labors.*

"Who are you?" he asked.

—*Sleeping kings of old.*

Not my kings, the Bridgebuilder thought, but he had too much respect for the power of the dream to speak thusly.

Soon after, he refused to hear a case. A man was set to die for some pointless heresy, and the Bridgebuilder could have freed him. "The choice of rotten fruits does not appeal to me," he haughtily told the delegation of local priests. Saleh had smiled at him from the shadows, but he never saw her again.

In time, the Bridgebuilder realized that she, too, had been part of the dream; prophecy gone wrong without him ever knowing how to set it to rights.

The angel recorded as faithfully as only one of its kind could do. Mindless in their devotion, they were not made to question. That was the province of men and women, those failed echoes of the creator. Words twisted as much as they ever had, crossing the bridge of meaning between intent and actuality. Still, the page held them.

The Fourth Sleeping King

The maid buckled her armor. She was so very tired. The messenger angels did not come so much anymore. It had all been so clear in the years before she'd picked up a sword. Voices in the hayloft, visions of light by night. God spoke through His servants and she listened.

She was the maid. This was the way of things.

Now she was accounted an enemy even by the very people she'd saved. The invaders from across the water, of course, said terrible things of her. The maid knew to expect that. Scullery girls argued in the same fashion. In a way, it was an honor to have her name on the lips of enemy nobles. She was the only woman they did not ignore.

But her own countrymen had turned away from her as well. Their hate bloomed the red-gold colors of mounting flames as surely as the leaves turned away from summer when autumn stole across the forests. This she could not understand. Had she not pressed the fight at Orléans and Jargeau? Had she not saved the very life of the Duke of Alençon?

There was the truth, of course. To be saved by a woman was more disgraceful than to have been defeated by a man. Their ears were open to the charges whispered from across the water, spread in those places where the armies met and mingled on saints' days, in whores' beds, at market towns, around council tables.

God had not forsaken her, but her own people had.

Still, she wore these good greaves and chain over a surcoat. Still, she had the helmet dented by a dozen arrows, each turned away in the last moment by an angel's hand, even while those closest to her fell. Still, she had this sword. The ultimate blasphemy, far beyond the worried mutterings of the priests—that a woman should take up the most male of weapons and prove herself able to cut and thrust her way into the body of the enemy soldiers and their army alike.

With that thought, she sat to oil and whet her blade. This had not been in the morning's plan. Mist rose off the fields outside her tent, the smell of horses and campfires, the little sounds of an army waking to a battle day. Even the sound of footsteps echoing on stone was not enough to deter her from her task, though it reminded her that the rest of this was memory, or dream.

Stroke the blade. Metal gleamed in the oil, a false brilliance which dried all too soon, but for a while made this a sword of heaven. The whicking sound of the whetstone against the edge. The heft of the pommel, more familiar to her now than the hand of any of the lovers she'd never taken in her years among men. The rotten straw reek of the cell where she knew she slept, even as the dream-sword found its edge.

—*There is no more to be done.*

She stiffened, the sword falling away from her hand even though there was no clangor of the blade striking the ground. The stuff of dreams, as real as it had been. This was the first time the Lord's host had spoken to her in . . . how long? "I am content," the maid lied.

—*No one is content facing their end.*

"The end of my life on earth is but the beginning of my place in heaven," she replied piously. Though in truth, she'd long doubted that as well. Too many of the men she'd killed were simply men. Not demons or devils, but ordinary persons with wives and children, who ate too much and farted and slept uneasily and cursed their serjeants and prayed upon their knees to the same God she did.

Could she truly climb to heaven on a stairway made of the corpses of men who'd died with the Lord's name upon their lips?

—*Yes.* Of course the angel could hear her thoughts.

With that the maid once more knew this for a dream. The messenger spoke in the words of the enemy, which was not so different from her own Frankish speech, but always before they had whispered to her in the writing tongue of angels, which is far more like the stirring of snakes in some nest, or the rising of a locust horde, than any simple words from the mouth of a woman or man.

Had the conversations always been dreams?

—*Yes,* the angel said again.—*But what does it matter? The world is but a dream of God. You will be a king in the history of this dream.*

"A king in death?" she asked aloud. "Surely a queen."

—*No* simpering queen drew on armor and sword, the angel told her reproachfully.

Queens do not simper, the maid thought, and turned her face away until she tasted straw in her mouth and awoke to a bright morning with the memory of a sword's heaviness on her lap. The gaze of the priest before her smoldered, and the maid knew she, too, would soon smolder.

The angel paused in its labors. Its kind *were* Divine intent, in the most literal sense, and so the purposes of the Tetragrammaton were never a mystery. Still, the words spreading from its pen introduced an unheralded glimmer of doubt.

Doubt was heresy, doubt was the casting out, a star fallen from the crystal heavens to the deepest lake of ice far beneath the middle world of God's creation. Shrugging off the unaccustomed sense, the angel resumed its toils.

The Fifth Sleeping King

The old man sat amid the willow trees and stared out across the Potomac. The waters of the river ran muddy, almost oily, seeming tired as they slipped home toward the sea. He'd been many things. The cicadas in the trees hummed the story of his life.

Planter.

Surveyor.

Soldier.

Political.

General.

President.

"But never king," he told the approaching night. In truth, surveyor had always been his favorite.

—*Of course you were a king.*

The old man looked up at the voice, which had carried over the cycling buzz of the insects. An angel stood before him—of this he had no doubt, for all his lifetime of tepid faith. Not recognizing this creature as one of God's messengers would be like not recognizing the ocean as being made of water.

It stood before him, a composite of mist off the river and the singing of slaves and the smell of the smokehouse and a few swirling leaves caught up in the hem of its robe. The old man knew he was dreaming then, but knew also that this, alone among all the dreams of his lifetime, was more real than even his waking moments.

"I beg your pardon," he said. "I went to some trouble never to be crowned."

—*Kingship is not a matter of a circlet upon the brow.* There was something almost prim in the angel's tone.

A question stole unbidden from his mouth. "Is my time at hand?" He was immediately ashamed of the fear that had asked it.

—*I am not that messenger.* Kindliness guttered in the angel's eyes, warming coals for the cold hands of the old man's soul.

He resolved to ask no more questions. That revelation should choose to come to him in the sunset of his days was no more, or less, surprising than any of the other things which had overtaken the old man down the now-vanished years. "I thank you for the visit, at least. Most who come to see me want something. Asking, always asking."

—*I ask nothing of you that you do not ask of yourself.* The angel moved, drawing the wind with it as a cloak, so the waters of the Potomac stirred in a way that would have alarmed any waterman.

"I ask nothing of myself." *Children,* thought the old man. Issue of his loins. A swift ending to the fractured mess the politics of his young nation had already become. A brake for the pride of those who had succeeded him in office both high and low. "Though sometimes I ask much of the world," he admitted with the same ruthless self-honesty that had so often been a stumbling block in his life.

The angel bent before him. Kneeling?—*Here is the secret of your life,* it whispered in a voice of willow leaves and the whippoorwill. When it began to speak again, all the old man heard was the dank,

close sound of darkness, and the fading of Martha's crying. He stared
at his trembling hands and wondered how long she would mourn him.

The pen scratched on. Scribing, scrying, painting futures in the ink of
the past, though all time was one from the vantage of the angel's copy-
desk. It had recovered its equilibrium. Angels were pendulums, mark-
ing the endless moments of the mind of God, messengers bridging the
ineluctable gap between perfected intent and the imperfect matter of
Creation.

It had never questioned why God, who was all things everywhere,
should require a book to record His doings, or the doings of His creation. It is not the nature of angels to question, only to answer. It is not
the nature of angels to devise, only to record.

The Sixth Sleeping King

What the hell was the matter with people? No respect, that was it. His
mother had been right. No one ever listened to him like they should.

The man who had been commander in chief poured himself another drink. He wasn't supposed to, had given it up years ago so far
as anyone knew. The gap between what he said he did and what he
actually did had ceased to matter so long ago that the ex–commander
in chief rarely considered it anymore. What he said, what he *believed*,
was the truth. The messy details were just that: messy details. No one's
business.

Disappointment, that was it. So many things which should have
happened never did. Promises from Scripture and politics alike had
been betrayed by niggling traitors. No one saw his goodness, his recti-
tude. Not even Laura, who'd always stood beside him, shrouding her
thoughts in a smile.

He really ought to have married a girl like Mom. A man could rule
the world with a woman like that at his side. Daddy had, damn him.

The ice in his glass clinked like the fall of coins. The outside sweated
cold and heavy. He knew then he was dreaming, he really hadn't touched
a drink in years. Not really. Not that counted. The ex–commander in
chief simply didn't stand around mixing a highball.

He had people to do it for him.

Even in his dreams, a man had to laugh at himself.

A young fellow in a suit stepped close. Dark skinned, but not obviously any particular kind of colored. The ex–commander in chief didn't recognize the guy, though he wore the regulation gray suit and translucent earpiece.—*Sir.* The fellow's voice slipped through another layer of dreaming into a space of soaring naves and thundering sermons and the safe, blind glory of prayer.

"This is about the red heifer, isn't it?" Where had *that* come from? He wasn't supposed to talk about it. The glory would come, in his lifetime, he'd been promised. He *knew.*

—*Sir.* Something hung in the fellow's eyes, expectant as a launch code.

He felt his breathing grow shallow and hard. "Is it time?" The promise, it was coming to pass!

—*Sir.*

A familiar peevishness rose inside him, that his handlers had so long fought to banish. Too bad for them, he was the boss here. Always would be. Didn't matter how he got to the top, nope. He was here now and not climbing down. No sir. "What is it," the ex–commander in chief demanded. "Speak up!"

—*Sir.* The voice sounded haunted, as if coming from an empty hallway far away.

He tried to shake off his dream, to wake up gasping amid the sheets. He hated the feeling of being wrapped in self-doubt, and always shed it as quickly as he could. Mother said too much thinking was bad for a man. The ex–commander in chief had learned to trust his gut. Facts changed depending on who brought them to you. Feelings were the hard truths.

Right now he was feeling very worried indeed.

—*Sir.* A terrible fire blossomed behind the fellow's gaze. The ex–commander in chief threw his drink at the flames, but they only passed outward along the arcs of liquid and ice and shattered glass until his dream was consumed by fire and a great voice echoed from the heavens, asking him if this was truly what he intended.

Still, he did not doubt himself. Not him. Nope. No sir.

The angel finally set aside its pen. The book was done, or would be until it was opened again. Words were the oldest, greatest magic. God had spoken in the beginning, and He would someday unspeak the end, swallowing Creation down in a sweeping blur of undoing: oaks shrinking to acorns; cold cinders swelling first to red giants, then reduced to their starry births; old men climbing from graves to step backwards to life until they climb puling and mewing back to the salty delta from which each had first flowed.

As done, undone. As lived, unlived. Time, helical, alive, autophagic, endless as a circle, with as many corners as an egg.

All of this best stated in the language of dreams. Consciousness was too linear for even the angel itself to properly comprehend the sweeping swirl of God's Creation. How so for His poor creatures of clay and sweat and breath?

It smiled, preening a moment, feeling a rare sense of accomplishment before moving on to the next task: to bear the book away so it might someday be read.

The Seventh King

She is just a girl. She doesn't know her parents, though there are people who live in her house and clothe her and feed her and call her by a name not her own. At night a favorite uncle crawls out of the wainscoting, thin as a shadow, heavy as a star, and whispers to her the dreams of sleeping kings long dead.

Someday she will be so famous that they will have to write down her dreams. When she grows into her power and announces her true name, darkness will settle like a cloak, bringing the nighttime of the soul to all those who have plunged her into darkness.

Which is to say, all of everyone.

For now, dreaming is enough. There is no higher truth.

The Fall of the Moon

My grandfather Lake was a man whose presence in my life was as great as the moon's pull over the tides. In a very indirect way, this tale is about me and him.

Hassan polished the twisted beech keel of his boat. The vessel had been a-building for years, assembled only from holy wood—thrown up by the raging Sea of Murmurs which even now coiled on the western horizon frothing like blood—and his grandfather's bones. It was not a large boat, but Hassan was not a large man. All he intended was to ride the Tide of Spring.

His work of late had been mostly in waiting. His grandfather had passed as all men someday do, with a familiar smile on his old man's face and a strange woman's name on his young man's lips. Hassan had carefully burned his grandfather's flesh to send the soul spiraling toward the outer moons, then baked the flensed bones in an oven built from clay mixed with his own blood.

The old man had emerged grinning and polished, pale and harder than he had ever been in life.

Now those bones were fitted into the ribs of the beech-keeled boat. It cost a soul to sail upon the Sea of Murmurs, a sacrifice endlessly renewed upon the smoking waves. Hassan had whispered his grandfather's name as he'd fitted each knuckle, each rib, each long bone, until the syllables had vanished from his mind with the final setting of the jaw in the tiller lock.

His grandfather had become the boat. A soul to sail on the sea, while Hassan remained a breathing man with his eyes open six feet above the welcoming soil.

"I will live forever," Hassan told his grandfather.

The boat said nothing, though Hassan thought he could hear it breathing.

"You listen, boy. You've ears to hear." The old man's hand was a crab's claw, twisted fingers bent together to grab young elbows in pain. "There's more to this world, and more, even as God wills us to be here."

Hassan smiled. "Drink your tea, Grandfather." He passed a little clay tumbler over to a shivering hand. They lived in a small hut hard by a cypress, as far from Telos as anyone did.

Alone together, thinking thoughts, the two of them.

"Tea." His grandfather grimaced. "This isn't real tea. More like seaweed soup. Tea grows in little sacks on bushes tended by coolies on the sides of steep mountains."

"What are coolies?"

After a long pause, his grandfather puffed out a ragged breath. "I don't know, boy. I don't know either."

Obsidian cliffs towered behind the village of Telos, a wall sheer and hard enough to daunt even the most adventurous boys. Each day their dark glass reflected the setting sun in a multiplicity of dim fetches, a small, stubborn galaxy brought down close to the land for casual inspection. They made a mirrored hell of the Little Moons and the Great Moons on nights when the entire sky danced.

If a boy risked all to tramp across the sands at low tide, he could turn back and see the carved tops of the cliffs. There was a city there, a thousand thousand times greater than Telos had ever dreamed of being with its three waterfalls and single corral.

The contrast between the glittering ramparts high above and the little driftwood homes below could strain even the most stoic heart. Very few ever chanced the damp sand and the red-boiled wrath of the waves for a glimpse.

Otherwise the village and lives of its people unfolded in the strip of hay meadows and salt marshes and twisted cypress trees that stood as stubborn as life between the glassy cliffs and the burning sea. It was a world that reminded folk of their place with each ragged breath and staggering step.

Only Hassan's grandfather had been different, and through him, Hassan.

The night Hassan's grandfather died, Etienne the hetman burned the village library. Hassan stood in the flickering light of blazing paper, watching sparks arc from the useless, melting datacubes.

"It does us no good," the hetman told Hassan. The village leader was an older man, blocky and stolid, uncle to Hassan's late mother, and had always claimed a soft spot toward Hassan.

"It's what we know," Hassan muttered.

"No." Etienne's voice was a quiet, intense reflection of his grandfather's. Like a version of the old man kept in a bottle. "We know the tides, and when the sea burns and stings, and to avoid the splinters of the cliffs. We know how the rains come and when they stay away. We know when to plant the maize and when to walk the fields plucking the borers from the stalks. *That's* what we know. Not the names of kings and admirals and who discovered each of the metals."

Hassan stared into the spitting fire. "He always said we were lost."

"Maybe. But here is where we are found. Here is where we will stay."

"Here." The obsidian cliffs gleamed in the night as Hassan raised his eyes to the empty stars.

"It's a good life," said Etienne.

The hetman had missed one book. When Hassan went to fold his grandfather's bedroll for the last time—Martine needed it for her middle son—he found the ragged volume beneath. It had a spine of split bamboo, that had been bound and rebound many times.

His grandfather had taught Hassan much about what few books they had. But Hassan had never seen this one.

He turned his find over in his hand. The cover was stretched leather, perhaps an eelskin, though he couldn't be sure as it was worn with long handling. When he opened the book, the pages crackled.

Whatever the original creators had meant to say had been long lost to the scribings of dozens of others. Writing crabbed across the pages, up, down, sideways, on a slant, in the colors of different inks and the soft gray of clay and the dark red of blood.

Voices from the past.

He even recognized his grandfather's hand.

Hassan sat down to read.

"Boy," it said in the old man's shaky block printing. Hassan had never been able to master writing himself. "First, you'll need my bones."

Once there had been boats which sailed the seas, both the mercurial Sea of Murmurs and the seas of ordinary water that stretched on all the worlds dreaming in the harsh light of the evening stars. Once there were boats which sailed the air, some fast as forked lightning that split the night, others slow as thought. Once there were boats which rode the tides of light that bound the stars together.

Now there were no boats at all.

The book told stories under stories. With practice, Hassan could pick out each hand. As he prepared his grandfather's bones, then searched the beach for the right wood, he would take moments and read the different stories. The hand which had written rounded letters in blood could be picked out of the confusion of the pages just as Maryam's drum could be heard beneath the singing of the village on Round Moon Festival.

Each story was a voice. The book was a chorus. Hassan knew that he would be the last.

The book told him many secrets:

"We are bound here between life and death. The black city on the cliffs behind us is our past. The deadly sea before us is our fate."

"You will need to spend a soul to cross the fiery waters. Do not trade your own."

"Our life was never meant to be this way. I cannot believe that either God or any man intended such for us."

"Love while you can, live as you must."

"I will be free beyond the horizon."

"Beechwood thrown up by the sea will make a suitable keel. Cypress smokes until the oil bursts into flame."

"This is the way to build a boat: attend to the pictures of my poor hand."

"Sail away."

"Live forever."

"Sail away."

Etienne came to Hassan in the month after his grandfather's death.

"The old man needs to be within the soil," the hetman said.

"He goes there piece by piece," Hassan whispered. It had been among the first lessons of the book, marked with some urgency.

You will need to spend a soul.

"There is talk in the village."

"There is always talk in the village. I do my duty."

Etienne grabbed Hassan's shoulder, squeezed it, a sort of distancing hug. "You are not healthy out here. Move into the town. Woo Maryam. She sees you as being . . . of interest."

I will be free beyond the horizon.

"No. I bury him in pieces, in all the places he loved." Such a lie; Grandfather had loved nothing but books. "He returns to soil."

"You are as strange as he."

Hassan had no answer for that.

A few weeks after Hassan found the beechwood for the keel, the Sea of Murmurs ran with mice and rats. The surf came rolling in oily sheets, tumbling the screaming animals to the sand. All of Telos scrambled along the beaches with nets and pots to harvest such a bounty of meat and pelts. In the normal course of life the village had only goats and a few surly chickens too precious to eat and too troublesome to roust out of the papaya trees.

This was a feast, one of the sea's rare gifts among its endless curses.

The bounty ended suddenly in a wave of larger things with teeth like needles and a dozen scampering feet. These creatures slaughtered the survivors of the rodent tide, then had to be driven back into the sea with sticks and shouts and some injuries.

Still they feasted, though many limped and Majid the Younger lost three toes and a piece of one calf.

"Boy," his grandfather said. "Wake up."

Hassan blinked. Had he been sleeping?

The old man was young, younger than Hassan had ever known him, his fingers strong and supple as he shook Hassan's shoulders. "There's a Tide of Spring coming. After that, fires and the fall of the moon. Be ready, boy."

"I'm ready," Hassan said, but he spoke only to the empty hut. He went out to work on the boat by moonlight.

The book had this to say, in a reeling purple hand which spoke but rarely throughout the threaded pages:

"A moon will fall in time, as it has before. The black city was broken by a bright fist from above. The red sea was poisoned by a dark fist from beneath. All life changes."

All life changes.

The night after his grandfather came to him, Hassan carved those words in his chest with a bone needle and some fire ash, then cried for the old man for the first time until the pain and blood-slicked sweat sent him into fever dreams of green fields of tea and giant brass coolies with the slack faces of apes, the wicked eyes of goats, and the tears of a lonely young man.

Etienne's visits became fairly regular, usually while Hassan was polishing his grandfather's bones or fitting pieces of bone and wood into the boat.

"Maryam will soon wed Majid the Younger," the hetman said one day. "They have trod the corn together, and he has already captured a gull for the feast."

"Don't like gull meat." Hassan tried to grin at Etienne. When had he last seen Maryam? "Stringy and sour."

"You likewise." Etienne patted the boat's gunnel. "I know what this is."

"It's a boat."

They both glanced toward the Sea of Murmurs. The water was a violent blue today, silver-finned mermaids singing sweetly perhaps half a kilometer offshore. Deadly.

"Such . . . craft and dedication . . . would serve Telos well. You could build a new council house. With your name upon the door for generations to read."

I will live forever.

But Hassan said nothing.

After a while Etienne deposited a sack of papayas, squeezed Hassan's shoulder, and departed.

One day the boat was done. Hassan simply knew that. He measured its length in three paces, its breadth in one, sighted down the oars carved so painstakingly in accordance with the rare picture drawn in a stained brown hand in the last book. Then he covered it over with a woven mat, walked into Telos, and began to survey the ground for a new council house.

It was something to do while waiting for the Tide of Spring.

Etienne misunderstood.

"So you are finally done with the old man," the hetman said. "Perhaps you would sup with my family tonight? Crazy cousin Hassan is come to town, my daughters are saying."

Love while you can, live as you must.

"I will see the children," Hassan said quietly. He was surprised to find his voice creaking so.

Something like a shadow flitted across Etienne's face. "They have not been children for a while."

One evening as Hassan worked at carving out the notch in a crossbeam just so, he realized that the world felt different. Wrong.

It was the light.

He looked up.

The Round Moon was just bellying over the obsidian cliffs to the east. First and Third Little Moons danced in the mid-sky as always. But al-Maghrib, the Soulful Moon of Paradise, was too large, too low.

"The Fall of the Moon," he whispered.

Hassan dropped his tools and sprinted from town. He had to get to his boat. Behind him people shouted, cried out, called to one another. Even as he left their words behind, Hassan could hear it was him they spoke of, not the Soulful Moon.

It did not matter. He would ride the Sea of Murmurs beyond the horizon and live forever.

Dragging his boat down the sand was back-breaking work. Small as it was, the craft was heavy. His grandfather's soul seemed to serve as an anchor, a tether. Had Hassan misunderstood it all?

"You are too late for doubts," he told himself.

The Sea of Murmurs rumbled behind him. It sounded almost gravelly, running thick tonight.

"I follow your secrets, Grandfather."

"Hassan."

He looked up. It was Etienne, looking much like his grandfather by some trick of the moon's light. The hetman had half a dozen others with him, including two of his daughters.

"Leave it off, Hassan. Come home."

"I must take my boat down to the sea."

"No. There is work to be done. None of us have much, so each of us is precious. Leave off your grief."

"It's hope, not grief!" Hassan shouted.

When they came for him, he laid to with the oar until he broke ribs on one of his girl-cousins.

As she screamed, Etienne waved the others off. "Please, Hassan. Come home."

"No." Secrets spilled from his lips like rain from a careless cloud. "This is the Fall of the Moon, and the Tide of Spring. I must away before the world ends. I must be free."

"Come home and be free."

Hassan threw the oar back into the boat and returned to his dragging. After a moment, Etienne leaned into the stern and pushed. "Come on," the hetman shouted, "the sooner he sinks his silly boat, the sooner we all go home."

But the growing light of the Soulful Moon gave lie to the words and hope to Hassan's heart.

I will be free beyond the horizon.

The Sea of Murmurs ran with sand and soil, a foam of wiggling worms atop the heaving brown tide. Was this the Tide of Spring? Hassan couldn't imagine how the boat could navigate such a muddy, almost-solid expanse.

Most of Telos had come down to the beach to watch the madman and his boat. Some cried, casting him hot looks, especially those tending his injured girl-cousin. Others stared at the blazing moon. Wind drove along the sand, carrying soil from the sea and an unexpected heat.

Hassan could believe this to be the end of the world.

"Look!" someone shouted.

There was color in the sea. Flashes here and there, like fire sparks on a distant stretch of beach.

The Tide of Spring?

Then all the muddy water burst into bloom, a thousand million billion flowers exploding on the Sea of Murmurs in a riot of color and scent. Hassan grabbed the bow of his boat and ran. It was light as a palm leaf, floating across the sand behind him. When he glanced back, he saw many hands helping.

His feet met the sea on the first spray of petals from the incoming tide. Hassan ran until the flowers were up to his knees. There was still water down below, a thick syrupy nectar, but even below the surface it was filled with the soft nudging of blooms. The boat slid in among the raging color as if made for the task, and Hassan tumbled into it. He would cross the horizon. He would live forever.

"Who will you take with you?" asked Etienne, waist-deep in flowers, his face glowing sad and hard by the blazing light of the Soulful Moon.

"Grandfather," Hassan answered. He sat down on the single bench, nodded to the gleaming bones worked in among the planks of the boat, and bent to his oars. Each stroke broke the surface of the Sea of Murmurs with a spray of perfumed scent that shivered his spine.

Behind him, they cried on the beach as the Soulful Moon fell. When he looked over his shoulder, Hassan saw that lights winked on one by one in the black cities atop the obsidian cliffs.

Then Hassan turned his face to horizon, and freedom, even as the moon fell and the air burned and flowers carried him in his grandfather's arms to someplace he never could have known before.

A Critical Examination of Stigmata's Print
Taking the Rats to Riga

Jeff and Ann VanderMeer asked me to write a story for them. I did. They hated it, telling me the story did everything they wanted, but in a way that did not work for them. So I wrote this story instead. See how many genre writers you can spot in here somewhere.

Perhaps the most quotidian detail of the print *Taking the Rats to Riga* (1969) is the eponymous rats themselves. This is somewhat uncharacteristic of the work of the artist Stigmata (b. Crispus Chang-Evans, Nanking, China, 1942; d. Khyber Pass, Pakistan, 1992). The artist was notorious for eschewing both representation and naturalism, noting in a 1967 interview with Andy Warhol, "The dial ain't set on sketch, and I'll never be a d**ned camera" (*artINterCHANGE*; vol. III, no. 4; 1968).

The unusual inclusion of such readily identifiable elements strongly hints that *Rats* is based on an actual event. The precise nature of this event is obscured by our distance in time from the origins of this print, as well as Stigmata's notoriously poor record-keeping. Lambshead's own acquisition notes on the print are strangely sparse as well. Art-world rumor whispers that the print depicts a scene from *Karneval der Naviscaputer*, an occasional festival of deviant performance art held within East Berlin's underground club culture during the mid- to late 1960s.

The astute observer would do well to attempt deconstruction of some of the other elements in *Rats*. Art unexamined is, after all, art unexperienced. In this case, even a close examination is unlikely to reveal the mundane truths behind the print. The emotive truths are, however, most certainly available.

Consider the chain that the rats are climbing. Why do they ascend?

From where have they come? A hook dangles or swings not far below the lower rat. It appears ornamented in both shape and detail. Bejeweled, this cannot be an artifact of the working man. Nor does it conform to the Continental notion of *kunstbrukt,* that design should be both beautiful and functional. This hook is curious and attractive, but hardly something to lift a bale of opium from the decks of a shabby Ceylonese trawler. One must also consider the possibility hinted at in the print's title, that these are the plague rats Renfield carries into the world for his master Dracula, as depicted repeatedly in cinema.

Examine the chain itself. In Stigmata's rendering, this could just as easily be a motorcycle chain as a cargo chain or an anchor chain. Were that to be the case, we might assume the rats were being drawn upward, toward the top verge of the image. The dynamism of their forms suggests that they are more than mere passengers. Still, is that no different from a man walking up an escalator?

Once we have evaluated the context in which the rats appear, the image begins to lose its coherence. Most observers consider the smaller lines in the background to be more distant chains of the same sort the rats are climbing, but Priest has advanced the argument that those may be strings of light bulbs (*Struggles in European Aesthetics,* Eden Moore Press, London, 1978). Her assertion is undercut by the strong front lighting on the primary figures in the composition, but given Stigmata's well-documented disregard for artistic convention, this is an inherently irresolvable issue.

The most visually dominant element in *Rats* is the tentacled skeleton in the left side of the image. Sarcastically dubbed "The Devil Dog" in a critical essay by Robyn (*Contemporary Images,* Malachite Books, Ann Arbor, 1975), this name has stuck, and is sometimes misattributed as Stigmata's title for the work. In stark contrast with the climbing rats, there is nothing natural or realistic about the Devil Dog. Rather, it combines elements of fictional nightmare ranging from Lovecraft's imaginary Cthulhu mythos to the classic satanic imagery of Christian art.

Priest (op. cit.) nevertheless suggests that the Devil Dog may, in fact, be representational. Presuming even a grain of truth, this theory could represent the source of Lambshead's interest in acquiring *Rats* for his collection, given the doctor's well-known dedication to his own extensive *wunderkammer*. It is difficult for the observer to seriously credit Priest's notion, however, as she advances no reasonable theory as to what creature or artifact the Devil Dog could represent. She simply

uses scare words such as "mutant" and "chimera" without substantia-
tion. The burden of proof for such an outlandish assertion lies very
strongly with the theorist, not with her critics.

Robyn and other observers have offered the far simpler hypothesis
that the Devil Dog is an expression of Stigmata's own deeper fears.
The open jaw seems almost to have been caught in the act of speech.
While the eyes are vacant, the detail along the center line of the skull
and above the orbitals can be interpreted as flames rather than horns
or spurs. For a deep analysis of this interpretation, see Abraham
(*Oops, I Ate the Rainbow: Challenges of Visual Metaphor,* University
of New Mexico Press, Albuquerque, 1986). The tentacles dangle, hor-
rifying yet not precisely threatening to either the artist or the observer.
Rising above and behind is an empty rib cage—heartless, gutless, a
body devoid of those things that make us real. This is a monster that
shames but does not shamble, that bites but does not shit, that writhes
but does not grasp.

The most important element in *Rats* is, without a doubt, the hand
rising up to brush at the Devil Dog's prominent, stabbing beak. It is
undeniably primate, and equally so undeniably inhuman. Still, a strong
critical consensus prevails that this is Stigmata's own hand intruding
to touch the engine of his fear. While the rats seek to escape up their
chain, this long-fingered ape reaches deeper into the illuminated shadows, touching the locus of terror without quite grasping it. The paral-
lels to Michelangelo's *Creation of Adam* (ca. 1511) are inescapable
and disturbing. Who is creating whom here? Is Stigmata being brought
to life by his own fears? Or does he birth them into this print, as so
many artists do, to release his creation on an unsuspecting world?

We can never answer those questions for Stigmata. Reticent in life,
he, like all who have gone before, is thoroughly silent in death. Each
of us can answer those questions for ourselves, however, seeing deeper
into this print than the casual horror and blatant surrealism to what
lies beneath. Much as Lambshead must have done when he bought the
piece from the court-appointed master liquidating Stigmata's troubled
estate, via telephone auction in 1993.

What wonder lies in yonder cabinet? *Taking the Rats to Riga* is a
door to open the eyes of the mind. Like all worthwhile art, the piece
invites us on a journey that has no path nor map, nor even an end-
point. Only a process, footsteps through the mind of an artist now
forever lost to us.

From the Countries of Her Dreams

WITH SHANNON PAGE

This is a story set in the world of Green and her misadventures. It introduces some characters who become important in my novel Kalimpura. *Plus it shows a bit more of the theogeny of this place, which always seemed important to me.*

Laris, of late priestess of the goddess Marya, now priestess of Mother Iron, awoke with a sweating, fearful trembling. Solis had been at her side once more, though Laris had laid her sister into the ground two months past. Winter gnawed at her little whore's apartment over the tack shop in Set Ring Alley. Even with rags stuffed around the shutters the wind found her, while the tapping of the smiths and farriers down below set a rhythm to her days of sleep.

Prostitutes worked nights. Priestesses never stopped working. It was all she could do to rest in daylight. And here came Solis again. Not a true ghost, nor a sending, Laris was certain, though later she would sacrifice a cup of grain spirits and a silver nail to Mother Iron to be certain.

No, these visits of her dead sister were from the countries of her own dreams, not the realms of spirit.

Even worse, she thought she knew why.

Sleep was gone now, vanquished by the biting chill that cut through her blankets, and the light leaking past the rags and shutters. Winter in Copper Downs was not for the faint of heart nor the flat of purse. Laris reached down by her feet and found her thick woolen gown—skirt buttoned up the front and back for easy access—and slid the garment over her cotton undershift without first turning down her covers. Then she slipped from her bed, kneeling before her tiny iron stove to build a small fire of scavenged scrapwood in hopes of warming both her hands and a bit of washing water. Lucifer matches were a rare luxury in her life.

Laris sighed. Being priestess of a goddess whose worshippers were by definition destitute and desperate left a great deal to be desired insofar as the offertory went. As further insult, their women's temple was a jumbled pile of bricks that had taken Solis's life when those saffron-robed bastards had come goddess-killing.

"Enough," she whispered, her breath fogging in bright ribbons from her mouth. She could think in circles for hours without finding a better answer. Instead she concentrated on coaxing the little flames to life within their ironwork. Breaking the skin of ice from the top of her water jar. Dipping a small cup's worth into the tarnished copper pot. All of this, step by step, without thinking of her sister or the death of the goddess Marya or the whirling bricks of the temple as they flew like flower petals before a storm raised on the ancient hatred of men and their gods.

"Outside," Laris gasped. Wondering if she was being driven mad by her sister's death and the savaging of winter, she stumbled from her little room and down the narrow stairs to seek food.

The lazaret on Bustle Street was the only place in Copper Downs where a woman could seek medical help without inconvenient questions being asked, or permission being required of a husband, father, or brother. The thick-walled, anonymous building served other purposes as well. One of them, quite simply, was a large pot of soup that never seemed to boil dry, but mutated in season from fish stock to stewed pigeon to a vegetable slurry and on and on. A woman could always get a bowl. Though it might taste strange, and sometimes sat poorly on the gut, the soup was ever warm and filling.

Besides, Laris needed to talk to someone. Neela, the old woman who ceaselessly tended the pot, was a good listener. The priestess took a turn behind the short, splintered counter, filling bowls while Neela chopped something stringy and gelid, occasionally tossing slivers into the great iron kettle.

Patients and their nurses shuffled by, as did one or another woman off the street. "The blessings of Mother Iron on you," Laris muttered with each bowl. Marya had been the women's goddess here in Copper Downs, all Laris's life and for generations before hers, but those days were gone. Desire, titanic goddess from the beginning of all things and mother to all the daughter-goddesses of women, had raised Mother

Iron in the place of lost Marya, and so Laris served the new goddess, strange as she was.

Some of the women made Marya's hand sign—whether old habit or protest, Laris could not say. Others popped their thumb upward from a lax fist, the nail symbol of Mother Iron herself. Still more made no response at all. All of them took their soup, though, which Laris took to say more about the needs of women than any amount of prayer or sacrifice might do.

"You never comes without a reason," Neela said behind her, startling Laris. "You eats, as they all does from time to time, but you only comes this side of the counter when you needs."

"Like praying, I suppose," Laris replied, recovering her wits. Had she been drifting off?

Neela huffed. "I wouldn't be the priestess with the knowing of prayers."

"Blessings on you, as well." The line had faded away, so it was only the two women, a stack of scuffed pottery bowls, and the big pot bubbling quietly to itself while the smells of the dock seemed to play in the steam.

"Huh. You always was fresh." The knife, honed so thin it would surely shatter into flakes soon, slammed into the block. "So was your sister."

Thusly, Neela cut to the heart of things. "I dream of her," Laris blurted.

"Aye, and who doesn't dream of their dead?" Sympathy stained the old woman's voice, though her expression was curdled as ever.

"She comes, she begs."

"And you gives, yes?"

"No." Laris turned a bowl in her hand, seeing it with her fingers rather than her eyes. Glaze rough in some places, worn smooth in others so that the soapy texture of the clay met her touch. Heavy but unbalanced, much like life itself. Chipped at the rim. "I cannot give what she wants."

"That boy, ain't it." The words were not a question, coming from Neela.

"That boy," said Laris miserably. She'd bedded hundreds of men for coin, loved a few of them for spite, but the hearts of women always drew her closer. Solis had been of a more generous spirit and traditional tastes. She'd had an understanding with Radko, a grocer's boy—though years past the age when that term was anything but a job title—with a simple outlook on life and a seemingly endless supply of fresh vegetables.

Laris had never been able to stand Radko. She'd tolerated him for the sake of the food he brought when he came courting, and the happiness Solis seemed to find in him.

"Ain't you talking to him since herself was kilt?"

Two months, thought Laris. "I didn't let him come to the funeral. That was women's business." *I have not spoken to Radko in the two months since Solis was killed.*

"Course she's crying." Neela was matter-of-fact. "She ain't said good-bye to him she loves." The paper-thin knife came close, not a threat, just a pointer at the flaw in Laris's own heart. "On account of you ain't let her."

As always with Neela, she only repeated the things you'd already told her. Truth from another's mouth was so much more damning than the doubtful thoughts that chased themselves through Laris's quiet moments. "Thank you," she said.

"Go thank yourself," groused the older woman. She handed a long wooden ladle to Laris. "And stir a while. I must take me to the small room."

She didn't seek out Radko that day. Knowing and doing were not the same thing. Her years before the altar had taught her much about the difference.

Instead Laris spent her afternoon tending the temporary fane of Mother Iron, in a Temple Quarter alley behind the temple of the Frog God. They still had rights to the lot where the old temple of Marya had stood, but no money or labor to clear away the wreckage, let alone rebuild. The Frog God priests had taken pity on the women—their concerns stood outside the politics of daughter-goddesses—and allowed Mother Iron's followers the relative shelter of their midden area.

One could make much combing the trash of wealthier people, but mostly Laris was glad for a stout wall with a small chimney that almost always blasted warm, smoky air. A light framework of scavenged timber, topped with ragged strips of sailcloth sewn together, made up the sanctuary. The altar was little more than a clump of still-joined bricks lugged from the nearby ruins, topped with an increasing pile of rusty iron nails.

No one had yet vandalized it. Women came by in the cold afternoon in ones and twos—mothers and daughters and maids and maidens and cooks and prostitutes and an actress off a foreign ship and a banker's wife and one woman cloaked so tight Laris had no sense of her, except that she walked wrapped in that strange insulation that money creates about the very wealthy.

Each brought their mite or measure. Each prayed for guidance, or protection, or just sobbed a while. Laris listened to those who would speak, and comforted those who would take the circle of her arms around them, and shivered in the cold between times. She never counted the offerings, not until it was time for her to pack away what could be packed and seek her own living in the taverns by night.

Food in the form of withered apples, a strip of dried fish, and several stale rolls—enough for her to eat the next two days. Also three copper taels, half a dozen iron nails, and improbably, one silver obol. Laris was certain that last had not come with the wealthy woman, and probably not the banker's wife. People with money always understood just how little was needed to get what they wanted from people without.

Laris set the coins in an inner pouch for the strongbox back at the lazaret where Mother Iron's meager funds were kept against the future. The rest she put in a roughspun bag before heading for her usual evening haunt.

Winter crimped the flesh trade as surely as it crimped shipping or any other pursuit that required men to bestir themselves out of doors. Also, working without her sister seemed to make Laris less desirable, less interesting, except to those so drunk or bemused that any woman with a damp sweetpocket was good enough. Unless she was starving, she never went with such men. Half of them turned violent, the rest cried for their mothers and would not leave her bed when their time was up.

She sat at the shadowed end of the bar in the Poison Fish and sipped from a tumbler of watered wine. Undine behind the bar had given it to

Laris on credit, but when she turned a man, Laris knew the drink and the cost of an upstairs room would leave her with little more than she had now.

The bowl of mashed chickpeas had been pure kindness.

Then Radko came stumbling from the frozen street. A voice murmured in her ear, and for a shocked moment, Laris thought Solis was still beside her. "What, sib?" she whispered in return, unsure if she was more afraid of an answer or the lack of one.

He brushed fresh snow off his tan corduroy coat, then slipped out of it, hanging it on one of the hooks alongside the door. The man didn't even look toward her—Laris was relieved that he hadn't pursued her into the Poison Fish with a purpose, at least—as he placed his hat, gloves, scarf, and face mask in the pockets of the shapeless jacket, leaving his upper body clad only in woolen undershirt, long-sleeved work shirt, and stained sheepskin vest.

When Radko stepped to the other end of the bar, under the hissing lantern Undine hung there to better see each new customer, Laris got a good view of his profile. Slightly hunched at the shoulder, as if he were half a lifetime older. Long, narrow nose out of alignment thanks to some argument with a teamster years past, if she recalled the story correctly. Curly hair greasy-dark with the sweat of labor, that he washed in the spring and again in the fall each year. Thick eyebrows under a deep forehead that hid eyes she knew would glimmer a dull brown.

Dull brown, that was the man. She'd never known what Solis had seen in him.

Still, her late sister's hand on her elbow propelled Laris into the light, struggling against the few steps toward that end of the bar.

"Oh, hullo," Radko said, looking up at her.

Exasperation outpaced caution to Laris's lips. "Hullo? That's all you have for me now, two months after *she* died?"

He shrugged, accepted a pewter tankard of ale from Undine. Laris smelled the yeasty, liquid-bread stink of it. Radko traced a finger through the foam. "You don't never talk to me, ma'am." A shrug. "She died, you didn't want me around. Didn't matter what I had for you."

Laris felt a pang of guilt, followed by another burst of anger. Her heart was too troubled for this conversation. But Neela had held the right of it on her sharp tongue as well. "I was wrong," she said slowly. The words were ashen in her mouth. "You grieved her, too, and I was wrong to turn you away."

Another shrug. "Ever'body turns me away. 'M used to it." A long pull on the tankard. Radko seemed to find something fascinating floating in his ale.

"Sh-she needs to say farewell," Laris blurted.

That drew a long look from Radko, with an expression that implied there might yet be a measure of shrewdness behind those dull eyes. Finally: "Solis needs that, or you?"

You cut me, and I bleed. Laris tried to think like a priestess, though she was tired and cold and broke. "All of us need that, perhaps."

Radko returned to studying his ale. His right index finger made nonsense patterns in the spill glistening on the worn oak bartop. "I'll go with you," he muttered.

"I . . . I haven't worked yet tonight." Somehow, her lack of clients suddenly seemed a deeply personal failing. Laris knew her beauty was fading with age and hard use, but there was always more to it than that. "I c-cannot leave."

The man reached into the inner pocket of his sheepskin vest. "You're four coppers, same as Solis, right?"

Laris just stared.

"For a flatback and half a candle's worth of time," Radko added, in case she had somehow not understood.

"Yes, but I—"

"I ain't going with you," he snarled. Now they were both embarrassed. "Just buying your time. So's we can say farewell to Solis together." Five coppers clinked onto the bar.

Well, thought Laris, *at the least I won't have to pay Undine for the room.* Against her better judgment, she reached shivering for the coins. She left one behind for the barback to take in payment for her abandoned wine, thin as winter blood and almost as cold.

They pushed through the night, walking into the chill, whistling wind. The snow had left off again, but the sky bellied low and full, where it could be seen at all in the darkness. Only the greater streets of Copper Downs were lit by the new gas lamps. On a winter's evening like this one, even the third watch was late enough for most houses to be shuttered. The light posts on the city's lesser streets were glowing cinders, or empty, their pitch-soaked torches stolen for someone's night fire.

From the Poison Fish to Laris's apartment was only a matter of fifteen minutes or so in good weather. Tonight, head down, her thin cotton cloak drawn close, she figured on twenty. In this weather the idea of taking Radko into her bed, just for the warmth of it, had a certain appeal. But this was *Radko*. Her sister's pet simpleton. She didn't even want to touch his arm as they walked.

They couldn't go to the new fane. The ruins of the old temple, where Solis had died, would be unbearable. Only in her room would it make sense to try to bid her sister farewell. Besides, that was where Laris saw Solis in her dreams.

Something caught at Solis so that she stumbled. A belated moment after, she realized it was Radko, tugging at her elbow. "You got a bully boy?" he asked, almost shouting over the wind to be heard.

"What?"

Radko jerked his chin back over his shoulder. Laris turned to look. Not a bully boy. Bully *boys*. Two of them, tall and walking swiftly. One was wide as a wall, the other almost too thin, and dark-skinned besides. One of those Selistani immigrants that the damned girl Green had drawn into the city.

Their singleness of purpose bespoke an immigrant-native comity that would be the pride of many a street-corner demagogue. Unfortunately, *she* appeared to be their single purpose.

"Not mine," Laris shouted, and turned to run.

Radko grabbed her elbow again, and pulled her close. She fought this betrayal, thrusting her knee into his groin. The only thing that saved him from collapsing in a groaning heap was the leather-and-canvas work pants, padded for outdoor days in the cold.

"Kiss me," he said, his voice thin. "Pretend, at least."

Again, she was a moment behind. *What* was with her head? A woman alone didn't survive long on the streets of Copper Downs by being slow. Step into a doorway, step out of their way. If the bully boys were bound elsewhere, let them pass unwitnessed.

She couldn't outrun them anyway.

Nuzzling close to Radko, Laris thought about her sister kissing this man. Touching him. Lying with him. Taking him into her body. Solis had always preferred to be taken as a boy, if there was a bit of grease to be had. Laris detested the way she felt after such sex, as if air had been forced through the entire length of her digestion.

But he had done this thing. To Solis. Did he want to do it to her?

Surprised, she found herself kissing him. Ale, and a bit of salt, and the frosty edge of night. He'd eaten fish for dinner, with some southern spice.

And this simple man smelled *very* complicated, when she got so close.

Rough hands ripped her from his grasp. Laris spun, praying now to Mother Iron—a goddess whose greatest virtue was perhaps that she walked the streets of Copper Downs in bodily form, at least on some occasions.

Hear the plea of all women, that the fist of men shall not strike me down.

Strength flared within Laris, where most people might have quailed. She'd taken more than one beating in her life for refusing to cringe.

The wide one had her in his vast paw. He didn't even look at Radko, who had slipped into the shadows. *Fool!* How could she have thought . . . ? Whatever she'd been thinking, for a moment. The thinner one leaned close, eyes gleaming with the sparkle of whitecrust, that was sold six copper taels a twist, enough to keep a man on the far side of the edge through two sunrises.

"I got a wo-wo-word for yoo-yoo-you." His accent was from across the Storm Sea, but something else twisted his voice, drawing the speech out like sugar candy on the vendor's metal fork.

The big one snorted. "Raji's been a little deep into the fairy dust," he said, as conversational as a man comparing potatoes in the market. "But it's his show." Fingers tightened until the joints in her shoulder cracked. Laris shivered, and would have dropped to her knees if he were not simply holding her up.

How strong was he? Where in all the Smagadine hells was Radko?

"Wo-wo-wo . . ." The skinny one had become terminally tangled in thought.

That was when Radko struck. The fool. He grabbed for the whitecrust addict, who slipped away like fire in a frying pan, then snatched at Radko so fast Laris didn't see him move.

Radko went down with three fingers tearing at his ear, a knife clattering to the frosted cobbles at their feet. The big one released Laris to hold back his companion. She scooped up the knife and pressed it hard, with both hands, into the big man's jaw from behind and below, at the base of his tongue.

The smell of hot metal filled her, and for a moment Laris knew the touch of Mother Iron.

He screamed, gargled and strange-sounding, then turned back to her with death in his eyes. She lost the knife in the movement, but it stuck out of the big man's head like a handle, so Laris danced away from him, grabbing for the one piece of leverage she could have on him. Behind her, Radko vomited.

The whitecrust addict came at her from around the big man's back—the man she had stabbed was staggering with pain, and not quite moving fast enough to kill her yet, though Laris was certain she saw her own end right there, right then.

Then Radko got the skinny one by the ankles, and he went down face-first. Nerve-wrangled and angry, the addict was too busy reaching for Laris to break his fall with his own hands. Something—several somethings—crunched inside his face instead.

She and the big man both paused a moment in their deadly dance as an eerie keen of pain rose from the Selistani. Radko broke the moment by slamming uselessly into the big man's knee. He kicked Radko away as if shaking loose a dog, then grabbed at the knife and pulled it free in a steaming, hot-scented gush of blood.

"You and your new goddess won't live to see the springtime." The big man's voice was thick with pain. He staggered into the night, one hand pressed against the wound, while the bloody knife clattered to the street.

Laris stood staring a moment, breath hard in her lungs. The whole business had taken less than a minute. She had no idea why she was not dead.

Neither did Radko, apparently. He scrambled for his knife, then gave the skinny attacker a booted kick in the fork of his legs. The keening turned to a grunt, followed by a moan.

"Enough," said Laris. "It's not for us to finish him off." She extended a hand to Radko. "Let's go."

He burst into tears. She understood the feeling.

"Now, Radko, let's go *now*."

They hurried arm in arm through the winter darkness, Radko's breath shuddering with his tears. When Laris glanced over her shoulder, she saw a short, lumpy figure with glowing eyes standing over the body.

Mother Iron. Her new goddess. Strange, that one, a peculiar choice after the slaying of the goddess Marya, but Desire herself—mother-goddess to them all—had spoken.

Nothing passed between them, no nod of recognition, but Laris realized her prayer had been answered after all.

At her apartment she sent Radko out for more water. They would need to wash the blood away, and look to their bruises and cuts. She hated to use another day's ration of wood, but there didn't seem to be another way. Besides, after paying Undine, she was four copper taels to the good. Perhaps she could spare it.

He came back with a full bucket of water and slush. Too much, really, for her poor fire, but it wouldn't go to waste. Wordless, Laris slipped out of her outer blouse and dropped the shoulder of her underslip as she turned away from him. "Tell me if you see too much damage."

Radko's big, blunt hands were surprisingly tender. Cold, from washing them outside when he was fetching water, but clean and careful. He pressed fingertips into her, poked a bit. When her breath hissed with pain, his touch eased and he worked his way around the damaged area.

"You got away okay," he finally said. Lips brushed her shoulder, setting the hairs of her neck on end and a shiver crawling down her spine.

"Thank you," Laris replied. "How are you?"

"Aches, ma'am, but they didn't cut me open none."

No, *she* had done the cutting open. But those two would have killed as easily as stared them down. What else could she have done?

"Let me have a look," Laris said sternly.

Radko's face was suffused with embarrassed shyness, and she could see the boy he had once been, not so far behind his eyes. He still shivered, almost violently now. Cold? Fear? Pain?

For Solis, Laris thought, and pulled Radko into her arms. They eased back onto the narrow bed together, and lay a long time until his weeping stopped. She found herself in no mood to let loose of him, and he did not seem inclined to pull away, so they held one another through the watches of the night.

Morning found them still abed. Laris had not slept well, but Radko had positively snored the night away in her arms. They were still clothed—she was four coppers to the good, and no trace of his seed within her sweetpocket, or her more fundamental regions, to show for it. Was there a living to be made holding on to sad, silent men?

Or just this one.

Radko opened his eyes, blinked, yawned. "We never did say goodbye to Solis," he muttered.

She kissed his forehead. "I think we already have."

"Hmm." A grubby finger traced her nose. "I got to work soon. What about those men?"

Laris shrugged. "They were after the goddess. She will protect, or she will perish. I survived the death of Marya, I can survive the death of Mother Iron."

"Mother Iron's never going to die," Radko said with an almost-pleased finality.

The point was well taken. The new goddess was an old, old figure, surviving centuries in the tunnels beneath Copper Downs, deity from an era so long past as to be forgotten, only lately risen to her new role. Laris laughed, a little. "Then perhaps I shall never die, either."

"Will I see you again?" he asked plaintively.

Laris glanced away at the light leaking through the shutters. Her emotions were complicated, swirling. He was not so bad. And that scent. Truly, Neela had been right. Solis had been crying for Radko.

"My work is in the evening . . ." The man was used to prostitutes, after mooning over Solis so long.

His face fell, so she added hastily, "But we will find a time."

Radko struggled to his feet, smiled crookedly, and limped out her door, heading for his own day's wage. Laris pulled her robe about her and contemplated the four copper taels and the knife on the floor next to her bed, all neatly wrapped in a scrap of lace. She did not recall doing any such thing last night. She did not even own any lace.

"Solis?" she said softly. "Mother Iron?"

There was no answer. That was good enough for Laris. She rolled back into her thin covers and breathed in Radko's scent, then settled in for a few more hours of sleep. For the first time in months, she was ready for a quiet journey through the countries of her dreams.

Unchambered Heart

This is the story Jeff and Ann hated. Luckily for me, not every-
one else did.

One of the more controversial pieces in the collection is a print
by the famed forger of art, currency, and graffiti, Alois Redpath
(b. Minot, North Dakota, 1936; d. Xian, China, 1994), who
signed his work Redman. Redman's most famous work, of
course, was an exact replica of a section of the Berlin Wall,
built overnight on a lot in East Berlin in the summer of 1965.
The Stasi are said to have authorized an assassination order
against the artist in retaliation, but by then he was living in a
commune just outside Phuket, Thailand, beyond even the long
reach of the East German secret police.

This print, known as *Unchambered Heart,* is said to be a
copy of one of the lost paintings of Mercer Amistad (b. Taos,
NM, 1934; disappeared in Papua-New Guinea, ca. 1971, possibly infected with kuru). Amistad and the infamous gray market art collector Dr. Bentley Maxon toured Europe together in
1964 and 1965, seeking medical curiosities that had been stolen by the Nazis during World War II and secreted in a series of
illicit museums operated by Himmler's notorious Section Goat.
The secretive paramilitary unit was responsible for much of the
Nazi psychic war effort. Himmler and his spiritual advisors
placed great faith in the accrued mystical powers of such artifacts as the Bottled Siamese Twins of Turin, the Bile Ducts of
St. Boniface, and the sadly distorted skeleton of that Swedish
unfortunate known as the Walrus Man.

Amistad's interest in such material ties into her long history of representing the unspeakable through the lens of art. Maxon's pursuits at that time naturally go without saying among the cognoscenti of his life and work. We can only speculate, of course, but Amistad and Maxon could surely have met Redman somewhere in Mitteleuropa during the time their travels overlapped. Internal evidence in the print suggests it may have used another artwork or sketch as its source, which would be consistent with Redman encountering a Bohemian artist wandering Europe with her sketchbook, in the company of a mad doctor.

Controversy arises from two sources. First, the provenance of the print is dubious. Maxon's own records regarding the piece are uncharacteristically vague, given the doctor's more typical prolixity. This leaves open the possibility that *Unchambered Heart* is a forgery of a forgery, or a pseudo-copy. Second, Maxon's interest in the print seems to be connected to his brief and unfortunate tenure with the transgressive German performance art troupe known as Golden Dusk, an episode in the good doctor's biography for which he has more than once publicly stated his deep regret.

In other words, an unlikely vignette of which to hang a reminder in the front hall of Maxon's Long Island conservatory.

—Unsigned curator's notes on *Unchambered Heart,*
from the unpublished catalog of the Roosevelt Island
Medical Deviance Exhibition of 1997

The venue was the basement of a pawnshop that had once served as a bank, centuries earlier. Barrel-vaulted ceilings made for small rooms separated by iron bars in the oddest places. Curious drains interrupted the floor periodically, as if the place also included "abattoir" in its résumé.

Maxon circulated easily through the curled smoke. He identified the usual marihuana, cloves, and tobaccos, but also several rarer hallucinogenic substances. By the end of the evening the crowd was going to be very wired indeed.

The performers had yet to identify themselves, so the audience mingled anonymously. Many wore domino masks or face paint to obscure their identity. Mostly young and beautiful, these were the children of

Europe's post-war money. And in truth more than a few scions of wealth built on gold fillings picked from Jewish corpses during the war.

Those latter were of more interest to him and Merce, of course. He had permitted himself to be distracted by the unusual and bizarre, as was his wont, but neither of them had lost sight of their essential objectives.

A pair of men wrapped themselves into a clinch in a dark corner— American officers from the look of their bodies and the cut of their hair. Maxon smiled indulgently. If any place might be safe from persecution, it was the moveable space that was instantiated whenever these events were held.

He pushed into the chamber where the main tank was located. It reeked of rust, saltwater, and a thick, animal musk. Ratty red velvet curtains remained drawn over the glass, but the low, sonorous rumblings from within were promising. Likewise the blood-crusted chains hanging from the ceiling. A winch had been bolted up there as well. Russian military surplus, and capable of hoisting several tons, if he was any judge.

Maxon noted a tense young man who held himself out from the increasingly drunken and naked crowd. No cameras were permitted in here, of course, but the fellow sketched furiously with charcoal pencil in a loose-bound book of foolscap paper.

Drifting over, the doctor took a look.

"Who the hell asked you?" growled the artist, covering the page with his forearm. He spoke in German, badly, with an American accent.

"No one whatsoever," Maxon replied in the same tongue, well aware of his own overly academic diction. "But then, you did not ask for authorization. Please, indulge me. I am a student of curiosities. Ever on the edge of epiphany."

"Redman." The artist's voice was grudging.

"My pardons?"

"Name's Redman." The young man had a truly magnificent scowl. His heavy, dark eyebrows would have given Frida Kahlo pause. He switched to English, with a decidedly Midwestern American accent. "This is the part where you tell me your made-up name, then we pretend to get along."

"Oh, I assure you that there is nothing made up about my name."

The doctor offered his hand, for a shake or a kiss as seemed appropriate. "Bentley Y. F. Maxon. Physician, collector, world traveler."

Redman did not take the bait, instead eyeing Maxon's hand suspiciously for a moment. "You part of this freak show?"

Maxon put aside the temptation to say he *was* the freak show. In any event, that was not true. At least not here, not tonight. And youth was not to be blamed for its callowness. "I play my roles in life," he said. "Really, I must insist you permit me to view the sketch on which you are working."

With a final, blistering glare, Redman pulled his arm away and showed Maxon the sketchbook while still keeping a firm grip on it.

Surprisingly, the scene was not naturalistically representative of the increasingly raucous and abandoned crowd. Maxon recognized the face of the woman in the foreground. Here on paper, her breasts were pointed, each nipple exaggerated into the nosecone of a V-2 rocket. But when last he'd seen her, while she had indeed been naked, she had not been astride an orthocone cephalopod like some unicorned squid out of the depths of time. Nor had there been thousand-eyed Buddhist demons in Soviet uniforms dancing behind her.

Admittedly, anything was possible here.

Maxon glanced around to be sure. Then, "Do you plan to sketch the performance?"

"These are studies," Redman said defensively. "Cartoons. In the old sense of the word."

"And excellent studies they are." He reached out to lightly grasp the young man's elbow. "I am a patron of the arts. Please do not neglect to inform me of whatever work proceeds from your evening with us tonight."

A few minutes later, Maxon located Mercer again. She had stripped and was painting her body with whitewash in preparation for the show. It was a surprisingly sensual process with even more surprisingly attractive results. As such Merce had drawn the attention of a portion of the crowd.

He stepped in close to speak low, pitched for her ears only. "Watch for the angry young man with the sketchbook. You should like to meet him."

"I love artists," Merce replied. Maxon wondered if she would use a human canvas to make her body prints tonight. If so, he had an inkling whom the woman might be rolling back and forth across.

A quiet signal from the ringmaster summoned the players to their places. Rather to his surprise, Maxon noticed Redman tucking his sketchbook away into a niche in the ancient, slime-crusted stones of a pillar and moving into position.

Really, the whole point of Golden Dusk was that you never did know.

When the red velvet parted like the lips of a woman's vagina in the moment of passion, the thrashing tentacles within were a most satisfying sight indeed. The audience screamed.

It was only a beginning.

Three days later, a fussy little man from the Swiss embassy made Maxon's bail. He'd seen or heard nothing about Mercer Amistead while in the custody of the *volkspolizei,* and had so declined to ask questions lest he draw unwanted attention to his traveling partner.

The bruises from the drubbing he'd received still smarted. The tear gas, thankfully, was only an unpleasant memory. Maxon still was uncertain whether the raid that had ended the show was planned or unplanned, but he had to admit it was a spectacular conclusion to the whole affair. He hoped the American officers had not been caught up, or at least had been fully clothed by the time they were. The U-Bahn would have saved them if they'd escaped. Courts-martial could be such a messy business.

His only regret had been his fascination with the specimens. Some of them were clearly part of what he and Merce had been searching for. Possibly even the legendary unchambered heart cross-bred between cephalopods and rodentia by Section Goat's veterinarians.

The streets of East Berlin were as obsessively clean as ever. The air was smoggy but cold, a curious combination. As always in this season, the city was redolent with diesel fumes and the pungent aroma of boiled cabbage.

He determined to head for West Berlin and find a *bierstube.* Some decent food would be welcome after the GDR's institutional hospitality.

Expunging the arrest record was a problem for later. Maxon knew he would have to take the necessary steps; otherwise the Basil Chantilly passport would be useless. He liked that identity, had taken quite some trouble building it out in the sort of elaborate and meaningless detail that made such things convincing.

Merce caught up with him near the tram line. "Enjoy your stay in the vopo hotel?" she asked with a grin, speaking Arabic to maintain some privacy for their conversation.

"Naturally," he answered in the same language. There had been some fine specimens of abnormal psychology among his fellow prisoners. Maxon was never one to pass up an opportunity for a little field research, even under uncontrolled conditions. "I trust you managed to retain your own freedom."

"I have just spent three marvelous days with that vile little creature you discovered at the affair." She took Maxon's hand.

"So at least you profited from the business in the basement." Maxon found himself blushing, both for the messiness there, and for the lingering sense of her in the chambers of his own heart. He was *not* a jealous man. "I am sorry to have lost those amazing creatures in the tank. Wherever did the ringmaster find them?"

Mercer shrugged. "This is East Germany. What can't you find here? But I do have a surprise for you."

"I am not so fond of surprises."

"You will like this one. I am in the midst of a painting that recaptures the spirit of that evening. Redman is drafting a pen-and-ink piece from the same theme. We shall see which you prefer."

"Something was saved, then," Maxon said. "Will we ever see their like again?"

"They will live forever in art," Mercer replied joyously.

His own heart pounded anew. "So shall we all, my dear. So shall we all."

Angels iv: Novus Ordo Angelorum

Here are more angels, wrapped in archetype and heaven's light.

Desire

The angel of Desire bares her breasts, nipples hard in the dreaming wind of night. Her hair flows from her head like smoke in the autumn sky. It is every shade of black and gray—desire is the province of each age of life, not just callow youth nor addled dotage nor even obsessed middle years.

Desire's wings stretch wide as any angel's, but their plumage is rare. They look to have been patched together from a very congeries of birds: the mountain teratornis and the lammergeyer, the great golden eagles of the Arabian desert and the condor in his snowbound fastness. Every child dreams of flight, waking to be mocked by the birds. Her wings bear the burden of those dreams, which unfold in later life to the wretched obsessions that drive men mad.

But it is in her eyes, the gaze of Desire, where this angel's true power lies. They are rimmed with kohl, draped with lashes like a dark spray of rust. Their brown depths are drowning pools of lust. To catch her glance is to feel your heart stop, to feel blood cold in your arms and hot in your groin. No one, no age or gender, is safe from her eyes, so Desire wears a mask of silk and leather with a coiled snake worked upon it in tiny rubies formed from the blood of those she has loved.

In her hooded beauty she reminds us that Love is the greatest and most terrible of God's gifts.

Despair

Desire's fraternal twin, Despair, is a young man with hollow eyes and a sunken chest. His hair is the eerie pallor of the starving, the icy white frizz grown by a corpse in its coffin. His skin is so pale as to be almost blue. Despair looks like every student pulled from a morgue freezer, caught on the wrong side of that balancing point between potential and disaster.

His wings are different from his sister's, composed of what might be called the ghosts of feathers, only brittle shafts and lacy ribs, without soft plumage to fill them out. Despair wears them wound close and tight to his body, just over the leather greatcoat that flaps around his calves. He dresses in torn black denim and an array of ropy scars. Everyone who ever cut themself in his name has inflicted their own wound upon him.

Despair's power is in his body. Even in shadow, the angle of his repose can cause a man to slump, a woman to turn away with tear-burned eyes. To meet Despair full on, his every muscle broadcasting the hopeless music of the world, is to lay down meek in the street and end your struggle.

He is both God's invitation and warning to stray from faith.

Chance

There is another angel, distant cousin to those already named, the angel of Chance. Chance is an elegant young man. His blond hair flips back in a wave. He favors pastel polo shirts and stylish white slacks. His wings are discreet, a clever accessory to be admired by the matrons of River Oaks or Telegraph Hill, while granddaughters at the country club blush behind their Shirley Temples and whisper youthful scandal of Chance's single silver earring.

Chance is not concerned with wagering, or the lottery, but rather the common happenstances of life. A missed flight, that relieves the annoyed traveler of death by burning jet fuel hours later in an Iowa cornfield. The flat tire that keeps the family Camry from a patch of black ice, leaving slick, spinning death for someone less favored. Hands bumping together over a book on sale at Powell's, leading to coffee, then pizza, then a wild night of passion followed by a lifetime of contentment.

You could pass Chance on the street and never really know him except by the twenty-dollar bill you later find stuck to your shoe. Chance is God's reminder to us that order is not one of the forces of the world.

Flora

Flora is the angel of plants and flowers. Her work is found among the world's oldest and quietest citizens. She wears flowing silks borrowed from her friends among the mulberry leaves, and crowns of whatever blooms that hour and season, be it the moss rose or the orchid. Her wings are spiders' webs, pale traceries glimmering by moonlight. It is the sight of Flora moving through the gardens of night that gave rise to legends of fairies.

Flora's hair is all the colors of the natural world, a rainbow turned to river. Her eyes are the brown of soil one moment, the blue of water the next. Her smile is tiny, pursed, a soon-to-open rose. Her heart is just as thorny.

Do not mistake Flora for a benign power. Trees with their roots rend the mightiest works of man. The least lichen is the death of rocks. Your bones will someday be her province, once the worms have cast you out. More patient than Time, she carries worlds in her hands and love of all that grows in her heart.

No one knows what God thought when He set her into the world, but remember that it was sweet Flora who set the order of the plantings in the Garden. It was she that tended the orchards. It was she that placed the fig leaves where a shamed man might find them, and it was she that grew the apple tree where a woman of intellect might climb on advice of a snake.

Word

Word is the oldest angel of all. He is sometimes called "God's grandfather." He carries his age well. It shows only in the webbing of lines around his pale, blind eyes, and the stiffness in his step. He has a shock of red hair that lifts in a mutable fire from his head, so that Word is always as tall as he needs to be. His skin is dark as well-baked bread. His face is the face of Everyman.

Blind as he is, Word needs no cane, for his wings serve him well.

They arch high as a house, more like the wings of a moth than a bird. Their sensitive fibers build for him a picture of the world. He wears no clothes for textiles would block his wings and pain his senses. Even in his nakedness Word is wrapped in glory.

For you see, in the beginning Word made the world upon the waters when God spat Word from His mouth. Later, Word made flesh. Without their tongues, men would be no more than animals. Without Word, men's tongues would be no more than meat.

Word is the beacon of our minds and the light of our days, withered proxy for an absent God.

Descent into Darkness

The Tentacled Sky

This story is me lightly channeling H. P. Lovecraft and enjoying the generalized weirdness of the life of cities.

The first note was scribbled on a piece of old cardstock, fountain-pen ink splattered carelessly across the fuzzed textures as if it had been written in haste by someone's elegant grandmother. The handwriting itself was hardly Palmer Method, instead being as sloppy as the inkwork. Again, signaling haste.

I turned the slightly irregular missive in my well-protected hands, looking at the back where a scrap of printing could just be made out to read "EALOU" in faded vermilion ink that reminded me of old blood. *Jealous?* I wondered. Or some portmanteau product name such as *Sealout*. The faint smell of roses emitted from the cardboard, though I was put more in mind of a funeral home than a florist.

Significantly, neither my name nor my address was on the reverse. Only the faded printing and some wear scars. The note itself simply read, "TUESDAY 7:13 P.M."

Unsigned, undated, unadorned. Stuck into my door, just above the latch where I'd be sure to find the note immediately upon my return from my errands about the city.

Note to gentle readers: I should not like to reveal more about my erstwhile whereabouts for fear of endangering you. Please forgive my lack of specificity concerning such an otherwise elementary matter.

Later on, the rain descended. The matter of climate had much been bruited in the newspapers of late, for so far in the course of this year barely halfway past we had challenged most prior records for annual precipitation. The weather-wise were declaiming that by the end of August this year of rain in the city should be one for the record books. The weather-foolish were proclaiming a need for honest citizens to provision themselves with boats for their porches, and flotation devices that the children might yet swim to school when the curriculum resumed in September.

This year's rain had been in general possessed of a distinctly unaqueous elasticity. Instead of washing the streets and clearing the air, the water clung with a nigh gelid tenacity to buildings, gutters, trees, and even the unfortunate birds. I was put much in mind of studies recently published in several lower-tier journals of academics and science regarding the polymerization of water. Ordinarily such drastic pronunciations about novel states of matter are thinly disguised pleas for funding or continued sponsorship, and as such I pay them little mind.

Our rain of this year in the city was revising my opinions on this particular matter.

I sat to watch the street through the cracked glazing of my front window. Naturally it was surgically clean on the inside, smelling faintly of surfactants and rubbing alcohol. However, on the outside the glass was somewhat obscured by the persistent sheet of water clinging like a drowning man to the last rope of his hopes. Though I had largely ignored the note of the previous weekend, it continued to perch on my mantel, ungainly harbinger of vague portent.

My grandfather's railroad clock had struck the seventh hour of the afternoon not so long ago. Now I peered into the street, looking through the rain that fell like clear aspic to see what might be in store at the hour appointed by my anonymous correspondent.

A single figure shuffled along the thoroughfare, eschewing the sidewalks in favor of the cobbled expanses where the day's traffic had so recently wound down to the usual evening trickle. I had to laugh, for the approaching entity was as something designed by children in pretense of threat—long leather car coat that flapped in the wind, the figure beneath shrouded in shadow and rainfall; a wide-brimmed hat pulled low over the face until nothing could be seen from my second-floor vantage except crown surmounting shoulders; and a shambling gait of which any bedtime-story boogeyman would be proud.

Could this jack-o-the-streets be my mysterious correspondent? Or an agent of theirs?

No one else appeared—no autobus or taxicab, no private automobiles rushing for medical aid or cruising for the evening air. Just this creature who dropped below my line of sight. I heard my apartment building's front door creak open, that bad hinge ever worsening in the endless rain. I heard a heavy tread upon the stairs. I heard the floorboard outside my door squeak as always it did when I had a visitor.

I tensed, waiting for the knock that would doubtless be a thunderous echo. My heart raced despite my airs of amusement, and my breath was harsh in my throat.

I counted to a hundred, but no knock came. Neither did the floorboard squeak again. Taking my courage in hand, I crept to the door and pressed my ear against the varnished wood, my nose reporting old oak, turpentine, and mold. I expected stentorian breathing, or some harsh life-noise of rough trade waiting to spring upon me.

Silence.

Noting that the clock now reported 7:15 of the evening, I rallied my intestinal fortitude and cracked open the portal, keeping the stout brass chain in place. I cannot say who or what I expected to find without, but no one stood in the hall.

Only the broad-brimmed hat lay there, upside down as if carelessly discarded before my door. Another piece of cardstock had been dropped into the inverted crown.

I listened a moment, for surely the visitor had not departed. I'd heard no footsteps, the floorboard had not squeaked, neither stairs nor front door had echoed in their invariable manners. Still, I heard no breathing, nor the rustling silence that usually shouts of a person holding themselves still and secret.

Either my visitor was a practitioner of one of those Asiatic arts of noiseless assault and stealthy concealment, or they had contrived to noiselessly vanish from the upstairs hall of my building. Into the apartment of one of my three immediate neighbors? I'd heard no knock, no click of latch, no usual murmur of polite social intercourse.

Once more summoning my courage, for by now I was deeply and obscurely disturbed, I pushed my door to, unsecured the chain, then opened it to step out into the fearful precincts that were my own front hallway transformed.

Only a hat threatened me. Damp, silent, inner band still warm from someone's head, with a further bit of cardstock left carelessly therein. An afterthought, missive from an uncaring universe. I pulled on a latex glove from the supply I keep always in my pockets and carefully lifted the card.

Unadorned, unaddressed, this time smelling of pocket lint and damp wool, one side proclaimed "UTTON," the other simply read "FRIDAY, 10:17 A.M." in the same hasty hand and splattered fountain pen.

With a sigh, I took my prizes and retreated to the dubious safety of my apartment.

I washed my hands a good long while with three different soaps while contemplating my next move. Clearly some game was afoot, though I understood nothing of it yet. Just as clearly this was not a matter for the authorities. What complaint should I bring to the police? That someone had gifted me with a hat and a pair of odd notes? Unfair as it might be, I was already aware of my reputation in certain sections of the city. The compromise of my dignity through the mandatory psychiatric confinement of two years ago was unjust, as any reasonable person could see, but neither the courts nor the medical authorities were overly concerned with reason, preferring instead their petty little rules and straitened expectations.

No, I could expect no help from those quarters. I was, as usual in this life, set upon my own devices once more.

Properly cleansed, I examined the hat with stainless steel tongs and a lacquered chopstick. Under my patient and persistent prodding, the headgear revealed no particular secrets. It was a fine-grained leather, lined with dark maroon silk. There was no maker's label or stamp on the inner band, though the threading indicated high-quality work, most likely a bespoke effort.

My children's monster in the street had been a fashionable fellow, for all his or her air of menace.

After much thought, and no little steeling of my resolve, I tugged on a latex skullcap. My hair, auburn ringlets of which I allowed myself small vanity, fit well enough beneath. This was little different from those times when I dressed myself to be someone else in the world. After spraying the inside of the hat with disinfectants, I gingerly placed it upon my head.

Gloves and skullcap, I reminded myself. It would not touch the flesh of my body.

I stood and regarded myself in the mirror above the mantel. Adjusting the brim, I thought I could pass for the stranger in a view from above. Should that ever be necessary.

Passing was a skill of mine, carefully cultivated against necessities both dire and trivial. Binding or padding my breasts, lifts in my shoes, a change to the curve of my spine and shoulders, the proper wig—I could be anyone.

Except yourself, a voice whispered. After a moment's startle, I recognized it for my own.

On Friday morning, the city was gloomy but no longer half-drowned. Not for the moment, at any rate. I sat by my window, the broad leather hat totemically perched upon my head. My street was busier than at the previous visitation; crowded with the usual midmorning traffic of rag pickers, letter carriers, delivery men, and harried mothers with preschool children.

I watched for the shambling visitor, and was not disappointed. Soon the mysterious figure appeared from behind a dark brown package truck disgorging some mercantilist sending into the home at 1406, near the beginning of my block. They shambled once more, this time bareheaded as any clown, curled hair moving in slight breeze outside. The car coat flapped, and their pace seemed more vigorous today. Of course, if my visitor cultivated anonymity, a slow, menacing gait would not be their best choice at such a busy hour.

Once again they disappeared from view just below me. Once again the front door swung open with the squeal of distressed hinges, the steps echoed, the floorboard outside my door squeaked. Once again there was no knock, only a psychic miasma of menace. Once again I stood, listening, waiting with the patience of snakes until the old railroad clock struck half past the hour.

I threw the door open in an outburst of showmanship to find a pair of tall leather boots in the hall, another cardstock note propped between them.

Elusive, once again.

Through the entire afternoon I scanned the sky for serpents. Sometimes I glimpsed the bladed and bloody future, another aspect of my life for which neither the civil authorities nor the medical establishment had any patience. The world to come leaves its tracks around us in the frost on hearses, railroad car graffiti, visible-but-secret patterns in park plantings and concert posters plastered to brick walls. One needs only attune oneself to read this.

I mostly keep my distance from these truths. They disrupt the flow of my life and introduce fears that can overwhelm. But the emergent structure of mysterious notes and visitations reminded me all too much of my prior visions.

So I watched, and waited, trying to catch sight of what might yet come.

Nothing emerged from the watercolor clouds but rain and more rain. No writhing tentacles, no bleary eye of God staring down in indifferent judgment. Haruspication is a lost art at the best of times, and my own small precognition has rarely served to provide more than trouble.

I was not sure this was trouble. Yet, something still moved.

"REED" was scheduled for "SUNDAY, 4:44 P.M." I spent the day scrubbing down the apartment. I was out of lye, but was able to compensate with some additional HCl at 32 percent concentration. I wanted to be ready, and the cleansing always aided my thinking. The idea of installing small cameras in the hall seemed logical enough, but was beyond my means both fiscally and technically. I was reluctant to wait outside and watch. My usual horror of the filth of the world was very much at issue, but also an inner sense on my part that if I broke the pattern, so would my visitor.

So I scrubbed and thought, thought and scrubbed, and focused on what would come next. Perhaps I should throw open the door as soon as I heard footfalls on the stairs? Or wait for the creaking of the floorboard?

Except this had already assumed the aspects of ritual. Breaking a ritual was a fearful thing. I could not even bring myself to vary the order in which I filled my small basket at the grocery store every Sunday afternoon. How could I violate this implied trust?

In the end, I waited in the window, boots upon my clingwrap-coated feet, hat upon my latex-capped head. Just about 4:40 my visitor appeared, walking more slowly due to the crowding of the street. Visibly female now, her car coat flapped behind her, her bare head flashing with auburn curls. From my vantage, she appeared to be barefooted.

I waited until she passed out of my sight into my building, then leapt to my door, a scrubbed and polished fireplace poker in my hand. The usual noises proceeded in the usual order, until I heard my neighbor's door creak open. Mrs. Willets, in 2B, across the hall.

She must be even now encountering my mysterious visitor at the head of the stairs! I heard the murmur of voices, but could not make out what was said, even as I strained. The tones seemed to be those of guarded familiarity, not challenge.

I realized then with sick horror that everyone in my building was in on the conspiracy. My visitor left her gifts before my door, then slipped silently into Mrs. Willets's apartment to outwait me.

No one was to be trusted. I'd learned that lesson practically in my cradle. But I'd let uncouth familiarity dull my wariness of those on whom most suspicion should naturally fall—the people around me every day. They were most in a position to deduce the patterns of my life, find my secret vulnerabilities, coöperate in a clandestine manner with the police and the doctors.

Angry now, I hurled open my door, poker at the ready.

Nothing was before me but a folded leather car coat and a piece of cardstock.

Frustrated, I stalked up and down the hall twice, but there was nowhere to hide and no one hiding there. Mrs. Willets was gone. The visitor was gone.

I used the tip of the poker to pick up the car coat—it took several tries—then kicked the cardstock through my open door. I retreated, shutting, chaining, and double-locking myself into the now-dubious safety of my apartment.

I did *not* want to have to move.

When I dumped the car coat onto the floor, I saw that the tip of the poker was mucky with some foulness. On close inspection, it was a mix of blood and hair. I whirled around, weapon at the ready, to see a naked woman slumped in my flowered wingback chair. Her neck was bent at an odd angle, while blood caked the right side of her face. Oddly, she wore a latex skullcap just like mine, and latex gloves no different from my own. Her features were as familiar as my mirror.

No, I thought. *Not again.*

I hurled the incriminating poker away from me. It clattered against the steam heater, then wound up beneath, leaving a deep maroon smear on my hardwood floor. Heedless, I picked up the cardstock and looked at it.

"URDER," it read. "TOO LATE NOW."

I understood that message well enough. It could be translated as, "We are coming, beware."

Stepping to the window, I checked the sky for signs. Serpents flew from the house of the sun. The first of many sirens wailed in the distance.

Bare-headed and bare-handed, I shrugged myself into my car coat, donned my leather hat, pocketed my stack of cut-up cardboard and my father's fountain pen, and stepped out into the glittering barbs of the gimlet-eyed future.

The filth of my life I left behind me.

Such Bright and Risen Madness in Our Names

And this is me directly writing in Lovecraft's world. Which is great good fun, if you're feeling creepy enough.

I

"Long have we dwelt in wonder and glory."

The passwords are ashes in my mouth. The last of the First Resistance was crushed eight years ago, when shoggoths swarmed the final submarine base hidden in the San Juan Islands at the mouth of Puget Sound, but the Second Resistance struggles onward, ever guttering like a starveling candle flame.

My contact nods, his—or her? Does it matter anymore?—head bobbing with the slow certainty of a collapsing corpse. The Innsmouth syndrome transforms so many of us, who were once human. The voice croaking a response bespeaks more of the benthic depths than any child of woman born. "Such bright and risen days these are."

And simply as that, I am admitted to the tiled lodge here at the mouth of the Columbia, amid the ruins of Astoria. We meet with our rituals and our secret rooms in imitation of Dagon and the Silver Twilight, because their rites *worked*.

Oh, we were warned. Lovecraft, Howard, Smith—they had a glimpse of the truth, which they disguised as fiction. Who believed? People actually made up *games* about the Old Ones. As if the mile-long shattered corpse still rotting across the Seattle waterfront nine years after the U.S. Air Force's last bombing run could be made into a joke, or a rattle of dice.

All that saves us now is inattention. Cthulhu, Yog-Sothoth, all are like children in their godhood. Dead, they lay so long dreaming that they lost the habit of attending to the world, except through such rites as move them.

The First Resistance fought the elder gods themselves. But how does a B-2 fly against something that can warp the very fabric of the stars with the power of its mind? The Earth's new masters did not need their priests to awaken them to those dangers, not after the Dunedin and Papeete nuclear strikes.

The Second Resistance struggles against the priests instead. Dread Cthulhu could snuff my life with the merest of thoughts, but he will no more bother to do so than I will snuff the life of a single amoeba deep within my gut. Traveling across 600 million years of time and space, then slumbering aeons beneath the waves in lost R'lyeh, does not equip one for such minutiae. His priests are the immune system, seeking to eradicate the last, hopeless glimmerings of human liberty and free spirit.

This lodge meets within the battered Sons of Finland hall along Astoria's deserted waterfront, in the shadows of the ruined Astoria-Megler Bridge. This was once a thriving coastal city of nineteenth-century sea captains' mansions, twentieth-century fisheries, and twenty-first-century tourism.

No more. Not a mile out on the bar of the Columbia River loom the unearthly non-Euclidian geometries of one of the cyclopean Risen Cities, strangely angled walls that endlessly glimmer a feeble green while screams echo across the water. Our priestly enemies hunt far and wide, but even under their noses we are scattered and furtive. We never see the stars anymore, and little of the sun, for the Old Ones' emergence and the nuclear attacks of the First Resistance wrapped the Earth in permanent winter that varies only a little by season. A man may walk from Oregon to Washington across the frozen Columbia seven or eight months out of the year.

We are in the old ballroom now, a baker's dozen of us. That number would once have been deemed unlucky, but Cthulhu and his fellow, rival gods have drained the world of luck.

The doorward drops his cowl. He is newly come among us, and must prove himself. Now I see he is a woman, as she lifts off a crowning mask that has misshaped her head. Beneath she is actually a reasonable-seeming human being, albeit as grubby and hunger-raddled as the rest of us. She slips from her robe as well, unhooks a padded hump, releases bindings on her legs, and stands straight, clad now in only blue jeans and a faded black T-shirt advertising a band called Objekt 775.

This is like looking at a piece of the past. I wonder where her parka is.

Inspired, I slip my cloak free and let it fall, along with my own fatigue coat, until I am clad only in ragged thermal underwear and combat boots. I am barely transformed, my hands overlarge and my fingers overblunt, but the change seems to have stopped there, as can happen with we who resist strongly enough.

Around me, others remove their cowls and hoods and cloaks, until we stand as an array of human and formerly human faces. Some eyes are bulbous and unblinking, others scowl furiously, but we all have the full measure of one another for the first time in years.

Also for the first time in years, as I look at our doorward, I feel stirrings in my groin. A natural woman . . .

"I am come from the lodge in Crescent City," she announces. Now her voice is blessedly normal as well. "Bringing news from Mendocino and further south." There are no lodges in the formerly great cities of the world, because none of those cities remain whole and unpolluted. "A lodge along the Sea of Cortez has made an important discovery. We have found a poison that will harm even the undying priests amid their armors and their spells."

"Despite the Old Ones' protection?" I ask.

"Yes." She smiles at me, and I am erect for the first time in years.

II

Just as foretold, the Old Ones are stripping the Earth from pole to pole. They are in no hurry, not by human standards—surely they perceive time so differently from us, this past decade may all be a single moment not yet passed to them, one thunderous tick of the clock of the long now.

Strangely, in places of some technology where electricity can still be induced to function, odd corners of the world away from the attention of the priests and their gods, we find that many of our space assets remain in order. Curiously, this is despite the abilities of the Byakhee and Mi-go to traverse the emptiness between planets. The last cosmonauts starved on the ISS seven years ago, and the station has since fallen burning from the sky, but their observations had proved invaluable.

Likewise weather and spy satellites, not all of which have yet strayed from their courses or lost their mechanical minds.

The world's cities were crushed or blasted or sickened, sometimes by human effort in the First Resistance, more often by the Old Ones themselves when they finally stirred from their watery graves. Now great, slow waves of fungal rot progress across the continents like a nightmare tide, swallowing forests and prairies and bottomlands alike. I've been as far east as Estes Park, and looked down on the Great Plains being scoured to bedrock. The mountains and coastlines are yet spared, but surely that is only a matter of time.

With this data, and a tenuous network of wanderers and observers, the Second Resistance has our guesses about how many years are left to do something against the priests who focus the lamps of the Old Ones' eyes like mad projectionists beaming death about the world. That the gods themselves are narcoleptic was perhaps the world's saving grace, before someone, somewhere, finally succeeded in summoning them to shore in their fullest strength.

We must believe it happened thusly, for if they returned only because the stars were right, well, no one can fight the stars.

Even the most optimistic of us do not bet on more than two decades remaining, and the general consensus is less than ten years. The loss of biomass may have started an irreversible decline in the atmospheric oxygen budget. What isn't killed by the growing fungal tides, freezes to death instead. We might win, by freakish luck and blind chance, only to perish as free men instead of slaves.

No, we are not even slaves, for slaves have value. We are but an infestation, an annoyance or perhaps a sport to the priests, less than dust to the Old Ones.

Still, we make our plans, and we gather our data, and we try. What else can we do? The human race is terminal, a cancer patient at full metastasis, every organ riddled with rot, the specter of death crushing a bit more air from every heaving of the lungs.

So I listen to this plan to cultivate an obscure type of jellyfish venom. Surely, like the fungi, it is those jellyfish who far more resemble the Old Ones than the cephalopods and amphibians old Howard Phillips Lovecraft was so fond of citing. This beautiful, as-yet untainted young woman—how?—whose name we will never know and who must have been a child when the end first came, explains how the vial she carries can be cultivated in long, low trays of saltwater, with an admixture of organic nutrients to sustain the jellyfish cells that produce the requisite toxin.

It is Julia Child by way of *War of the Worlds*. We plot the downfall of humanity's most vile traitors via kitchen science, and hope to blind the Old Ones back into restless slumber in doing so.

III

I stay that night in the lodge, for my string of boltholes doesn't begin until about fifteen river miles inland, at Knappa, Oregon. As is our usual practice, most of the others leave. Those far along into the trans-formation, including Madeleine Gervais whom I'd known quite well back before the end, are far more nervous about this plan. The girl from Crescent City is unable to tell us how the poison might affect *us*, only that it has worked on captured priests, who cannot be slain except by extreme violence, followed by reduction and burning of the corpse.

We can make them die unknowing. Oh, the joy that thought brings me. These traitors who have already brought the deaths of billions are beyond any redemption of suffering or vengeance.

Curling in my little nest of borrowed blankets in one of the old base-ment saunas, I am quite surprised when the girl comes to me. I know her by her footsteps and her scent already.

Her fingers brush my shoulder, the light pressure of them through the fabric of the blanket the first human touch I have known in almost nine years. We do not hug, or even clasp hands, in the Second Resis-tance. "I saw that you understood," she whispers.

The hairs on my neck prickle, as my cock strains like a clothyard shaft. "I do," I whisper, then immediately curse the echoed meaning of *those* particular words. I still wear my wedding ring, though my finger has grown around it until the band is almost invisible. Most days I cannot recall the faces of my wife and daughter.

"It is darker here." She squats back on her heels, shadows against shadow, barely an outline through some stray bit of light elsewhere in the basement. It is enough for me to notice the swing of her right breast beneath the concert T-shirt, and I recall enough of women to know she has done this on purpose.

"Darker than California?"

"Yes." She shivers slightly. I realize her nipple has stiffened to something pleasingly mouth-filling. "So many of the Old Ones love their cold."

"They are creatures of space, and night, and the darkest depths." For no good reason, I add, "Such bright and risen madness in our names."

That hand touches me again as the breast strains against its enclosing fabric. "Are you lonely?" she asks in a soft, lost voice. I am too taken up in her to wonder at the question, for already I am lifting my blanket to shew her just how lonely I am.

IV

The woman is gone the next morning, a note telling me she heads north for the Aberdeen lodge, if it can still be found. Here in Oregon we've had no word from the Washington side this year since the river thawed in May, though in past years they've come across at Longview two or three times a month by boat during the free-flowing months. Priests burned out the Lincoln City Lodge last December, the members stripped and broken and laid before the dark tide of shoggoths, digital prints of their deaths tacked to walls and telephone poles all up and down the Northwest coast as a warning to the remaining feral humans.

No such word of Aberdeen, for good or ill.

I should go back to my own routines, but there are vats of jellyfish toxin to establish. Someone will have to scale the odd-angled walls of the Risen City and carry the stuff in. Or allow themselves to be captured, and pray for a slow enough death to be able to spread the poison first.

In any case, the sauna room smells of sex and me and her, and I know I shall never again experience the sweet caress of a woman. The scent-memories are precious, while they remain.

I work for days, as Madeleine stays with me after the last stragglers depart. She knows that I touched the girl with my body, just as I will never again touch her lidless, staring eyes, and damp, spotted skin. The painful memory returns, that it was she who gave me the wedding band I still wear.

Can she be jealous now, beyond the end of all things?

Still, the little cells grow, the trays glowing slightly in a curious echo of the walls just offshore. Madeleine's lips are no longer well formed for speaking, and neither is her larynx, but she grunts her fears to me.

The toxins will kill us all, or at least those of us who are transforming. Her. Me. Everyone but the girl from Crescent City. Or perhaps the toxins will kill no one, and this is all but a cruel hoax. Maybe the Old Ones toy with us, even now.

Finally I take her into my arms one night, in the old sauna. Though true coupling is not possible for us, I make love to my memory of who my wife once was, while her lidless eyes weep acid tears to scar my chest and shoulder.

V

In the morning, I find her shriveled corpse next to the toxin trays. A faint smear still glows around her lips. I wonder if I should cry, but tears are years gone.

There is nothing more to be done. I gather my strength and purpose. As we were instructed, I press the cells in old cloth, so the toxin can be more easily spread by air or contact. As it dries, I bottle the stuff into old light bulbs from which the metal stems have been broken off, then bind them with duct tape. If the priests beat me upon my capture, they will be very surprised.

I leave detailed notes and diagrams shewing our work, for when others of the lodge return. Eventually I step outside into the chilled mist and stare across the water at the Risen City. I shall take a dory and row me down to that watery hell, bringing blindness to the Old Ones, and death to my immortal enemies.

As I ply the oars, I wonder if the girl and Madeleine planned this for me. The waters around me roil with evil, the sky is Armageddon-dark, and I find it does not matter.

"I love you," I tell the world. Then I row some more.

Her Fingers Like Whips, Her Eyes Like Razors

I always thought the fair folk Under the Hill were creepy as hell. So I set about showing that.

Mother never has been patient. Old as she is—and there are hills Above of which she can remember the birth—time has never blessed her with the sort of wisdom lore informs us is inevitable with the assumption of the grace of age.

This does not bother me. I am not one of the mabkin. They toil at her leisure, they sweat to her pleasures, they suffer to her pains. Sooner be a worker ant in a burrow than one of those pretty, pretty, doomed butterflies. Mother always pulls the wings off her children and eats them in the end.

No, my purpose in this life is different. Someone must keep the Doors, after all. The great copper hinges on which the boundaries of night and day swing do not clean themselves of verdigris. Neither do the shadowed locks forged by Chronos himself in the time before the light first came into the world oil their own tumblers.

You who live Above tell stories. I am never certain if this is a sickness or a blessing, though in my weaker moments over a glass of lifewater I have confessed a time or two to envy. I have even caught the way of it from you. Everyone who comes begging at the Doors launches their plea on the wings of some tale. They tuck their feet beneath their knees amid the riot of spring flowers, or a moment later they huddle fast amid the snowdrifts and the winter wind, or a moment after that lean with the stiffness of their aging against some patient draft animal and croak out a querulous plea against the final bloody sunset of their mayfly days.

The Doorkeeper listens to all. The Doorkeeper hears all. The Doorkeeper is the keyhole to Mother's heart, here Below. Mother is not patient, but I am, for I hold her heart in my left pocket along with a hawk feather, three apple seeds, and the list of True Names, which is so short and infinite that it has been scriven on the inside of a silver thimble.

Come, then, and tell me your story, for Mother will never listen, and I always will. Like the icy seed of winter hidden inside a summer rain, Below is always here. Like the golden fire of summer hidden inside a winter freeze, Below is always here. And you will never be on the right side of the Doors, unless your tale makes the seahawk fly from my vest, the three trees bloom, and the thimble whisper your True Name in the voice of the distant, amniotic sea.

Then Mother's heart will take another beat, she will age another day, and we will all be a moment closer to freedom.

Come. Tell me.

The chemo port implant scars on Addison's right chest still ached a little, and she ignored the continuing sensation that the surgeons had left a Bic pen inside her. Another twinge, to the chorus from her ribs and the partial thoracectomy that had removed her tumor. Besides, she was away from all that now, for a little while. Or maybe longer, despite the appointments next week back in Laramie.

The day here was fine and cold, the wind brisk, and she was outdoors. Addison climbed through what felt like more bracken than any hills had a right to be covered with. A week earlier, she hadn't even known what bracken was. Ferns and flowers?

Hills without mountains seemed strange to her, but she was a long way from Wyoming. The last few nights camping in her little tent, she'd felt a long way from anywhere. It had taken her great mental effort to remember the name of the little airport she'd flown into over the weekend, after changing planes four times and crossing an ocean.

"I'm not worried," she told the empty sky, over which not even a hawk circled. The sky held no answers.

She slipped a half-eaten Clif Bar from her pocket, which slowly became a three-quarter-eaten Clif Bar before her gag reflex kicked in. *Figs, who the hell ever thought figs were a good idea?* Addison was eating less each day, which was odd, because she wasn't really at any significant altitude.

Just the top of the world, from this view.

Her grandfather Locke's words kept coming back to her.

Start at the Heartbeck
The sunset behind you
Always climb higher
You'll find your way true

He'd sung her to sleep with those words when she was a baby and a little girl, and later on made her memorize them. Addison had spent her winters with Grandfather Locke in the little house in Laramie, while her parents and brothers worked their high-country ranch. She'd been too weak for the deep snows, she'd been told all her childhood. Too delicate a constitution.

Addison had never had a cold a day in her life. Not a moment's illness.

Not until now.

She crossed a ridge so low and subtle she almost missed the fact she wasn't climbing anymore. The sun stood overhead, directly at its zenith. The scent was different here—the slight rank of bracken overwhelmed by the underlying acidity of the stony soil and a damp tang of metal.

The smell of magic, when you feel like you've been chewing wires.

Where the hell had that thought come from? In Grandfather's voice.

There wasn't any higher to climb. Not here, not now. No beck to put at her back, either. The watercourses had vanished to rivulets a day ago, and she was carrying her last two quarts on her hip. All she saw in front of her was a shallow bowl of a high valley, a place that by rights should have cupped a little tarn reflecting the blue sky with the indolence of water.

Close your eyes and follow your nose.

Grandfather Locke had died last winter with a smile on his face, looking no older than he ever had since she was born. Not even tired, just finished, as if his life work had been carving a young adult Addison from the stuff of childhood.

Now he was talking to her.

So she listened. That's what she was doing here, right? Walking east from the Heartbeck.

Addison closed her eyes and breathed in the place she stood. Trace of bracken. Soil. Wind, bearing a bit of damp from some more fortunate locale. The droppings of something small and herbivorous. Metal.

Metal.

Copper.

Mouth open, she turned, facing first one way then the other, until she thought she knew where the metal tang was strongest. She advanced slowly, her hiking pole a cane now. No point in breaking an ankle in the one gopher hole for forty miles on this high, hollow hill.

Did they even have gophers on this side of the Atlantic?

Step, sniff. Step, sniff. Step, sniff.

When she bumped into the solid mass on the ground, Addison was not the least bit surprised.

She opened her eyes to see a pair of copper slabs stretched before her. No, not slabs, doors, for all that they were flat against the bottom of the little valley. They looked like nothing so much as the blast doors to a Wyoming missile silo, if the air force had been hiring Italian espresso-machine designers to build the Cold War infrastructure.

The margins of each door were worked in high-relief chasings of snakes and trefoils, which themselves seemed to form a script, though not one she recognized. Tiny eyes winked between the leaves. Tiny mouths screamed ecstasy and terror. Battles and seductions worked their way across the vast spaces between the margins. The doors seemed almost alive.

She looked about to find a girl who hadn't been there a moment before sitting on one corner of the doors, twenty feet away. A young woman, much her build and age, wearing a rather smart denim miniskirt and a hunter green ragged wool vest far too large for her. And apparently nothing else, which made Addison's heart skip a beat before she looked away from the curve of exposed breast, then found herself drawn back again.

The girl was the girl in the mirror.

"Hello," the stranger said. Her voice was soft, familiar, though the accent was strange, like nothing Addison had ever heard.

"Uh, hello." Addison's own voice sounded odd in her ears now.

They stared at one another, ordinary brown eyes locked on ordinary brown eyes. She'd never been anything special, had always longed for the fiery red hair and green eyes of all the brave servant girls who were future queens in the books she'd devoured from the library, but Addison's looks had remained resolutely plain.

On this girl in her ragged, open vest, here in the crown of the high hills, those looks were as exotic as any raving beauty on the page. Unthinking, Addison plucked at her own hair.

"Do you bear sorrow or joy?" asked the girl.

"You—" Addison blurted, then stopped. "You look like me."

Laughter that could have rung the bells of morning. *Why don't I laugh like that?* "Better to say you look like me, stranger." A long, thoughtful pause, something deceptively close to compassion in those brown eyes. "No one finds these doors by accident. Well, almost no one. But surely not you."

"No, no . . ." Addison paused, stared at her own slender, callused fingers a moment. She was still thirty feet from the other girl, but she could *smell* her. A far-too-familiar scent somewhere between sex and sleep. It was . . . disturbing. "Grandfather sent me."

"Whose grandfather?" Now the voice was gentle.

Why was this question important? She'd fallen into some modern version of the riddle game, like talking to her therapist but with such different, unknowable stakes. Addison stalled by walking around the verge of the doors. There was certainly no way she was going to set foot *on* them.

The other girl was patient. Addison got the impression the stranger would have waited a decade for her to round the corner and walk face-to-face to answer the question.

"My grandfather. Grandfather Locke."

"*Morfar* or *farfar*?"

"Excuse me?"

"Your mother's father or your father's father?"

"Oh. Mother's. Daddy was a Keyes."

Something stirred in the girl's vest pocket. She glanced down in apparent surprise, looking into a dark place that seemed much deeper than the ragged woolen vest could contain. "Lock and key," mused the girl.

"I'm Addison Keyes."

The pocket shifted again. Was she carrying an animal in there?

The girl just stared back.

Eventually Addison filled the silence. "And you are . . . ?"

The answer was prompt if unhelpful. "Waiting."

"For what?"

She patted the copper doors. "Locks and keys."

Something shifted in Addison's head, half-forgotten words of Grandfather Locke's. Another verse.

Until you are truly lost
You will never be there
Always climb higher
And never ask where

He really had been a bit strange . . .

"I can take the hint," Addison said. "Nominate determinism is just silly, but if you want me to be, I am both a Locke and a Keyes."

"If you think names do not count, then you have learned nothing." This close, the girl touched Addison's hair, then sniffed. A spark passed between them, like petting a cat during thunderstorm weather. Addison didn't jump, but was surprised at the tingle inside her breasts and groin. "You were raised by a mabkin."

"What?"

"Your *morfar*. Locke? He is a mabkin. I can smell him on you."

"He passed away last summer."

"Really?" She smiled sweetly at Addison, though there was nothing but menace in those pearly teeth for a moment. Addison wondered if she, too, were almost-fanged. "Did you see the body?"

"N-no. He died in the hospital, and the funeral was closed casket."

The smile was positively evil. "If you dug it up, you'd find a dead wolf and a few stone of rags and feathers. He hasn't come home yet, but he will. *I* would know."

"And *I* would know if he was alive!" Addison shouted, suddenly enraged. "He never was going to come home, damn you. That's why he told me all the stories, and bought me a plane ticket before he died, and spent all his time filling me with ideas about wearing my clothes inside out and carrying pebbles in my pockets! He was crazy and I love him."

"You're not wearing your clothes inside out," the girl pointed out quite reasonably, ignoring Addison's anger.

"And the only rocks I have are inside my head, I swear." Addison huffed, trying to settle down. She had not come this far to fight with some imaginary twin. "He's dead, girl-whoever-you-are-in-waiting. I watched him slip away. Colon cancer, and they took it out of him three times until he was shitting in a plastic bag and eating nothing but oatmeal. Whatever a mabkin is, no one noticed on the operating table. Or in the CAT scans."

"The crab disease." This was the first time the girl seemed taken aback. "A mabkin, in the presence of a grimalkin, was struck down by the crab disease . . ."

Grimalkin? An old cat. The CAT scan? Riddles, and more stupid wordplay. Addison stuck to the point, for fear of talking in mystic circles. "What, you people don't get cancer here?"

"We die of nothing but grief or the sword. Sometimes at the same moment."

"Grandfather Locke died on the sword of cancer, then. But I held his hand when he was done. I don't think he grieved."

"Did he call for Mother?" the girl asked gently.

"Yes," said Addison, and burst into tears.

Later they sat close in front of the primus stove while Addison boiled water for ginger tea. The girl, who would answer to "Door" but called herself nothing that Addison could determine, had been delighted with a white chocolate macadamia Clif Bar. Their shadows lengthened eastward, and Addison kept wondering if she would camp up here. She wanted to see where Door would go at nightfall, because experience had already taught her about the rapid descent of frost on these hills.

Door seemed unconcerned about the passage of time, or really, anything else other than Addison's camping gear.

"You carry fire with you in a little bottle. This is so much more clever than wooden sticks."

"I have matches, too," Addison admitted.

"Surely. Monkeys are clever."

"I am not a monkey."

"Not you." That almost-fanged smile. "But you were raised among them, and you have brought back their clever ways."

"I've brought back something else, too," Addison admitted. She touched her chest, just below the right clavicle.

"Yourself, of course." The later the day grew, the more feral Door seemed to become. At noon she'd been almost reserved. Now she was tricksy.

Ignoring the chilly air, Addison slipped out of her fleece vest, unbuttoned her wool shirt, and dropped the shoulder on her thermal top, tugging the sports bra's band with it. "See this," she asked, pointing at a red-lipped seam on her neck and another on her chest.

"I could do much better." A copper blade shaped like a rhododendron leaf appeared as if from nowhere in Door's hand.

"Stop it," Addison said, slapping the girl's wrist. *Feral, feral.*

The touch caused another spark to leap between them.

With that, the blade vanished. Door cocked her head, looking for all the world like a curious robin. "What, then?"

"It's a chest port. I start chemotherapy next week back at home."

Door looked puzzled.

"Cancer. The crab disease." Addison sighed. "What killed Grandfather Locke. It's trying to kill me." She wasn't supposed to think of it that way, her therapist had been very insistent.

Now Door seemed completely taken aback. Addison wondered if the other girl's preternatural confidence faded with the light. "You have come to the Doors bearing the crab disease?"

"Well . . . yes?"

"Some come here seeking life eternal. Some come here seeking the true death of the soul, for fear of the same thing. Some come seeking riches. Or a lost love. What do you hope for here?"

Whatever Grandfather Locke set me to find, Addison thought, but did not say. Her fingers brushed her chest where the port implant ached. "He . . . He always told me I would discover where I belonged."

"You belong wherever you are," Door said simply. For the first time, Addison thought she heard compassion in the other girl's voice, but when she looked up, all she saw was the gleam of the Primus flame in Door's eyes. It was like staring into a tiny, liquid hell.

"I don't want to die," Addison whispered.

"Ah, life eternal." The smile flashed, even more fanged in the encroaching gloam. "We don't have that here. Chronos is long since fallen. We merely abide endlessly without the benefit of time."

"Cancer is a disease of time."

"*Life* is a disease of time."

Another touch, their third, and on this occasion the spark was like summer lightning. Door drew Addison into a close embrace. Like hugging herself, but not. Like masturbating, but not. Like a mirror so close one could step into it.

"Would you go Below?" Door whispered in her ear. Inside Addison's head.

"Would I come back?"

"You would carry the disease of time into the Quiet Lands. Is that what you want?"

More of Grandfather Locke's words came to her then.

Be my sword, little girl
Carry over the ocean my will
To the Mother of us all
So that she may someday lie still

Had she only ever been his pawn as well? Was even the cancer her morfar's gift to her? "I would not wish this on my worst enemy if I had one," Addison whispered to herself.

"Time is everyone's worst enemy," Door whispered back from within. "The sword of ruin. That is why it does not pass beneath these hollow hills."

"Cancer is the sword of ruin, thrust through the body." Addison thought back on Door's words. "Both grief and the sword." The disease of time, indeed.

"Your story will sweep open the doors," Door replied. "They may never shut again."

Did she want to? Who were the people under the hill to her? Mabkin, her grandfather Locke's folk, but he'd never spoken of them. Just filled her head with stories, filled her heart with his death, and filled her hand with a ticket to elsewhere.

Addison wasn't certain what choice she was making. To go home and slowly poison herself, while poisoning the cancer a little faster. Or to pass beneath these copper doors and come to face her great-grandmother, who lived outside time.

Sooner pass between the pages of a book.

You always did want to pass between the pages of a book, girl, her grandfather Locke said. *And someone must break the chains under the hill, someday.*

Though Door's fingers barely touched the copper, the slabs swung upward as if pressed forward by hands the size of houses. They smashed into the ground on each side with an echo that Addison felt deep in her bones. The inner faces of the doors were decorated just as ornately as the outside, though in the last of the twilight, the carvings seemed alive, fields of men fighting flowers while winged archers sailed overhead laughing.

A stairwell descended into darkness. The steps themselves were carved from the stone of the hill, each one bowed and worn with generations of passage. There was no light at all below, but the air smelled of roses and grave dust and meat.

It was an invitation.

A vector of change now, aimed at the deathless heart of the unchanging, Addison touched her woolen vest, fingered the seam of her denim skirt, and set off into the darkness below with an ache in her chest and her grandfather's memory in her heart.

Mother will learn patience now. If the monkeys know anything we do not, it is that death is the greatest teacher life can set before us. I am not one of the mabkin, but I have sat at the borders of Mother's realm so long I might as well be one.

That a monkey came for me is one of those blessings which can only be the world playing with its own sense of humor. Her stove burned me a little, but I got the hot tea off and into my belly. It will be strange, eating their food, but I have a ticket that will take me somewhere else.

Change is coming Below, where change has never been welcome. I wonder who set the Locke and the Keyes on their course, or if that is just another of the world's little jokes upon itself.

Leaving the flame behind to light the night, I follow Addison Keyes's scent back down from the high hills. As Above, so Below. Mother's fingers may be like whips, but they will never tear at me now. Mother's eyes may be like razors, but they will never cut at me now.

I thank my sister, I thank myself, and I sing a song of crabs and cats as the bracken whips at my hiking boots and my monkey pants and I bounce down into the wider world armed with bright teeth and a copper knife.

I am coming. I might even become a Mother myself someday, in Addison's high Wyoming hills.

Are you afraid? Or are you laughing?

Mother Urban's Booke of Dayes

This is the only story I ever wrote in which my daughter appears directly, as herself, though under another name. I always thought I could do more with the character, but she grew up too fast, and every time I thought I understood her, she had become a different young woman.

In a basement that smelled of mold and old cleansers, Danny Knifepoint Wielder prayed down the rain. The house wasn't any older than the Portland neighborhood around it. Most driveways were populated with minivans, children's bicycles, heaps of bark dust and gravel accumulated for yard projects postponed through the dark months of winter. None of Danny's neighbors knew the role he played in their lives. They would have been horrified if they had.

Not making it to church on time carried scarcely a ripple of consequence compared to what would happen if Danny didn't pray the world forward. Lawn sprinklers chittering, children screeching at their play—these were the liturgical music of his rite.

"Heed me, Sky."

Danny circled the altar in his basement.

"Hear my pleas, freely given from a free soul."

Green shag carpeting was no decent replacement for the unbending grass of the plains on which the Corn Kings had once vomited out their lives to ensure the harvest.

"I have bowed to the four winds and the eight points of the rose."

Woodgrain paneling echoed memories of the sanctifying rituals that had first blessed this workroom.

"Heed me now, that your blessing may fall upon the fields and farms." With a burst of innate honesty he added: ". . . and gardens and patios and window boxes of this land."

"Daniel Pierpont Wilder!" his mother yelled down the stairs. "Are you talking to a girl down there?"

"Mooooom," Danny wailed. "I'm buuuusy!"

"Well, come be busy at the table. I'm not keeping your lunch warm so you can play World of Warships."

"War*craft*, Mom," he muttered under his breath. But he put away his knife, then raced up the steps two at a time.

Behind him, on the altar, his wilting holly rustled as if a breeze tossed the crown of an ancient oak tree deep within an untouched forest. Oil smoldered and rippled within the beaten brass bowl. Rain, wherever it had gotten to, did not fall.

That night Danny climbed up the Japanese maple in the side yard and scooted onto the roof. He'd been doing that since he was a little kid. Mom said he was still a kid, and always would be, but at twenty-two Danny had long been big enough to have to mind the branches carefully. If he waited until after Mom went to her room to watch TiVoed soap operas through the bottom of a bottle of Bombay Sapphire, she didn't seem to notice. The roofing composite was gritty and oddly slick, still warm with the trapped heat of the day, and smelled faintly of tar and mold.

The gutters, as always, were a mess. Something was nesting in the chimney again. The streetlight he'd shot out with his BB gun remained dark, meaning that the rooftop stayed in much deeper shadow than otherwise.

Sister Moon rising in the east was neither new, nor old, but halfway in between. Untrustworthy, that was, Danny knew. If Sister Moon couldn't make up her mind, how was Sky to know which way to pass, let alone the world as a whole to understand how to turn? This was the most dangerous time in the circle of days.

He had his emergency kit with him. Danny spent a lot of time on his emergency kit, making and remaking lists.

— Nalgene bottle of boiled tap water
— *The Old Farmer's Almanac*
— *Mother Urban's Booke of Dayes*
— ~~Silver~~ stainless steel knife
— Paper clips
— Sisal twine

— Spare retainer
— Bic lighter (currently a lime green one)
— Beeswax candles (black and white)

That last was what he spent most of his allowance on. Beeswax candles, and sometimes the right herbs or incense. That and new copies of the *Almanac* every year. The *Booke of Dayes* he'd found at a church rummage sale—it was one of those big square paperback books, like his *The Complete Idiot's Guide to Magic,* with a cover that pretended to look like some old-timey tome or grimoire. The entire kit fit into a Transformers knapsack so dorky looking he wasn't in any danger of losing it on the bus or having it taken from him, except maybe by some really methed-out homeless guy or something.

Danny had figured out a long time ago that he'd get farther in life if he didn't spend time worrying about being embarrassed about stuff.

This night he lay back on the roof, one foot braced on the plumbing vent stack in case he fell asleep and rolled off again. The black eye he'd gotten that time had taken some real explaining.

It hadn't rained in Portland for sixty days now, which was very weird for the Pacific Northwest, and even the news was talking about the weather a lot more. Danny knew it was his fault, that he'd messed up the Divination of Irrigon specified in the *Booke of Dayes* to shelter the summer growing season from Father Sun's baleful eye. That had been back in June, and he'd gotten widdershins and deosil mixed up, then snapped the Rod of Seasons by stepping on it, which was really just a dowel from Lowe's painted with the Testor's model paints he'd found at a rummage sale.

You could never tell which compromises the gods would understand about, for the sake of a good effort, and which ones brought down their wrath. Kind of like back in school, with his counselors and his tutors, before he'd quit because it was stupid and hard and too easy all at the same time.

Anyway, he'd gone the wrong way around the altar, then broken the Rod, and the rain had dried up to where Mom's tomatoes were coming in nicely but everything else in the yard was in trouble.

Since then, Danny had been studying the almanac and the *Booke of Dayes,* trying to find a way to repair his error. He was considering the Pennyroyal Rite, but hadn't yet figured out where to find the herb. The guy at the Lowe's garden center claimed he'd never heard of it.

He'd finally realized that having offended Sky, he would have to ask Sky how best to apologize. And so the rooftop at night. Sky during the day was single-minded, the bright servant of Father Sun. Sky in darkness served as a couch for Sister Moon, but also the tiny voices of the Ten Thousand Stars sang in their sparkling choir. Sometimes a star broke loose and wrote its name across heaven in a long, swift stroke that Danny had tried again and again to master in his own shaky penmanship.

Tonight, as every night for the past week, he hoped for the stars to tell him how to make things right.

A siren wailed nearby. *Fire engine*, Danny thought, and wondered if the flames had been sanctified, or were a vengeance. More likely someone had simply dropped a pan of bacon, but you could never tell what was of mystic import. Mother Urban was very clear on that, in her *Booke of Dayes*. Even the way the last few squares of toilet paper were stuck to the roll could tell you much about the hours to come. Or at least the state of your tummy.

He listened to the trains rumble on the Union Pacific mainline a few blocks away. Something peeped as it flew overhead in the darkness. The air smelled dry, and almost tired, with a mix of lawn and car and cooking odors. The night was peaceful. If not for the scratchiness of the roof under his back, he might have relaxed.

A star hissed across the sky, drawing its name in a pulsing white line. Danny sat up suddenly, startled and thrilled, but his foot slipped off the vent pipe, so that he slid down the roof and right over the edge, catching his right wrist painfully on the gutter before crashing into the rhododendron.

He sat up gasping in pain, left hand clutching the wound.

"That was not so well done," said a girl.

Danny's breath stopped, leaving his mouth to gape and pop. He tried to talk, but only managed to squeak out an "I—"

Then his Transformers knapsack dropped off the roof and landed on his head. The girl—for surely she was a girl—leaned over and grabbed it before Danny could sort out what had just happened.

"Nice pack," she said dryly. He was mortified. Then she opened it and began pulling his emergency kit out, piece by piece.

Miserable, Danny sat in the rhododendron where he had fallen and looked at his tormentor. She was skinny and small, maybe five feet tall. Hard to tell in the dark, but she looked Asian. Korean?

Though sometimes Mexicans looked Asian to him, which Danny knew was stupid. She wore scuff-kneed jeans and a knit top with ragged sleeves.

He had no idea if she was twelve or twenty-two. Of course, Danny mostly wasn't sure about himself. He knew what his ID card said, the stupid fake driver's license they gave to people who couldn't drive so those people who were completely undeserving of pity or scorn could get a bus pass or cash an SSI check. His ID card said *he* was twenty-two, but lots of times Danny felt twelve.

Almost never in a good way.

"This your stuff?" She turned the retainer over in her fingers as if she'd never seen one.

"Nah." Danny stared at the broken branches sticking out from under his thighs. "They belonged to some other guy I met up on the roof."

She laughed, her voice soft as Sister Moon's light. "You should tell that other guy he'd get farther with a silver athame than with a stainless steel butter knife."

"It's the edge that counts," Danny said through his pout.

The girl bent close. He could almost hear the smile in her voice, though he wouldn't meet her eye. "You'd be surprised how many people don't know that," she said, so near to him that her breath was warm on his face. "A sharpened paper clip and grass cuttings will serve for most rituals, if the will is strong enough and the need is great."

Now he looked up. She *was* smiling at him, and not in the let's-smack-the-stupid-kid-around way he'd grown used to over the years. Then she reached into her sleeve and pulled out a short, slightly curved blade that gleamed dully under the gaze of Sister Moon. "Try this one," she said, handing it to him, "and look on page 238 of the *Booke of Dayes*."

Danny stared at the knife a moment, then glanced up again. She was gone. Not mysteriously, magically vanished—he could hear the girl singing in the street as she picked up a bicycle and pedaled away with the faint clatter of chain and spokes. But still gone.

The knife, though . . . Touching it, he drew blood from his fingertip. *Wow,* he thought, then raced inside to read page 238 by flashlight under the covers.

Reversal of Indifference

Betimes the Practitioner hath wrought some error of ritual, perhaps through inattention, or even a fault of the Web of the world in disturbance about zir sacred space, and so the Practitioner hath lost the full faith and credit of the kindlier spirits as well as the older, quieter Forces in the World.

Zie may in such moments of tribulation turn to the Reversal of Indifference, which shall remake the rent asundered in the fabric of the Practitioner's practice, and so invite the beneficent forces once more within zir circle of influence. Thus order may be restored to the business of the World, and the Practitioner rest easier in zir just reward.

Zie should gather three mice, material with which to bind their Worldly selves, and all the tools of the Third Supplicative Form before attempting the exercise in the workbook for this section.

Danny didn't have the workbook—he'd only found *Mother Urban's Booke of Dayes* by accident in the first place. He'd checked, though; the workbook wasn't available on Amazon or anywhere. So he'd done without. Most of the time he'd been able to sort out the needed ritual, trusting in his own good faith to bridge any gaps. This was not so different. He understood the Third Supplicative Form well enough. Still, he'd never noticed the Reversal of Indifference before.

It was such a big book, with so many pages.

Mice, and binding, though. There were mice in the basement, in the heater room and sometimes in the laundry closet. He went to set out peanut butter in the bottom of a tall trash bucket, built a sort of ramp up to the lip of the bucket out of a stack of dog-eared Piers Anthony novels, then considered how to bind the sacrificial animals once they were his.

The answer, as it so often seemed to be, was duct tape. Danny was excited enough to want to try the Reversal of Indifference that same night. He had his new athame, and the star had certainly sent him a detailed message in the mouth of that strange Asian girl. A practitioner could only be so lucky, and he aimed to use his luck for all it was worth.

Danny had harvested four mice within the hour, so he left one inside the trash bucket for a spare in case he made a mistake. One by one, he took the other three and wrapped them in duct tape. They were trembling, terrified little silver mummies, only their shifting black eyes and quivering noses protruding.

"Sorry, little guys," he whispered, feeling a bit sick. But magic was serious business, the lifeblood of the world, and he *had* failed to call down the rain.

No one would miss a few mice.

Then Danny made himself sicker wondering if one of the mice was a mother, and would little mouse babies starve in some nest behind the walls.

He shifted his thoughts away with the heft of the athame in his hand. The knife was tiny, but nothing felt like silver. The Third Supplicative Form—as best as Danny understood without the workbook available—was a long chant followed by the delivery of the sacrifice. Usually he sacrificed a candy bar, or maybe a dollar bill. In tonight's case, the sacrifice was obvious.

This time Danny remembered to take the battery out of the smoke alarm. Then he lit his candles, purified his hands in the bowl of Costco olive oil, and began the chant. The mice shivered on the altar, one little mummy actually managing to roll over and almost fall off onto the green shag. He nudged it back into place and tried to concentrate on magical thoughts instead of what he was about to do.

When the moment came, the mice bled more than he thought they could. One managed to bite his finger before dying. Still, he laid them in the hibachi, squirted Ronson lighter fluid on them, and flicked them with the Bic. The duct tape burned with a weird, sticky kind of smell, while the mice were like tiny roasts.

Guilt-ridden, Danny grabbed the trash bucket to go free the last mouse into the yard, but halfway up the basement stairs he had to throw up. By the time he got outside, the last mouse had drowned in the pool of vomit, floating inert with the potato chunks and parsley flecks from dinner.

He washed his mouth and hands for a long time, but still went to bed feeling grubby and ill.

Morning brought rain.

Danny lay in his little bed—he had to curl up to even lie in the blue race car, but Mom kept insisting how much he'd loved the thing when he was seven—and listened to water patter on the roof. Portland rain, like taking a shower with the tap on low. It didn't rain so much in August, but it was never this dry either.

He'd done it.

Sky had heard him, and returned blessings to the land.

Danny didn't know if it was the girl's athame, or the mice, or just more careful attention to the *Booke of Dayes*. He wanted to bounce out of bed and write Mother Urban another letter to her post office box in New Jersey, but he wanted more to run outside and play in the rain.

Then he thought some more about the mice, and looked at the red spot on his finger where one of them had bitten him, and wept a while into his pillow.

It rained for days, as if this were February and the Pacific storms were pouring over the Coastal Mountains one after another. Danny performed the Daily Observances and leafed through the *Booke of Dayes* in his quiet moments to see what else he'd missed besides the Reversal of Indifference. Mostly he let Sky take care of the land and wondered when he'd see Father Sun again.

Mom seemed distracted, too. Danny knew she loved him, but she was so busy with her work and taking care of the house, she didn't always remember to hug him like their therapist said to, or feed him like their doctor said to.

That was okay. He could hug himself when he needed, and there was always something to eat in the kitchen.

So mostly Danny mooned around the house, watched the rain fall, and wished he could take the bus to Lowe's to look for new magical herbs in the garden center. He wasn't allowed TV, and there wasn't much else to do except read *Mother Urban* or one of his fantasy novels.

Except as the days went by, the rain did not let up. First Mom became angry about her tomatoes. Then he saw a dead puppy bumping down the gutter out front, drowned and washing away in a Viking funeral without the burning boat. The news kept talking about the water, and how the East Side Sewer Project wasn't ready for the overflow, and whether the Willamette River would reach flood stage, and which parks had been closed because the creeks were too swollen to be safe.

Danny watched outside to see if the Asian girl came by again on her bike. He wanted to ask her what to do now, what to do next. There was no point in climbing the roof to ask Sky—the only answer he would get there was a faceful of water and Oregon's endless, feature-less dirty cotton flannel rainclouds.

If anything, Sky was even less informative in such a rain than when Father Sun shouted the heat of his love for the world.

So Danny sat by the dining room window looking out on the street and leafed through *Mother Urban's Booke of Dayes* for anything he could find about rain, about water, about asking the sun to return once more.

He read all about the *Spelle for a Seizure of the Bladder*, but real-ized after a while that wasn't the right kind of water. *Maidens' Tears & the Love of Zir Hearte* had seemed promising, but even from the first words, Danny knew better. Still, he'd studied the lists of rose hips and the blood of doves and binding cords braided from zir hair. Closer, in a way, was the *Drain Cantrip*, though that seemed more straightfor-ward, being a spell of baking soda and vinegar and gravity.

Danny tried to imagine how much baking soda and vinegar it would take to open up the world to swallow all this rain.

The news talked about people packing sandbags along the water-front downtown. All the floodgates were open in the dam at Oregon City. A girl drowned in the Clackamas River at Gladstone, trying to feed bedraggled ducks. A grain barge slipped its tow and hit a pillar of the Interstate Bridge, shutting down the Washington-bound traffic for days.

All his fault. All this water.

He prayed. He stood before his altar and begged. He even tried the roof one night, but only managed to sprain his ankle slipping—again—on the way down. And he read the *Booke of Dayes*. Studying it so closely, Danny realized that Mother Urban must have been a very strange author, because often he could not find the same spell twice, yet would locate spells he'd never seen before in all his flipping through the book.

Meanwhile, his own mother complained about the weather, set buckets in the living room and bathroom under the leaks, and sent Danny to the basement or his bedroom more often than not. Some-thing had happened to her job—too wet to work outdoors at the Parks Department—and she stopped using the TiVo, just watching TV through the filter of gin all day and all night. He wasn't sure she slept anymore.

Danny was miserable. This was all his fault. He never should have listened to the Asian girl, never should have killed those mice, not even for a ritual. If only he could bring them back to life, or set that stupid, fateful star back into the sky.

He couldn't undo what was done, but maybe he could do something else. That was when he had his big idea. It couldn't rain *everywhere,* right? If he worked the ritual again, somewhere *else,* the rain would leave Oregon behind to move on. Things would be better again, for Mom, for his neighbors, for the people fighting the flood. For everyone!

Excited but reluctant, Danny caught five more mice. He put them in a Little Oscar cooler with some newspaper, along with cheese and bread to eat, and pounded holes in the lid with a hammer and a screwdriver so they could breathe. He gathered the rest of his materials—the silver athame, duct tape, the brass bowl, the bottle of Costco olive oil, the Ronson lighter fluid—and stuffed all of it in his dorky Transformers knapsack.

All he needed was money for a bus ticket to Seattle. They wouldn't even notice the extra rain there. Mom never really slept, but she was full of gin all the time now, and spent a lot of her day breathing through her mouth and staring at nothing. Danny waited for her noises to get small and regular, then crept into her room.

"Mom," he said quietly.

She lay in her four-poster bed, the quilted coverlet spotted with gin and ketchup. Her housedress hung open, so Danny could see her boobs flopping, even the pink pointy nipples, which made him feel weird in a sick-but-warm way. Her head didn't turn at the sound of his voice.

"Momma, I'm hungry." That wasn't a lie, though mostly he'd been eating the strange old canned food at the back of the pantry for days.

She snorted, then slumped.

"Momma, I'm taking some money from your purse to go buy food." There was the lie, the one he'd get whipped for, and have to pray forgiveness at the altar later on. *Mother Urban's Booke of Dayes* was very clear on the penalties for a Practitioner's lying to the Spirit Worlde.

But without the money, he could not move the rain. Besides, surely he'd buy food on the way to Seattle. So it wasn't *really* a lie.

He reached into her purse, pushed aside the pill bottles and lipsticks and doctor's shots to find her little ladybug money purse. Too scared to count it out, Danny took the whole thing and fled without kissing his mother good-bye or tucking her boobs back in her dress or even locking the front door.

Danny's pass got him on the number 33 bus downtown. Even in the floods, Tri-Met kept running. The bus's enormous wheels seemed to be able to splash through deep puddles where cars were stuck. The rain had soaked him on the way to the bus stop, and at the bus shelter, and even now its clear fingers were clawing at the window to drag him out. Danny clutched his Little Oscar cooler and his Transformers knapsack and stared out, daring the rain to do its worst.

If he made the rain mad enough, and Sky, who was both mother and father of the rain, maybe it would follow him to Seattle even without the Reversal of Indifference.

The Greyhound station downtown had a sign on the door that said NO SERVICE TODAY DUE TO INCLEMENT WEATHER. Danny wasn't sure exactly what "inclement" meant, but he understood the sign.

He sat out front and stared at the train station down the street, crying. It was in the rain, no one would notice him in tears. The Little Oscar emitted scratching noises as the mice did whatever it was mice did in the dark. He knew he should draw out *Mother Urban's Booke of Dayes* and try to work out what to do next.

Then the girl on the bike showed up again. She came splashing through puddles with a big smile on her face, as though this flood were a sprinkler on a summer lawn. The bike skidded sideways in front of him, splashing Danny with grimy water. She leapt off like she was performing some great trick, and let her bicycle fall over into the flooded gutter.

"So how's your edge, Danny?" she asked brightly.

He couldn't remember that he'd ever told the girl his name. It wasn't like he knew hers. "Th-this is all your fault!" he blurted.

Somewhere out in the rain a ship's horn bellowed, long and slow. The bus station was near the waterfront, Danny knew.

The girl's grin expanded. "Somebody's going to hit the Broadway Bridge."

"You s-set me up."

"No, Danny." She leaned close, her hands on her knees. "I just told you how to do what you wanted. *You* set you up. A Practitioner must know zir Practice."

He was startled out of his growing pout. "You know everything about the *Booke of Dayes,* don't you? Tell me, how do I fix this?"

Another laugh. "Think," she said. "Smart kid like you doesn't have to go to Seattle to stop the rain."

"I been doing nothing *but* think for days!" The tears started up. "People been drowning, that p-puppy, Mom's got no w-work, the to-matoes are rotting . . ." Danny screwed his eyes shut to shut the tears off, just like Mom always made him do.

When the girl's voice spoke hot-breathed in his ear, he squeaked like a duct-taped mouse. "What's the name of the ritual, Practitioner?"

"*R-reversal of Indifference.*"

"What does that *mean?*"

He wasn't stupid! Danny concentrated, like they'd always tried to make him do in school. Reversal . . . reversal . . . The meaning hit him suddenly. "You can turn something around from either direction," he said with a gasp.

She clapped her hands with glee. "And so . . . ?"

"And so . . ." Danny let his thoughts catch up with his words. He could see this thread, like a silver trail in the sky, tying a star back into place. "And so I can make Sky stop thinking about rain on Portland, make Sky take the rain back."

"Bravo!" Her eyes sparkled with pure delight.

"Wh-what's your n-name?" he asked, completely taken in by the girl's expression.

"Geneva," she said, serious but still amused. "Geneva Fairweather."

He squatted on the bench in front of the Greyhound station and opened the Little Oscar. Five sets of beady eyes looked from a reek of piss and damp animal. Danny already had his duct tape out, but when he reached for the first mouse, he remembered that it was the edge that counted. Geneva Fairweather had said you could work most ritu-als with a sharpened paper clip and grass cuttings.

So maybe he didn't need to kill three mice. Or even tape them into tiny mummies to bind them. His fist would hold the mouse. The athame was sharp enough to prick three drops of blood from the mouse's back. The poor animal squirmed and squealed, but it was not dead. He folded the blood into a corner of paper torn from *Mother Urban's Booke of Dayes,* and followed the ritual from there.

Within moments, the rain slackened and Father Sun peeked down for the first time in three weeks. Danny turned to Geneva. "See? I could do it!"

A distant bicycle splashed through the puddles. She was gone.

Still, it didn't matter. Danny knew he'd done something important. Real important. And Geneva Fairweather would be back, he was sure of it.

As for Danny, if he could do this, how much more could he do?

What effect would a Reversal of Indifference have on his mom?

Clutching his bus pass, Danny walked back toward the Tri-Met stop. He would study *Mother Urban's Booke of Dayes* all the way home.

On the bus, he noticed for the first time the tiny illustration of a girl on a bicycle that appeared somewhere on every page of *Booke of Dayes.* Sometimes inside another illustration, sometimes tucked within the words, sometimes on the edge.

Had she been there before?

Did it matter?

The mice rustled in his jacket pocket. A pungent odor told Danny they were already making themselves at home there. That was fine with him. Smiling, he pricked his finger with the athame, right there on the bus, and watched the blood well like a fat-bellied ruby. Once he got home, some things would begin to change.

Angels V: Going Bad

The last of the angel stories, and probably the nastiest. I've always had a fascination with the mythology of the Rapture, and the idea of what the world would be like under demonic reign. Or maybe this is just how I see life in Portland.

"Innocence always was a recipe for disaster." Sesalem kept one hand on the issue .38 that protruded from the holster at his back like a warm, black egg stuck halfway out of the hen.

A nervous habit.

Corpses made him nervous.

Fork-Foot, his Infernal Liaison, walked around the body, kicking it with needled claws. Sesalem winced at this contamination of evidence. Eight feet tall, jeweled with glittering scales, and armored with Infernal Immunity, there was little the detective could do to influence the demon.

"Not innocent." Fork-Foot growled like machine screws in a blender. "Stupid."

The alley was narrow, three stories of age-blackened brick on each side lined with greasy Dumpsters. Portland had been a nice town, back before the Rapture. Now they were lucky just to keep the murder rate down.

It was no comfort that a good number of the victims got up off their tables at the morgue and walked out. Or sometimes clawed their way from the earth, much later.

"She came down here," Sesalem said. He framed his thoughts into a narrative as he always did when working a case. "For . . . something. To find help, to offer help. Not to score, I don't think. Though someone scored *off* of her."

The victim was perhaps sixteen, African-American with short, wiry hair. She'd been carrying a canvas bag from the Albina Church of God in Christ All-Saved and wearing a white sundress. At least, they assumed it had been a sundress. Covering her head, the bag had been tugged off by a forensics tech who now waited for the detective to finish his meditative contemplation.

Sesalem couldn't imagine any local nut-cutter carrying that bag. It had to belong to her. Logo aside, it was too clean for downtown.

"Stupid," rumbled Fork-Foot. "I tell you, you listen. People never listen." His voice faded to a ritualistic grumble.

"Was the perp one of yours?" If so, case closed, and move on. Make a call to her parents, if she had any they could find.

"No. Aura's no good."

Demons killed for sport, about like people ate and slept—automatic as breathing, hard to get through the day without. Most victims were in free-kill zones, where there was no call for investigation. Even when not, the crime was usually so obvious as to merit only the most cursory review.

People killed for sport too, some of them far too emboldened by the demon-haunted world of the Rapture. That was still illegal. In theory.

"What about one of the Damned?"

"No." Fork-Foot offered no further explanation, but his word was literally law.

Sesalem sighed. "One of ours, then." He nodded at the forensics tech. "Okay, Jackie. Do your stuff, tag and bag her, then ship her to county. Somebody text me if we get a positive ID from this mess. And . . . be kind." Sometimes it took a soul a while to realize it was finished with life.

He walked back to his parked car, ignoring the stabbing pain in his kidneys. Those who hadn't rammed broken-necked through the roofs of their houses and cars to go to Jesus during the Rapture were mostly Afflicted since. Kidney stones sucked, but it beat having snake hair or tear ducts that dripped shit.

Fork-Foot leaned on the fender of Sesalem's car, a short-wheelbase Toyota Land Cruiser painted to resemble a zebra—if zebras had balloon tires and bull bars. The metal groaned, eliciting a sympathetic wince from Sesalem.

"Not one of yours, either." Fork-Foot's tongue shot out of his muzzle to lick one eyeball.

"Not one of ours?" Sesalem asked. "That doesn't leave a lot of options."

"Them." Fork-Foot pointed at the sky. He locked his thumbs to make butterfly wings. "Bird brains."

Not butterfly wings, Sesalem realized. Angel wings. "I don't believe it."

Fork-Foot shrugged, then jumped straight up to the top of the building they had been standing in front of. Sesalem watched the demon leap across the stunted skyline of the Pearl District. It was headed downtown, presumably for the local demons' nest in Pioneer Courthouse.

"Angels." Sesalem shook his head. "No way."

The instant message came through on his cell phone's tiny screen about two hours later. Sesalem was eating a pork burrito in front of a little trailer on Southwest Fifth.

"Alley vict Sheshondra Rouse 17 yrs Albina resident cause of death heart failure. Mutilation post-mort."

Post-mortem mutilation? Not demon work, then. Pre-mortem was their style. They definitely preferred to prolong the suffering.

The pay phone a few yards to his left began ringing. Sesalem glanced at it, then at the *vieja* running the trailer. She shrugged. Cell phones had continued to work pretty well since the arrival of the Legions of Hell, but the land lines had really suffered. They mostly worked by Demonic—or sometimes Divine—intervention.

Rational people didn't answer ringing phones.

Rational people didn't work Homicide in a demon-haunted world, either. Sesalem walked over and picked up the receiver. "Hello?" he said cautiously.

"Detective Sesalem." It was a distant, tinny voice, the line crackling with static and crosstalk in some guttural tongue. "This is Control."

Control. What the few agents of the Divine still on Earth called their semimythical upstream management. Parallel to the demons' New Jersey headquarters, in a sense. Either this was some joker with brass balls the size of coconuts or Heaven was calling.

Under the circumstances, Sesalem went along with it. "Sure. Go ahead, Control."

"Back off the Rouse case. Let it go, and return to doing good works."

"Good works my ass," Sesalem snapped, his own self-discipline slipping. "Too damned late for that." He slammed the handset down onto the hook. He truly hated being told what to do.

Then he sat down to finish his burrito and think about why a bird-brain would commit murder. The pay phone rang again, but he ignored the noise.

It had to be murder. Otherwise Control wouldn't have bothered to call him. And it wasn't a demon. Notoriously dishonest as they were, he couldn't figure why Fork-Foot would bother to lie.

But Fork-Foot had hinted at something.

Sesalem needed the demon again, needed to know what Fork-Foot knew. He walked far enough away from the still-ringing pay phone to dial Fork-Foot's pager from his cell phone.

Fork-Foot dropped to the bricks of Southwest Fifth like a runaway freight elevator. Sesalem flinched from the cloud of chips and dust accompanied by a stench like an electrical short. Brimstone would have been an improvement.

"Nothing to liaise here," said Fork-Foot in his metal-shredding voice as he looked around. "You got something personal to discuss?"

Cut to the chase, thought Sesalem. Don't extemporize, don't apologize. Just look him in the eye pits and talk. The detective took a deep breath. "Why would an angel have murdered Sheshondra Rouse?"

Fork-Foot shrugged. It was like watching an earthquake ripple through a wall. "Why not?"

"They're forces of good."

Fork-Foot laughed. At least Sesalem thought it might be a laugh. "Read the Bible, little man. Angels are no different from demons. Just prettier wardrobe, better public relations."

"This isn't Gomorrah. It's Portland. She was a good kid from the Albina neighborhood. There's no *reason*."

"Even angels got to play."

"Sport? That's all you think it was? A sport killing, like one of your hunts through Old Town?"

"You better off believing that."

What the hell did that mean? "Better off than what? Some dead black kid?"

"Better off than some dead black detective," said Fork-Foot.

"Tell me," hissed Sesalem, his voice dropping like it did when he was sweating a perp.

"Already did," said Fork-Foot. "Don't need to page me no more."

Then the demon was gone in a swirl of brick dust. All around Sesalem, phones were ringing, from office windows, from passing cars, his own cell.

Back at the crime scene, Sesalem left his cruiser blocking the mouth of the alley. There was nothing left but draggled police tape and some empty film canisters. Forensics still hadn't gone all digital.

He stood where Sheshondra Rouse had screamed her last. Black paint had been hastily slopped over whatever stains had resisted the quicklime and hot water the cleanup crew normally employed. It was still sticky, already crisscrossed with boot prints, clawed demon feet, and a motorcycle.

"Why'd you die here, baby?" he asked the brick walls. Somehow this didn't seem like angel play.

"Angels are no different from demons," Fork-Foot had said.

Did they ever change sides?

As if summoned by the thought, a rush of warm, moist air blew in, Leviathan itself breathing upon the alley, followed by a flutter of wings. The angel landed next to Sesalem in a straight drop eerily reminiscent of Fork-Foot's most recent appearance.

It was almost seven feet tall, cadaverously thin, with junkie arms— all slack, stringy muscles and blue tendons. It wore leather pants with buckled motorcycle boots. The angel's bare chest was covered with an ornate tattoo of Michelangelo's *Pietà*. Great gray wings swept behind the angel, matching greasy gray dreadlocks and sea-gray eyes. The angel had silver rings on each finger and he smelled like an overheated motorcycle.

"Just because we're good," the angel said, as if picking up a prior conversation, "doesn't mean we're nice."

"The good don't kill the innocent." Sesalem palmed his .38. Even loaded with silver bullets dipped in holy water and myrrh, the gun wouldn't do much for him now. It still made him feel better.

"The good do what they can in these late days." The angel glanced at the sticky paint on the pavement. "She would have met someone.

He would have been the wrong person, led her places she shouldn't go. She had power in her, Detective. Power that could have blossomed into something terrible."

"People get crucified on traffic lights in this town," said Sesalem. "I got a new definition of 'terrible.' So why not just turn her around and point her home? Or better yet, kill that wrong person. He might have deserved it."

The angel shook its head. "There were no good exits from this alley for Sheshondra Rouse."

"You needed him," breathed Sesalem in a burst of insight, "him but not her. He's a source or a contact or something. She had some spiritual power, loose in the world. Disposable."

"My war never ends, Detective. Does yours?"

Was it a man Rouse had come to see? An angel? Or a demon?

There didn't seem to be a difference.

"One of your people went bad," Sesalem said. "She died for it."

"Almost correct," said the angel. "One of theirs went good. But he needed a soul to carry him upward."

Then the angel vanished, leaving a swirling gray feather perhaps a yard long. Sesalem holstered the gun, snatched the feather from the air, and trudged back toward his Land Cruiser.

All four tires were flat, slashed by needled claws. Sesalem looked back down the alley in time to catch a beam of light, a young black girl standing in it, talking to a tall, bejeweled demon—Fork-Foot?

Then they were gone.

It was a long walk home. He threw his cell phone in the river to stop it ringing, following it with his badge, but kept the feather. "How good is good?" he asked it.

There was no answer.

The End

The Cancer Catechism

This is the end. Really, there's not much more to say. Never walk this road I have walked if you can help it. If you must do so, take my hand. Maybe I can help you a few steps along the way.

People say there are no atheists in the foxholes, but people are idiots. It's awfully tough to believe in God when you're knee deep in mud, blood, and other men's guts. Combat is the Problem of Evil on the hoof.

But if you really want to feel the stress of divine regard, spend time in an oncology unit. The half-hidden whispers and the strained smiles and the whirring click of the infusion pumps form a choir of pain every bit as agonized as the howls of the damned in some imagined hell.

> *i: I believe in the dark miracle of uncontrolled cell division, creating tiny, undifferentiated embryos of hate who are nonetheless children of my body.*

You enter your days like everyone else. There is an alarm clock sometime before dawn, an electronic voice calling to you through the fragmented wilderness of your dreams. There is a moment of blessed relief as you take the day's first piss. There is that odd echo of flowing warmth in your shower. You shave, perhaps your face, perhaps your legs, depending on your hormonal balances and grooming preferences. You stumble into hopefully clean underwear and minimally food-stained clothes. You microwave yesterday's coffee and choke down a pair of brown-sugar-and-cinnamon Pop-Tarts.

Ablutions, evacuations, and alimentation taken care of, you move out into the wider world.

Sometimes you wonder why you do it this way. Two hundred and forty work days a year. Fifty years of a working adult life. Twelve thousand days of this routine, more than half of your allotted twenty-two thousand. Ninety-six thousand hours out of your life, a quarter of the waking hours you will ever experience.

For what? A paycheck? Friday nights spent drinking with your college buddies before they drift off earlier every year, consumed with bleary-eyed guilt toward tired spouses and squalling children?

Still, you do what everyone does. Then sometimes you do it differently. You take a weekend to the coast. You fly away at the holidays to visit aging relatives who *still* think a sweater vest is a good idea for a gift. You go camping up in the hills and throw out your back sleeping on rocks that were pebbles when you lay down but boulders when you woke up.

Because, really, what else is there? Life is years of sheer, endless boredom punctuated by occasional bouts of the mildly interesting. Not much to do, not much to believe in. Just eat, sleep, shit, breathe, breed, grow old and die.

Somewhere along the way, you acquired your own partner. Or two or three or four, usually in a row with minor overlaps. Serial monogamy is the American way. Changing relationships has become like switching from Cheerios to Rice Krispies. One or two of those partners helped you produce sprogs, either by donating a small amount of warm, sticky fluid to your own efforts, or through dint of nine months of vomiting and backaches and blameful mood swings.

There's not much to believe in except your kids, and in truth, what are they going to grow up to be? Assuming video games don't corrupt their plastic little souls and global warming doesn't drown them in their beds with rising sea levels, they'll just turn out like you.

Then one day you find blood in the toilet while stumbling around amid receding somnolence. Maybe you ignore it for a while, maybe you dart in immediately to see your doctor in a grip of panic. Still it comes back again and again until you do seek medical advice, that little harbinger of terrible things to come which you cannot yet admit to yourself.

Because that day, you have finally found something to believe in. Something *real*. Something intensely personal. Death doesn't play chess for souls anymore, or sit down to an unfriendly game of Texas

Hold 'Em. Death approaches along a pathway built from silvery needles and grim lab reports and the hum of CT scanners.

It's a different game now, and some blood in your morning shit has proven to be your table stakes. You'd best believe you're playing for your life.

> *ii: I have faith that my body will do its best to marshal my immune system against these invaders from within, but I also surrender myself to the tender ministrations of the scalpel and the loving embrace of oncological poison that the days of my life shall be filled with terror, nausea, and fatigue.*

Oncologists must take classes in how to deliver difficult news. Their medical specialty is as devilish and soul-crushing as a loaded pair of casino dice is to a drunk's last dollar. You can see the distress in the doctor's eyes as she comes into the room, not quite meeting your pathetic attempt at a frank gaze.

You've promised yourself you'll be open, accepting, strong enough to deal with whatever comes. The blood work was no big deal. The CT scan with its strange bodily warmths and curious surges was almost entertaining. The PET scan was just strange, like a B-list superhero's origin story writ mundane. The colonoscopy, well, the less said the better, but at least it didn't hurt. The best way you've been able to describe *that* procedure was as resembling a small-budget alien abduction experience.

Tests, tests, tests, to prove that it's really all okay.

You're young. Sort of.

You're healthy. Mostly.

You have the love of family and friends. At least, that's what they tell you.

Whatever this is, you will get through it. Whatever this is, you won't let it beat you out of all those precious moments that you've suddenly realized make up your life.

"I'm sorry," she tells you, finally locking eyes with you for a moment. "It's definitely colon cancer. The good news is that there doesn't seem to be any metastasis. The bad news is it appears to have interpenetrated the colon wall, which means the disease has spread past the original site. I'll be referring you to a surgeon in the Digestive

Medicine group for a resection. After that, we're probably going to have to prescribe a course of chemotherapy."

At least she delivers the information concisely, using words you can mostly understand once your sense of horrified denial has settled somewhat. There are so many questions, but you can't ask them all, not right then. Cancer's got your tongue.

You feel the demon settling in where it clings to your back. Its long, barbed tail circles your waist then slides into your anus and upward along the Hershey highway to begin the slow, mortal feast that will eat you out from within.

The world is different now. You have something to believe in after all. Your oncologist is your psychopomp. Your surgeon will be your ferryman across that river of dread.

There's another side of life, and you suddenly realize that you have seen it far too soon.

> *iii: I confess that I am but a sinner in the hands of an angry cancer. There is no way through this thicket of tumor and metastasis save to go forward to whatever end cancer has prepared for me, to feast at whatever table cancer has laid for me. My loves, my family, my friendships; they will all be placed as sacrifices upon this, the altar of my suffering.*

Surgery takes you strangely. Going in you joke and smile bravely and pretend this doesn't concern you very much. The surgeon and his assistants have disclosed risks to you, side effects, the various debilitations and deaths which can befall anyone unlucky enough to be splayed beneath the scalpel upon an operating table.

Still, you don't know what to expect, so you try to expect nothing except a new experience. Cold and naked under a ragged little swatch of oddly printed cloth, smiling strangers wheel you away down vacant corridors into the countries of the knife.

It is the anesthesia that puzzles you most. Even in sleep, you know if you're warm or cold. Your bladder tells you when to get up for at least a few stumbling moments. Time still passes. A crying child or a lover whispering your name will wake you.

Anesthesia, though . . . It's a little death. Not in the sense of the

French *petit mort,* but a preview of finally dying of this dread disease. Like a movie trailer for the blank nothingness that is eternity once consciousness has been extinguished. One minute you are counting backwards to a frowning woman in a surgical mask, the next minute you are swimming in fog, surrounded by curtains, hearing machines peep and bing the measures of your metabolism.

"I'm still alive," you say. Your aunt chuckles and squeezes your hand and tells you that's the fifth time you've said those words in the last twenty minutes. *It must be important, then,* is all you can think in reply, but self-consciousness has returned with the rest of your awareness, so you just smile and squeeze her hand.

You lie there laced with needles and tubes and think about the irony that you have for a few hours touched that far shore, and can remember nothing of it except a blankness so profound it cannot truly be called a memory.

Cancer has brought you another lesson closer to finally understanding death.

A few days later, home from the hospital, you slyly enquire how the surgery seemed to other people. Your friends tell you they knew you would be fine. Your mother pretends not to weep. Your spouse rolls their eyes and tells you not to make so much drama of it all. Your kids hide from you, needy and avoidant all in the same moment in that way only children can manage to be.

It takes you a week to be able to get yourself out of bed. Your morning shit turns into hours of sitting, waiting for gravity and intestinal gas to do what peristalsis cannot manage for far too long after the surgical insult to your colon. You have a lot of time to think while perched on the toilet. You think about softer toilet seats and moisturized toilet paper, but you also think about how people don't tell you so many things lately, how even many adults are as avoidant as the kids, even if they're more subtle about their abandonment. You think about what it means to go through this, and what chemo will do to you, your family, and your friends.

You think that if you were finally going to find faith in your life, it could have been focused on something more constructive and less disturbing than *fucking cancer.*

Someone comes into the room because you were yelling without realizing it. You can see the fear naked in their eyes. It doesn't matter

314 LAST PLANE TO HEAVEN

who this is, because that same fear has stripped itself bare and slipped into the eyes of everyone who cares about you.

That is something you can believe in as well.

iv: I acknowledge that my life will be spared or spent by the dark arts of medical science, at the mercy of statistics that can never tell my true story but only tell the story of my cancer cohort as a whole. I understand that my fate is in the hands of the cancer god, and that no matter what we do or how well we do it, I may never see an effective treatment. Or I may outlive you all. I accept what the statistics say about that, as well.

Chemo is an entirely different chamber of horrors than surgery. You find new fields of pain and loss there, novel revelations to feed your burgeoning faith in cancer. There are needles, of course, but you have rapidly grown accustomed to them. The drugs aren't so bad the first time or two.

But where surgery dropped you swiftly into a hole which then took a month to climb out of, chemo lowers you slowly, inch by inch, week after week, into a hole which you may never climb out of. Starting with your dignity and ending with your sense of self, chemo takes everything away from you.

Those mornings of yours grow later and later. You begin to miss work and misunderstand your spouse and children. The smallest things become difficult and the largest things become impossible. You never knew how large a thing standing in the shower could be.

You can't drive, and you don't have the energy to be a passenger for long, so you stop going out even when people are willing to give you rides. You stop seeing your friends unless they make the time to come to you. Your kids avoid you because you smell funny, like sweat and puke and chemicals. Your spouse doesn't hold you at night anymore because they are afraid of somehow hurting you.

You become ingrown, a tumor on the body social of your family and friends. Silent, mostly quiescent except for the daily violence of various fluids irrupting. You straddle the line somewhere between deadly and dead.

The worst thing is that chemotherapy robs you of your mind. You lose the ability to focus properly, to create, then to consume. In time you are reduced to watching reruns of old shows on Netflix streaming, because you can process nothing new. You repeat yourself when you speak at all. You feel desperation.

Cancer has covered over your life, a blanket damp with sweat and blood. You are tired beyond measure, like the day after a bad flu combined with the worst hangover you have ever had, and it does not end. Day after day, week after week, month after month, alone with your increasingly muddled thoughts and the whispered gospels of cancer being recited with every beat of your heart and every momentary flow of your blood.

"*Memento mori,*" it tells you. "*Respice post te! Hominem te esse memento!*"

"Remember that you will die. Look behind you! Remember that you are only human!"

Death becomes a kind of friend. It rides on your shoulder like a carrion crow. This skeletal bird remains as invisible to the people around you as your tumor ever was, but it affects them just as much. You are branded by its talons, blinded by the peck of its beak, deafened by its silent screeches, but this bird and you become closer than school chums, closer than lovers.

In time it grows into a sort of comfort. One way or another, this will all end. The story will go on, and be seen as a tragedy by some. But the promise of chemo is twofold. In death's own language it whispers to you that you might survive, or that you might come to an end. That far shore which surgery showed you unremembered glides past the sinking raft of your suffering. You can see all too well its towering black cliffs and crumbling ravines.

Someday, probably someday soon, you will go home to that place you've never been before.

> *v: I know that cancer is my fate and my friend and my boon companion. Whatever becomes of me, cancer has remade my life as surely as the forge remakes the sword, as certainly as rain and sun remake the seed. Even in dying, I am reborn.*

There is no devil mocking you. God didn't give you cancer to punish you. Colon cancer has come to you through a combination of losing the genetic lottery, cosmic rays, and perhaps too much bacon in your younger days.

Coming out of chemo finally, you know these things. Your life has been stripped down and annealed. Some friends have drifted away out of fear or a sense of frustrated helplessness. Your spouse might have left you in the face of the disease. That happens more often than even oncologists want to admit. Your kids cry because they're afraid you're leaving them soon. Your parents' eyes are haunted by this potential reversal of the natural order of birth and death among the generations.

Still, you are alive today.

When a Christian friend in mortal fear for your soul begs you to get right with God before the disease claims you, you want to tell him you have already found another faith. You believe in the end of all things, and though it is bitterly disappointing to face that far shore, you aren't so frightened as you once were. Death is no longer abstract. It's now a personal companion. The bird on your shoulder stays with you, and you want to share that with your Christian friend, but this is not a faith for which you can proselytize.

Cancer, like combat, is the Problem of Evil on the hoof. You have met the enemy and he is yourself. Your tumor children may yet claim you, but now you have a dark sort of faith to guide you through these, your darkest hours.

You still dream of that far shore and the blankness that will keep you from ever seeing it. That journey once made will never be remembered except in the echoes you leave behind in other people's lives.

There are no atheists in the oncology unit. Only the catechism of cancer, and the difficult comfort it brings even amid the worst of times.

Afterword

Once upon a time, I read a book.

It was on a college roommate's shelf around 1984 or 1985. I picked the paperback up in a moment of careless boredom, sat down to idly turn a few pages, and was hooked forever. On the author, on the language, on the notion that fiction could be joyous, transcendent, and substantial. That novel was quite literally why I became a writer.

The book was *Shadow of the Torturer,* and the author was Gene Wolfe.

Once upon a time, I sold a story.

It was one of my first major market invitations. I was thrilled to send the manuscript to Peter Crowther of PS Publishing. The acceptance put me over the moon. Then the signature sheets for *Postscripts* issue one came around in the mail. This was one of the first times I'd ever had to work my way through a stack of a thousand loose papers. And the other names on the page. Oh, my. A who's who of American genre fiction, from Ray Bradbury to Joyce Carol Oates and beyond. And some newcomer named Jay Lake.

The last name eventually to be signed on the page was that of my favorite author, Gene Wolfe.

Once upon a time, I went to an awards ceremony.

It was the Locus Awards in 2007 in Seattle. They were also holding an induction ceremony at the Science Fiction Hall of Fame. I was wandering about in the EMP building poking at things when I realized that one of the inductees had entered the hall early, presumably to rest his weary feet. I approached to congratulate him when he broke into a huge smile, turned to his wife, and said, "Rosemary, do you know who this is?"

I literally looked over my shoulder to see who it was that Gene Wolfe was so pleased to see. There was no one present but me.

Once upon a time, I contracted a fatal disease.

I am dying of metastatic colon cancer. Chances are very good that by the time these words reach print I will either be on my deathbed or in my grave. I don't write anymore. A career that was first born in the 1980s as the merest dream, and blossomed in the 2000s after years of diligent effort, was finally stopped by a small mutation and some clusters of runaway cells that wouldn't fill a cereal bowl.

Putting together my final collection, I was discussing with John Pitts who I might ask to write the introduction. We bandied about various names of people I liked and admired. John asked me who I would have if I could have any writer.

My answer of course was Gene Wolfe.

When I wrote him to very politely inquire of his interest, his response was instant and enthusiastic.

So I have come full circle, from following Severian the Torturer through the distant future past of Urth, to putting the finishing touches on a manuscript introduced by the man who introduced me to the idea of what writing could ever be.

My debts to the people in this field are immense and unredeemable. So many have helped me. So many have given me a hand. So many have given me the literary equivalent of a good thrashing when I needed it.

But my gratitude to the man who is almost literally my patron saint for helping me introduce this final collection to you knows no bounds. Neither does my gratitude to you for reading it.

I love you all. It has been a real privilege to know you.

Jay Lake
Portland, OR